HUNT
FOR ORION

GUARDIANS OF ORION BOOK THREE

S. L. RICHARDSON

S. L. Richardson

www.slrichardson.com

Available in these formats:

ISBN: 978-1-7340644-5-2 (eBook)

ISBN: 978-1-7340644-6-9 (Paperback)

Cover Design: Natalie Narbonne at Original Book Cover Design - www.original-bookcoverdesign.com

Book Formatting: Cait Marie

Editing: Roxana Coumans–5 Dogs Book Editing

Published by Flasheila Press | Friendswood, Texas

For Flash

My husband
My rock
My everything
You are the savior of my universe

PROLOGUE

Symedek ~ The Ancient One

S acred blood dripped from Symedek's sword, glistening against the sharp metal's edge as he raced down the corridor.

Angel blood.

Silver. Translucent. Divine.

Like mine.

But in blood only.

A violent storm raged outside the palace. For days its deluge had turned the city's hard packed dirt roads into muddy rivers. Harsh winds pushed fat raindrops through the small windows high up the stone wall. His feet slapped each puddle, shooting a cold spray against his bare calves. He sneered, realizing the water cleansed him of the filth of battle from which he fled.

Shadows from the sconce's flames danced against the rock walls, chasing him like the angelic forces hounding him. The floor buckled beneath him as chunks of rubble rained down on him, along with the cries of the Nephilim; his brave, beloved children, fighting against their enemies, buying him time to complete his task. He stumbled, rage boiling within him. Each agonizing wail pierced his heart, pushing his legs toward a truth only he must know about. If he doesn't complete his life's work on Earth, it will be for not.

A waste.

A defeat.

I will not let that happen.

I will live on...

Symedek thrust his sword into its sheath, silver blood painting the leather opening. Another cry tore through the air, spiking his urgency. He pushed the heavy wooden door open and found his cherished mate. Arayana lay on a bed of bright pillows. Her light brown face glistened with sweat as she arched her back against her pregnant belly.

Good. The child is not yet born.

She gazed over at him; her soft brown eyes glazed over with the pain of childbirth. She stretched her hand out to him. "Symedek," she moaned. "You live. I feared I'd never lay eyes on you again. I trembled with fear for you, more even than childbirth."

He staggered across the room. Falling to his knees, he grasped her sweaty hand. His crescent moon ax, churning with red fire from handle to head, still lay where he'd left it next to her. With his free hand, he brushed her forehead and pushed the damp hair away from her face. She sighed, closing her eyes as his fingers slipped through her thick, rich black tresses. Memories flooded his mind of his fingers entwined in her hair during their passionate nights spent as one.

Would we ever be together again?

"Yes, my love, I am here. Listen to me carefully, know what I say has grave consequence. I have a mission for you. One of supreme importance." He glanced up at the two servants, their heads bowed before their master. "Leave us now. Make haste!" They scrambled to their feet, exiting through a narrow door at the room's shadowy edge.

"I will do whatever you ask," she grimaced against the pain. "How can I help you? My time is here. I'm useless until our baby is born."

"Shh. Be brave. Do you trust me?"

Arayana nodded against his palm; eyes bright as she held his. "With my life."

"Good." Her eyes rolled back as another wave hit her, tightening her hand around his. The roars of battle waged closer, their looming sounds threatening his thinning patience, waiting for her pain to pass. "God has come for me, but I have a plan to thwart him."

She cried out, her body folding on itself. He was losing both her and precious time. His fingers tightened on her scalp, turning her head to face him. Her eyes snapped open; a single tear slipped from its corner.

"This child is our future—my path to life once again for eternity. You'll be the sacred mother of my secret lineage. Each generation shall birth a girl who will carry the wondrous secret within them, and birth another girl who will continue to be the holder of my truth. You alone will carry the knowledge of my legacy and keep it alive when you share it with our daughter. She will pass it on to her daughter and down through the ages until, one day, I will find a way to come back to this world and retrieve what is mine. I'll be whole again and resurrect my sacred race and rule over humanity once more."

She shook her head, eyelashes fluttering as she tried to concentrate through her suffering. "I don't understand how I—"

"Don't fear what I'm about to do. Receive me freely, my love, and you'll be a part of the ultimate sign of strength and divine power."

"I'm ready," she panted, her breath hot against his face.

He blocked out the surrounding chaos and searched for the ethereal essence buried within him. "Heed my plea!" It sparked when it received his call, awakened by the ancient language of the angels.

"Do as I demand! Break in two, oh divine soul of mine. Separate and come up to me. Let me plant you in my child to be carried down, soul after magnificent soul, until I can reunite with it again and finish what I started!"

The command echoed in the chamber, oppressed by her pain and his frantic, daring tirade. He arched back and threw his hands up. Trembling with an illicit excitement, a bright flash of light exploded behind his eyes. A tremendous rip tore through him. He didn't fight the sensation of being ripped in two. He rode the powerful wave, weightless, as the unholy storm lashed inside him. A blaze of energy sliced his soul as it severed in two. But another crack ripped through the room. The air sizzled, ripe with the odor of a foul intruder.

No!

He can't be here.

It was too late to stop what he'd started. One part of his soul ripped away from the other and worked its way up into his throat. He leaned over her, parting his lips wide as an orb of his soul burned a glorious path into his mouth. She gasped at the bright light between them. He lowered his mouth to hers, silencing the scream laying on her lips. His body shuddered as the rent soul rippled from his mouth into hers. Arayana seized at the insult, but his elation overrode any concern for her fear or shock. When he laid his hand on her taut belly, the baby kicked. He jerked up, stealing a glance of her illuminated womb. The child arched inside the primordial womb of water and blood. Awe stuck him when the orb settled where its heart nestled. Smug satisfaction swelled. He'd completed his task of infamy and immortality.

I did it!

I've won!

"What have you done, Symedek? Still trying to play god among these hateful humans?" His low chuckle brought a sneer to Symedek's face. He glanced at Arayana, her face and body momentarily slack from the orb's invasion. He grabbed his sword, stood up, and calmly faced the invader. Eying the malevolent dark prince, he dare not underestimate his casual stance or playful tone. There was nothing innocent about his malicious gaze at Arayana.

The room shook as the battle advanced closer inside his palace walls. He'd built this magnificent compound on the backs of simple humans, who had been so easily inspired by his words of unearthly wisdom and his display of absolute power. Mating with the females and creating his Nephilim helped to hold his subjects in place. Their giant stature and ferocious nature intimidated God's creation. The floor vibrated under his feet as good and evil collided.

Hold on my fierce children...

"Why are you here? Have you finally come to your senses to fight against God above ground?" Symedek's sword tingled in his palm, its red flames sparking with his anger.

"Why so hostile? You know I support your work on Earth. I've been your secret ally through it all. My guidance and knowledge of God's fools is why your reign has been a triumph. Without me—"

"I don't have time for your boasting. If you didn't bring an army with you, leave me so I can fight alongside my children."

"Awww, yes. Your cherished Nephilim. The reason God has brought his wrath upon you. Did you really think there would be no consequences for mating with females? How could you? They're so... beneath you. And their stench." The prince shuddered, glancing at Arayana. "Revolting."

Symedek clenched his jaws, stifling the sharp reply that would get him nowhere. Arayana cried out as she brought her knees up. He stepped in front of her, wanting to shield her from the prince's gaze. "To each his own. I find them beautiful—fascinating. Now, raise your weapon and fight with me. We can defeat them before you escape back into your pit—"

"Oh, I'm in no hurry. I'll ask you again. What have you done to the child?"

Symedek remained silent as the prince made his stealthy approach.

"No answer for me?" His harsh laughter cut the air as a smirk crossed his marble-like face. He placed his massive hand on his sword's hilt. "I recognize what you've done, for I am a Seraphim, too." His six black wings ruffled as if mocking Symedek. "Only we have the power to split our soul. Is that what you have done? Split your soul and implanted it in your seed? You truly are an unscrupulous rebel, aren't you? I understand your plan now. You hope to come back—continue where you left off and rebuild your so-called destiny. God won't like that. He'll never allow you to return."

"That's where you're wrong," Symedek smiled. Six inky white wings, streaked with crimson feathers, burst behind him. "I stayed longer and learned. I understand him better than you and the Fallen. You were all impulsive cowards to not stay and learn his ways."

The room's air charged with wicked energy as the prince removed his sword. "The only coward in this room is you. *You* were with us. *You* also have a contempt for his abomination. Not only are you a traitor to us, but you're a liar, too. I saw you back away and point your disingenuous finger at us, deny your conspirator words and action by striking down those you had aligned with behind His back."

Symedek readied his stance to strike first. "Of course I did! Why would I want to live a life under Lucifer's depraved, moronic rule, locked in his warped pit, when I could rule my kingdom in the light—have it all here on Earth and create my race with my seed! I'm just as powerful—"

The stone walls shuddered. Symedek's blood surged against the alarm rising in him. He desperately needed to end this waste of time. Was this the prince's plan? Delay his escape with confusion and pompousness?

"This is why you're here, isn't it? Distract me with your hollow accusations." He lunged forward, aiming his sword at the prince's heart. The prince pivoted and flew to the other side of Arayana. Symedek gasped at his error. Her body now lay between them.

"I dare say I was curious as to your escape plan. And now I know, but I can't believe you think you'll survive." The prince cocked his head. "I wonder what punishment he has planned for you. Your plan for escape will not come to fruition. But I do admire your efforts. Leaving your soul alive inside your lineage—a hostage until you retrieve it. Brilliant. But what if you can't return? What if God kills you and the Watchers who made the grave choice to follow you? What then?"

Full-blown panic hit Symedek.

What if he's right?

My soul lost, never to see the light of day... never to live freely again.

His eyes darted between the prince and Arayana. "The baby's coming!" She reached between her legs and grabbed the emerging infant. It wasn't long before its first wail burst from its lungs, galvanizing Symedek to make a desperate plea.

"We could work together. You and I. Protect my seed and help me fight to live another day. After a time, we come back—together to Earth. I will raise an army here and you secretly raise one in Hell. When the time is right, we'll attack and reclaim what we wanted!"

Enraged shouts bellowed from behind the wooden door, not meant to hold back charging Angels. The prince glanced at the door and sheathed his sword. An evil grin spread as he raised his hand to summon his portal.

"Making a deal with me? Although it's tempting, you seem to forget that I don't need you. I could wrench your soul from this useless creation, and be done with it." His contempt for the infant was clear. "But I tell you what. I'll watch over your... seed, give it my protection, and make sure no one finds out about your *secret*." The air cracked as his portal opened, revealing the cavern of hell behind him. The prince crouched down and ran a black, thick talon down Arayana's cheek before he snatched Symedek's ax. "But it won't be for you. You *will* perish today. When the time is right for *me*, I'll seek your soul. I'll absorb you into mine and we'll become a greater force than anything ever created. Our souls combined will rule. We will be invincible! *Two become one*. It is the only way. Say yes to this, Symedek." He raised the ax above Arayana. "Now—before I kill what you hold most dear!"

Helplessness washed over Symedek as his dreams emptied from him like blood from a gutted pig. Arayana's sweat-drenched face turned to Symedek, cradling the newborn to her breast.

"Do as he says! Save our child!" She begged.

"No answer for me?"

Symedek glared at the prince with loathing churning inside of him. "I agree, but only if you don't resist me when I come for what is rightfully mine. I will not die today." He spoke between gritted teeth.

The prince threw back his head and cackled while he shoved the ax inside his belt. "We shall see, but temperance was never my virtue." He stepped inside the portal. The red ax burned bright against the smoke. It snapped closed, silencing the prince's taunting laugh, but left Hell's stench clogging the air.

Symedek rushed to Arayana and fell to his knees. The walls boomed as stone and dust spit down around them. "Go! Escape with your women and leave this place. Remember what you heard and saw today. Pass it along so the lineage knows to beware of the prince and his treacherous desires. I'll do everything in my power to return. This will not be for nothing." His hands clasped her face while he laid a chaste kiss on her full lips. "Be brave and remember who you are. The queen of our race." He grabbed her by the arms and helped her to stand. She leaned heavily on him as they shuffled to the back door. The handle was cold in his feverish hand. He yanked it open. Rain pummeled down and water ran like streams off the rooftop. Only the clashing chaos of battle was mightier.

She turned to him. Courage and fear warred in her eyes. "I will protect her with my life, certain you will prevail, my love." She cupped his cheek.

"As will you." He grabbed her hand, bringing her palm to his lips. He gazed at the delicate lines of her face and etched them into the walls of his memory. Hungry lips kissed her palm before he stepped back into his chamber. "Now fly, my dove, before the will to let you go leaves me."

Tears ran freely down her face. Her maidens materialized from the side of the palace and rushed to surround her. They whisked her away around the corner in a flurry of sodden linen dresses. He nodded in encouragement before he closed the door when she disappeared from his sight.

She must survive...

He turned and ran toward the chamber's door. He pulled out his sword, fury boiling at his impedance to do nothing more than throw himself at the mercy of his nemesis. An unseen force blew the wooden door open, knocking him back to the dusty floor. Light flooded the dim room. A kaleidoscope of brilliant colors played against walls. The colors shone of the Angels, not his Nephilim. He tried in vain to shut out the flurry of images rising before him of his dead children. The pain was too much to bear.

"Get up." Strong hands gripped him, yanking him off the floor. His eyes, flat with despair and hatred, stared into the cobalt depths of who he knew clutched him.

Michael.

"Is he still here? Is that how you achieved all this with Lucifer's help?" Michael shook him, anger rolling off of him.

"I didn't need Lucifer's help. This is my work! My creation! Don't you dare lay my perfection at his feet!"

"Stop lying to me! This room reeks of the Fallen." More Angels poured into the room. The dark blood of his children dripped from their armor; swords raised to kill more.

"There is no one here, you paranoid fool!"

Raphael came up behind him and took his sword. Symedek clenched his fists, wishing to smash them into Raphael's sparkling emerald eyes. Translucent chains emerged in his hands. Raphael wrapped the cool metal around Symedek's wrists and feet, never rattling as their angelic powers seeped into his skin.

"No!" Symedek seethed as the powers that made him a Seraphim leeched from his pores and into each link until it emptied him of his precious lifeblood. The shell of a Seraphim remained, even his wings lay limp around him. "You can't steal my essence! It's mine—"

"You worry about your essence when it's your *life* I wish I should end? You've defiled the sacredness of the Angels with your heresy. If I had it my way, I'd wipe you and the Watchers from the face of the Earth. But that isn't God's will."

Symedek barely stood, weakened by his lost lifeblood now locked inside the chains that bound him. Still, a dark hope bloomed within him. Michael was not here to kill him.

"I see the conspirator's light of hope rising in your eyes, but there's no escape for you. Not now. Not ever."

Raphael gripped Symedek while Michael raised his arms. He swung them wide, splitting the room's space to expose another. Heaven's glory blazed before him. Symedek trembled, trying to hold on to his feeling of revenge and rage. A bright light struck him and wrapped around him like an icy embrace. He couldn't fight it seeping into his pores, stripping away his thin barriers, leaving his sins transparent to the Heavenly Hosts.

"No," Symedek's groan was lost in his harsh, rapid breathing.

Raphael pushed him forward. Symedek stumbled on to the endless translucent floor of Heaven. Fellow Watchers joined him. Some trembled while others raged. His lavish palace, erected to him by his innumerable slaves, disappeared when the window to his world gave way to a blanket of stars. He may have lost everything, but he'd never grovel at God's feet. He'd been a god, and in his death, he'd remain a god.

"But you aren't a god, and never were." God's voice boomed, shaking his resolve. "You and the others only showed man sin with your wicked and vile teachings. You turned them away from the goodness I infused inside each of them so you could play god. Death is too swift a judgement."

The light's heat ceased to warm his skin. A sweeping cold filled him inside this paralyzing cocoon. Panic clawed, driving a need to thrash against the shackles, but the effort was useless. His body didn't obey his commands, locked in the chains fused to his skin.

"Never will you see light again. Never will you feel heat again. Never will you be seen of again. You will spend eternity in bondage, imprisoned in a black abyss of ice, with your traitorous Watchers, left with nothing but each other's wails and whimperings."

Horror spiked as he envisioned his future. From the mountain-top, a lightning bolt sizzled through the air. A thunderous boom cracked when it sliced through the stars. An opaque portal yawned open. Frigid air whistled through and blasted his face.

"You deserve nothing less. You have no honor." Michael's condemnation doused him with a numbing truth.

I'll never reunite with my soul.

The same bright force that had ripped him from his home, lifted him off the floor. Its power hurled him through a blanket of streaking stars. He thought of Arayana, his dead Nephilim, and the child he hoped would escape the evil prince's grasp. The portal's inky opening grew wider until it encapsulated his vision. His mouth dropped open; the scream heard only within his horrified mind. Static burst around him before his body punched through an invisible force field, then slammed to a halt inside a prison.

Silence.

Black.

Cold.

Endless...

His fellow Watchers joined him; each face etched in its own macabre nightmare. He locked eyes with Eonlysis, his ally from the beginning, hating the acceptance and regret hollowing his eyes. Symedek slowly turned his head away from him, not wanting his friend's acquiescence to defeat the last vision he'd see. The force released him, leaving him suspended in mid-air. Its light withdrew and narrowed as it retreated. With only a pinprick of light left, he hardened his mind to fight back the panic clawing at his every fiber.

I will escape from here.

I will get my soul back.

I will kill the traitor prince.

Complete darkness now claimed his tomb, filled with the wails of the newfound hopeless.

CHAPTER
ONE

OLIVIA

For a school assignment one year, each student in Olivia's class had to create a bucket list of twenty things they wished to achieve before turning thirty. Excitement had zipped through her as she composed her dream list. At the top of her list was skydiving.

Exhilarating.

Daring.

Heart stopping...

With a parachute.

But Olivia wasn't wearing a parachute as she plummeted through the sky.

Her back lay exposed to the ground rushing toward her, defenseless to the bone crushing effects of her body smashing against the unyielding earth.

And still she tumbled.

Olivia's dark-blond hair whipped around her, lashing her cheeks. Her arms flailed into the sky, fingers grasping at the fluffy white clouds overhead, as if one could end her swift descent.

But it didn't.

Her mouth hung open; a scream frozen in her throat. She tried to gulp a chilly breath of air, but her lungs had already seized, gripped in terror as the world below rushed ever closer. It appalled her she'd chosen to tip over and fall off of her beloved Griffin.

"You must master this skill. If it happens in battle, trust your link with Aureus to catch you."

Melchior's words roared in her head, colliding with these seconds of sheer terror, stretching out like a lifetime. Melchior was her trusted Magi mentor of all matter's warrior and her linage in the Guardians of Orion. But surging panic threatened to overrule her logic to trust his words.

Where are you, Aureus?

Did our link fail?

You're a guardian, Drake... trust in yourself and Aureus!

A faint noise broke through the wind, whistling in her ears. Were those his long, powerful wings flapping in the air or just her wishful thinking that he was coming for her? A bird-like cry pierced the air. She scanned the sky through her strands of hair and caught sight of his lion body soaring above her. His wings of gold dipped left, out of her sight. Her eager hands stretched; her fingertips ached to grab his thick fur. A warmth shifted the air beneath her. He called to Olivia again. His massive frame disturbed the air and radiated his much-needed body heat.

They spoke no words. Their communication filtered through their shared link. Their hearts beat as one and their minds synced on a primal level, anticipating what the other would do. His body nudged her back. The rioting air became less turbulent, allowing her to turn and face the ground. Gold tinted feathers covered Aureus's neck and white, luscious fur coated his body. Reaching out, she entwined her fingers; the tips sinking through to his tough hide. Her grip locked onto the fur. Waves of relief flooded as she straddled his back, thankful for her devoted magical beast.

"You're incredible!" A thrill tingled down her spine as she leaned over and nestled against his neck. He squawked in return, his steady heartbeat pounding with hers. "Thank you, my friend! I hope we don't have to practice this too often. Although it might not be as stressful the next time." Her stomach dropped when he dove towards the rolling green valley bordering her new home.

Home of the Magi.

The dark, jagged line of the canyon's rim dominated the horizon. A mighty, racing river sliced through the valley, carving out the canyon's majestic walls. Aureus turned right and aimed for the gray granite church commanding the skyline where the guardians trained, meditated, and now slept. The forest's trees blurred beneath her as he skimmed over their pointy tops. She squeezed her thighs, anchoring herself against him. A sly smile stretched across her face, loving the freedom of unencumbered flight. Never in a million years had she thought she would fly like a bird.

My life is definitely unique.

Other animal cries filtered through the valley. Zach and Sergio came into her peripheral vision. Zach rode his Pegasus, Malik, his orange-streaked wings pumping across the sky. Sergio rode Sadira, his red-flamed Phoenix, leaving a wispy trail of crimson like fading contrails from an airplane. Both hugged the backs of their magical beasts as they flew towards the church. Her heart swelled with pride and respect for her brave fellow guardians. The battles and fellow-ship they experienced were precious, theirs alone to fight against the terrors the Fallen would unleash upon humanity. She could never combat this evil alone. She'd learned that lesson the hard way in her confrontation with Delilah. Zach, Sergio and Lucia had run to her side along with Michael, Raphael and Gabriel. Each fought unselfishly, and it almost cost them their lives. But they defeated Lucifer, and the Fallen that full moon night at the Valley of Fire. The forgiveness each gave her afterword in the church was a tremendous gift she'd never forget.

What happened to Delilah and Zar?

An uneasiness settled in her gut, wrapping a sense of foreboding for her future. Her fear of them had dwindled, but they could never let their guard down. When their enemies returned, they'd be ready. The guardians used the Fallen's impending attack as motivation to work as hard as possible to harness their newfound skills and powers.

Evil can't win.

Olivia felt Aureus's pulse spike. He peeled away from the tree line where a pasture lay at its edge. Tall grass swayed as they flew closer. Olivia didn't know what had caught his eye, but she trusted him to guard and guide her with his life. He landed softly and trotted back toward the forest's dark edge. The pine trees and underbrush were thick, hiding its inhabitants' secret from onlookers. Olivia scanned the darkness, wondering what had attracted him. He stopped and stood alert, staring into the dense forest. No birds flew or critters scurried in the dense thicket. It was as if the forest itself held its breath. She dismounted, her curiosity increasing with each passing moment.

There...

She paused as a magnificent white tiger emerged from its crouch. It exited the forest's edge, like parting a curtain from dark into light. Sunlight reflected in large gold eyes peering at her, blinking in a lazy demeanor that spoke of no fear or trepidation. With a tail swish, its body line blurred and transformed from tiger to human girl. Olivia smiled when Lucia waved at her. Clad in her black skin-tight armor, Lucia was as threatening in human form as a tiger. Her shoulder-length hair, as black as a cave opening, lifted in the breeze. Power and confidence vibrated in her friend.

God, she's so cool.

Lucia jogged over and hugged Olivia. To think that only a month ago, Lucia was in a wheelchair from a bicycle accident she had as a young girl. Now, she was a fellow guardian, a true warrior in spirit and mind. "Hey, how ya doing? My heart stopped when you fell off Aureus and hurled through the air. I appreciate you're supposed to practice the situation, but—whoa, I don't know if I could do that!"

Olivia chuckled and released Lucia. "I had a hard time letting go. I trusted Aureus would catch me. The free fall was nuts—loud and frightening. Now that I learned what happens, it's not too bad. Actually, it's thrilling in a daredevil kinda way."

A low squawk emitted from Aureus, alerting her like a warning. Olivia and Lucia swiveled and faced the forest the Griffin spied with intention. A stillness remained, thick with unseen power, yet an air of reverence remained for whatever lay inside the foliage. Olivia heard approaching footsteps. The leaves rustled with each stealthy step. She couldn't imagine any danger here, but her hand reflexively moved to the dagger at her hip. Her breath caught when a lion's face materialized. Sunlight highlighted the glorious caramel-colored mane, thick with green streaks running through it. Lucia gasped when its entire body came into view. It was larger than any lion she'd ever seen. Collapsed wings of emerald green feathers fluttered from its front shoulders. It paused at the edge, the eerie darkness behind it magnifying its power and beauty. Aureus sat down, nodding discreetly to the magical beast. The lion returned the sentiment and turned its gaze to Lucia. She cocked her head, as if listening to a faint conversation only meant for them to share.

"Lucia," Olivia whispered. "What is going—" Lucia raised her hand, silencing Olivia's question on her lips.

She held her breath when Lucia took a step toward the magical beast. Lucia's hand stretched out as if aching to run her hand over its thick fur. She took another step, carefully closing the gap between her and the lion. Her stride never wavered, even though the lion's tail swished, its long tongue licking over its mouth. The lion's wings erupted from its shoulders. Electricity charged the air.

Olivia's arm shot out. "Wait! Don't move—"

The lion's roar drowned out the rest of her words as it lunged at Lucia.

CHAPTER
TWO

OLIVIA

The forest absorbed the fierce roar, but its underlying cautionary vibes rippled through Olivia. Mesmerized by the yawning cavern of its mouth and the long sharp teeth guarding the entrance, Olivia stood rooted in place. Lucia's trembling fingertips grazed over the bridge of the lion's nose. His green eyes twinkled at Lucia as if acknowledging her courage to touch him. She yanked her hand away when he shook his head, the glorious mane fanning out around it. He blinked and crouched back on his tawny haunches. Two massive wings pumped as he leaped forward, nearly grazing the top of Lucia's head. Olivia instinctively ducked, but Lucia remained standing tall. Her black hair whipped around her face, caught in the turbulence created by his exit. Both girls gazed into the bright blue sky and followed the creature's path. The huge tan body glided as deft as a bird. Another roar boomed over the forest, then he disappeared over the horizon.

The girls turned and stared at each other, open-mouthed at what had just happened.

Olivia rushed to Lucia, her golden-brown eyes shifting to scan the sky. "What was that all about? He barely glanced at me... only had eyes for you. Have you seen him before?"

Lucia shook her head, wonder still sparkling in her eyes. "No. I haven't seen him before, but I've recently felt like someone... or some-thing... has been watching me while I trained. A few days ago, Balt-hazar and I were sparring in this very field. I knew immediately unknown eyes were upon me, so I shifted into a tiger. My fur bristled as I scanned the forest. The shadows moved like a mist, but I couldn't lock onto whatever stalked us. The forest held its inhabitant in a cloak of silence. Soon, the forest returned to life and I no longer sensed eyes on me. I shifted back and found Balthazar staring at me with a huge grin. He scratched his beard and raised an eyebrow. I asked him if he saw anything and he shook his head no. He told me the forest has many creatures that call it home. One of them has captured my attention. I asked him what that meant, but he raised his sword and said I would find out in due time. I guess I did. The lion's stare had the same intensity I felt that day."

"Wow. He's incredible, but very intimidating. Maybe he's watching you like our magical creatures watched us?"

Lucia shrugged, her eyes flickering to the forest once more. "I guess so, but the Magi said I am my own magical beast because I can shift into a tiger." A sly grin crossed her face. "I'd really love to have one pick me. Honestly, when I watch you and the boys fly, my heart leaps with wonder and a bit of envy. I want to feel what you feel. The wind in my hair—the freedom of flight." Her eyes were luminous with unshed tears. "It must be amazing."

Olivia grabbed Lucia's hand. "Well, I'm your fairy godmother today. How about you fly home with me on Aureus? He can defi-nitely handle both of us. Right?" She glanced over her shoulder. He gave a quick squawk and shook his body like he was readying himself for his riders. "See," Olivia laughed. "It'll be fun!"

Lucia squeezed her hand and giggled. "Sounds amazing! Armor off." Her sleek black protection uncoiled from around her and disap-peared, going to its home on the shelves inside the Weapons Room.

"Let's go!" Olivia winked. The girls ran to Aureus and climbed onto his back. Lucia sat behind Olivia and wrapped her arms around her waist.

"Hold on tight. Free falling isn't all that it's cracked up to be." Lucia laughed, the joy in it melted Olivia's heart. "Fly, Aureus! Show her what you can do."

He trotted for a few feet, thrusting his wings up and down. When his feet lifted, Lucia whooped with excitement. The forest grew smaller as they rose above the sprawling field. He banked slightly and made a lazy circle over the forest, as if to catch the attention of all who called it home. Olivia's heart pounded in sync with his powerful rhythm.

"It's gorgeous up here!" Lucia yelled. "I feel like my heart is going to explode!"

"Hold on tight!" Olivia warned, knowing Lucia hadn't even begun to feel the full rush. "Sometimes, I wish I could stay up here forever." Lucia's head nodded against her back.

Aureus headed for the deep canyon. Olivia leaned forward, tightening her thighs and digging her heels into his side. He dove over the granite canyon's jagged rim. Lucia gasped as he raced for the river below, tightening her grip while matching Olivia's movements. Aureus skimmed near the river's surface between the rapids crashing over rocks on the river's banks. Deep inside the canyon's walls, long shadows cast over the riders, sending a chill over her skin. Olivia's cheeks ached from a smile she didn't think could grow any bigger while the racing wind chapped her skin.

"This is incredible!" Lucia yelled.

A wide, blind curve loomed ahead. Aureus slipped down, letting his enormous paws drag across the tips of the rapid's crest. Lush greenery growing through crevices in the gray walls blurred as he built up speed. Lucia gave another squeal of delight when he soared around the corner. Just ahead, spanning the chasm, was the enormous stone bridge to the church. Both girls cried out as he streaked through the massive arched pillars. Aureus let loose a cry of seeming joy at the sight. Olivia understood he, too, had been thrilled by his daring feats. He slowed and soared out of the canyon. He circled the church once, then landed by the back entrance.

Lucia jumped off his back and raced to face the amazing beast. Olivia dismounted quietly, watching her fellow Guardian throw her arms around his thick, feathered neck. Olivia felt her heart swell in reaction.

"You're magnificent," Lucia murmured, her forehead rested against his lowered head. "I'll never forget this day. Thank you." She dropped her hands and stepped away. The feathers on his wings rustled, reflecting shards of gold within them. He took flight and rose over the church. Olivia lost sight of him when he passed through the church's tall spires, spiking into the sky with the sun in its late afternoon descent. Olivia would also never forget this day. Aureus had revealed his virtue of humility, his gift of service to Lucia shined through his color of gold. But she also knew inside his giving heart there was a fierce fighter who would do anything to protect his rider in their joined battle against evil.

Olivia came up next to Lucia, who still scanned the sky. "Well, that was kinda boring, don't you think?"

Lucia's infectious laugh wrapped around Olivia while she gave her a hip bump. "So boring, my mind almost exploded. When he dipped down and touched the water, I think I stopped breathing! Thank you, fairy godmother. I'll remember this day for as long as I live."

Olivia gave her a hip bump in return. "Same for me... and Aureus. I felt his response to you. I think he would have blushed if he were human."

"He'd be a cutie, too," Lucia winked. The girls giggled and made their way to the huge wooden door.

Behind it lay her new home.

Her training grounds.

Her mentors.

And Zach.

~

After a long afternoon of training, Olivia dragged her tired body down the dim hallway of smooth stone. It reminded her more of a medieval castle than a church. She certainly never expected to call it home. Her room was the last door on the left before the hallway curved and stairs led to another level. Many times, she'd wanted to explore the commune the Magi created, but her time didn't allow for much of that. Her days were crammed with training, going on hunts, and going to school. Graduation was fast approaching, as were more decisions about her future. She'd always imagined going to college and pursuing a law degree, but could she achieve these goals with the demands and dangers of the guardianship? She shook her head as she opened the door.

Can't think about it right now, just want to sleep.

She sighed and closed the door behind her. Leaning back, she inhaled the fresh scent of her simple bedroom. A double-sized bed, a dresser, and a desk with a chair filled the room. A white comforter was the perfect canvas for exotic pillows looking like they were plucked from a Mediterranean market. She walked across the Persian carpet and sat on her bed. The room held the same flair as Balthazar's room where he retreats to meditate. She didn't even want to tug on the thread of how it all got here. It didn't matter in the end... she loved it. One wall had arched windows, giving her a breathtaking view of the exquisite landscape. Her eyes narrowed as she gazed at the forest, its tips gleamed silver under the bright moon. It was dark and foreboding at night, but she was not afraid to enter it. Her night vision took away the shadows where something could lie in wait. But today's visitor had been an intense surprise and a little unnerving to think of all the magical creatures she could stumble upon.

Is the lion meant for Lucia? I hope so.

She lifted the edge of her shirt, but a knock on her door stopped her hand. Her brow creased, wondering who would come by so late. She opened the door to a grinning Zach. Tension ebbed from her when she noticed the twinkle in his emerald eyes. His smile grew, highlighting the single dimple in his cheek.

"Did I surprise you?" He asked, rocking back on his heels.

"Ya, you did. I wasn't expecting you since we just left each other in the training room. Is everything okay—"

He stepped past her and grabbed her hand. He pulled her close, leaving no space between them. "Yes, but I couldn't very well do this." His tall frame leaned down and touched his lips to hers. A thrill of excitement swept away the surprise of his kiss. His lips remained gentle. Demanding nothing more or less of what she was willing to give in return. She released his hand and slipped her arms around his neck. Her fingertips grazed over the faint webbing of scars left from the horrendous flames of Lucifer's dragon, Abaddon. Her heart stammered when she thought of how close she'd come to losing him. His agonizing screams as the flames licked over his body rang in her ears. Pushing the terrible memory aside, she entwined her fingers in his thick brown hair and drew him closer. A shiver ran through his body as their kiss deepened. A sudden heat flared between them, igniting a flame that demanded more fuel.

I could do this all day...

A part of her wanted to completely let go, get lost in her growing feelings for Zach. Let the unspoken desire she had for him take over. But she couldn't. Those steps could divide her focus and distract from her purpose.

Guardian of Orion.

Demon slayer.

Protector of humanity.

She pulled away before she lost control. "I agree. This would have caused a stir, but I'm glad you came by where we have more privacy." She smiled up at him. "I really don't know how private it is, though. I have a sense of always being watched."

"Well, shame on them. Let's give them something to make them blush." He leaned back down, but she rolled her eyes and playfully slapped his chest.

"Uhm—I don't think so." She tried to pull out of his embrace, but his arms locked tighter around her waist. When their eyes locked, she found the hard glint of determination back lit by his budding passion.

"I'm serious, Liv. I don't like all this sneaking around in hopes of quick moments alone with you. We need more, and I want more for us. Think about all we're giving up to be Guardians; a normal life as teenagers, hanging out with friends, even time with our families. I don't also want to give up how it feels to be your boyfriend. Sometimes, you are more important to me than the guardianship."

Her eyebrows shot up. "Don't say that—"

"You know what I mean, Liv. Of course, it's important, but our parents found each other and were able to be couples. If they could do it, we should make it a priority, too. You're my future just as much as the guardianship is."

She remained silent as warring emotions bubbled inside of her. Dreams of a future life with Zach were so precarious, and sometimes frightening for her. She'd spent most of her life not trusting many people, especially boys. But since her dad had come home, she'd broken through the lack of trust barrier. It left her secretly wanting the love and commitment both their parents had for each other. Zach had shown he was worthy, but was she ready to be completely vulnerable to him?

But is now a good time to add that to the mix?

She swallowed through the nervous thickness clogging her throat. "I understand what you're saying and I believe it, too."

He jerked with excitement. He unlocked his arms from around her and gently placed his warm hands on her face. "Then let's—"

"But we both know that Lucifer is coming back and he will hit us hard. Until we know what happened to Delilah, Zar, and even Asura, we can't let our focus become divided. The consequences are too great." Zach sagged as he closed his eyes. She pressed her lips together, hating herself for putting up boundaries that a part of her didn't want to have in place.

"God, I know you're right, but it's hard to ignore my feelings for you. I know this may sound corny—"

"Because you are," she chuckled.

"Okay. Guilty as charged." Zach shrugged his shoulders and laughed. "Look, what if we tried to have dates—" his fingers made air quotes, "—times for just us. I've got a few ideas of places where we could go here in Magiland. Together. No one else. How does that sound?"

Olivia reached up on her tiptoes and gave Zach a chaste kiss. "That sounds delightful."

"Good." He gripped her chin. "I'm holding you to it," he whispered and kissed her again, leaving her reeling with the unspoken promise it held.

He dropped his hand and opened the door. Stepping aside, he gave a lopsided grin.

"Sweet dreams, Liv."

"Night," she managed before the door closed.

Olivia flopped down on the bed and stared up at the ceiling. She placed a hand on her stomach, trying to calm her butterflies.

What are you planning, Zach Paxton?

Am I ready for it?

CHAPTER
THREE

OLIVIA

Bacon.
  Waffles.
Coffee.

The aromas of a perfect breakfast trifecta enticed Olivia when her portal opened up in her bedroom. Deliciousness wafted up from the kitchen, along with the clatter of cooking. Thunder lifted his head, curled up on her blanket. He rose and stretched, arching his back as he spied her with his huge green eyes.

"Morning, kit-kitty." She walked over to her bed and stroked his long, gray fur. "Let's go get some breakfast. I'm starving."

The sizzle created by the portal's closing didn't make her near as giddy as the sizzle of bacon. Her stomach growled as she took the stairs two-at-a-time. Once she hit the foyer, she darted around the corner and let her nose lead the way, Thunder's soft pattering of footsteps behind her. The hushed tones of her mom and dad talking interlaced with the comforting harmony of their morning routine. During Dad's first months back home, it irritated her and raised her suspicions about what they were discussing. Words died on their lips when Olivia entered the room. That had been the true dagger to her heart. Feeling like an outsider in her own home.

Their lies were crushing me. I couldn't take much more of their secrecy.

Thank God we're past it.

She smiled as she entered the bright, cozy kitchen, now pleased to find her parents working and chatting side-by-side. Their motions continued like they knew each other's next move. Comfortable. Compatible. In love... like it should be. Like how she'd imagined it when she was younger. This new reality sent a warmth through her heart, a place that had been cold for too long.

"Morning, Livvy," Dad saluted her with his coffee cup.

"Hi, honey," Mom placed the spatula on the counter and moved in for a hug. The arms that wrapped around her were lithe, but stronger since her car accident. Olivia returned it with a big squeeze before stepping back. "How was your day?"

Olivia slipped onto the barstool, accepting the cup of coffee Dad handed her with a salute of her own. She closed her eyes and inhaled the rich aroma. Because of her angelic powers, she didn't need the caffeine anymore, but that didn't stop her from loving the taste. She took a quick sip, letting the robust flavor roll over her tongue.

"Well, Mom, it was riveting, to say the least. For starters, I fell from Aureus in flight... on purpose."

Mom stopped piling food on the plate and cocked her head. "Um, things you should probably not share with me before I finish my morning coffee." She winked and placed the plate in front of her.

"Thanks. You guys spoil me with these delicious breakfasts." Olivia's mouth watered as she slathered butter on the golden waffles and covered them with maple syrup. She ate a few bites, reveling in their flavors melting in her mouth.

"Anything else?" Dad asked over his coffee cup's rim.

"I took Lucia for a ride on Aureus. He totally showed off, flying over the forest near the church before zooming through the canyon. Lucia had a blast, but I think she yearns for a magical beast for herself even though she can shift into a tiger. That... is something I'd love to do. But the *really* big event of the day happened when a huge, winged lion emerged from the forest. He was majestic and fearsome, but wasn't interested in me, only Lucia. He let her touch him, but then flew away as quickly as he had appeared. I wonder if he's curious about Lucia? I guess we'll find out if he shows himself again."

"A winged lion, huh?" Dad scratched his close-cropped beard. "That *is* interesting," he mumbled, placing his cup in the dishwasher.

Olivia wanted to ask him more, but her phone vibrated in the charger. She wiped her hands on the napkin and grabbed the phone, wondering who would text her so early. Most of her friends had faded away, but that was her fault.

Callie.

Leaning closer, her pulse quickened. She hadn't heard from Callie since she quit Cuppa Joe's.

Hey. I know I haven't reached out, but do you think you can stop by Joe's after school?
We're fine, but I need to talk to you about my "problem". Hoping you can help.
Thanks.
XO

That could only mean one thing. Her ex-husband was harassing her, and she needed help. She clenched her fist, remembering when she made Callie promise to contact her if she ever felt threatened by him. Sparks of anger flared when she pictured Callie and her daughter, Chloe, being subjected to that brute's cruelty.

Absolutely.
XO
Stay near Joe

Her fingers hovered above the phone as she considered if she was overreacting. She didn't care and hit send. If Callie was nervous enough to contact her, then something big had happened. Glancing at the time, she shoveled in one more bite before she pushed away from the counter.

"I'm late. Thanks again for breakfast!" She waved, snatched the remaining piece of bacon, and jogged into the foyer. She grabbed her backpack and was out the door. Being late drove her nuts, but the text from Callie overrode her irritation during the drive to school. Tightening her grip on the steering wheel, worse case scenarios swirled in her mind.

He better not have hurt them or there will be hell to pay.

Excited murmurers broke out and books slammed shut when the last bell of the day rang. Olivia guessed she'd been successful today at hiding her distracted thoughts about Callie from Ms. Thomas, her prim and proper history teacher. Whatever sixth sense went on behind her teacher's tortoise-shell glasses for her had not pinged during class. Instead, she smiled at the students filing out of her room. Olivia slipped next to her friend, Alisha, and into the crowded hallway.

Phew... maybe she's just as ready as we are for this school year to end.

Graduation.

And then what?

"Hey, did you hear me?" Alisha rolled her eyes and whispered in her ear again. "Here comes your boyfriend... and Sergio." Olivia's head jerked at Alisha's breathy tone when she said *Sergio.* She stopped and grabbed Alisha's arm, pulling her closer. Students suddenly changed direction like water around a boulder.

"Uhm—what's going on? I've never heard you say his name like a swooning groupie. Have I missed something?" Alisha's brown eyes twinkled as a conspirator's smile stretched across her beautiful, dark skin.

"Come on, you know I always thought he was cute, but something is different about him. He's—"

Olivia's body lurched forward as someone slammed into her shoulder from behind. She glanced up to find Ryan, with an ugly sneer on his freckled face, staring back at her. "Always in the way. Standing around like God's gift to the world—" his mean eyes raked over them, "—I won't miss seeing you." He hollered before he blended back into the crowd.

Olivia curled her hands into fists instead of blasting him with a spear of fire or throwing him across the hallway. No matter how good that would feel, showing her powers would only hurt her in the end.

"Jerk!" Alisha belted out. She shook her head, her ebony curls catching the overhead lighting. "He's such a creep."

"Yeah. I guess some people never change." Olivia remembered the day at Cuppa Joe's when she saw her first demon. A wrath Fallen had attached himself to Ryan. When Ryan picked a fight with Sergio, the demon tried to attack her, Zach, and Sergio, but someone killed him before he could kidnap her and take her to Berith. At the time, she didn't know who Berith was. She does now. The reigning Prince of the Wrath Realm. In hell... One of seven princes who serve directly under Lucifer.

Who killed him and saved us that day?

Ryan's red hair bobbed above the crowd. She'd always hoped when a demon was killed, the person it stalked would change their course in life. It didn't appear to be the case with Ryan, who still wore his anger like a badge of honor. Ryan and Zach locked eyes as they passed each other, but neither made a move to escalate the issue. Zach had honored his word to let her fight her own battles.

The girls moved and waited against the metal lockers lining the hallway. Olivia couldn't help but smile when Zach's gaze found hers. She hitched her backpack higher on her shoulder, feeling a little silly for mooning over his approach. Where she would have turned away before, she happily stepped into his outstretched arms and returned his embrace.

"Hey, you." Zach's breath stirred the hair on top of her head. "Ryan stirring up trouble again?"

Olivia scoffed and pulled away. "Isn't he always?"

"Hi, Alisha, you—uh... look nice today." Sergio shifted his feet while clearing his throat. "I mean—"

Alisha giggled and bumped his shoulder with hers. "I'm glad you noticed. You know, I was thinking about getting some ice cream. Want to come?" Olivia caught the subtle hopefulness in her friend's raised eyebrows. When Sergio stood there like he was dumbstruck and shrugged his shoulders. Alisha glanced away, her eyes darting to the exit door. "No biggie, I'll see later." She turned and hustled away, her back ramrod straight as she weaved through the thinning crowd.

"Are you crazy, or just dumb?"

Zach's question pulled him out of his stupor. Sergio slapped his hands over his face and moaned. "Both!" came his muffled reply. His hands slid down his face. He turned and stared at the closing exit door. "Why didn't I say yes?"

"Yes, to what?" Lucia maneuvered her wheelchair next to Zach and Olivia. She cocked her head. "Well?"

"Your brother lost his tongue and apparently his nerve when Alisha asked him on an ice cream date." Zack chuckled when Sergio leaned back into the lockers and softly banged the back of his head against them.

"*Wow*, is all I have to say." She wheeled closer. "I'm going to smack you around in training and maybe knock some sense into you." Olivia joined Zach's chuckle as Sergio glared at his sister.

"Look, I blew it. I know. When she asked me... I froze. I can't believe I just stood there. I've wanted to—" he shook his head, "—it doesn't matter anymore. She'll ghost me for sure now." He shoved himself off the lockers. "Come on, Papa's probably waiting for us. See ya." He made a half-hearted wave and left without waiting for Lucia.

"Have fun with that," Olivia smiled at Lucia. "Don't go easy on him, either."

A mischievous grin spread as she placed her hands on the wheels.

"Don't worry, I've got a laundry list of reasons to knock him down a peg." Olivia admired Lucia's moxie. If anyone could help Sergio find himself again, it was his sister.

He needs to get rid of his harboring rage over Manny's death.

"I wouldn't want to mess with Lucia. She might go *tiger* on his sorry butt!"

Olivia slipped her hand into Zach's. "Now that would be a sight to see."

They headed for the parking lot, Olivia picking up the pace when the metal door closed behind her. "You're in a hurry." Zach tugged on her hand. "What's up?"

"I need to stop by Joe's. Callie texted me this morning, asking me to come see her after school. She didn't say much, but I think her ex is giving her problems." Her stomach twisted, thinking about what Callie might confess to her.

"Okay. Let me know if there is anything I can do to help her."

"Thank you." Olivia placed her hand on his cheek and kissed him. "That means a lot to me. I'll fill you in later."

She dashed off to her faded green Explorer and braced herself for the worst.

CHAPTER
FOUR

OLIVIA

Familiar aromas of fresh coffee and baked treats mingled with hushed conversations welcomed Olivia to Cuppa Joe's. Nothing had changed since she stopped working here, but it felt different. Brightly colored eclectic tables and chairs filled the room. Couches and classic video game consoles lined one wall, and customers relaxed with their favorite cup of coffee. A pang of sadness hit her. She left working at Joe's because of the guardianship.

But she wouldn't leave the people.

Joe waved to her as he made his way from behind the counter. He had once intimated her with his watchful eyes and reserved demeanor, but her former boss was a kind man with an amiable smile once she'd earned his trust. His fit, lean frame easily weaved its way through the tables towards her. Olivia's shoulders relaxed when he scooped her into a quick hug.

"Hi—it's so good to see you! It's been too long." He stepped back, holding her at arm's length. "How ya doing? School going well?"

"I'm doing great. This last semester is busy with finals and deciding on a college. Mom's fully recovered and so happy that Dad's back home." Olivia cracked a grin. "We're getting to know each other again. I'm used to having him around now, and he's pretty cool. Just one big happy family. But I miss it here. Thanks for understanding—"

Joe shook his head, his thick brown hair falling across his fore-head. "I get it. I was once your age, too. Life moves on and your future is big and bright. Although, it's been a rocky road replacing you." He glanced over his shoulder at a teenage boy working next to Callie behind the counter. His t-shirt stamped with, *Life without coffee is scary,* hung loose on his tall lanky body. "Simon is finally getting the hang of it, but he's not you." Joe's hazel eyes creased in the corners as he grinned at her. "What brings you by?"

"Well—to say hi of course, but I was also hoping to catch Callie during her break and catch up. Is that alright?"

As if hearing her name, Callie glanced up and locked eyes with Olivia. Her jet-black hair pulled back into a ponytail, accentuating her sharp cheekbone, but the dark shadows under her crystal blue eyes gave Olivia pause. Callie perked up with a smile before she leaned over and whispered in Simon's ear. He glanced our way and nodded, letting Callie by behind him.

"Sure, that's fine with me." He nodded, his face softening while Callie made her way to them. His quick gaze border-lined on mooning over her, but his posture stiffened with a protective nature. Olivia couldn't blame him. Callie's striking, petite stature made heads turn, but she never paid much mind to the not-so-subtle flirts from customers. They passed each other with an unspoken look, some-thing they've done a hundred times under this roof.

I wonder if she even knows how Joe feels?

Olivia's radar was up again when Callie hugged her, the bones in her ribcage too pronounced for her liking. "Thanks for coming by. I know you're busy—"

"I'm never too busy for you. Don't ever think that. I'm glad you reached out. It's been too long." Olivia glanced around the cafe. "Want to talk here or go outside?"

"Let's go out back. There's something I want to show you." Callie led the way down past the game rooms, then pushed open the door. She walked into the sunshine flooding the hallway and into the warm desert heat. Olivia stopped near Callie's compact sedan, watching her friend rub her hands over her arms. Callie stared into the distance as if she was trying to find her words. The silence stretched out between them. Finally, Callie released a heavy sigh. Her eyelids fluttered shut, but a single tear escaped through the crease and tracked a wet line down her cheek.

"I remember the day I told you my divorce was final. I was so relieved to finally move on from him. Chloe and I could start out fresh. I could finish college." She opened her eyes and faced Olivia. The pain on her face was clear, but the palatable fear in her eyes was unacceptable. "At first, Jared left us alone. But I started feeling like I was being watched, a tickle at the base of my neck. Sometimes at a store or walking to my car after class at night. I found no one, but it unnerved me. Then my tire was slashed after work. That pissed me off. But when the day care called, it scared me to death. A worker noticed Jared lurking at the fence line. Then the phone calls started. He either yelled and called me names or cried because he wanted us back. I was stupid and tried to talk to him, but it always backfired. About a month ago, he broke into my house." She scoffed as she leaned against the trunk. "He stole a stuffed bunny he'd given Chloe and—"

"What did he do?" Olivia placed her hand on Callie's arm.

"He found an old photo album and laid it open on our kitchen table. A few pictures of Chloe were missing, but... on one picture from our honeymoon, he had stabbed it with a knife. I threw up in the kitchen sink, terrified by the black handle protruding from the album."

"Tell me you called the police," Olivia asked through gritted teeth.

"I did." Her voice vibrated with anger. "I got a dog and a restraining order. He had a lame alibi and was smart enough not to leave prints. Nothing happened for a few weeks. I thought the police and restraining order had knocked some sense back into him, but—"

she licked her lips "—I did something reckless I wanted to do for a long time. I went on a date with Joe."

About damn time!

"That's not reckless! That's fantastic!" Olivia squeezed Callie's arm. "I thought you and Joe—"

Callie shook her head, whipping the ponytail behind her. "No, you don't understand. Joe walked me to my front door and kissed me. I was so lost in how amazing it felt, I didn't think about us being seen until Jared's truck revved by us and peeled around the corner. I was so undone, Joe insisted he spend every night on the couch. He's been amazing through this. Chloe loves him, but—" she shoved away from the car and opened the driver's door. She reached inside and came out with an envelope. She came back and handed it to Olivia. "This came in the mail yesterday."

Olivia recoiled at the subtle stench of sulfur Callie probably couldn't detect. She took it from her as blood rushed in her ears.

A demon is with Jared.

It made perfect sense to Olivia. The escalation of threats and stalking were being driven by a demon. She opened the envelope and pulled out a single photo. Her stomach dropped when she saw the red bullseye drawn over Callie's face.

"You said to contact you if I was in trouble. Well, I am, so how can you help me? I'm desperate—I haven't shown this to Joe yet. He'll lose his mind. I have a bad feeling about this."

She slid the picture back inside and handed it to Callie. Olivia had to come up with something quick, because telling Callie she was a demon slayer was out of the question. "My dad started up an old business. He's doing some P.I. work again. How about we come by tonight? He can set up security cameras, monitor the house while you're out. He'd love to help you after all you did for me while Mom was in the hospital."

Kinda true... Dad was always watching out for people and would love to help.

"Would he really do that?" Callie caught Olivia off guard with a big hug. "You don't know how relieved I am." Callie's voice hitched with a sob as her body sagged against Olivia. Callie pulled away and scrubbed her hands over her face, wiping away her tears. "Thank you."

"Absolutely." Inhaling through her nose, Olivia released a cleansing breath. "Dad and I will come over later tonight. He'll set everything up and hopefully I can see Chloe before she goes to bed. Sound good?"

"Perfect. I'm sure she'll be up. She's a regular night owl. I better get back to work." They hurried inside, Callie peeling off toward the counter while Olivia headed for the front door. She waved at Joe, hoping he bought the smile Olivia planted on her face and missed the fire burning in her eyes. She pushed open the door, trying to keep a lid on her emotions. Yanking open her car door; she couldn't believe a demon was so close to her friend.

I should have been around more.

Maybe living with the Magi is a bad idea...

A buzzing cut through her thoughts. She pulled out her phone and found a text from Zach.

How did it go with Callie?

Anger poured off her in waves when she thought of Callie's revelation; fear for herself and her daughter from a jealous ex-husband incited by a demon.

She's being stalked by her ex. I'm pretty sure a demon is behind it. Feel like going on a hunt with me tonight?

His text popped up, making her laugh.

You are the perfect date.

She drove home, devising a plan to help rid Callie of Jared. She and Chloe deserved to be safe and not live in a constant state of fear.

The only catch was making sure her Guardianship remained a secret.

CHAPTER
FIVE

OLIVIA

"I hope you know what you're doing. If her ex shows up, you'll be vulnerable. Or worse, he pulls a stupid stunt and you have to reveal your powers," Dad said, shifting in the car seat.

"That's why I brought you and Zach." Olivia sat in her dad's truck parked down the street, away from Callie's small ranch-style house illuminated by a nearby streetlight. The quaint neighborhood was older, with mature trees and big hedges. The residents kept it tidy and cozy, leaving one with a sense of living in a safe, peaceful community. But streetlights and landscape created long shadows, a maze to cloak an approach for someone up to no good.

"If he shows up, you call 911 and Zach will go after the demon," Olivia said, turning towards her dad. "I need to get inside her house and see if I can sense a trail. If nothing happens, then I'll get Jared's address and we can hunt him there." She shifted her gaze to the backseat and found Zach staring out the side window. "Ready?"

"Always, but I can't shake this nagging feeling. My mark isn't tingling, but the neighborhood is too quiet, like it's waiting for something to happen," Zach said, casting a wary eye at her.

So, I'm not the only one with a bad feeling.

"Well, let's go find out. Zach, walk around in your shield and check things out while Dad and I go to the house." Both nodded, and they exited the car. Zach grinned at her before he raised his shield and disappeared into the night.

"Poof," Dad muttered. "Zach is gone. I loved going invisible to the world... except to the Fallen."

"Makes the hunt and kill much easier when I don't worry about who's watching." Olivia said.

"Those were the days." Dad scoffed.

Olivia and Dad crossed the street, his bag of hardware swinging at his side.

"Thanks for coming and helping Callie out. The wave of relief washing over her was huge."

Dad chuckled and lifted the bag. "I'm happy to help, and it got me thinking. This P.I. gig you made up might actually be a good idea for me. I can still help people and fight the bad guys on a different level."

"Conner Drake—Private Investigator," she said, chuckling with her dad. "Has a nice ring to it."

"We'll see—"

Olivia grabbed her dad's jacket sleeve when her mark of Orion sparked to life. "Wait. A demon is near." She scanned the shrubbery, but found no movement in the thick shadows. Her pulse spiked when frantic barking erupted from inside Callie's house. Olivia's heightened hearing picked up the muffled shouts of surprise. Olivia turned to Dad. "Stay here and call 911. I'm going in."

Dad grabbed her arm, tension in his grip. "Please be careful, Livvy."

"I will... just call the police," she urged before she ran for Callie's house.

"Shut up!" yelled an unfamiliar male voice. Heart pounding, Olivia reached the front door. The barking stopped with a painful yelp.

Only lowlifes hurt a dog.

Infuriated, she turned the doorknob. Locked. Chloe's muffled crying turned her anger to fear. Without thinking, she surged a fire pulse through her hand, melting the metal enough to turn the handle. She shoved the door open, startling the occupants when it slammed against the wall.

The scene would stay forever burned in her memory.

Terror lay thick in the crowded living room. Jared stood near the kitchen counter with a gun leveled at Joe's chest. Callie stood behind him, holding a distraught Chloe straining against her mom to reach a curly-haired, tan dog cowering against the couch.

But it was the smoky wrath demon who hovered next to Jared, penetrating the room with evil. The bitter odor of sulfur left a tang in her mouth. Its red eyes shifted to Olivia, first with surprise, then with hatred.

Where are you, Zach?

All heads swiveled, along with the gun, now aimed at her.

"Who—" Jared's eyes narrowed. "Well, if it isn't the coffee store brat. What are you doing here? Oh, wait—I know. You're here to spread more lies about me. You've been bad-mouthing me since the beginning." He sneered. "Well, welcome to the party."

Olivia slowly raised her hands. "I just came by to say hi. I'm not here to cause any trouble," she said. Zach emerged from the hallway, unseen in his dimension except by Olivia and the Fallen. "Why don't you put the gun down? You're scaring your daughter."

Jared took a quick peek at Chloe. Her sobs filled the room. He licked his lips, eyes darting between everyone in the room. The demon roared at Zach and mutated into a Fallen. Zach backed down the hallway, raising his sword, swirling with green electricity. Clad in black with two crimson horns twisting from his temple, the demon leaped towards Zach. They disappeared down the hallway in a clash of swords and shouts. With the demon gone, she could make her move.

"I told you, Callie, no one else could have you. You're mine! I'm taking Chloe and there's nothing any of you can do to stop me." Jared turned his gun away from Olivia. Terror coiled inside her as the battle between Zach and the demon appeared in the backyard.

Jared's eyes went flat, jaw set as he leveled the gun at Joe. "You should never have kissed—"

It all happened so quick, but time moved in slow motion. Through the sliding glass door, Olivia glimpsed green, spinning water blades slicing through the demon before Zach plunged his sword into the demon's chest. Her elation was short-lived. She thrust her hand out and sent a wave to shove Jared off balance. A gunshot exploded in the room a second before her force pushed Jared against the counter. An anguished cry rang out, piercing Olivia's ears and heart. Joe was thrown back and collapsed, blood blooming from his upper chest. Callie dived to the floor, screaming as she tried to scramble away to protect Chloe. Shock registered on Jared's sweat glistened face. He shook his head, dazed, raising the gun still locked in his grip. Rage boiled within Olivia, fueling the next strike. She shot her hand out again, and like an imaginary claw, ripped the gun from his hand and tossed it back towards her. But it wasn't enough. She felt the beginning wisps of fire swirling in her palms, her mark pulsating against her skin.

I should kill him... look what he's done.

He doesn't deserve to live.

Footsteps thundered through the door. Shouts of *police* and *hands up* broke through her heated haze. Two police officers raced around her, pointing their weapons at Jared. He rolled onto his stomach; his gaze locked with hers. "How did you do that?" He hissed; dark eyes filled with malice. An officer stepped in front of him, breaking the contact as they read Jared his rights.

Joe...

She dashed over to Joe and fell to her knees beside him. He lay on the floor, his face too pale against the blood pooling behind him.

"He needs an ambulance!" Callie yelled, rocking Chloe on the floor, tears streaming down her face.

"One's on its way, ma'am," the officer said as he kneeled next to Joe. He moaned, his eyes fluttering open. "Callie."

"Livvy, get two towels from the kitchen." Olivia glanced over and found her dad behind her. "Hurry! We need to put pressure on his wound." She jumped up and ran into the kitchen, slamming drawers open and closed until she found the towels. Dropping them into Dad's hands, she stepped back, praying sirens coming up the street would get to Joe in time.

"Olivia, can you hold Chloe?" Callie's chin quivering against her daughter's dark hair. "I need to see Joe. This is all my fault—" She squeezed her eyes shut, pressing her lips together.

Olivia bent down and carefully scooped Chloe into her arms. "He'll be fine... he's strong—" Callie shook her head and pushed away from the couch. She leaned over Joe, whispering in his ear, words meant only for him to hear. The room became too crowded when the medics rushed through the doorway. Chloe's arms closed tighter around her neck.

"Teddy," Chloe muttered. The sweet-faced dog jumped onto the couch and licked Chloe's wet cheek. Olivia rubbed circles over her back, feeling some of the tension release from Chloe's tiny frame.

"How about we take Teddy to the backyard?" Chloe nodded against her shoulder. Olivia rose and skirted the outside of the room, keeping Chloe's face turned away from the nightmare that shattered this sweet little girl's world. The dog followed at their heels. She opened the sliding glass door off the kitchen, inhaling the fresh night air that bathed her face. Teddy bolted out as if shot from a cannon. Sliding the door closed behind him, she scanned the small backyard for Zach.

"Hey," he said, leaning against the side of the house. Chloe's grip tightened as they turned to his voice.

"It's okay, sweetie. This is my friend, Zach. Do you want to go play with Teddy?" Chloe nodded and squirmed out of Olivia's arms. She flipped on the porch light, illuminating the two innocents, finding some joy despite the traumatic situation. It didn't take long before a distinct set of arms wrapped around her and pulled her close. She breathed in his fresh scent as her heart slowed down from its frantic pace. Sliding her arms around his waist, she felt a tremor pass through him, but his heart continued its rapid beat against her ear. He remained quiet, allowing her to gather in the devastation and disappointment she felt in herself. Knowing she couldn't hide in his arms any longer, she released him and pulled away.

"How's Joe doing?" Zach murmured; half his face shrouded in a shadow.

Olivia glanced through the glass door. Joe lay on the gurney being wheeled out of the living room. She swallowed past the thick lump in her throat. "He's hurt pretty bad. Hopefully, he'll be okay... I don't know. This is my fault. I waited too long to stop Jared because I didn't want to show my powers. That split-second hesitation on my part could cost his life."

"Don't kick yourself, Liv," Zach said, wrapping his warm hands around her face. "You couldn't have known he'd really pull the trigger with his daughter watching. Who does that? But that wrath demon— the hate rolling off it—it was the strongest I've faced. There was also this odd giddiness about him too, as if he felt emboldened."

Zach's face paled. His hands fell away, but not before she felt the tremble of his fingertips against her face. She cocked her head. "Are you okay—"

The door slid open. Callie's tear-streaked face peeked through the gap. Her eyes traveled over Zach without a word. Instead, she locked onto Olivia, her hand swiping under her red nose. "They're taking Joe to the hospital. They won't tell me if they think—I need to go—" she pressed her lips together, briefly squeezing her eyes shut. "I called my mom, and she's on her way. Can you stay here until she arrives?"

"Absolutely. I'm so sorry about Joe."

Callie raised her hand. "Please, none of this is your fault. It's mine." She drew in a shuddering breath. "Thank you for your help." She paused as if to say more, but slid the door closed before Olivia could respond.

What if Joe dies?

"Listen, I'm sorry, but I told Kylie I would help her with a homework assignment tonight. I better get going," he said, stumbling back from her. "I'll see you later."

"Wait... what?"

All too quickly, Zach stepped through his portal and was gone in a swirl of green lights.

What's up with him?

Confused by his abrupt departure, she watched Chloe throw a ball for Teddy, his little furry body a blur across the yard. Olivia realized, once again, that someone she cared about got hurt when she thought she had the situation at hand. She learned from her mistake when she didn't bring the guardians to face Delilah, but it didn't seem to matter. This time, she brought help. Zach killed the demon and Dad called the police. But *she* had failed to stop Jared, and Joe got shot because of it. She closed her eyes, trying to shut out the image of Joe's body jerking as blood bloomed on his shirt.

Horror washed over her, its icy tendrils stealing away the fragile peace she'd built.

What if we aren't enough to stop Lucifer and the Fallen?

Are all our efforts going to come up short?

Will more people I love get hurt because evil will do anything to win?

CHAPTER
SIX

ZACH

Familiar scents of clean linen and his dog, Hank, wrapped around Zach as he stepped through the portal into his bedroom. Hank's soft woof and tail thumping against the carpet welcomed him home. He missed the comforting warmth of his family and home, but protecting the guardianship made the decision easier to live with the Magi. The portal sizzled closed, leaving the two alone in the quiet darkness. He stepped toward Hank, but a tremor that had started in Callie's backyard snaked through his body while prickly sweat broke out on his forehead. Painful, terrifying visions swam in his mind. He stumbled a few feet before crumbling to the floor next to Hank.

Jared pointing his gun at Olivia while the wrath demon snarled, raising his sword at him.

Ash and black blood spewing into the air, obscuring his view when a gunshot boomed in his ears.

Joe bleeding, Olivia kneeling over him.

Cody's head bobbing in the rushing water.

Choking on fear and cold water as the current whisked Cody away from him.

Lying on the river bank, despair and shame numbing his core.

A wet nose nudged his face. Zach's shaking hand reached for Hank, grasping his scruffy neck. He pulled his dog closer and sunk

46

his face into his fur. Hank whined gently, placing his paw on top of Zach's arm like a comforting hug. Zach's heart raced, bombarded by repeating images, relentlessly pounding home his failures.

"I know, boy—just give me a minute," Zach muttered. He gritted his teeth as he fought to shut the mental slide show, wreaking havoc within his mind and body.

Olivia's alive.

Olivia's alive.

Olivia's alive.

The mantra slowly calmed him, helping the horrible images to fade away. Running his hand down Hank's back eased his hand's trembling, but a stunned heaviness pushed down on his shoulders. He'd never reacted like that after a battle. Satisfaction at defeating his nemesis had allowed him to keep his emotions in check. Why this reaction now?

What's happening to me?

A stream of light panned across his room when the bedroom door opened. Zach's body froze. A long shadow cast across the carpet.

"Zach? Are you there?" He relaxed, recognizing his dad's voice.

"Yeah, I'm here—" The door fully opened before he could finish, exposing him cradling Hank on the floor. He released his dog, but not before Zach received an affectionate lick on his cheek.

"I heard Hank whining? Is everything okay?" Dad paused in the doorway. Back lit by the hallway light, his big frame looked more formidable than ever.

Do I look okay?

Zach sat up and leaned back against the bed. "I thought I was, but—" he shook his head, "—now I don't know." He stared through the doorway leading to his bathroom. How many times had he stared into that mirror, wondering if he was worthy of this life, worthy of his family's love, worthy of the guardianship? Hadn't he broken those chains, or was he doomed to be shackled to them forever?

Dad closed the door and crossed the carpet with the barest of a whisper. His years of military training still defined his movements and the way he held himself. He settled next to him and stretched out his long legs, mimicking Zach.

"If you want, you can tell me about it, or we could just sit here till it passes."

Zach turned and regarded his dad's profile. His keen night vision took in his sharp, angular lines, highlighted the haircut he kept in military regulation. Zach swallowed; nervous his dad might suspect something. Did he want to share what happened tonight? Maybe he was tired from a long day.

"I'm okay—"

"You think you're the first person I've found suffering trauma... in the throes of the aftershock from the stress of battle? Curled up into themselves, fighting off their demons soaked in their own sweat? If you don't want to talk, I respect that. But don't kid me or yourself." He twisted to face Zach. "It's too important to ignore, son."

Zach released a pent-up breath as he struggled to find the courage to begin. They'd come a long way in mending the trust between them after Cody's death. Bringing it up now could pick at the scab of an old wound, but his dad didn't act angry or disappointed with him. Zach rubbed his hands down his jeans, thankful his hands didn't shake anymore.

"Tonight, Olivia and I, along with her dad, went on a hunt," Zach said, feeling his dad's body tense next to his. "Her co-worker, Callie, was being stalked by her ex-husband. When she talked to Olivia about it, she noticed the faint smell of a demon on a picture Callie handed her. Olivia fibbed and said her dad was a PI and could rig her house with a security system. Olivia asked me to come in case there was trouble... and boy, was there trouble," he scoffed.

"Like what?" Dad asked.

"When we got there, her ex had a gun and a wrath demon clinging to him, spurring on his anger. Things happened so fast. The demon and I began fighting outside while Olivia tried to calm the situation, but her ex was too far gone. Just as I killed the demon, a shot rang out. I froze. All I could think of was Olivia's dead. The demon would have easily killed me as I stood there. My heart pounded against my chest so hard." Zach reached up and rubbed his chest to ease the ache.

"Anyone hurt?" Dad's voice was gruff, but his body sprung tight.

"The ash cleared and there was Olivia kneeling next to her boss, Joe. He was the one who got shot. A sick wave of relief washed over me because the blood wasn't hers. My knees turned to jello, so I leaned against the house and gulped in deep breaths. By the time Olivia came outside, I had my act together. On the inside, I felt like I was one moment away from being pounded by a tidal wave. I left as soon as the ambulance took Joe to the hospital. I barely made it through the portal before I broke out in full body tremors and sweat. Visions kept punching me, cries chasing me. I pulled Hank next to me and buried myself into him until it finally stopped." Hank laid his face on Zach's legs. He scratched him behind his ears, a knot clogging his throat.

"What visions came to you?" His dad's soothing tone helped ease his tension.

"At first, just snippets of what happened in the house, but then it shifted and blurred into Cody. That instant on the river when I lost him. Ever since I shared the story with Olivia and Sergio, I felt some relief. But when he pointed the gun at Olivia and the shot echoed in my ears, it was like—" Zach felt his sense of control slipping.

"Like?" Dad laid his hand on his shoulder. "Don't keep it inside. It'll only fester."

"Like she would be gone too, and once again, I couldn't stop it. Forever trapped, watching someone I love die in front of me. I thought I was better but—"

"It's not surprising what's happening to you. Many men and women struggle with this... PTSD. When I was in Iraq every day we cleared neighborhoods—knocking on doors, never knowing what waited for us on the other side. We lost a few people in ambushes. The hardest thing I ever had to do was tell the next patrol to do the same mission. Many times, I went through first. I couldn't ask them to do it, if I couldn't do it, too. Some soldiers come home affected and others don't. I could compartmentalize it all... deal with the effects on my terms. Without knowing what would happen, losing control was the hardest. I couldn't stop someone from getting hurt or killed. Ironically, for me... and I'm only speaking for me... I had to learn to give up my desire to control every aspect of a mission. I trained them until they dropped, mission planned, until my eyes bled, and gave them the best weapons possible, but in warfare, at the most basic level, each person controls their actions. There's no rhyme or reason — why someone lives and someone dies. It sucks." Dad exhaled, leaning his head back against the bed. "It came down to my faith and what I believed in. When I questioned God or raged at the machine, it only landed me back in the same place, staring at the same set of hollow eyes in the mirror. Faith got me through the rough spots, in believing their souls would go to Heaven. Do you believe that, Zach?"

His dad's words infiltrated his pain and confusion, like a balm over a burn. "Yes, I do. I think about Cody in Heaven. After the Magi showed us Heaven, I knew he was there... probably cracking a joke." They chuckled, easing some of the tension. "But my guilt remains."

"And that's feeding on what happened to you tonight. When the gun went off, your sense of guilt or lack of control transferred to Olivia. The Magi trained the guardians to use the unique powers to fight the enemy. Set yourself free to do this mission... this quest. I know what I'm asking you to do. I had to do it with your mom and now—with you. You can do it. I have faith in you."

Zach reached over and hugged him. His dad's muscular arms wrapped around him and held him tight. "I'm so proud of you, Zach," he whispered into his ear. "Whenever you need to talk or just sit in the dark, I'm here."

A tear slipped down Zach's face as the knot in his chest gave way. Dad didn't talk much about going to war or the scars it left. Hearing what he faced and how he conquered his fears gave Zach hope. "Thank you for sharing and understanding. I needed it."

"Glad I was here to help." Dad patted him on the back and

released him. "Now you better get going before the Magi have a fit. They're mother hens at heart."

"True that," Zach snickered as he rose from the floor.

Dad made his way to the door. "See you in the morning. Love you," he said, glancing over his shoulder before he closed the door.

"Love you, too," he murmured. Raking his hand through his hair, Zach replayed their conversation. He wasn't dumb enough to think his fears would miraculously go away, but at least his reaction tonight made sense to him. The talisman in his pocket radiated heat. Zach raised his portal to return to Magi-land with a restless night ahead of him.

CHAPTER
SEVEN

SERGIO

Sergio's sleek armor clung to him like a second skin. Sweat trickled down his face as he wielded his sword, Nisroc. Gold sparks flew from its metal edge when it clashed against Balthazar's sword. Every day, he fought and trained with his mentor, his only goal was to defeat him. Sergio absorbed the lessons he learned, pushed himself to win a sparring match with Bal. Each day he came up short.

I'll win today.

His body hummed, arms absorbing the weapon's collisions. He fought the urge to let them buckle under the strain. Grunting against his mentor's strength, he leaped off the floor, pushing Balthazar off balance. Sergio twirled and sliced the sword through the air, hitting his opponent's side. Surprise flickered in Bal's eyes as his body caved in on itself. Bal crouched to the floor, waning light from the weapon room's stained-glass windows played a kaleidoscope of colors over his back. Sergio landed behind him; a grin twisted on his face.

"Ready to call it quits?" Sergio boasted.

Balthazar exploded from his position with a back kick to Sergio's stomach. The air whooshed from his lungs as he stumbled back, bringing Nisroc up in defense. It was too late. Bal swept his foot behind Sergio's calves, sending him sprawling to the floor with a thud. Before he could move, Balthazar stood over him, his sword's tip hovering over Sergio's heart.

"I think it is you who are done." Balthazar flashed a smile, his white teeth bright within his long, black beard.

Sergio glared at his mentor's powerful body framed by the shimmering, iridescent film cascading down from the huge, ornate arches circling the room. Disgust with himself churned in his gut as he scooted backwards until his legs cleared the glistening sword.

How did that happen? I had him!

I'll never beat him.

Sergio stood on stiff legs. The heavy weight of once again losing pressed down on him. "You're right. I'm done." He turned toward the shelves where a menagerie of many weapons lay waiting. Nisroc's blade of polished gold felt heavy in his hand, disconnected from the oneness they shared when he fought with it. Balthazar followed; his footsteps unusually loud behind him. His firm hand grabbed Sergio's elbow, yanking him to a stop. Sergio's eyes widen when Balthazar came in front of him and blocked his way. He'd never seen his mentor's eyes blaze with such a fury.

"What do you mean you're done? You can't handle losing a lesson? Why is this time different?"

"I'm always losing a lesson to you. It's a beat down every time. Just once, I want the last move. I've beaten demons, but I can't beat you." Sergio's shoulders sagged, his gazed shifted to the white flames flickering in the fire pit. "I'm tired of—" he shook his head, "—I'm just tired."

Balthazar sheathed his sword with enough force that it surprised Sergio the sharp tip hadn't pierced the scabbard. He rested his large, dark hand on the hilt and leaned in close to Sergio. "You want me to let you win so you can feel better about yourself? That's not my job. The reason you defeat the Fallen is that I push you to your limits. The day you best me is the day our training is done. But we don't have to worry about that day now, do we, since you want to quit, right?"

A heat crept up Sergio's neck. "Don't talk to me like a child. I'm not a child! I'm a guardian!"

"Then act like one! You had me back there. You should have had Nisroc's tip to my back or tucked under my neck, but you asked me if I wanted to quit. Those precious seconds caused you to lose. Why do that with me, but not with a demon?"

Sergio stood frozen by his question, sucking air between his teeth. His response came out like a long held back eruption. "Bad things happen to me, to those I love! I caused Manny's death. I'm the reason Gabriel had to follow me into Hell and almost died. If I can beat you, maybe my luck will change and people I love will stop being hurt."

Balthazar's hand slipped from the hilt. The hard lines of tension disappeared from his brow. "Beating me will not change the destiny of any man… only man himself can do that. You can't be held responsible for circumstances out of your control or for choices others make. But letting fear rule your warrior heart *will* get you hurt. Are your heart and mind not working as one?"

Sergio ran his hand through his hair, frustrated by the thoughts that undermined his every move.

Maybe he's right. Maybe my fears are getting the best if me.

"I don't know anymore." Sergio turned to walk away, but Balthazar's words stopped him in his tracks.

"You have the biggest heart of any guardian I've ever trained. Your compassion is a gift, but it's also your biggest vulnerability. You've experienced tragedies. Everyone does. The problem is you hold them in your heart and they're with you when you fight. It steals your strength instead of being your fuel. It gives me no pleasure to harden you, but I do it because I want you to live and fight for those you love so deeply."

Sergio's throat constricted, wanting so desperately to be the guardian Balthazar saw in him. Yet the mental anguish he put himself through exhausted him, leaving him drained and uncertain.

Why can't I get past this?

Is holding onto the ax part of my problem?

Sergio shook his head. "I guess I'm not cut out for this after all. Besides, you have Lucia now. You don't need me." He couldn't be the cause of another death. If he had to do it, he'd walk away.

Balthazar reached out and laid his hand on Sergio's shoulder. The golden glint in his eyes turned softer as he spoke. "We need you more than ever. Lucifer is near—his army is nearly ready." Sergio closed his eyes, trying to shut out what he knew to be true. "You don't believe me? Let's go meditate and you can see what I see. Hell bursting at its seams with rage and vengeance."

Panic gripped his core. Ever since his descent into Hell, Sergio fought the tether lurking in him since he had linked with Lucifer, becoming an unknown participant of his Fallen hive. The ax was left in his room for this reason. He didn't want it close anymore to hold and feed the insidious darkness inside of him. He couldn't risk it.

"No. I never want to see that horrible place again. The smells and cries still haunt my dreams."

Balthazar nodded as he squeezed his shoulder. "You know better than anyone what we're up against. We can't let the Fallen loose on humanity. The burden must be so heavy you want to crumble under its weight. I feel it, too. When I succumbed to Lucifer, I broke the trust of my fellow angels. I don't want you to live with the same guilt. That is why I push you so hard, why I use every trick I know against you. The time for the guardians to face Lucifer is here. I can't make you stay, but the guardians are not complete without you... and your heart."

Sergio swallowed the lump in his throat. "How do I get past this —this feeling like I make everything worse?"

A wry grin played over Balthazar's lips. "I wish I had the words of wisdom to free you of your pain, but that would mean I'd have to follow them, too. Pain is part of living. You can choose how to heal. For me, my friend, healing comes from working with you and past guardians. My wings—being an angel in Heaven. The sacrifice is worth it to serve you and God. You made the choice to become a guardian. Your personal desires and needs only distract you. Your need to protect Lucia only puts her in harm's way and insults her ability as a guardian." Sergio jerked back as if Bal had struck him.

"That's not my intention—"

"And your desire for vengeance for Manny is a poison eating away at your goodness. And beating me in battle will not make you invincible. Giving your life may be the ultimate end. Releasing yourself from these chains of worry and anger is your sacrifice." Balthazar pointed his finger at Sergio's heart. "Your heart and your mind must work as one. The day you stop fighting yourself is the day you become a great warrior."

"You think I'll be a great warrior?" His eyes widened. "Me?"

"You survived Hell. What bigger test do you need?" Balthazar stepped back and nodded at the weapon's rack. "I think that's enough for tonight. Meet me at sunrise in the pasture. You'll ride Sadra and work on your air bombs in flight." He walked away; his stride once again light as he crossed the room. Sergio watched him disappear through the film, parting the flowing film like a curtain. He stayed rooted in his spot, turning over Balthazar's surprising words.

He thinks I'll be a great warrior?

Something eased inside Sergio, a loosening of a choke hold around his heart. He moved without thought as he took off his amour and left his precious sword on the shelf. His words of quitting rang hollow as he ran a fingertip over the blade. Giving up the guardianship meant never holding Nisroc, never riding his beloved Sadra, and never fighting against the evil that had nearly destroyed him. Balthazar's confidence in him had cracked the hard shell he'd hidden inside, too fearful to set himself free. His hard but true words of wisdom shone a light on the falsehoods he fed himself. He strode back to his room, unpacking Balthazar's hard truths. By the time his hand wrapped around his bedroom's doorknob, a fragile, renewed sense of purpose enveloped him.

Balthazar was right. Lucifer's army would not be denied for much longer. War would be upon them soon. He couldn't let his emotions rule his world anymore.

His price for freedom loomed in the dark recesses of his closet at home, a pull to forget his promises he made as a guardian. Once he brought the ax out into the light, the past would fade to black... his lone promise to fight for only Manny and avenge his death no more.

Sweat broke out on his upper lip as he pulled up his portal. Gold light swirled over his bedroom walls and the closet hiding the ax. He walked through, heart pounding faster with each tentative step.

I have to do this.

I have to let Manny go.

But am I ready?

CHAPTER
EIGHT

LUCIFER

Heat billowed from the endless pits of Hell and flowed over Lucifer as he circled high above his kingdom on the back of his dragon, Abaddon. His long, powerful legs clung to the beast's black-scaled body moving beneath him with each magnificent stoke from wings of iridescent ebony flames. The Seven Realms glowed like jewels cast within the scorched terrain. Each lava pool spilled its blood life over and churned down the ancient canals until the fiery mass emptied into the moat surrounding his tower. Its massive black structure loomed highest among all the dark buildings; its spiked spires pierced the hazy smoke blanketing the atmosphere above him. Jagged mountains cradled his domain. The hollowed-out tunnels and caverns pulsed with the Damned encased inside of every crevice. He sensed their vibrations and undulations, anxiously waiting for their release in order to fulfill their purpose and decimate humanity.

Soon...

Lessors brought an abundance of tainted human souls to their final destination with him, expanding his army. The Fallen, driven with a newfound intensity, worked the Realms below him. They forged weapons from the moat's lava, corralled the newly formed Damned into the mountains, and trained with weapons on the ground or while flying malicious beasts. He closed his eyes and inhaled the pungent odors of smoke and sulfur, reveling the wails of the newly christened souls bombarding his ears. The frenzied activity thrilled him, knowing they slaved for his vision, for his world... for him.

"The time is ripe for war. We'll ride together, my friend, glorious and invincible against our enemies. With a few surprises for them?"

Fire flared from Abaddon's nostrils as a tremor traveled over his sinewy body. Lucifer chuckled and stroked his marble white hand over Abaddon's neck. "Yes. I'm ready too, but first, a few more pieces have to fall into place. Let's begin, shall we? To the Main Hall."

Eager anticipation tugged his lips into a hard smile. He cast out the fiery link he had marked the Fallen with before they fell through the churning abyss, commanding their presence in the Main Hall. In unison, they turned away from their tasks and obediently answered their master's call. Dancing to his tune, they flocked to the hall to await his arrival. Abaddon made a lazy spiral around the tower, breathing fire into the thick air. Once all were amassed inside, he entered through one of the seven enormous arches. Abaddon landed at the edge of the pit where he had killed the traitor Sonneillon with a deadly fire blast. Lucifer glanced into the pit, remembering the desperate pleas of innocence from his former ally, who thought his place as the Prince of the Realm of Greed would conceal his deceit and protect him from recourse.

Your hunger for greed and power ruined you. I burned you to show the Fallen the consequence for any such betrayals.

Death.

Your replacement will not be as reckless...

Lucifer's six magnificent wings unfurled behind him to the awe of the masses. Taking flight, he circled above the jam-packed crowd oozing with the colors of the Realms. Their raucous cheers and thunderous pounding of chests and feet roared to a crescendo when he landed on a large semi-circular stone platform. Jutting out from one wall, suspended above the crowd, it entitled him a bird's-eye view of the pit's deadly battles while he scanned the occupants with a keen, vigilant eye. Behind him rose a throne of polished black granite carved in tongues of ebony fire with tips sharp enough to impale. He raised his hands. Silence fell over the hall, anticipation thick for his next words.

"To mark the beginning of the new vision of a world I seek for us, I called you here. My fellow Fallen, we are no longer bound to only exact revenge on God and the horrid Heavenly Host. We limit ourselves by thinking that this is all we can achieve. You see—we've raised an Army of the Damned. Molded by their sins, they've bound themselves to us to further our cause. The Princes of the Realms have worked tirelessly alongside you to mold them into ruthless, fearless, soulless soldiers craving the death of selfish humans who failed them during their bleak time on Earth. I share with you today that when we take back what was once ours in Heaven, we will then overrun man's world with war and devastation. The Realms will rule their lands, becoming our playgrounds of sin, hunt, and delight. *We* were told *we* would serve humans. *We* were banished because *we* dared to defy this vile lie and humiliation. But *we* will soon rise and return to our rightful place as masters of *His* abomination. This is our destiny. I vow to give this to you, rewarding you for your loyalty and undying devotion to me and our cause!" Deafening snarls and cries of approval enveloped him, validating his deepest desires of war and revenge that he let lay dormant for too long.

At last... my time is here.

"Do you stand with me?" The hall shook with intoxicating affirmation. He inhaled deeply the crisp, penetrating scent of blood lust exuding from the Fallen, born of carnal blood, thirsting for death. He stepped to the edge, quieting the hall once more. "Then let us begin."

He faced the Realm of Greed gathered in front of their arched entrance. Their varying shades of cobalt blue cast around them like waves of turbulent waters.

"The last time we gathered as one, I uncovered a traitor in our midst. Once the loyal Prince of the Realm of Greed, Sonneillon betrayed me with his treacherous plan to take my place as your leader. He shamed his Realm with his deceit and reckless actions. But the coward paid the price with his life. The valiant Fallen he failed and left behind do not wear his treason. They, too, were unaware of his selfish plans, disregarded in his play for power. They deserve a Prince worthy of leading them into battle. A prince who will rule their Realm on Earth in the glory of their namesake." He leveled his eyes to one who towered amongst them. "Mammon. Join me."

Hushed murmurs rippled across the Realms as her fellow Fallen opened a path for her. She walked with her chin lifted in statuesque beauty. Her long legs carried her with a warrior's power. Lucifer feasted upon her approach, knowing with every stride she made, his choice was perfect. She was like no other. As a Seraphim, her position at the top of the hierarchy was a given. But this wasn't what stirred him. It was the color of her blue. Unlike the other Fallen from her Realm that blazed with shades of cobalt blue, Mammon's color was like that of a glacier, almost opaque in its frigid, unyielding shade. It was as if her color hadn't burned in the abyss like the others. Skin so pale, her blue lifeblood traveled like roads over her arms until they pooled at her wrists, creating hands of blue. Her ice-colored eyes, rimmed in bright blue, were voids inside the pools of black. Reaching the front of the Realm, her six ebony wings unfurled, leaving no doubt she'd endured the fires of the Fall. A quick stroke put her in flight. Air swirled like it shivered with her arrival on the landing's edge. She bowed to him, two long pointed black horns stark against her cropped white hair.

"Master." The corners of her ice blue lips tugged.

The curves of her body, as sharp as the angles of her face, cut through the thick air with a cold assurance as she moved closer. He grinned at his choice while plucking a thick black feather from the top of his wing. A solitary drop of blood fell at her feet. He poised the feather above her wing. "Do you pledge to honor your Realm and lead it to victory?"

"Yes. It's my greatest honor to be their Prince." He stabbed the feather like a dagger blow into her wing. Mammon's eyes widen from the intrusion, but a wave of pleasure rolled in their icy-blue depth. The Realm of Greed cried out with approval.

Lucifer spread out his arms. "Do you swear your loyalty to your fellow Fallen?"

"Always!" she shouted, turning to scan the hall. "We are one!"

He nodded, letting the exuberant cheers echo through the hall. "Do you promise your fealty to me, your chosen Lord and Master, against all others?"

"I swear you are the one true Lord of all, and I'll destroy whoever opposes you and your vision."

"And so it shall be." His hand fell to his sword's hilt that hung at his side. Metal rode metal as he pulled it from the sheath and raised it high. "I present to you, Mammon, Prince of the Realm of Greed."

Each Fallen raised their personal weapons of destruction in a return salute, turning the Hall's floor into a metal armory. Mammon's blue hand freed her sword, exposing a long silver blade that curved at the end. Her chest heaved as she thrust it into the air, matching their shouts with her own.

Lucifer lowered his sword and turned to her. "Return to your Realm, Prince." His eyes narrowed slightly, moving closer to her. "Don't disappoint me."

She shifted, returning with an icy stare. "I'm nothing like Sonneillon. You have nothing to fear from me."

He raised his eyebrow. "Oh, but you see... I fear no one because I am the only one to fear."

Mammon bowed her head. "My Lord." She lifted off the platform, her icy blue form lost under her inky wings. He imagined she glowed, suspended above them all, hypnotic in her triumphant return to her Realm.

Last, but not least...

Another delicate matter needed Lucifer's attention. This one more precarious than naming a new Prince.

Asura.

Crowning an unwilling, hostile queen was a delicate matter. A warrior beauty who had done little to ingratiate herself to him. Instead, she stayed away from his tower, choosing her Realm over his company. When he called upon her, the thin facade of toleration she displayed was almost comical. Oddly, it didn't infuriate him... yet. She presented a challenge to him. One he'd gladly accepted. Making her queen was easy. Having her trust and loyalty again was the tricky part. He needed an unshakable alliance. A Master of all and his lioness queen. A Fallen would think twice before considering dethroning him.

"Asura. Come to me."

He knew exactly in which direction to extend his hand. Since her unbecoming late arrival, she'd bored holes into him with a tiresome, stony glare. Gold crackled within the mass of thin braids that framed Asura's ebony face. She took flight in a flurry of black and gold, landing before him without taking his hand. He cocked his head, daring her to deny him. Her nostrils flared, but she reluctantly put her hand in his, radiating a heat fueled by more than the hot hall. As he thought about his new queen, he hummed with anticipation.

Taming you will be a great pleasure.

"I once announced, here in this very hall, my desire to make Asura, Queen of the Seven Realms. No Fallen is more deserving of this honor. Today, I make good on my promise." Lucifer's aide, Saxem, emerged over the platform. Cradled in his hands laid a gold crown carved with seven spires of twirling flames. Embedded at the top of each gold flame was a brilliant jewel, each representing a vibrant color of the Seven Realms. Asura's eyes widened, lips parted as she gazed at its beauty. Lucifer held back the smirk lurking at the corners of his mouth, reveling in watching Asura betray herself. She was, after all, from the Realm of Pride. The crown's significance and beauty were hard to deny. Lucifer took the crown and lifted it before the Fallen.

"This crown represents each of the Realms by its unique jewels, while the flames represent the fire that burns deep within us." He faced Asura and raised the crown over her head. Her skin crackled with gold streaks, but he didn't miss the fists clinched at her sides. He placed it on top of her golden braids and then took her hand. "I pronounce you Queen of the Seven Realms. We will rule together for eternity."

The hall's walls echoed with clamoring cries until they started chanting her name. She turned to the crowd with a slight crease in her brow. Taking advantage of her uncertainty, he tugged at her hand. When she turned to him, he struck quickly with a hard kiss. A wave of fury washed from her as she held the kiss until he released her.

"Just because you've made me your queen doesn't mean I'll be your lover," she hissed, her eyes churning with contempt.

His chuckle rumbled in his chest as he leaned into her ear. To the crowd, it looked like an intimate whisper. It was no such thing. "There will soon come a day when you will beg to be in my bed. It will be I who will decide if we will be lovers," his voice grew harder with each word. "I have much to enlighten you with. And when I do, you'll come to realize that every vile word you believed... spilled from a traitor's lips. When that dawning clears the web of lies clouding your senses, you'll beg for my forgiveness and do anything to protect me and our future. On that day is when you truly become my queen." She gasped when he nipped her ear before pulling back.

A sneer marred her lips when he faced her. "There is nothing you can tell me to change my mind about Sonneillon. He was no traitor to you or the Realm."

"We'll see about that." He signaled Abaddon. The dragon leapt into the air and came towards the platform's edge. "I think it's time for your first unmasking."

Her chest rose and fell as if she'd just finished a battle in the pits, but she remained silent as they climbed onto Abaddon's back.

The Fallen watched them exit through an arch. Beneath him, they scattered from the Main Hall and returned to their Realms, attacking their previous tasks with renewed vigor. He led his dragon away from the Realms toward the mountain's smoky peaks. Excitement churned as his destination grew near, shrouded in darkness born of heavy mist and black terrain.

Asura grew tense, seated between his arms. "Where are you taking me? We are past the caverns of the Damned."

"To a place I created for those who need, shall I say—intense retraining."

She twisted, her crown's golden flames flashing in the dark. "For the Fallen? I have not heard of it." Surprise flickered on her face.

"Of course you haven't," he scoffed. "Because only a rare few survive. Those that have learned the invaluable lesson of silence."

Abaddon started his descent into a narrow canyon barely noticeable between the jagged mountains. Lucifer smiled as she shifted back in her seat.

You have much to learn, my queen.

And a few valuable lessons, as well.

CHAPTER
NINE

DARK
PRINCE

T he Dark Prince's claws slashed into the Damned's flesh. Rivulets of black blood left trails down the brutalized body. Her screams had silenced long ago, her mouth hanging open behind the tangled mass of red hair. In the quivering firelight cast from the torches behind his prey, he envisioned Delilah's face. It provided a twisted entertainment at the prospect of her death at his hands. But taking out his frustrations on this look-a-like didn't fuel his fire now.

No.

Lucifer's ludicrous display at the Main Hall had driven him into this rage filled frenzy. The way he strutted on the ledge above them, preening with his blatant stunt to appease the Realm, sickened him. Lucifer had drawn two potent Fallen into his inner circle. It would take more than his accusations of incompetence to influence either of them to see the cracks in Lucifer's facade.

Mammon was dangerous. Her icy demeanor hid a fiery taste for blood and revenge.

She is glorious, more worthy of wearing the crown than Asura.

The Ancient One spoke inside his head, but the Dark Prince was used to his untimely interruptions. His body hummed, muscles bulging as he landed the final blow. "Asura was a lover, a confidant from his past. He has a soft spot for her, maybe even a blind spot we could exploit. Mammon was a Fallen of loyalty and power, one we need to make sure bears no suspicion against us. She's worthy of the Prince of the Greed Realm, but her eyes are not on being queen. Ruler over all is more her style. She'll be my first kill when the Realm is ours."

And Asura? Will she remain queen? Her dark skin, crackling with gold, excites me.

So many questions. "What delights you is of no concern to me. Who will be queen is a misuse of time. There are more pressing issues at hand, like forcing Lucifer into war so we can begin ours."

The Dark Prince stepped back, inhaling deeply through his nose. The ruined Damned dangled limp from the shackles. This death was too quick to satisfy the hatred rushing through him. "Useless," he jeered, kicking the Damned's foot.

We could find another one… or two. Maybe a Lessor would bring more fulfillment. Your punishments help soothe me, hold me over until we fuse eternally as one.

An idea sparked in the Prince, one that could produce some peace and much needed respite from the Ancient One. "I have a better idea." He moved deeper into the cavern, past other mangled remains of the Damned, to an arched entryway carved out of the back wall. The small area was pitch black, but he knew exactly where and what laid in the crevices he'd dug out of the walls. His hands trembled with anticipation reaching into the deep space.

What is it?

"A present of sorts for you—a reunion from the past."

The Prince freed the large wooden box from its hiding place, but unease replaced his pleasure. Confused by its lighter weight, he crouched and set the box on the ground. He opened the lid and found it empty. Stunned, not believing his eyes, his hand thumped around inside the box. "Who would have dared to steal it from me?" Seething, he picked up the box and threw it against the wall, shattering it into wooden fragments.

Steal what from you? What was inside?

"Shut up!" He flexed his fingers, itching to clamp them around the thief's neck. "Let me think." His memory shuffled through the handful of Fallen who knew about his lair, ones who brought him victims and shared in the delight of their death. A face moved to the forefront, and with it, a sinking sense of dread. "Balik."

The thief?

"Yes. Balik. The only one who saw me use it. If I'm in a mood for a particular sort of Damned, I had a few chosen Fallen I would use to bring it here. Most would leave, but Balik would linger in the background, his presence lost to me. He must have seen me put it away and decided he wanted it for himself."

What did he see? My patience is wearing thin with your riddles.

"The day I came to you, before Michael imprisoned you, I took something of yours. Do you remember what I claimed for myself?" He didn't have to wait long before the Ancient One's answer.

My ax... created with my blood and feather. It belonged to me and you took it.

"Of course, I took it. You had no further use for it. It was mine to have." He needed to escape the cave's confines. He turned to leave, but the Ancient One's account stopped him cold.

Balik had no choice but to take the ax. When I created the ax, I inserted a spell. If it was ever separated from me, it would go through however many hands tried to own it until it could find its way back to me. When Balik saw the ax, mesmerized by its blazing red, he couldn't deny the compulsion to take it. Just like you did. You'll find Raum in his possessions and we will finally be reunited.

The Ancient One's slow roll of laughter grew louder, filled with harsh chords of humiliation.

"If it were still here, don't you think you would have sensed it?" The Dark Prince spoke the words through a haze of fury. "It's not in the Realm. Balik is dead. Killed by one of the Guardians. He must have taken it with him that night. One of the Guardians or an Archangel must have found it and now have it in their possession."

Do you understand what this means? It is bound to find a way back to me.

"Don't say it! Don't—" He bellowed into the cave filled with death at his hands.

Which is the discovery of you—of us! We must find it.

The Prince screamed at the destroyed box until it felt like the cords in his neck would burst. Even to his own ears, he sounded like a trapped animal ready to battle against its impending death. After all his planning, waiting, and wallowing in Lucifer's shadow, a simple weapon could ruin him. He raised his portal and stepped through, his pain and disbelief left echoing behind him.

CHAPTER
TEN

ZAR

The whip crackled in Zar's hand, thrashing back and forth across Delilah's body as if by its own volition. His static-like mental vision mapped her limp body hanging above him, ravaged with lashes laced across her flesh. His harsh breathing droned out the moans escaping from her lax jaw. Exhausted, his arm dropped to his side. The tip of the whip Lucifer had given him to impose the punishment for her betrayal, laid in her pool of blood. But Zar didn't share in the crowd's exuberance for Lucifer's pleasureful display of retribution. The blood pumping through him was driven by his own sense of betrayal by the angel turned Fallen that he'd dared to trust... and fallen in love with. He dropped the implement of torture and stepped away. A harsh reality squeezed his chest.

I've saved myself from Lucifer and the Fallen's scorn and humiliation.

But whipping Delilah didn't save my heart from her.

He felt numb to everything around him except the ominous turmoil splitting him apart.

The images shifted. Pain ripped through his neck as fangs dug into his flesh. White fur surrounded him. A wail burst from his lips...

Zar bolted upright, chest heaving as he tried to pull himself free of the dream that haunted him when he dared to sleep. The screams inside his head subsided as he dragged himself into the present, safe inside his small hovel in a mountain's tunnel. Raking his fingers through his hair, he shoved the macabre memory of Delilah back into his mind's recesses. He sagged back onto the hard-packed dirt floor and let the silence wash away the dream's last remnants.

Will Delilah or the white tiger ever stop tormenting me?

No.

With the nightmare's effects receded, a more recent event percolated into focus. Zar unwillingly heeded the call to the Main Hall, but had stayed hidden against the arched entrance. The displays from Lucifer in naming Mammon Prince and Asura his Queen disgusted him equally in both sham and audacity. He scorned at the farce of it all. Didn't Lucifer understand Mammon wouldn't be easy to manipulate? She was unyielding in thought and fierce in her desires. Her silent yet deadly retribution was legendary in the Realms. Swift in action, she rarely wasted her time with arguments. She preferred the pit's immediate gratification. With this newfound power, her strike would turn colder and more ruthless. All would be well if her goals aligned with Lucifer's.

Or rain chaos if it went poorly.

Where Mammon's veins flowed with ice, Asura's burned with a fire rivaling Lucifer's. If he thought he could tame her, he was sadly mistaken. She'd fight his unwanted advances and attempted domination with her whole being. He'd never win her over. It belied her essence.

Not my concern.

Zar had left the Hall, chased away by his inner demons. He'd abandoned his room, preferring the shadows while he wandered the Realms. Finding no solace, he took to the bleak mountains that matched his mood. He discovered little, except for various entrances hidden in the deep, narrow canyons availed to him because of his mapping abilities. Exploring occupied his mind. Someone had carved some labyrinths with mindless intent, while others gave him a sense of foreboding and left it uninterrupted. He took refuge in a small cave near the entrance after discovering the tunnel. Intrigued by its small opening that expanded to an impressive sized tunnel, he would explore it after he rested.

If the cavern is large enough, I could bring Cydanos.

No better time than the present.

A high-pitched wail sliced through the darkness, but was suddenly cut short. He jerked; his hand moved to the dagger at his waist. The cry reverberated in the tunnels until its depths swallowed it. Slowly rising from the floor, he waited for the next cry, but it never came. He shook his head, wondering if he'd imagined it. As far as he knew, no one else lived in these tunnels. But the hairs lifting on his neck alerted him that he wasn't alone. Careful to keep his steps light, he entered the tunnel, pausing at the endless void before him.

What do I care what's down there?

Because maybe this is where Lucifer's hiding Delilah.

He held his breath and listened for any shifting sound, but only tomb-like silence greeted him. The prickles on his neck didn't subside as he walked further into the tunnel. He scanned the area and pulled out his sword. He kept to the main tunnel despite the smaller shafts breaking off to the right and left. Dank air shifted over and brought with it a subtle scent. He frowned, the odor tickling a memory fighting to find its origin. He stopped and flattened himself against the rough walls. Fear coiled within him. His mind grappled to reconcile his memories and his current reality.

This is the unknown scent that clung to Delilah after she met with her ally unknown to me—the traitor.

Sonneillon.

How can this be? He's dead.

Dread of the truth fought a losing battle to his curiosity. He could be wrong about the origin, even though his gut said otherwise. Conflicted as he was, there was only one way to find the truth. Continue into the tunnel's depth until he found who screamed. He pushed off from the wall, but stayed close to it. He didn't know how far he had traveled under the mountain, chasing the scent like a predator sought his prey. Its oily essence clung to the air, alive with a malice so thick, he thought it would choke him. He pushed on, blood rushing in his ears, sword held high to plunge into the unknown enemy surely lying in wait to ambush him. But no demon or ghost lurked when he reached his destination. Only tortured remains. A body hung from the shackles around her wrists, her face shrouded in long, tangled hair.

No...

Frozen in panicked disbelief, his senses scanned the area around the small alcove. Satisfied he was alone, Zar lurched forward and stretched out his hand to seek the truth. He pushed the matted hair from her face, his fingers gliding over the face's sharp contours. His sigh echoed like a grunt when no familiar face mapped under his fingertips.

Not Delilah.

But someone who looks like her.

He turned to flee, but hesitated. He had to know if more were hidden. He took a few cautious steps deeper into the void. The answer loomed before him. A huge cavern emerged with walls like a black honeycomb. Some ripe with death, others empty vessels. He staggered back, swiping his hand across his mouth. This wasn't a dungeon of the Realms. This was someone's private hideaway, carved in secret, used for punishment or pleasure giving at any whim.

And now I know.

Zar had no desire to be found and ran back to where he entered. He didn't care what Realm the victims had come from—Fallen or Damned—or what they'd done to garner the punishment of death. His only concern was to flee... and fast. The traitor's scent faded, but not the feeling that Zar's own scent may have left a trail to be discovered by who he thought had perished in the pits. He didn't stop at the hovel's entrance where he'd slept, but pushed for the exit ahead.

Escape.

But not freedom.

Zar welcomed the blast of heat from the Realm to ward off the cold knowledge he'd stumbled upon. He sidled up against the mountain's base and glanced at his surroundings. Smoke billowed in the distance from the endless war machine, pumping out its ever-growing army. Would it be safe to return to the Realms and risk being discovered by the traitor, or should he continue his solitary existence? Was it possible to hide in plain sight?

Maybe.

Having made his decision, Zar flew to the mountain where stables housed the Degasus. Here the creature's sweat and fire would mingle with his own. There, he could use his senses to discover if his theory was correct.

Sonneillon wasn't the traitor.

Lucifer knew this, but killed him anyway.

Was it to possess Mammon, Asura, or both?

Or had Lucifer thought he'd executed the traitor, who was now still free to plot his next move?

Either way, Zar had discovered a dangerous knowledge. If he wasn't careful, he could end up burned alive in the pit as well.

CHAPTER
ELEVEN

DELILAH

S ilence.

A barren vacuum pressing on me.

Intensifying the tormented screams battering my mind from within.

Dragging me further into the internal hell that rivaled my external, cruel prison.

Delilah rolled over. The black earth scraped against the flesh laid bare by her shredded clothes. Time had lost all meaning as her body struggled to heal from her daily punishment. Memories floated by that she wished were nightmares instead of snippets of her horrid reality:

Her feet scraping tracks beneath her as rough hands drug her through a tunnel.

The cackle of her jailers as they slammed the heavy metal door of her cage.

Pain never ceased. It was as if each lash of the whip had leached her powers.

Wondering when death would finally come and put her out of her misery.

But her release never materialized.

Instead, she existed in total and complete exile. Nothing but an oblivion of haunted memories hounding her. She coughed, triggering a puff of black dust. There was no one to blame but herself and the disastrous choices she made in her childish hubris and revenge. Freedom to live her life... to chase her wanton dreams of vengeance against Conner, had shackled her to evil. Jumping into the Mar of Sin was supposed to be a leap of power and strength. But none of those ideals lived in Hell—in Lucifer. Blinded by her schemes, she stood before Lucifer, positive she was more cunning—that he would never discover her network of lies. Only a fool would assume they could stay one step ahead of the devil, especially when they struck a deal.

I am the fool.

Time allowed her to tug slowly on the tattered threads of her choices. Some teased her, drifting on the edges of her thoughts like a kite's tail. But she couldn't reach for them. Not yet. She could only digest her shameful actions in small bites. Her actions were a feast, rotten to the core.

She peered into the bleak emptiness that mocked her through thick prison bars. When she could finally move, she explored her cell, hoping to find a means of escape. But despair weighed down each step. Trapped inside a circular area, surrounded by unyielding bars and a deep moat. She was on an island in the middle of a vast cavern. Marooned forever.

Dread her undesirable companion.

Other, more hopeful memories tortured her as they chiseled through her haze. Painful in their beauty; she had carelessly cast away. Ones filled with light, peace, and love. Ones where her wings were white and flew among other Angels in a vast, warm light. She'd taken her life, her gifts, for granted. This was her reckoning. What she deserved.

I love you, Delilah...

God's last words to her before the Mar of Sin's vortex drowned out everything as she transformed from light to dark.

From peace to madness.

From love to hate.

What am I now?

Nothing.

But in her nothingness, she made a discovery about her unpacked truths. Her actions had set in motion a war between Heaven and Hell. She gave Lucifer the knowledge she should have kept sacred. Humans didn't deserve what he had planned for them. The Heavenly Host would suffer heavy losses. She must try to change this course, undo the wrongs her actions started.

The dark was her blanket as she planned and waited, hoping someone would remember a broken, exiled Fallen and return.

The ground vibrated beneath her with the sharp strikes of footsteps. Her eyes flew open, remaining still as she sought the source in the darkness. Lights emerged, flickering across the cavern's sloping roof. Dancing in sparkling gold, it spread but only to one wall like the vibrancy was absorbed by a black hole next to it. Her heart skipped to a pounding beat, terrified by an overwhelming scent. It belonged to the only one who embodied the Realm; fire, power, death.

Lucifer.

Delilah sat up slowly, wishing there was a wall at her back. But the dirt island held no such protection.

I'm a caged animal. Trapped. Exposed. Helpless.

Delilah rose to her feet and defiantly lifted her chin to greet her enemies. The lights took flight over the moat. She held back a snarl when Asura came into view because Lucifer dominated her attention. His white face glowed in the dark, stark against his wings, stabbing the air like shiny black metal. The evil that once excited her... electrified her, now terrified her. She took a step back and scanned the cavern for more Fallen. The void closed behind them; no one else was in sight. They landed between the moat and bars, kicking up dust. Lucifer's mirth filled the air, his black eyes dead in pools of churning fire. Asura stood beside him. A sneer marred her beautiful dark face; a hideous crown adorned her golden-laced braided hair. Delilah kept her face blank, hiding the hatred burning inside her.

"My, my, Delilah. Time here has not served you well. The smell of your filth disgusts me, yet brings such pleasure." He cocked his head while his eyes traveled over her, lingering where her arm once was. She'd never tell him about the horrors of shadow pain or the anguish of loss when only one hand rose to wipe away the tears. "How pathetic you are. Once so beautiful—full of promise. Now, broken and maimed as a traitor should be." He took a few steps away from Asura, contemplating Delilah through the bars. "Do you ever wonder why I didn't kill you? Your action certainly warranted death."

Delilah turned her body, mimicking Lucifer's movements to keep him in front of her. "No. I figured my languish was more enjoyable for you."

He stopped and faced her, a false smile thinning his lips. "It has brought me a sliver of pleasure, but you are still of use to me and my... queen." Delilah spotted the ripple of anger in Asura before she glanced back at Lucifer.

"I'm useless to you now. I can't help you or your queen—"

A punch of energy slammed Delilah's chest and sent her spiraling to the floor. She gasped for breath, watching Lucifer's hand lower through the strands of her ratted hair. He strode back in silence to Asura like a predator stalking his prey. Asura watched his approach with the same wariness. He grabbed a thin braid, raise it to his nose, and inhaled deeply. His sigh of pleasure rumbled through his lips while his long fingers rubbed the braid between them. "You have answers. I need to dispel my queen's denial that Sonneillon was the traitor."

Asura's head jerked as though someone had slapped her. Gold swirls ignited in her chest and swept down her arms. Lucifer let the braid drop when her face leaned into his. "I'll never believe a word that comes from that liar's mouth. And you shouldn't have either. Since the day she got here, she's caused nothing but trouble and has only spread deceit and mistrust among your most loyal Fallen." Her tirade ricocheted off the walls, but Lucifer shrugged, seemingly unphased.

"You've let your bond with him blind you. Delilah spun lies, but the truths about the guardians are real, as is her knowledge about Sonneillon."

Delilah's eyes grew wide when Asura's glare clashed with hers. "What could she possibly know about him?"

How did he find out?

"Well... shall you start, or shall I?" Lucifer asked, twisting his head toward Delilah.

"She's right. I know nothing—"

"Fine. We'll do this the hard way—for you." Lucifer took flight. His wings pumped in a leisurely fashion as he flew above the moat. "I created this hideaway an eternity ago, knowing one day I'd require a very particular prison, say, for... an angel. I'd almost forgotten about it until your treason came to light." He swooped lower. "Did you ever wonder why there wasn't any water in the moat? I don't suppose that matters, but I think it's time to fix that." He flew out of sight, spiking Delilah's fear to a new level. A loud creak infiltrated the cavern like he'd opened an old rusty door. Delilah expected to hear the rush of water. Instead, angry hisses rose from the bottom, with the unmistakable sound of thick creatures piling onto the floor, slithering over each other as they battled for space. The moat's walls glowed in purple pulses, the color rising closer to the edge. A small cry escaped Delilah when Lucifer emerged with a thick snake the length of his body draped around his neck. Its purple eyes sparked and a fork-tongue flicked at Delilah.

"These lovelies are a creation of Astaroth. To humans, their poison will instantly kill, but not for an unfortunate Fallen. One bite and their poison creates a painful delirium. He's found it an effective means of punishment." Lucifer stroked a single white finger down the shiny purple scales. "What Astaroth found most intriguing is that with each bite, the poison dilutes the blood until, after a long and extremely painful duration, death finally comes. He found it perfect for his needs, as do I. Tell Asura about the traitor and I'll spare you."

Delilah licked her cracked lips while her tightening throat threatened her ability to speak. The sounds from the moat grew agitated, matching their master.

"He speaks the truth. I wove lies. I wanted revenge against my enemies at any cost." Delilah's words tumbled out of her as the snake moved down Lucifer's body in a slow, curving motion. "I got worried and suspicious that I was losing Lucifer's ear—especially when you came back. Apparently, I wasn't the only one fuming about the rekindling. Sonneillon brushed by me on one of my walks and whispered for me to meet him at the base of the granite cliffs behind his Realm that night."

"You lie!" Asura's black hands grabbed the metal bars and shook them. "Sonneillon would never meet with you. He found you vile—"

"He said that to please you, spoke what you wanted to hear. But, he too, was spinning lies and making new alliances. He was tired of waiting for Lucifer to take action and go to war. He knew he couldn't stand by when the new World Order was announced. I met him and he took me to this... hideaway he built deep into the cliffs." Asura's hands fell from the bars, her head shaking in denial. Delilah stood up, buoyed by the misery on Asura's face. "He said you'd been there, too, but not for a while. But it didn't smell abandoned—"

"I'm going to kill you—"

"And he asked me to help him bring down Lucifer. So, I did and shared—"

An invisible hand seized Delilah's neck. "I think she's duly enlightened. Now it's my turn." The snake's inky body squeezed between the bars and coiled its length a few feet from her. Its head swayed, hypnotic in its motion, displaying a splayed neck flattened like a disk. "It's time you tell me what you've kept to yourself about the guardians." The force lifted Delilah until her feet dangled above the floor. She thrashed about in vain, striking nothing but air. "Tell me what you know or I set my friend free to sink his fangs into your flesh!" The purple tongue flicked again as if gauging striking distance. To her horror, the force let go. She screamed as she crumbled to the ground, waiting for the sharp pain of its vicious bite.

"Wait!" Wheezing through her battered throat, she scrambled away from the snake. She raised her good hand in meager defense. "He had—" she coughed and dragged in another gulp of air, "—a tattoo on his chest. The hunter in the stars, Orion. He said his powers lay beneath, given by an angel. I asked him who, but he wouldn't say more... said he'd already said too much. He swore me to secrecy and then shunned me." A muffled sobbed escaped through her quivering lips, leaving her shame complete.

If ice could form here, Lucifer was the glacier. "Michael," he hissed. "Only he would think of such treachery, using what I hate the most against me. But he doesn't know that I know his secret weapon. It will be me that uses it against him to his ruin!" He grabbed Asura's arm, the shiny creature still swaying at Delilah. "Goodbye, Delilah."

"But the snake—"

He glanced over his shoulder, casting her a parting blast of hate. "Did you really think I'd let you live? You never understood the essence of the Fallen. You will now. Each day, these creatures will fight among themselves for the right to climb their way out of the moat. Their bodies flailing, striking and slapping... deadly scales ripping their rivals' body, until only one earns the pleasure of sinking their fangs into your flesh, fulfilling their deep-seated hunger. It'll slither back to the moat. Through your haze of pain and hallucination, you'll hear this battle for your flesh to start anew. Your blood will thicken with their venom and slowly kill you. It will spread through your body like the poisonous lies you spread to take my throne. Your heart will stop beating, you'll gasp your last breath. And I will still be Lord and Master of Hell."

The snake struck with lightning force. Two fangs stabbed her calf before its mouth latched onto her. Ice ran up her veins, but a trail of heat scorched behind its path. She screamed; the walls reverberated her pain. A seizure claimed her as the floor spun and her vision tunneled. She sensed the release of her calf as she lay victim to the storm tearing her apart.

How could I have believed him?

I should have let myself die before I spoke the truth.

What have I done?

CHAPTER
TWELVE

OLIVIA

S ome smells invoke a soothing feeling, like a favorite candle burning or the hint of spring in a breeze. But the pungent smell of disinfectant mixed with unnatural pine made her stomach churn with anxiety and fear. As her feet slapped along the beige linoleum in the stark hallway, memories of her mom's near fatal accident rushed to the surface. She recalled holding vigil by her bedside while grappling with her dad's return to their lives; the harsh lighting, machines beeping, keeping her mom alive. What felt like a lifetime ago was only six months in the rear-view mirror. She stopped in front of the door, reminding herself her mom wasn't behind it. Instead, Joe laid there, recovering from a gunshot wound he received because she'd been too slow to act.

Please be okay...

Olivia knocked gently on the door before cracking it open. Peering around the door, her gaze met Callie's red-rimmed eyes cushioned in dark shadows. "Hi, I hope it's a good time—" Callie jumped up, making the chair's metal legs clatter on the floor. A few quick steps closed the gap for a hug.

"Hey, it's the perfect time." Callie's smile couldn't hide her worry. "Joe's been in and out, but he's doing better."

"I could come back later if you don't think he's ready for a visitor."

"No... please stay. The company will do me some good, and Joe would be bummed if he missed you." Callie squeezed Olivia's hand. "Come on, sit with me."

"Okay—good." Olivia's shoulders relaxed as she pulled up a simple vinyl covered metal chair next to Callie. The hard seat had never offered enough comfort for her during the long hours spent sitting, waiting for her mom to wake up. It was no better now.

Callie sat and laced her fingers with Joe's. "I haven't had a chance to thank you or your dad for coming over and saving us from Jared. I don't know what would have happened if you hadn't arrived."

Olivia's gaze lingered on the large white bandage peeking out from the hospital gown covering most of his shoulder. An IV dripped into a tube that ran down his arm, exposing a dark tribal tattoo around his bicep. Her mouth turned dry when she finally let herself look at Joe's face. Wavy chestnut hair fell across his forehead, dark stubble stark on his pale face. "I'm sorry we didn't get there sooner," Olivia muttered. "Maybe I could have stopped—"

Joe's eyes fluttered open, startling Olivia. "Better late than never," Joe said, his voice barely above a whisper. His hazel eyes crinkled in the corners. "So, you're not fired."

Olivia smiled as she hurried to the other side of the bed. "I quit, remember?" She grabbed the water cup from the nightstand and offered it to him. Dry lips wrapped around the straw, taking long sips of water. He sighed and fell back against the pillow.

"Yeah, I remember. I'm not that beat up. Place isn't the same without you. I even miss your snark," he chuckled. His face turned serious as he squeezed Callie's hand. "Thank you for your help. I don't think we'd be here if—"

Olivia shifted in her seat, uneasy with his praise. "Listen... uh—" she cleared her throat, "—I didn't save your life. The medics and ER staff did that. I'm afraid I made it worse when I barged in and startled him."

The room fell silent except for the monotonous beeping machines, a constant reminder of Joe's fragile status. The couple exchanged a glance, filled with more than the blush of new love. An unspoken conversation happened between them, born of time spent together, managing the stressful reality of an abusive ex-husband. Callie nodded, her blue eyes swimming in tears, when she turned to Olivia.

"Joe and I want to be honest with you. There's more to the story, more to us, and... more to you."

What? They couldn't possibly know...

Butterflies fluttered in her stomach as her mind raced to remember a time when they could have seen something. "I'm not sure what you mean by *more to me*, but I know you both have been swooning over each other since I started working at Joe's."

Grins split across both their faces, bringing a healthy flush to Joe's cheeks. "You're right. I thought Callie was the most beautiful woman I had ever seen when she walked in to the interview. I got so tongue-tied and flustered, I was certain she thought I was an idiot and would walk out the door and be gone forever. She took the job... thank God, but it didn't take me long to realize she was suffering in a terrible marriage. You came along and helped tremendously. I tried to keep my distance, not wanting to insert myself or act like a creepy boss. When I saw the bruises on her arms, I couldn't stay away. I confronted her about it after work. She was embarrassed and tried to brush it off, but when I wouldn't let her, the dam of tears broke loose. She finally shared the nightmare of Jared's abuse and how she needed to get out before he tried to hurt Chloe. So, we built a plan." His voiced faded as if he'd used up all his energy to speak.

"After the divorce, I hoped Jared would set me free. At first, he played along, but he began stalking me."

"Why didn't you tell me?" Olivia gaped. "I could have—"

"Your mom had just gotten hurt and your dad showed back up. I couldn't pile on. Besides, I had Joe."

Olivia leaned back into the chair, not liking the answer, but she understood why Callie had kept her in the dark. She would have been little help during that time. "Okay, so what happened next?"

"I got a restraining order. That worked... for a while. I thought he'd finally come to his senses and moved on—like I did." Callie ran her fingers through her black hair, glancing down at Joe. He squeezed their still clasped hands, giving her an encouraging smile. "I should have known it was too good to be true. What you don't know is Joe and I developed feelings for each other over those months and we fell in love. We got careless and Jared saw us like I told you. Jared's behavior ramped up so quickly, and that's when we asked for your help."

"Why now?"

"Because I know you're special." Joe whispered, but his words exploded like a bomb in Olivia's head.

"I don't know what you mean," Olivia reached up and twisted her dragonfly earring. "I haven't changed—"

"That day, at Joe's, when the lights went out... something happened." Joe's eyes locked with Olivia's. She wanted to look away, but the calm knowledge unwavering in his gaze held hers. "I saw something, too."

Olivia jumped up from her seat, a knot forming in her stomach. "You saw something? I think you're mistaken. It was a power glitch—that's all."

"I thought so, too. That's why I hurried to the breaker box in the back. But as I got to the hallway, I felt a presence... a warmth coming ebbing towards me. I paused and saw a light forming a faint body outline in front of the box. I was stunned, frozen in place, trying to grasp what I was seeing. Then I heard in my mind, *go back to her*. I numbly took a few steps back and turned, running my hand along the wall in the dark until I came to the counter. The lights suddenly came back on and I saw you, Zach, and Sergio cowering on the floor. That's when I bent down and told you I fixed the problem, but you were staring past me with a look of terror I've never seen on anyone before. I knew something unspeakable had happened and that a divine presence had saved you. Everything changed after that. Your dad came back, your mom almost died, but you—" Joe swallowed, "—you changed, too. A new glow surrounded you. I can't really explain it, but I sensed you... and the boys... had become something not of this world."

Olivia sank back into the chair, stunned by Joe's revelation. "How?"

"Ever since I could remember, I've always felt connected... sensed things that no one else did. My Mom said I was *touched*," he chuckled. "Whatever it is, I sensed it in you and the evil surrounding Jared. We don't need to know what it is, but you can't deny that I'm right. Before Jared shot me, you raise your hand, and a force shoved him. It was you, and it probably saved my life."

"When I saw Zach in the backyard with you, I wasn't surprised. He helped you, didn't he?" Callie's calm tone belayed the ramifications of their story.

Olivia felt trapped. How could she deny what they saw when she couldn't share her identity with them? Joe and Callie couldn't get mixed up in this. Next time, they might not escape the Fallen.

I can't put them in harm's way.

"Listen. I—"

"You don't have to say anything," Joe said, a smile tugging at his lips. "We just wanted to thank you and to tell you to keep doing whatever it is you're doing to help others. The world needs people like you to fight against the unseen evils. Your secret is safe with us, although why teenagers get to save the day is beyond me."

Tears formed in Olivia's eyes even as they shared a chuckle at Joe's words.

You don't know how badly I needed to hear that.

The door swung open, saving her from saying something she shouldn't. A nurse hustled in and scanned the room. "How's our patient doing?" she asked as she glanced at the monitor.

"Better than last night," Joe smirked.

"I think I'd better let you get some rest." Olivia stood and walked around to Callie. "Call me and keep me posted on Joe."

"I will. And don't forget what we said, okay?"

Olivia nodded and then hugged her. "I won't, and thank you." She whispered in her ear. Joe's eyelids had already closed, so she left the room, sending up a prayer for them.

Please keep them safe and let Joe completely heal.

She strode with a purpose down the sterile hallway, buoyed by her friend's words. A daring plan formed while she drove back home. No matter how badly it scared her, she knew it was the only way forward. Everyone would tell her no, but her gut told her she had to do it.

I need to connect with Delilah.

CHAPTER
THIRTEEN

OLIVIA

S hards of colorful light illuminated the vast white wall at the back of the church. The dark wooden cross absorbed the light, creating deeper hues across the huge beams. Its display mesmerized Olivia. The silence of the minimalist church slowed her racing heart. Her eyes darted to her backpack slumped against the pew. Inside lay the tool she needed to complete her task. It worked before, but knowing the risks made her nervous and worried the outcome may not be successful.

But I have no choice.

I have to do this so no one else gets hurt.

Glancing back at the cross, she willed the peace she found in this moment to take root. No more looking back. No more *what ifs* or *would have, should have, could have.* The time for action had come, but she learned doing it alone was a mistake. She wouldn't risk it again. She released her pent-up breath; the tension melting from her shoulders.

Here I go...

"Michael. I need you." Her plea echoed around the church as if searching for its subject. She shifted in the pew as the sound faded with no blue sparks announcing his arrival. Running a hand through her hair, purple and orange flashed in the corner of her eye from the ring her mom had given her for Christmas. Her words of wisdom, spoken in a firm but gentle voice, took her back to the last evening they shared before Dad came back into their lives.

It will enhance your intuition...

Help you better trust yourself...

Reveal the strength and energy of your inner fire...

She twisted the ring around her finger, hoping her next move would reflect the ring's meaning.

Streaks of blue crackled in the aisle before Michael appeared. His presence never ceased to steal her breath, with his stunning white wings dipped in blue, highlighting his warrior stance. But calm swept over Olivia when his brilliant blue eyes, filled with compassion, hit her core. Whatever Michael had been doing, he stopped and come to her as if she was the most important thing in the world. Still at a loss for words, she could only grin as his eyes scanned her from head to toe.

"Don't worry, I'm not hurt. That's not why I called you," she said, a flush creeping up her neck. "I need to talk to you about—uhm— what happened with Callie and Joe and what we have to do next."

The tension ebbed from Michael. "Alright. How can I help?"

Olivia moved out of the pew. She paced in front of him, trying to figure out how to start.

"Do you want to go for a walk or—" His deep voice stopped her in her tracks. "Just say what's on your mind. It doesn't need to be perfect."

She hooked a stray strand of hair behind her ear and squared her shoulders. "Are you ever afraid... I mean—well, unsure you made the right move. The attack on Callie and Joe hits so close to home. After Mom and Dad almost died from Zar's attack, I thought we—I had everyone protected by living with the Magi. But it didn't matter. A Fallen found Jared by chance because of his jealousy and rage at Callie attracted it. I thought I was in control, that we had the situation at hand, and we didn't. And for the first time in a long time, I became nervous again, realizing the battles between Heaven and

Hell are so much bigger than me. All my efforts seem small and reactive. This fear I'm carrying is stifling the good I feel about our purpose." Olivia paused, trying to gauge Michael's reaction, only to find a far off look on his face. "Am I wrong to feel this way?"

"No. Fear knows no bounds and humbles even this simple Angel," Michael's voice cracked as his focus returned to her. "I had never tasted fear until that fateful day when Lucifer tore Heaven in two. Angels that I've loved since the beginning of time made the choice to side with him and his evil ways. I stood in horror as Lucifer and his army raised their swords, wanting to destroy our way of life—over their hatred for humanity. I was overwhelmed with an anger I'd never felt before, and a sense of protection for those who stayed with God. As the battle raged, my goal was to get to Lucifer and destroy him. I thought if he's gone, his hold on them would leave too. He must have thought the same, because a wave of fire licked over his followers. And then, behind him and his army, the Mar of Sin erupted with churning dark clouds and a noise like a snarling, ravenous beast. Our swords clashed at the vortex's edge, swinging wildly to gain an advantage over one another. Lucifer's face contorted in rage as his army of fallen angels and beasts fell into the abyss. He stumbled and fell, his losing his weapon. I raised my sword, wanting to pierce his heart, but I froze for a fraction of a second, just long enough for the horrors swirling around to strike me numb. And then he spoke the last words."

Olivia's heart beat wildly. "What did he say?"

"'*You should have killed me while you had the chance. Blood stains a coward's hands.*' He dove over the edge, his last words striking me as he tumbled into the swirling mass. His arrogant laughter from the abyss still haunts me."

"He's wrong! You're not a coward. You fought him and won."

"Don't you see?" a bitterness wrapped around his words. "Lucifer lived. I thought he'd die when he went over the edge, never to be seen or heard from again. I was so wrong. There's so much blood on my hands from the Angels we lost in battle... all that I had loved." He raised his palms towards her as if to show her the blood he felt staining his skin. "More blood is a tragedy, but it's the price of battle and our free will. I never want to see another friend die or recognize a Fallen consumed with evil. What happens when Lucifer comes and we meet again and I fail?" He lowered his hands. "So yes. I'm afraid of failing. We all are. But it won't stop me. I have to be ready every day for his return, even as the responsibility of it seems too much. I can't run and hide or ignore the evil encroaching on our worlds. God made some of us to bear a mighty burden. That's why He created me... and you."

"Your burden, your blessing." Her lips trembled as she mouthed those fateful words.

"Yes."

Olivia's teeth tugged on her bottom lip while she considered Michael's reflection. A sense of relief washed over her knowing that an Angel who personified strength, courage, and wisdom empathized with her fears and uncertainty. Maybe her idea wasn't so crazy after all.

"Thank you for your honesty," she reached over and grabbed his hand. A soothing warmth spread up her arm. "Your truth makes me feel better about me and what I'd like to do next."

He grinned, releasing her hand. "Always the fearless planner... what is your idea?"

"I don't want to wait around any longer for Lucifer's next move. Reacting to events and looking for demons isn't helping us find out what he's up to. The waiting is driving me crazy, and after what happened to Joe and Callie, I have to get an upper hand." She paused, waiting for his reaction, but he remained silent, regarding her with a raised eyebrow. She strode across the aisle between the pews. "I want to meditate, but not just to scan Hell's activity. I want to connect with Delilah."

"No—"

"Just hear me out," she blurted over him. "Delilah is the key. She started this mess with her need for revenge against my dad. She betrayed the Angels and the Guardians by telling Lucifer the portal's secrets. When she fell through the Mar of Sin, I don't know if she truly understood what her selfish actions would ignite. But it's clear that she has Lucifer's ear and is still working with Zar. I hurt her pretty badly—she may have died. I need to find out. If she lived and is still close to Lucifer, then maybe I could learn about his next move. If she's dead, then I don't have to worry about her trying to hurt my family anymore. Either way, I have to connect with her again."

"Okay. There are too many traps she could set, hoping you'd try to connect with her again."

"But, I—"

"I trust you, Olivia. Your thinking is as wise as it is dangerous. It takes great courage to go into the unknown. I won't stop you, but you will not meditate alone this time."

Her shoulders sagged as she stood in front of him. "Deal."

He nodded and crossed his arms over his chest. "How will you connect with her?"

She bent over the pew, blood rushing in her ears as her hand reached for her backpack. The zipper's steel teeth opening sounded ominous in the silent church. She reached into the void, her fingers tentatively searching for the segway for her plan. Wispy ends fluttered against her fingertips like a butterfly's wings. Her eyes narrowed as her query emerged into the light. She turned and held it up to Michael.

"This is Delilah's feather when she was still an Angel. She left it for me when I was a little girl. I found her once by accident by using this. This time, it will be on purpose and I won't be the one surprised."

CHAPTER
FOURTEEN

OLIVIA

The feather's wispy edges fluttered as Olivia twirled it between her fingertips. She leaned back against the pew, trying to settle her racing heart and mind. The last time she'd meditated, she was searching for Zemira, her Guardian Angel, but the portal took her to Delilah. She barely pulled back before being discovered. This time, she *wanted* to find Delilah, hoping to get information about Lucifer's plans for war.

What if she's not alone?

What if she's dead?

Linking was as dangerous as walking into a battle blindfolded. You never knew who you'd encounter or if it might alert Lucifer. She needed to stay on the visual edges and peer through like a looking glass. The key was to unlink before being discovered. Hoping to find Delilah alone was dicey, but having Michael next to her boosted her confidence.

"I don't like this, Olivia," Michael's deep voice rumbled with a cautionary tone.

"I know. Can't say I'm thrilled about it either. Thank you for staying with me. I feel safer, like you're my shield... my armor."

He gently touched her, sending a much-needed surge of warmth up her arm. "That's the best thing I've heard today." He chuckled and stepped back into the aisle. "Are you ready?"

She swallowed, trying to dredge up some spit in her dry mouth. She brought the feather close; the ends dancing over her face. Closing her eyes, she cleared her mind and slowed her breathing. A picture of Orion filled the black canvas, its stars, bright beacons outshining the twinkling counterparts. She focused on Orion's belt, concentrating on the far-right star. The orb awakened under her mark as if it also was drawn like a magnet to the portal within Orion's belt. Blue sparks ignited her vison as her mind sped through time and space until the field of stars blurred away.

The transition from light to dark jarred Olivia. Darkness, like the depths of a cave, cloaked her vision until her night vision adjusted. The air was thick, wrapping around her like a second skin. A strange sound emerged. She couldn't decipher it, but her skin crawled in reaction. She moved deeper into the dark, hyper-aware that something or someone lurked outside her field. Unease grew, along with her doubt that she would find Delilah here.

What is this place?

An undulating purple light glowed in the distance, drawing Olivia closer. A black metal circular cage sat on an isolated island surrounded by a glowing purple moat. A limp figure lay motionless inside, huddled against the far bars. Olivia gasped in recognition.

Delilah...

But not the Angel of her memories or the Fallen she'd battled. The form laying on the dirt floor was a broken being tossed aside, solitary in punishment. Her once vibrant red hair was matted and dull, hiding her face. She had one arm tucked under her head. The other arm was missing. Flashes of their battle surfaced. She remembered the satisfaction of her sword slicing through Delilah's arm. Her ripped clothing exposed old wounds.

The hazards of battle...

Or was it?

This isn't how Delilah looked when she escaped through the portal.

Olivia cautiously moved closer. Deep purple veins on Delilah's white calves caught her attention. They traveled like vines up her legs before disappearing beneath her tattered clothes. Olivia held her breath, ears straining to make out the muffled words emanating from under the tangled hair. Her palms sweat, trying to decipher if the sounds were real or just her imagination.

"My fault," Delilah suddenly wailed, slamming her fist against the ground. "Have to fix this! Must stop—" She bolted up, clouded green eyes searched in Olivia's direction. "Who's there?" Delilah scanned the cavern as if looking for the same predator Olivia sensed was too close. "Is that you—Olivia?"

Trepidation thickened Olivia's tongue. How could she detect her? Does that mean someone else could sense her, too? Should she respond or continue to watch and wait? Delilah continued to gaze in her direction, setting her teeth on edge.

"How did you find me?" Delilah sagged against the bars as if she'd used the last vestige of her strength. The silence stretched between them, sucking Olivia closer despite her nerves. "I am losing my mind. Death must be near." Her breathless words echoed in the void.

Olivia's every nerve screamed to back away, but Michael hadn't called her back and she needed answers. Whatever state Delilah was in, she had to take the risk and make contact.

"Yes, it's me—Olivia," she said, barely above a whisper. "I found you through the white feather you left on my pillow when I was a little girl—the day my dad left our family."

"Aww, yes. The day I thought all would change and Conner would come back to me, but he deserted us both. Or so I thought. I forced him to make a choice, and he made the right one. He had to protect his family and the guardianship. I was incredibly selfish." Delilah drew her knees up against her chest. "And look where all that rage and hate has gotten me. In Hell... in this prison. To die alone.

This is my reward for causing the end of humanity. It's what I deserve after all the bad choices I've made... the lives I've destroyed."

Olivia reeled back, shocked by Delilah's confession. Could she really be sorry for all the pain and suffering she has caused, or is she just fishing for Olivia's sympathy to lure her into another trap?

I can't trust anything she says...

Yet, I believe her.

"What happened to you after our battle?" Olivia asked. Hissing grew louder in the moat. Undulating motions quickened as if excited by some unseen force. Her mark tingled, warning her danger was near.

Delilah swiped at the tangled mess around her face. Revealing the jagged scar running down the side of her face. "Lucifer gathered the Fallen into the Main Hall, furious the Guardian and Raphael had escaped. He whipped the Fallen into a frenzy and spoke of his vision for a New World Order. He plans to destroy Heaven and make the Earth a playground for the Fallen to use humans for their wicked pleasure. The Realm delighted in this possibility to abuse those they feel are responsible for the Fall. Lucifer banished Zar for his failure, yet he got the honor of whipping me to near death, because I betrayed them both. He locked me in here—" she doubled over as if gripped by pain, "—to die a slow death by... them."

"Who? Who is hurting you?"

"Can't you see them circling around me?" Delilah tossed her arm out, her bony finger cast at the moat. "Snakes bred by Astaroth. They bite me each day. The venom is poisoning me—killing me slowly, driving me mad."

A shiver traveled down Olivia's spine, sickened by what moved around the moat. As if on cue, a thick snake zig-zagged up the rocky slope, its triangular head weaving toward the edge. Olivia sucked in her breath, the landing almost within reach.

"One's coming—"

"There's nothing I can do to stop it, so I have little time left before it strikes. There's so much to tell you. I want to help you defeat

Lucifer. He can't win. I know how to stop him." The snake's head broke over the edge and hissed at its prey. "There's another force down here who matches Lucifer's power—"

"What? How can that be? We would have known—"

"No! No one knows but me—" Delilah froze, her eyes widened, locked on something unseen by Olivia. Her mark throbbed when the edges of her vision filtered with a dim light.

"You must go. Now!" Delilah spoke between clinched teeth. "Quick, before—"

"I can't leave you like this. Let me help you."

"You can't help me. It would alert them to your presence. Leave. It's the only way." Her hand gripped the bar, as if bracing for the inevitable. "He's coming."

Olivia... cut the link.

She couldn't ignore Michael's command, but she had to learn more about this other force. "I'll return. I promise. Fight, Delilah." Olivia snapped back through the portal. But she'd never forget the last thing she witnessed.

The snake's body arched back, head held high as its fangs dripped with purple venom, and the hopeless fear etched on Delilah's face.

CHAPTER
FIFTEEN

DARK
PRINCE

Black walls blurred as the Dark Prince flew through the cave, unnerved at how close it was to his lair.

We need to be careful... this could be a trap.

Swirling purple light vibrated in the distance, but it was the smell of fear and sweat mingling with Delilah's musk that excited him. Oh, how he wished his hand had caused her suffering. He wanted to take pleasure in her perfectly horrid prison. What he found did not disappoint him.

The snakes are a delightful touch. She will die at the hands of what she is.

"Yes. For once, we agree on something."

His wings pumped through the stagnant air, more eager than ever to get to her. A devious grin stretched across his face upon hearing her wail. "This will be fun."

The snake's fangs poised above her, seconds from sinking into her exposed calf. He flicked his wrist and sent the snake hard against the bars. Blazing purple slits found the culprit and coiled to attack the intruder. Sensing the power of the intruder, it slithered out of the cage and disappeared over the edge.

Kill her quickly before anyone returns.

"All in due time, Ancient One."

He landed on the rocky edge, sneering at her through the bars.

"My Delilah, you are a fright and a bit on the ripe side, too. Prison doesn't suit you, but it is what you deserve."

Delilah stared at him with uneasy regard even as a sneer pulled back her upper lip. "Of course, it's you. Who else would dare to have Lucifer followed? Have you come to gloat over my demise or appease your fears that I've kept our secret?"

"Is that how you greet a friend and a partner, no less?" He stalked the edge, running his hand against the bars, slapping each one. "I would have thought you'd be pleased to see me. Someone to rescue you from your dreadful circumstances."

"I have a feeling you're not here to free me. So, finish your gloating and leave me to my slow death." She turned from him and hid her face behind her filthy hair.

"Death by snake. I admire the irony," he chuckled, "but I'm only here to ask you a question. Why did you keep our secret?"

"How do you know I didn't tell him of your betrayals?"

"Because I'd already be dead." He gripped the bars with both hands, pressing his face between them. "Tell me what you are scheming and why? I wouldn't hold my tongue if I were you. My patience is at its end."

Silence was her answer, sending a spark of hate through him.

Do it now.

"Because I hate him and his arrogant queen with every dying fiber I have left. He's not worthy to rule the Fallen and Asura will turn on him as soon as the timing is right. I took great pleasure in reinforcing the lie that Sonneillon was the *true* betrayer. Her screams of rage filled my soul with a sweet victory. And Lucifer, so willing to believe in his ultimate genius, gloated in her denial as well. So, when you leave me, I will fill my thoughts with you and how you will triumph over him and become the true ruler the Fallen deserves."

He mulled this over as the snake pit came alive. A new plan awakened, weaving in his mind like the entwining serpents nearby.

"Will Lucifer return, or are you to languish in your misery until death?"

Her skeletal finger pulled the hair away from her face. Wary eyes stared at the spot where the snake had vanished over the edge. "It's difficult to languish when I'm bitten every day by those assassins crawling, circling me like vultures. Their fangs are so sharp, it isn't the bite I feel, but the poison injecting into me, stealing another day of life. I've learned something about my tormentors. I assumed their glossy scales were moist and cool, but as it travels over my body, it was not the sensation it leaves behind. Instead, the dry, raspy rubbing of its scales against my skin scald me before they slither back to the pit. The hisses... their never-ending reminder they despise me. It's all I hear as my body lays prisoner to the venom thickening my blood." She turned; her hatred flashed. "Kill me slowly? Yes, so he can punish me for my supposed betrayal of him, and still be free to grill me for more information on the Guardians." She slammed her fist against the floor. "But I have no more to share. I've told him all I know."

She got what she deserved. She betrayed Lucifer.

He ignored the insistent chatter from the soul he'd claimed for himself.

"If you're miserable, why aren't you begging me for your death?" he asked more to hear her say it, then really caring about her answer.

"Because I want to live. I want to find a way out of here. I'm not done with my revenge and neither are you."

He nodded, admiring the hateful streak burning inside her. "My, my... you truly are a Fallen."

"I thought you understood that when we met. We used each other for information and... pleasure. I have no love lost for humans or Angels. I would go through the Mar of Sin again, only I would have been smarter and more ruthless. My only regret will be that I will not see the look on Lucifer's face when you reveal your true self —your powers to him." Purple light blossomed from the moat, growing up on the shadowed sides. "Another snake is preparing to bite me since the last one failed." Her flat voice matched the resignation frozen on her face.

Don't believe her. Let her die, we have no more use for her…

He clenched his fist, wishing he could silence the voice. Once he stops having to keep his regular form, he will squash the Ancient One's voice.

No… never!

"I have a proposition for you that will be beneficial to us both. You'll continue to feed Lucifer and Asura disinformation about me. Feed his ego and drive his queen deeper into her rage. In return, I will give you my feather. It will heal you and grow back your arm. If we both do our part, it keeps Lucifer off my scent and you get to live to see him humiliated and killed in front of the Fallen. Do we have a deal?"

Fool… FOOL! Kill—

"But I could die before you give me your feather."

A deep rumble rolled from his chest. "Already distrusting me?" He swatted his hand toward the moat as if swiping away a nuisance. "I can do nothing about the snakes, but my time is closer than you think."

"How will I know?"

He exhaled heavily. "I grow weary of your questions. A simple yes or no will do."

"Yes." She stood up on shaky legs.

"Good!" His wings opened with a snap. "One more thing, the next time I return, I'll have some information I'll want you to feed to Lucifer. Things you've… remembered."

She nodded her head, but her eyes shot to the triangular shaped head creeping over the rim. She yelped when he waved his hand and flung the snake across the moat. He smirked at Delilah before he flew away.

That was too easy. She will betray you, I'm sure of it…

"Delilah is a game worth playing. She's an added shield I need to keep Lucifer off track. I know what I'm doing, so shut up." A tunnel of light bloomed before him. The Realm's air now dissipating the stench of her prison still clinging to him. He aimed for his Realm, but the excitement of visiting Delilah made it difficult to control his features. A grin grew as the perfect solution changed his destination.

My lair...

My sanctuary...

My secret...

The Damned he locked away awaited him.

For his pleasure and their death.

CHAPTER
SIXTEEN

LUCIFER

The spacious domain, his sanctuary, was the one place in Hell just for him. Lucifer closed the door, its echo a welcome note of silence and solitude. The vast window across the bedroom reflected the Realm's exploding colors. His long strides ate up the distance while the mirrored wall to his left mimicked him. He ignored the massive, empty bed, the silky covers undisturbed irritated him. Soon he would deal with Asura ignoring his desires. He stopped before the window and the view that normally brought him peace and pride. A strange unrest churned within, an unsettling when his dreams of war and domination seemed so close at hand. He closed his eyes, fighting the face flirting in his mind's eye.

Delilah.

Is she telling me the truth?

Is Michael plotting against him with the Guardians?

Opening his eyes, he glanced over his shoulder at the bed he once shared with her. An icy rage burned, but an insidious flame of desire still flickered for her. Had the wasteland of time made him pliable to her and the promising secrets she whispered of a renewed path to power? No one, not even Asura, had plagued him, burrowing under his hard exterior and discovering a soft underbelly he hadn't realized lay vulnerable. He let her wander Hell unchecked, plot with Zar, and even allowed her the fantasy of shared power. Ultimately, Lucifer believed her alliance remained with him. But when Delilah met with Olivia, seeking the secrets for herself and the traitor first, it shattered a wall of complacency and allowed a surge of mind exploding rage to take root. He rose Abaddon from his slumbering depths. The dragon could help him stamp out any doubts about who was the ruler of the Fallen.

Sonneillon's death in the battle pit left no room for doubt.

No one deceives me without a consequence.

He lunged for the bed, snarling as he shredded it and the taunting memories of the passions they'd shared. With his spurt of rage spent, he stepped away from the heap of tattered remains. He growled with satisfaction and replaced Delilah's pale body and hair of flames with Asura's ebony curves and hair of wild gold braids. She had stayed true to her declaration during her crowning to not be his lover, but taking her to Delilah's prison had shaken Asura's blind allegiance to her dead mate.

She'll come to me soon enough.

Watching her beg forgiveness will be such a treat.

"One day soon, I will teach her humility and the rules of being my queen."

He departed his sanctuary with a lighter footstep than his entrance and headed for his Throne Room for his next task.

"Zar," he murmured and sent his link to demand his appearance.

Lucifer stroked Abaddon's black scales, causing a ripple under his fingers. He admired the curled-up dragon lazing in the Throne Room. Its tail encircled the black marble throne. Abaddon's reptilian eyes were slits as he scanned the empty hall. A rumble emanated from his chest, echoing Lucifer's own discontent. He leaned back into his chair, admiring the massive room where he'd created his plan, indulged his serpent, and waited too long to take his rightful place as ruler of Heaven, Hell, and Earth. Tannin broke the pool's surface, his red-tipped fins bright against the opaque water. It swam around the pool's edges in search of food or prey.

"Sorry, my pet. Nothing yet, but I promise I will have a bounty of flesh for you soon." As if it understood Lucifer's vow, its serpentine body slipped to the depths until the tail fin waved in final salute to its master.

Lucifer's nostrils flared as he impatiently waited. Enormous arched double doors, each emblazoned with a red serpent, lurched open. Zar emerged alone and walked across the transparent bridge over the pool. His stride reflected a confident swagger that surprised Lucifer. Zar's body held no visible changes, but as he stopped at the base of the stairs, a hardening—a sharpened edge had chiseled away his vulnerability. It suited Zar and his eyeless pits.

Took long enough...

"My Lord," Zar bowed. Fire blazed down the stair's railings, reflecting brilliant reds and oranges off his long, platinum hair. This new, dangerous air intrigued Lucifer. Where had Zar been since the day he whipped Delilah in the Main Hall? Whatever he'd been up to had made him better prepared for his next tasks.

"You look well—better than the last time our paths crossed. It made me wonder about your condition since you took your time answering my call." Lucifer drummed his fingers against the chair's arm.

"My apologies. I have chosen to live in the mountains outside the Realms. The solitude suits me."

"I see. So, you have banished yourself from your fellow Fallen?" Lucifer cocked his eyebrow. "Why would you choose this instead of enjoying the Realm's pleasures?"

"I still come to the Realms and ride Cydanos. When I'm finished, I make myself unseen—stealth, if you will—and take in the happenings unnoticed by others. It sharpens my senses." Zar's small shrug almost went undetected. "Otherwise, the outskirts of the Realms better fit my needs."

Lucifer stood and mulled over Zar's careful use of words. He walked over to Abaddon and placed his hand against his body. "And keeps you out of sight. Maybe in hopes that the Fallen and I will forget your failures?" Zar's silence was all the answer he needed. "Do you spend your days and nights wondering why I didn't have Abaddon kill you, too?" The dragon raised his head as a small red glow emerged in his belly. "Why I spared you the death your failures earned?"

"Having me torture Delilah served your purposes better than burning me next to Sonneillon. I assumed you'd get around to my death soon enough. Is that why I'm here?"

Lucifer smiled, respecting Zar's attitude. "Spoken like someone who's not afraid to die."

"Death has been my shadow since my time with the mutant. I do not fear dying. The mutant stripped it from me, absorbed by the pit's dirt floor."

Lucifer left Abaddon's side and made his way down the stairs. Zar remained rooted in his stance, reflecting the truth of his words.

"Your honesty—it speaks a truth I wish more Fallen embraced. We have become soft, complacent in the Realms. We have prepared for war, gathered the Damned and sparred to keep up the blood lust for the humans. But as our invasion approaches, I sense the tang of fear in the undercurrent of shouts for victory. But you have beaten death, shaping you into the Fallen I'd hoped you become. I see in you what no one else does."

Zar cocked his head. "And what is that?"

"Perfection." Lucifer's fingertips glided down Zar's face, skimming over the scarred eye sockets. The flesh quivered as if awakened by his touch. "Your vision far surpasses the sight you lost. You sense what others don't. Predict your opponent's next move by the twitch of their skin. This is why you can beat the likes of Leviathan. This is why I need you—why I know you won't fail in this task."

"What is it?" A muscle twitched in Zar's jaw.

"The Guardians. Your nemesis. My future." Zar bared his teeth, eliciting a long overdue reaction from him. "I see you haven't forgotten about them."

"Never."

"Good," Lucifer whispered in Zar's ear. "Revenge has no time limit."

Zar growled with approval.

"I'm sending you back to Earth to watch the Guardians. Find their weakness. Everyone has a blind spot. I want to know more about them, draw them out—blindside and humiliate them in front of the God who finds them so precious."

"But the angelic goons will have them well protected."

"Therefore, I've chosen you and your unique skills to maneuver around them. When you retrieve the information I need, we will start our war."

"What about Delilah? Where is she?"

The question hung unanswered between them. Lucifer stepped past him and walked to the pool's edge. Ripples traveled across the water as Tannin skirted the edges. "You surprise me. I would have thought she was dead to you."

"My only interest in her is the information she still keeps hidden."

"Delilah is, well shall we say, wallowing amongst her kind. She no longer furthers my purposes."

Zar's footsteps were barely a whisper as he came up next to Lucifer. "I don't under—"

"And you don't need to. Our priorities lay with the Guardians and their secret portals. I must control those pathways, so the Fallen and Damned have unrestricted access. This is our—your only concern."

Zar turned his head, aiming his empty sockets at him. "I'd like to see her before I leave for Earth. She may share something with me, even in her anger, that she held back from you. She might be foolish enough to think she has something left to barter for her freedom."

Zar's concerns raised the memory of the last time he met Delilah.

She was scared, but was she desperate enough to hold back what he sought? "Suit yourself." He flicked his wrist toward at the exit. "Ask her all the questions you want, but I think you'll find her worth is nothing."

"Thank you, my Lord."

"I allow this for the Fallen's future, not because I want to satisfy your curiosity about her. Deep inside the Sloth's mountains, you'll find her prison. I'm sure your heightened senses will locate her." Lucifer turned, his long strides taking him to the stair's landing. He paused before taking the first step and peered over his shoulder.

"One more thing before you visit our disgraced angel." Zar's retreating form stopped, then faced him. "Your fledgling yearning for Delilah's love will get you killed. She can't give you what she doesn't possess. Leave whatever feelings you have left for her in the cavern where they can die alongside her."

Zar stilled, as if absorbing the reality of Lucifer's statement. He bowed and walked away without reply over the bridge, his platinum hair a siren song to Tannin's stalking form.

CHAPTER
SEVENTEEN

LUCIA

B lades of lush grass swayed across the vast rolling field. The dense forest was a blur of green and black on Lucia's left. On her right, the hills rose to meet the sky. Exhilaration pumped her wild blood as the speed of her run flattened her coarse fur. Freedom to roam the fields surrounding the Magi's home had become like an addiction to her. She spent a decade bound to a wheelchair, hiding her envy at everyone's ability to move however they pleased, taking for granted the mobility of their bodies. Now her spine had healed, thanks to the orb's angelic powers. All she wanted to do was run, jump, swim, or... well, anything but sit.

This is what I want to feel for the rest of my life.

Huge white paws trampled the grass and carved a path back toward the human waiting for her. Sam's earthy scent hinted at the breeze, but Lucia had no problem capturing it. Olivia's grandpa was also a Shifter, turning into a grizzly bear during his time as a Guardian. He wanted to teach her how to better control the shift instead of it controlling her.

But do I want that?

The wild power of the tiger was intoxicating, but the longer she remained shifted into the creature, the more she lost herself in its world. Wondering what her life would be like to stay a tiger filtered through her dreams at night, amplified by her shifting during the day. She didn't share her desires with Sam or Sergio, this dangerous draw to not shift back to her human form. No one needed to know. This was her sacred self. An internal story for only her heart and spirit to embrace.

A familiar creature entered her domain from the forest and gave chase. Her nostrils flared, inhaling the lion's earthy, primal scent. Her heart raced as his larger stride reduced the distance between them. His presence no longer frightened her after weeks of him observing her from the forest's shadows. He'd never left the cloak of the trees, but his stare always sent a shiver over her flesh. She never turned his way, even though a yearning to do so tugged deep within as if it would connect two kindred spirits.

This time was different.

Her head swiveled when he came up and ran beside her. His dark tawny mane flowed; muscles rippled under his fur as he returned her stare. A glimmer brightened his emerald-colored eyes. Lucia's muscles burned from the exertion, so she tried to slow the pace. What would happen then? They couldn't talk, but the attraction to him was deeper than words. Confusion struck her when his eyes darkened. Depths of sadness replaced the shards of light. A low growl rumbled from him before he made a sharp turn back for the forest. Her paws stumbled beneath her at his abrupt departure. Her conflicting desires to chase him or return to Sam tore at her as he neared his sanctuary's boundary. Human reasoning lost the fight.

And I'm good with it.

She pinned her ears back and charged across the field. The magnificent beast glanced back at her before he slipped into the dark canopy. She heedlessly crashed into the forest; afraid she would lose sight of him. Forced to slow her pace by the thick undergrowth and wide tree trunks, she scanned the area until she caught a shifting shadow and a streak of tan fur. The deeper they charged into the forest, the stronger the tiger's control over her human reason. She felt as if she was a passenger trapped on a runaway train, hurtling out of control. The wild beast within ignored her budding fear as it sniffed the air, tracking the lion. She knew she should stop and reach for the orb and shift, but the tiger's curiosity and desires swept her away.

The forest became devoid of light. No animals stirred, yet the tiger stalked fearlessly deeper. A low roar split the silence, morphing into a human-like sorrowful moan. It echoed around her. The tiger sniffed the air again, confused when she detected no human scent.

What is going on?

Sunlight filtered up ahead through the tree trunks and branches, setting the forest ahead in a glow. The tiger followed it until she stepped out of the dark edge. She paused at the wide circular clearing. In the middle, the lion sat on his haunches, his thick tail swishing across the dry grass. He didn't flinch when she took a few cautious strides towards him. Something drew the tiger and Lucia to his presence, daring her to abandon any remaining caution.

Why can't I pull away from the lion?

And do I want to?

The lion didn't wait for her. She froze as he trotted to the other side of the clearing. She bared her teeth at his departure, wishing to nip at him for leading her on a wild chase. What was the point of following him? He wasn't interested in making any sort of contact with her. The front of his body slipped into the murky shadows. She took a few steps closer, her heart hammering as the rest of him disappeared into the forest. She shook her massive head and scanned for any trace of him, because what faded away couldn't possibly be right. Her mind must be playing tricks on her.

It wasn't a lion who had run from her.

Instead, a man with tawny hair flowing down his broad, tan back.

Was he a shifter, too?

Could it be?

She wanted to chase him and demand answers. Who was he and why was he here with the Magi? Her head spun with questions. But there was a bigger problem at hand. She and the tiger were both exhausted. Lost in the internal struggle for what form was in control, fear took root. The tiger stopped resisting her pleas to leave the clearing even though Lucia felt it deny its own urges to stay and chase the lion. The tiger followed the trampled trail out of the forest, its power and sense of direction more reliable than hers. Pine needles and twigs snapped beneath the dirty paws. Finally, the forest thinned and the calming grassy field lay just beyond. A familiar scent drifted to her and waylaid the choking panic that she'd pushed too far beyond her boundaries.

"Lucia! Where are you?" His call ricocheted around her; the caller's urgent demand for her response remained unanswered. She had ventured too far, let the tiger rule over her for too long. If she didn't connect with the orb soon, she feared the tiger would take over and retreat to the forest.

Which do I want?

A numbing sensation crawled up her legs, signaling she could wait no longer. Using the last of her strength, she reached for the orb and fought to make the connection. The shift began, but her vision turned to black.

"Armor on," she mumbled before collapsing onto the grassy edge, uncertain if she was still...

A tiger.

A woman.

Or dying.

CHAPTER
EIGHTEEN

LUCIA

Calloused hands gently brushed aside the hair clinging to Lucia's damp face. The same frantic voice kept calling her name, but it sounded far away, like someone was yelling through a tunnel. Her head swam with a torrent of hazy visions vying for scrutiny, only to disappear in succession as another surfaced.

A lion racing next to her...

Dark, dense forest with a bright clearing just beyond its edges...

A man with a wild mane of tawny hair cascading down his massive back.

Lucia's eyes snapped open at the electrifying memory, only to find Sam staring back at her. He searched her face, then quickly scanned her from head to toe. The deep lines of concern etching his face relaxed when his gaze returned to hers.

"Are you okay?" He raised his brow. "You have your armor on."

She nodded and cautiously sat up with Sam's help. "I didn't know what would happen after the shift, so I thought putting my armor on might be a good idea. *Armor off.*" Embarrassed by her disheveled state, she averted her gaze back to the forest. She knew the lion, or man, wasn't waiting at the edges. The tightness squeezing her chest made her mad. What did she expect? He'd come out of the forest and explain himself and the connection she had for him?

Yeah, right.

Get a grip on yourself.

"I'm fine. I think." A half-hearted grin appeared as she made an internal check. The tiger's essence lay dormant, tucked away by the orb's power. No bumps or bruises, only questions needing answers.

"Well, I sure hope so, kiddo, because you about gave me a heart attack," Sam chuckled, and let go of her arms. "One minute, you're racing toward me at full tilt, and then a lion comes out of nowhere and chases you. When you ran after it, my eyes popped out of my head. Promise me you'll never do that again. This old ticker would just stop."

Lucia laughed and nudged his arm. "I think that heart of yours can handle a lot worse, but I'll try not to scare you again."

"You wanna tell me why you gave chase instead of doing the smart thing and coming back here?" Her laugh faded away. "You are still learning the boundaries of your shift, and by the looks of you, you've found it."

"I know. It wasn't very smart of me." She glanced down at her hands, remembering the sensation of the earth giving way to their strength. "But the tiger's primal needs wanted to take over... and I let it." Silence fell between them. She was thankful for Sam's patience and his not passing judgment, but she got the sense he would not let her off the hook, either.

"I'll tell you what happened, but can I ask you to please let me be the one to tell Sergio and Bal?"

Sam put his hands up. "Your secret is safe with me. I'm a firm believer that everyone should tell their own story."

"Thanks." She blew out a breath and wondered where to start. The beginning would be best. "The first time I saw him—the lion... I was with Olivia."

"Uhm. That's a surprise, but I guess there's no reason to think she would confide in me." A hint of sadness hung on the last word. "What happened?"

"He came out of the forest and watched us, but focused on me. I had just shifted and I think he saw me. There's this connection that's hard to explain. The world kinda tunes out and I'm only focused on him. He let me come right up to him and touch him, but then he flew away. Olivia was not pleased, but I never felt in any danger. I only wanted to see him again." She swallowed, wishing she had some water for her dry mouth. "You and I started training, and I kept hoping for his return."

"Lucia—"

"It's not a bad thing," she scoffed. "I mean—come on. This place is full of magical creatures and none of them are dangerous. I wanted one to seek me out... just like the others." She pulled out a long blade of grass and ran her fingers over it. "I know that's silly—"

"No, kiddo. I understand. Felt that tug a few times myself." His smile emphasized the deep lines on his face. "But shifting is pretty cool, too. I'm sure they wish they could do it." He nudged her leg. "Now, back to this lion."

"I noticed him watching me run and train with you. Sometimes so deep in the forest, I could hardly sense him, but he was there, coming closer every day. Today he showed himself again. I think it surprised him as much as it did me. But his flash of joy changed to sadness, and that's when he took off for the forest. I—no... the tiger tracked him deep in the forest until we came to a clearing. The lion sat there, waiting. He roared at us. Not in a menacing way, just sad. He jumped up and trotted to the other side and—"

Should I tell him?

He'll think I'm crazy.

"And?"

"And he shifted into a man just as he entered the forest." Sam inhaled sharply. "I know, there's no way that could have happened, but—" He remained silent, all the humor gone from his face. "What! Do you know something? Could he be real?"

Sam abruptly stood, shaking his head as he dusted off his pants. "Listen, I am more concerned about you and the shift. I don't think you understand how close you came to losing yourself to the tiger."

Lucia sprung to her feet. "I could still reach the orb—"

"Before you stick out that stubborn chin of yours any further, listen carefully to me." Sam leaned in until they were almost nose to nose. "You won't like it, but it might just save your life."

She blinked a few times, never having been on the receiving end of Sam's sudden intensity. Disguised under his easy-going nature, was a man with a fire still burning in his belly. "All right. I'm all ears."

"Good," he said, the corner of his mouth lifting. "You mean... a lot to me, kiddo. You're special, but shifting is a dangerous biz—" he swallowed, "—and I don't want to see you get lost to it. Some shifters can stay for very long periods of time in their animal form. That was me. If I'm correct, after what happened today, you have a time limit for your shift. The will of the tiger is strong and wants to remain. It's not meant to be malicious; some seem to have more dominance and their drive to fight is stronger. Monitoring how long you shift isn't enough. The key is to not lose your *will* to the tiger, or the power you feel when *it* is in charge. Does that make sense?"

"Yeah—too much," she said, glancing at the forest.

Like I'd like to become the tiger.

"If you lose your ability to find the orb, the roles will become reversed."

"You mean I would stay a tiger?"

"Yes. And the dominant wild doesn't like to shift back to human."

Lucia's jaw dropped. "How do you know this?"

He reached for his canteen and took a long draw. He offered it, and she took it. The cool water soothed her dry throat, while her mind raced to put together Sam's cryptic word. She watched him over the rim, conflicting emotions played across his face until one finally settled.

Resignation.

"There is a legend here, more of a myth, about such a creature."

Water sprayed from Lucia's mouth. "As in the lion I saw?"

Sam jerked to the side, barely missing her geyser. "Yes—"

"Tell me—"

"This is for Bal to answer, not me. Let's head on back."

She put her hands on hips, not ready to return, but to dig in and get some answers. "Look, I need—"

"Ask. Bal." His lips pressed into a thin line like he'd sealed them shut.

"Fine," she muttered. "I'll ask Bal." She took off across the field, his long stride stayed right behind her. She wasn't really mad at Sam; it was an irritation with how close she'd come to losing herself to the tiger. He let her stomp towards the church in silence. Needing one more question answered, she stopped and turned around, and almost collided with his chest.

"Whoa." He grabbed her arms, holding her place. "Forget something?"

My sanity.

My pride.

My heart?

"Can you please just answer this one question?"

"All right," he replied, crossing his arms across his chest.

"Did that ever happen to you—you know... losing yourself to the grizzly?"

"Can't say as it did. The bear was content to relinquish control. My fellow Guardians didn't worry about me when I shifted."

She nodded and walked toward the church, this time with Sam next to her. She peeked at him from the corner of her eye. Did she dare ask?

"Were you close with them?"

"Who?" he frowned.

"Your fellow Guardians... Helen and my Abuela?"

"You sure are nosy today," he muttered. He gazed at the horizon's fading light, staring off as if memories flashed before him.

Maybe I pushed too far?

"The three of us were very close. Helen and Camilla—I could hardly keep up with them. Fearless. Lord, they would climb over me if it meant first to the fight. They left me in awe. But don't worry—" he turned and winked at her, "—I held my own just fine."

Lucia chuckled. "I have no doubt."

"Near the end of our time together, well..."

"What?" She wanted to shake him until he gave her all the answers. The fortress's gray bricks were getting larger. "You don't like to talk, do you?"

"I'm told it's not one of my strong suits." It was his turn to chuckle, but his face quickly sobered. "Until Camilla almost died in a battle on the same night as Juan, your Abuelo. It all went south—"

"My grandparents? I don't understand."

"And it's not my place to make you understand. I've already said too much." He stopped in front of the metal door leading to the many tunnels under the church. "Look. I've had some very dark years, time lost, blurred by booze and self-pity. I tried to drown out the pain of my wife's death to cancer and my many failures. It didn't work. Never does. When I finally got sober, I learned to own up to them with my own voice, my backbone. What happened to Camilla? That's her story to tell you, not mine. No matter how badly I'd like to fill in the blanks for you... I can't. I won't. When she finds her voice, you'll be the first to know."

A numbness crept inside Lucia from all the information, leaving her dizzy with the need for more answers. "Thanks for helping me."

"You bet." Sam heaved open the door and nodded towards the dark entrance. "Come on, kiddo. That's enough introspection for one day."

Not for me.

My night of inquisition has just begun.

CHAPTER
NINETEEN

SERGIO

The ax rested on Sergio's lap in his bedroom's dimming light. Black scales wrapped around the red handle leading to the head's crescent-moon blade. Three red claw prongs emerged from the handle, clutching the ax's head. His finger ached to glide across the weapon, but he resisted the urge—the desire to have the malevolent tingle lick up his arm and ignite the flame of revenge for Manny. His chest tightened as the painful memories of the night of his death pummeled him.

Red blood seeping across Manny's white t-shirt.

Watching the life fade from his eyes.

Letting him go, never to hold his brother again.

Sergio made a vow to avenge Manny. His angry footsteps carried him away from the agonizing scene, all the while secretly stowing away the swaddled ax inside of Manny's jacket. Zar was first on his kill list, but any Fallen he slain would momentarily quench the insatiable monster inside of him that pushed him farther and deeper into a dark, lonely corner. He ran his fingers through his thick, black hair as he tried to calm his thrashing heartbeat. He focused on the good that had happened since that tragic night.

Training hard and fulfilling his role as a Guardian.

Being a team with Olivia and Zach.

Lucia becoming a Guardian and walking again.

Lucia...

Beads of sweat prickled his hairline from the ax's pulsing heat. He glanced down, remembering the new oath he'd made to himself last week after his training session with Bal.

Fight the ax's call to darkness and reveal it to... who?

That's the problem.

Don't want to disturb Gabriel.

I don't want to witness Bal's disappointment again.

Papa would be furious.

Olivia and Zach would be hurt and probably a little pissed at me.

That leaves Lucia.

She's the one to tell first. The one who understands him like no other.

His twin.

His other half.

Two shall become one.

Sergio silently questioned Gabriel's words. They were already one. What more than being Guardians together could bring them closer? He drew a blank, but having her by his side when he tells the others will make the blow back he'll receive easier.

I hope she understands.

A sharp knock at the door had him shoving the ax under his pillow. "Just a min—"

"It's me," Lucia announced, opening the door. "I have something to tell—"

"You can't just barge into my room. I could have been changing clothes or napping or—" he waved his arms around, "—whatever."

She put her hands on her hips. "Okay... sorry, but I need to tell you something right now."

"All right," his brow furrowed, not detecting any bad vibes from her. "I'm all ears."

The mattress bounced when she plopped down beside him. "You won't believe what happened to me today. I was training with

Sam in the field and that's when I sensed him in the forest. He chased me—"

Sergio jerked. "Wait. Who chased you?"

"The lion. The one I've been telling you about." She rolled her eyes. "Anyway, he chased me, but abruptly turned into the forest. I followed him—" Sergio's jaw dropped, "—into a clearing and I swear to you, he shifted just as he went back into the forest. I was so exhausted by the time I made it out of there, I almost couldn't shift back. Thank goodness Sam was waiting for me. That's when he told me about the myth—"

Sergio clasped his hands on top of his head. "You're making my head hurt with your speed talking. I'm still stuck on you couldn't shift back."

She huffed, stood up, and paced the small confines of his room. "Sam told me there is a myth about a lion that is a shifter that lives here. He said I had to ask Bal for the rest of the story because he didn't know much about it." Lucia whirled around and faced him. "He then spilled the beans that Abuela has something she's been keeping secret—" She stopped, her eyes darting around the room.

"You can't stop there. Tell me!"

"What's that smell?" She wrinkled her nose. "Did you go on a hunt? You know we aren't supposed to—"

"No. Of course I didn't. I don't smell it." He shook his head as his pulse hammered in his ears. Was he ready to unveil the ax? No. He needed more time to plan. "Come on, let's go eat. You must be famished." He grabbed her arm and pulled her towards the door.

She yanked her arm free. "Don't lie to me. I've sensed this before... at home, but I thought it was the lingering odor from a hunt. But we aren't hunting now."

Sergio fought against his rising panic. His eyes darted to the pillow. Lucia lunged for the bed, but he shoved her away, surprising them both. She gasped; mouth open as she blatantly shot daggers at him.

"You'd better have a good reason for doing that."

"Lucia, please." A flush crept up his neck as he lifted his hands up. "I'm sorry. This—uh... well." His words died on the end of his tongue.

Lucia rose. Whatever anger she felt slipped from view. As if sensing he needed a nudge, she reached out and took his hand. "You can tell me anything."

Of course, I can...

A heaviness lifted from his shoulders. He let go of her hand and reached beneath the pillow. Closing his eyes for a moment, his long fingers wrapped around the handle.

No more would this be his burden alone.

No more would this dark weapon have a hold on him.

He held the ax with both hands and faced her, presenting it like an offering.

She recoiled and placed her hand over her heart. "Where did you get that? Is that from a Fallen?"

"Yes," he said, barely above a whisper. "The demon who killed Manny left this behind. I found it under his car while I cradled his body."

Lucia fell back against the bed, focused on the ax.

"I grabbed it and instantly a dark urge for revenge took hold, flooding me with an anger and drive to fulfill my oath." A tear slipped down his cheek. "But I don't want to be filled with these emotions anymore. My rash actions almost got me killed, along with you and everyone else. I want to be free of it." His voice cracked as he sat down next to her.

"Why didn't you tell me?" Hurt flashed across her face.

"At first, because I didn't want to. It was mine. I thought the vow to avenge Manny made me a better Guardian. I was so wrong. There were many times I wanted to tell you, but I chickened out, still not ready to let it go."

"What changed?"

"Bal finally penetrated my thick skull last week," he scoffed. "Once I decided it was time, I knew I had to tell you first, but I didn't know how to start the conversation. I guess it's a good thing you barged in here after all."

She nudged his shoulder. "And to think I thought I had big news."

"There's something else. I think there's a reason he left it behind."

"Why?" She cocked her head.

"Just a feeling, but it's the only thing that makes sense. After we kill the owner, the weapons evaporate, but not this one."

Lucia jumped up and pointed to the door. "Come on. We must tell the Magi now."

"Hold on! I need a better plan than storming their rooms. Give me a minute—" He grabbed his backpack and shoved it inside.

A quick rap at the door startled them.

"Wait a minute!" Sergio's tone was too sharp for his liking.

Jeez... no privacy at all.

"Hey, it's me," Zach said. "Can I come in?"

Sergio tossed the backpack under his bed before he answered. "Yep."

Zach opened the door and peeked around the side. "Everything all right?"

"Just fine. What's up?"

Zach's gaze shifted between them. "Well, obviously, something is going on between the two of you. Olivia has asked for a meeting in the Weapons Room. I can tell her you—"

"I'll be there," Lucia piped up first.

"Me, too."

An awkward silence fell over the room. Zach shrugged and stepped back into the hallway. "See you there," he said, before shutting the door.

Lucia rounded on Sergio and leaned in close. "Promise me you'll tell the Magi soon."

"I will. We'll see what's up with Olivia first, okay?"

"Fine. But if you don't tell them soon, I will. There's too much at stake."

"Wow. How about a little faith, *hermana?*"

"Oh, I have faith because I'll be there with you, *hermano*. Let's go."

With a lighter step, Sergio followed her out of his room, leaving his worries about the ax temporarily behind him. He was thankful for whatever reason Olivia had for calling a meeting.

It can't possibly be as awful as the reason I need to call one.

CHAPTER
TWENTY

OLIVIA

O livia paced around the fire pit, its white flames casting an iridescent light over the Weapons Room. The curtains shimmered like a waterfall, making the large space feel intimate and peaceful. Memories overwhelmed her consciousness of the day she, Zach, and Sergio received their weapons in this very room. Their fateful journey culminated in becoming the Guardians of Orion.

Michael blowing across the blade, illuminating an angelic scroll.

Him handing over her sword crackling with blue energy.

Your burden and your blessing.

Weapons of every shape and size vibrated with various jeweled colors, as if each contained a heartbeat. She glanced at Sandalphon. Her hand itched to grab the cobalt blue hilt and pull it off the shelf. She rubbed her palm against her leg and ignored the urge to wield her sword. Something more important weighed on her mind. The next step she was certain she needed to take, but only if her fellow Guardians agreed with her risky plan to make an allegiance with someone who was not worthy of it.

Delilah.

Bile rose in her throat when the last snapshot of Delilah flashed before her. The demon snake poised to strike the already battered leg, dripping fangs bared, determined to sink into Delilah's flesh. What hit home with Olivia was the complete horror, yet resignation, paralyzing Delilah. No one can fake those pure moments of desolation. This was why she believed in her utterances of help and remorse. She had fought against and despised Delilah for the destruction she'd caused and the evil she'd chosen, but she could not condone that kind of torture.

To believe Delilah was one thing. To dare trust her was a step she could take only with the Guardians supporting her.

Are they willing to take that chance?

Am I?

Footsteps tread lightly on the staircase, winding down toward this sacred place where trust and oaths of alliance were pledged between Guardians over the eons. Would the friends she holds so dear grant her one more, or reject it? She closed her eyes and sent a quick prayer.

A tan hand parted the barrier. Lucia and Sergio stepped inside, followed by Zach. Eager grins greeted her as they glanced around the room. The barrier silently closed behind them, sealing them in a quiet cocoon.

"Hey," Sergio said, sliding his hands into his pockets. "What's up with the meeting? Someone coming out of the flames to tell us Lucifer has given up because of our awesomeness?"

Lucia strolled past him, rolling her eyes. "He's so dramatic." She hugged Olivia and whispered in her ear. "Hope everything's okay?" Lucia pulled away, but those inquisitive eyes roamed over her to check for herself. Olivia nodded, but sensed a wave of tension between the twins. It was rare for Lucia to take a jab at her brother with no humor in her voice. She glanced at Sergio, surprised to find a frown aimed at his sister. The brewing knot in her belly hardened. Her goal to get them all on the same page became more difficult if something was amiss between them.

"Visitors would surprise us both. In fact, that's why I wanted to meet here. I thought it was the best place for privacy."

"Well, you've got my attention, too." Zach cocked his head. "What's going on and how can we help?"

Olivia's shoulders relaxed, thankful for Zach's encouragement. Deep down, she was counting on him to see her plan's potential, not just the dangers. Her cheeks puffed when she released her pent-up breath.

Here we go...

"I went to the hospital to see Joe yesterday. Callie was there, too." She licked her lips as they stood still with anticipation. "He's awake and feeling better. We had a quick, but troubling conversation. Turns out they have been secretly dating. Jared found out and lost his mind. He started stalking and harassing her. That's why they turned to me, because they thought I could help."

"That's curious." Lucia said. "Callie should have called the police before you. What did she think you could—"

"Because they know—or at least suspect something different about you." Zach rubbed his neck, briefly closing his eyes. "Is that it?"

"Yes." Her reply was so soft she wasn't sure they heard it. "Joe saw a presence when the demon attacked us in the coffee shop. He also noticed a new light in us and surmised something mystical had happened. He shared his thoughts with Callie, and they decided to ask for my help."

"That's why Callie wasn't surprised by me in the backyard."

Olivia nodded and returned Zach's gaze, letting the gravity of the situation settle among the Guardians. "They're very thankful for our help and didn't pry me for more answers. They also promised to keep our secret and I believe they will. There's no reason to suspect the Fallen would go after them."

The corner of Sergio's mouth lifted. "Your friends are faithful to you, *chica*. I'm glad Joe will recover and he and Callie are together. Besides, I'd really miss his chocolate chip cookies at Cuppa Joe's."

Zach shoved his shoulder while Lucia sent him a withering look.

"What?" He held his hands up. "Jeez, you know I'm just joking— trying to lighten the mood in here."

"I count on you for that," Olivia smiled. "Joe left me speechless and a little unnerved. The outcome could have been worse if they hadn't reached out. There are other reasons I asked you here. There's more I have to tell you, something I did without you."

She felt the weight of their gazes, but it was Zach who flashed hurt in his green eyes as his jaw set in a firm line. Raising her chin, she readied herself for a fight she couldn't afford to lose.

"After I left the hospital, I called Michael to the church and told him what happened. I also shared the fear of failure eating at me. All I could think about was... I can't keep those I love safe. We train, but in hiding. We wait for Lucifer's next move instead of making our own moves. I can't *be* this anymore—letting this fear cloud what we are meant to do."

"Fight," Lucia said.

"Exactly."

"Did Michael have any suggestions?" Zach asked.

"I was the one with the idea. I told him I wanted to find Delilah."

"You did what?" Sergio's reply rose above the cacophony of protests.

"Listen. He didn't like it either, but he let me do it, anyway." Their abrupt silence was just as deafening as their denials. "I had the white feather she'd left on my pillow for me. With Michael by my side, I meditated, and I found her. She was in a cage deep inside a cavern. Poisonous snakes circled her in a moat. Lucifer has one bite her every day, causing her a slow and painful death."

"Which she deserves," Zach spoke through gritted teeth. "My sympathies can only go so far."

"I felt the same until we talked. She's half dead, but her words shook me. Before she knew I was there, she was mumbling words of regret, of her fault, and that she needs to fix what she has done. When she sensed me, she begged me to let her help us. She said she knows how to stop Lucifer. There's another force in Hell, more powerful than him, and she's the only one who knows he exists. I didn't get any more from her because someone—or something was approaching and I had to leave."

"You don't believe her, do you?" Sergio raked his hand through his hair. "She's the cause of all this! She's done nothing but lie. Manny is dead because of her." His voice cracked as he pointed to Lucia. "Tell her she's crazy."

Lucia's pale face turned to her. "I'm having a hard time understanding, believing she is anything different from who we battled. I want to trust her story, but—" she shook her head, "—but I think it's just another trap to get us killed."

Olivia accepted their perspectives, knowing the pain of Manny's death was still so fresh for her and Sergio. "I get it. The hurt and distrust. I almost lost my mom, too. I saw and heard things that can't be faked. I'm asking you to trust me on this."

"I trust you, Liv. We all do." Zach pointed to the flames burning behind her. "An oath was made here binding us together to fight the Fallen, not align ourselves with them. You tried that once, and it was a disaster." He touched his jawline. "I have the scars to prove it. I would think you'd be smarter this time."

His words cut deep, sparking a desire to strike back and defend herself. But what's the point? All they had done was unmask the fear and uncertainty she was already feeling.

Was Delilah playing me for a fool... again?

Olivia recalled the brief encounter with Delilah, shoving away the panic making her hands shake. She searched for deception in Delilah, but came up empty.

"Don't you think I've struggled with that? I've done nothing since I saw her except replay our encounter and shred myself over it. In the end, it didn't change my impression. Delilah knows how to bring down Lucifer."

"What did Michael think?" Lucia asked.

"He was appalled by her circumstances, but uncertain there could be another force more powerful than Lucifer. He said it was up to us to decide to pursue it any further. That's why I called the meeting."

"So, what do you want to do?" Zach paced.

"I want to contact her again, with all of you there, so you can decide for yourself. If any of you find a hint of deception, we walk away and let Hell keep her. If not, we find a way to work with her."

"That's a big ask," Sergio scoffed.

"I know. Please, just think about it." She didn't know what else to say. Forcing them wasn't what she wanted. She needed them with her, and right now, none of them were.

"We will." Lucia turned and grabbed Sergio's arm, leading them both to the exit. She kept her eyes on them, not wanting to return Zach's heated stare. When she finally met his gaze head-on, she threw up a wall to hide her hurt.

"You could have told me. I could have been there with you."

Olivia's anger flared. "I don't have to tell you everything first. There are things you've kept to yourself as well until you've worked them out. I knew this would be harder for Sergio and Lucia, but I thought you—"

"Would forget about my scars—my pain?" Zach threw up his hands.

"Have forgiven me." She stormed past him, needing to put some distance between them.

"Liv—wait, stop."

Olivia paused, but didn't turn around. She wouldn't let him see the tears threatening to fall.

"Meet me under the bridge tonight after practice." His voice was a mixture of urgency and hurt.

Because she wasn't sure of her answer, she left without giving one.

CHAPTER
TWENTY-ONE

ZACH

He shifted his feet, stirring the gravel under the stone bridge looming above him. The soothing sound of the river helped to calm Zach's jitters. Just like the waters would collide with the boulders downstream, so would he crash against the force of Olivia. Zach rubbed the tight cords in his neck. He remembered the hurt etched on her face in the Weapon's Room when he argued with her. Brutal honesty was his only avenue to drive home his adamant point.

Delilah is dangerous.

They all knew what she was capable of, and each was a victim of her malicious games. How could they not presume this was another ploy to get the Guardians to show themselves? She'd shown she would stop at nothing to get what she wanted.

And I have the scars to prove it.

He grazed his finger along the faint burns scarring his jawline, trailing like a spider web. He'd kept them, barely visible to others, as a reminder to never let down his guard and to trust his gut. The problem with Olivia's plan was that he couldn't discern whether his gut was churning because Olivia could be in harm's way or if it was his distrust of Delilah.

Definitely both.

He scoffed, wondering if he could ever separate his desire to protect Olivia from any of his other emotions. They jumbled together like a Gordian knot he couldn't untangle. Olivia deserved the right to fight for herself and her beliefs. She'd done a damn fine job of it. She didn't need him getting out of his lane and into hers. He respected her too much to undermine her abilities as a Guardian... and a woman he couldn't live without.

What if she doesn't come?

What if I've—

Olivia's subtle vanilla scent drifted to him in the cool night air. He tingled with anticipation, thinking of how her body melded with his when they embraced. How her soft lips answered his when they kissed. How complete he was when he was with her, making it harder each time to let her go. He sighed, thankful her footsteps were light, not heavy with anger.

"Hey," his voice cracked. She stopped; her faint shadow drawn by the moonlight. "I'm glad you're here. I wasn't sure if you'd come." He stayed under the safety of the dark arch, keeping his rioting emotions hidden for just a moment longer.

"I wasn't sure either." She tilted up her chin. "But I didn't want to go to sleep upset with you. It's too important to wait until morning."

Zach bent down and grabbed the surprise he planned for them before their rift happened. He gripped the handle and stepped out of the darkness, feeling vulnerable under the moon's glow. He picked a path to her until he stood an arm's length away, his olive branch between them.

"Whatcha got there?" Her eyebrow arched as she crossed her arms.

"It's a little basket I swiped from Mom. There are some goodies inside, and a blanket for us to spread on the ground. I wanted to surprise you with a night under the stars—like a date." He swallowed, desperate to rid the lump in his throat. "Tonight didn't start the way I'd envisioned, but maybe there's a chance it can still have a great ending."

"Yeah, my plan didn't get the reception I was hoping for, either."

"I'm sorry about my reaction. It was certainly a lot to take in. You deserved better from me. I think everyone needs a little time to think about it. We can talk about your plan some more." He raised the basket. "There's this little grassy area, tucked away by the cliffs, where we can talk—" he rushed on, "—or say nothing and look for shooting stars. I'm in for whatever you want to do. Just don't leave. Please."

When a smile tugged at her lips, a glimmer of hope bloomed inside him. "Star gazing sounds relaxing, and then we'll talk."

Fist pump!

"Great!" He took her hand and led the way before she could change her mind. They walked in silence, letting the rustles of nature and the rushing river do the talking. Strolling parallel to the cliffs, gravel gave way to a gentle rise of a grassy carpet. Boulders dotted the hilltop, guarded by patches of trees. He dared a glance over his shoulder and broke the comfortable quiet.

"We're almost there," he nodded toward the grove, quickening his step.

"I'm in no rush." She smiled back. "I like it out here at night. We spend so much time inside training, I forget how it feels out here—something primal about how it calms me."

The basket's contents clanked against each other as the hill grew steeper. The spot he'd picked came into view. His nerves tightened, trying to organize his thoughts. He needed to get his feelings... and his past... off his chest. He didn't want to mess it up. It was too important not to get it right the first time. When they reached the top, he pulled her up alongside of him. The large odd-shaped boulders were laid out in a haphazard circular fashion, yet close enough together to give a sense of privacy. The moon light was just bright enough to cast the tree's shadows swaying over the area, giving it the appearance of a slow dance.

"Here we are," he squeezed her hand.

"I haven't seen this before," she gasped.

He chuckled as he took another step. "I was hoping you'd say that."

Her low laugh floated around him. This was the Olivia he wanted to bring out tonight. He led her to the middle and set down the basket.

"How did you find this place?" Olivia twirled once before gazing back at him.

"I glimpsed the boulders when I was riding Malik." He fanned out the blanket and sat down. "I checked it out the next day on foot. The trees disguise most of it from the air. It's way more open when inside the boulders. One day, I want to build a fire and camp overnight. There have been times when I couldn't sleep. I thought about coming out here. It was enough to close my eyes and pretend... you're here snuggled next to me." Zach turned; her expression hidden in a shadow. "Will you do that now?"

She didn't say a word as she lowered herself onto the blanket, tucking her legs beside her. He reached out and took her hand. His fingers twisted the ring she always wore. "Do you ever take this off?"

"Only a few times when we were first training. I thought it would interfere with my grip, so I didn't wear it. Instead, it felt like something was missing, distracting me. I put it back on and haven't looked back." She entwined her fingers with his and tugged. "Are we here to look at the stars or my ring?"

"What if I just want to look at you?"

Olivia laughed, rolling her eyes. "There you go again with your corny comments."

"What? You asked," he said, laying back on the blanket while gently pulling her with him. "And for the record, it's not corny if it's the truth."

She didn't answer, but her shoulders relaxed as she drew closer to him. He turned his head and gazed at the blanket of stars twinkling against the night's black canvas. The earlier fears and trepidations holding him captive ebbed from him as he absorbed the outside elements where he felt so at home. Try as he might, he couldn't calm his heart rate, certain Olivia heard it pounding in his chest.

"Do you remember the night we went to Red Rock and looked for Orion?"

"How could I forget? It blazed above us, like now." Her arm stretched up; finger pointing to the same constellation branded on each of their chests. The seven dots tingled as if responding to its mirror image. "Sergio was so mad at us; thought we were wasting our time—until the bikers entered the lot."

"Along with the demons attached to them. Man, I was scared. When the demons swirled around my truck, making it shake, and then they came after us." Zach exhaled. "I thought we were goners."

"Until Michael, Zemira, and Eliphaz came streaking down like shooting stars and saved us. I knew then that the demon seeing us at Joe's wasn't a fluke. We were different... meant to do something bigger than ourselves. I never fathomed how much our lives would change." Her words were but a whisper, but reverberated through to Zach's core.

He rolled onto his side and waited for her to turn to him. His gaze darted to her lips, parted slightly as if words were left frozen on them. Leaning down, he kissed her with a gentleness that unbound any remaining knots of doubt. Their kiss deepened; her soft moan was almost his undoing. A flash of heat burst within him, making his skin burn hot... his need for her threatening to steal away any reason to not ask Olivia for more. He pulled away before he did something he'd regret. When he opened his eyes, he found hers sparking with a passion equal to his. He wanted to sink his hands into her hair and dive back into the kiss, but he rested his forehead on hers and tried to unscramble his brain while easing the ache within him.

"Zach?" her breath fanned his face, arms winding around his back.

"I need to tell you some things that I've wanted to share with you for so long. It's been locked inside of me and I've never shared it with anyone. I only want to tell you. You're the most important person in my life. The one who matters most. I want nothing hidden between us, even if shame or disappointment tries to silence our voices."

A seriousness washed over her. "Whatever it is, we can handle it together. It's safe with me."

He mouthed *safe* like it unlocked something within him. "Some days, these feelings are all I think about. One lays heavy on my heart while the other wants to set my heart free. Trying to find the perfect time and place became impossible with things ramping up with Lucifer—"

"There's never a perfect time... just tell me." She stroked her hands up his back, leaving a trail of heat.

He sat up and brought her with him, needing to be face to face with her to gauge her reaction. "The first one is about Cody. There's more about what happened when he died." The rest of his words dried up in his throat.

Olivia straightened; her face bright with encouragement. "I know it's difficult..."

He swallowed and braced himself for whatever reaction came his way. "Everything I told you, guys, was true. Cody and I went down the river and got caught up in the rapids, but he didn't fall out and hit his head... at least not then. When the canoe flipped, we fell out together. We came to the surface close enough where I could just about touch him. There was so much turbulence we were both panicking, trying to reach for anything and for each other. Cody was yelling about his leg and kept getting pulled under. I was frantic, gulping in water, but I finally grabbed his arm and he quickly latched onto me. He came back up sputtering, crying for help. I told him I had him and I wouldn't let him go. He went under again, but this time he brought me with him. I kicked and got us to the surface, but he was really struggling to stay afloat and hang on. I kept thinking we have to get through it, but that's when Cody's body struck a boulder. In my mind, I hear him gasp and look at me for the last time, eyes glossed over with pain. I called out to hang on, don't give up. I don't know if I was yelling *No* or if it was the screaming inside my head.

We went under again. I tried with all my might to hold on to him, but he was too heavy, and the rapids were ripping us apart. I had to let him go, or I was going to drown, too. So... I let him go. As soon as I did, I tried to get him back, but he was gone. I told him I wouldn't let go, yet I did. The currents swallowed him up. That's the picture burning in my memory. I let him go, and he died. I never should have. My best friend died because I couldn't keep my promise." He didn't realize he was crying until the salty tears fell over his lips. "He's dead because of me." A sob escaped, releasing the flood gate of his buried guilt.

"Oh, Zach," Olivia wrapped her arms around him, squeezing him tight. "You did everything you could. You dying too, wouldn't have saved him. What you did was what you had to do. Save yourself and live. You have to forgive yourself and stop carrying the weight of this burden."

He pulled away and looked at her, trying to believe what she said was possible. "I've tried so many times, but when I replay it, his death presses in on me. It changed me forever and I don't know how to stop it."

She lifted her hands and cupped his damp cheeks. "His death was tragic, but not your fault. Stop searching the past. It changes nothing. I know. I did it with my dad, and it just kept me angry. Being a Guardian helped me to move on and shed that old skin. You can, too. What we do together—have together, that is our present and our future. I think Cody would be very proud of you and would not want you to live a life in the shadow of his death."

An old ache clutching his heart loosened. He wanted this war inside of him to stop, to move on from the horror of Cody's loss. It felt almost selfish to do it.

Would Cody be proud of me?

Dare I even believe it?

I have to let him go... again.

He brought his hands up and covered hers. "Thank you, Liv. It feels good to tell you and see that you're not disappointed in me. For you to say we have a future together is all I've ever wanted to hear."

She grinned and released his face. "I meant the Guardianship—" Olivia giggled and squirmed as his arms encircled her, tickling as they went around her.

"I want you to know something. If I have you in my grasp, I won't let go. I promise you that." Zach said.

"There was never a doubt in my mind."

"There's something else I want to tell you."

After all, he'd just unloaded on her, he was amazed she waited patiently for more.

He brushed his lips across her forehead. "Your mind dazzles me like no other."

Her eyelids fluttered closed beneath a chaste kiss he placed to each. "You see the world with a clarity like no other."

He grazed a kiss across her lips. "You speak with a conviction and truth like no other."

He moved down her chest. Her breathless gasp was music to his ears. He eased aside her scooped neck t-shirt and kissed the warm skin over her heart. His lips lingered, absorbing her pounding heart beneath them. "And have a courageous heart like no other." Looking up, her eyes were large and luminous as their eyes locked together.

"I love you, Liv," his voice cracked as he shifted and hovered over her lips again. "You are my future... my life, for however long it lasts."

Deafening silence fell between them.

His world froze, narrowing into a moment so fragile, he might shatter waiting for her reply.

As the seconds stretched, his body went numb.

Does she not feel the same?

CHAPTER
TWENTY-TWO

OLIVIA

"I love you, Liv."

Time was swallowed in a vacuum of complete stillness.

Her mind stuck on those words like a rock lodged between moving gears.

Only her heart, skipping to its new frantic beat, made it clear time never stopped.

"I love you, Liv."

This simple phrase, his gift to her, terrified Olivia more than the evil she battled.

Evil she understood with its clear black and white boundaries.

Love was confusing to her, an abyss of gray with edges shifting at will.

"I love you, Liv."

Love was a lethal weapon one could wield against another in anger, hurt, or revenge.

They expected love to be returned fully to the giver, without strings, guarantees, or demands.

Love was putting another before self, giving up control.

"I love you, Liv."

And yet Zach, who struck her with an instant attraction, drew her to find the source until their eyes met across a crowded school hallway. They shared a destiny, but was it to be partners in love as well? He was giving her all of himself, jumping off the cliff into an unknown world of loving her.

This was true courage.

Zach stared at her with a hope and vulnerability she could crush in an instant.

As the sounds of leaves rustling in the breeze came to life, so did another realization. The bubbling panic to run away or tell him he couldn't possibly know what love was never bloomed.

Instead, a warmth of pure joy and peace spread throughout her body.

Her trembling fingertip brushed over his lips as a single tear slipped from the corner of her eye. "I never thought I'd want to give my heart to another... that I could trust someone enough to understand how fragile it really is. But I was wrong. You unlocked my heart, so my heart I give to you." Her hands caressed his face. "I love you, Zach," she whispered.

A sob of joy burst from his lips, closing the precious gap between them. The kiss fanned a fire in her belly that had been on a slow burn for too long. Her fingers entwined in his hair, pressing them into a deeper kiss full of love and need, wishing its searing heat would seal them as one. Now that she had given her love to him, was she ready for the physical surrender, as well?

The kiss abruptly stopped, the cool air dousing her heated lips. Her eyes flew open at the swiftness with which he sat up, bringing her dizzying body up with him. "What—"

A roar split the air, ripping apart their lover's cocoon. They jumped to their feet as another one rose louder, like a challenge to the wild. Zach turned to Olivia. "That's not Lucia."

"No. And it doesn't sound happy." Chills ran down her spine as she called up her portal. "Come on. We better go. It sounds like it's in the field behind the church."

He nodded, stealing a quick kiss before he took her hand. The crackling blue portal opened, and Zach stepped through first. Pausing for a moment, she glanced over her shoulder. The unopened wicker basket and rumpled blanket called for her return to the magical moment that had slipped away from them. Olivia took a snapshot in her mind's eye of the place where they'd professed their love... where she'd done something she thought impossible for her.

I gave my trust and love completely to another soul.

To Zach.

The portal's current zipped over skin as she stepped through, raising the fine hairs along her arm. It snapped closed behind her. The church's gray walls were a dark mass to her left as the grassy field lay open to the rise leading to the forest rising in the distance. A prowling lion stopped and turned his deadly stare in their direction.

"What's the beast doing?" Zach whispered.

"I don't know, but it's the lion from the forest. The one Lucia and I saw—"

Another roar tore from the lion's cavernous mouth. Sharp white fangs glistened in the moonlight. The curves of the lion's body began to blur. What once was fur became skin. What once was a lion became a man. He mouthed something as his glare shifted to the back door. Shadows shifted around his legs, turning into baggy pants. His long strides ate up the ground between him and the door.

"Caspar!" He bellowed with clenched fists. "Come—"

The church's backdoor flew open, spilling golden light over him. Long, thick waves of brown hair brushed past his shoulders. His broad chest puffed out, his legs braced as if ready to pounce or withstand an attack. Caspar emerged first and stepped in front of the stranger. Balthazar and Melchior came out next, but stayed by the door. Melchior caught Olivia's attention and gave her a quick shake of his head.

Zach leaned in close. "What the hell is going on?" he murmured.

"I don't know, but... if he's a shifter, could he be a..."

"Guardian?" Zach finished her sentence with the same amount of disbelief.

Olivia's eyes widen when Caspar placed his hand on the

stranger's shoulder. He didn't flinch, but he still looked ready to either fight or fly. "Peace be with you, Amal. It's been too long since you've graced our door step. What brings you to—"

"Lucia, wait!" Sergio's plea echoed from within, but to no avail. Lucia bounded out of the door at full speed, darting past Balthazar and Melchior. She ran up next to Caspar, casting a shadow next to Amal. He stepped back, Caspar's arm dropped from his shoulder.

"I knew it! It is you." she pointed her finger at Amal's face cut with hard lines. "I haven't seen you since the day you drew me deep into the forest, only to disappear. And now you're back late at night, yelling for Caspar? I don't understand."

When Sergio burst through the door, Olivia wouldn't wait on the sidelines any longer. "This could go south if Sergio loses his temper. Let's go." They jogged over and stood by the Magi.

Sergio barged between Amal and Lucia. He jerked his thumb at Amal while he faced his sister. "Is this who you saw... the lion-man... who put you in danger?"

"She was never in any danger from me." Amal's low voice rumbled.

Sergio wheeled around and leaned into his face. "Really? Your little cat-and -mouse game of leading her into the forest may not have been dangerous for you, but it was for Lucia. She almost lost herself to the shift. If Sam hadn't been there—"

"That's enough." Caspar's command sliced between them and moved them a part. "We'll discuss what happened later, but right now, Amal came here looking for me. Everyone else go back inside so we can talk."

Amal shook his head. "They are welcome to stay. Their presence is why I'm here." His shrewd green eyes assessed them.

Caspar nodded his head, even as uncertainty flickered across his face. "If that is your wish."

An eerie silence fell over the group. Amal's gaze drifted back to Lucia. His shoulders sagged, but remained silent.

"What is it?" Lucia touched his forearm.

"I'm sorry I put you in danger. It was reckless of me. My life here —" he waved his arm at the forest behind him, "—is a lonely one... by choice. I rarely come out of my sanctuary, especially when the Magi bring new Guardians to train. But something tugged at me, pushing me to come out of hiding. When I saw you shift into a tiger, I was stunned. I thought maybe I had finally lost my mind and created a mirage. Each day, I crept closer until I couldn't stand it anymore. I had to find out if you were real."

"When I was with Olivia and Aureus." Lucia murmured.

He nodded. "Your touch frightened me, but awakened a part of me I left buried for too long. The human part... and the Guardian part."

Zach turned to Olivia. "Whoa," he mouthed.

"Why hide here? Why didn't you go back to your life?" Olivia asked, stepping forward.

Amal's mouth parted, but no answer came, only a far-off look where something played before him.

"I know." Lucia's gentle tone beckoned Amal to face her. When he did, his hard edges softened. "Because you became lost to the shift and couldn't go home."

"Yes," He swallowed hard. "I could not return."

"So why now? If it's because of my sister—"

"Stop speaking for her. My respect for her is the reason I'm here." Amal's eyes narrowed. "And I want to help her... all of you."

"We are thankful you've come back. We need all the help we can get." Balthazar came up from behind, his words silencing Sergio.

Questions swirled inside of Olivia, but each one pulled on a different thread attached to more questions. Amal's presence unnerved her, his primal energy palatable under his quiet demeanor. "When were you a guardian?" Olivia blurted out.

"Long before your time, but that's not important. This group of Guardians is different. There are always three, but there are four of you." He cocked his head. "And you all live here. That's new, too. I can only think of one reason this would happen. Lucifer knows about the Guardians, which puts them in peril."

"And the Mar of Sin. An Angel took the fall to tell Lucifer her knowledge of the Guardians." Bal said.

Amal flinched like he'd been hit. "Why would an angel do such a horrible thing?"

"Revenge against my dad, who was also a Guardian." Nausea turned her stomach from the lingering guilt of her dad's actions. "Lucifer and the Fallen are desperate to find us so he can open the Mar of Sin to finish what he started."

The edges of Amal's body blurred. He stumbled backward out of the door light's halo. "I've spent too long in the land of unliving. The Fallen cannot win—" The rest of his body faded as he completed the shift. The lion raced for the forest, his form melting into the darkness.

"Amal, wait!" Lucia cried out.

When he didn't stop, anger darkened Lucia's features. She pushed past her brother and stormed back to the church. Sergio followed in her wake.

Olivia found the spot where the lion had disappeared into the forest. Amal had complicated motives and a deeper story that Olivia needed to understand before she felt comfortable working with him. From Lucia's reaction, she also wasn't sure if Amal would be a good or bad influence on Lucia.

"Meeting in the Weapon's Room. Now." Balthazar's clipped tone left little doubt the *whole* situation displeased him.

And I haven't even dropped my bombshell about Delilah.

But Zach, I'll keep to myself, for now.

CHAPTER
TWENTY-THREE

OLIVIA

White flames snapped behind Balthazar, matching the anger crackling in his gold eyes as he scanned the room. When his glare paused on Olivia, she paled as his gaze lingered. They narrowed before he continued to Sergio, Zach and Lucia with the same intensity. Melchior and Caspar stood behind him like warrior statues. The Magi's displeasure with them was blatant, and she couldn't blame them. Amal's arrival and Lucia's run-ins blindsided them. Olivia braced herself because what she had to share would surely spark another firestorm.

"I think I speak for Melchior and Caspar when I say it surprised us when Amal came out of hiding and interacted with you." His large hands rested on his hips. "It seems Lucia's arrival has awakened him from his slumber. It was long overdue. We should have been told of this development. Amal is very... complicated."

Lucia stepped forward. "I should have told you, and I'm sorry. I guess I got caught up in him being a shifter, and wanted to learn more about him—about what makes us so different." She glanced at her feet. "It's lonely—confusing being half human, half tiger." Lucia's soft-spoken words surprised Olivia. Being a shifter seemed so incredible to her, she didn't consider that it would also make her friend feel isolated.

Balthazar's visible anger slipped from his face. Two long strides closed the gap between them. His hands enveloped her when he took them in his. "My child, your blessing weighs heavy on you, but burdens are meant to be shared. Until Amal sheds his past, he may not be able to help as you desire."

"Who is he, and why is he here?" Lucia pleaded. "I need to know."

He let go of her hands and turned to the other Magi. Bal patted Caspar's shoulder as they passed by each other, his spry footfall heavier. "He is from the ancient time... the time when the Watchers twisted humans into believing they were gods."

Lucia gasped; her hand slammed against her chest. "But he looks so young."

"Time stopped for Amal in both body and spirit. He wasn't much older than you when he married. A babe was born not long before the Watchers' tyranny ended. The city was in chaos and battle raged at the pretender's palace. Amal had to find his sister and get her to safety. He found her shivering, wading through water outside the palace walls. He portaled her to safety, telling her to tell the man he's sending her to, that Amal asks that he give her a safe voyage as a favor to him."

Olivia's ears buzzed as the only possible name scenario bubbled to the surface. "Noah. She was on the ark."

"Yes," Caspar's green eyes filled with sadness. "But when Amal portaled home, he found his wife dead, struck by a stray arrow, and his baby crying inside his basket. Amal was enraged, devastated by the loss of his young wife. Raphael felt his pain and brought him and the baby here. Lost and alone, the shift became a place of comfort from the pain. When his grief grew unbearable, the lion became the place he wanted to be. So, he stayed here to roam in the forest."

"What happened to the baby?" Sergio asked as he put his arm around Lucia's shoulder and pulled her next to him.

"We brought the families here as the flood raged. His brother raised the son until it was his time to become a Guardian."

"Okay, I'm lost." Zach scrubbed his hand over his face. "Amal, who is like my infinity grandpa, which, by the way, blows my mind—is still a shifter. If his orb is gone, how can he shift?"

The Magi exchanged glances, but Olivia had seen this communication before, which means something big was about to drop.

"An orb still resides within Amal. A new orb was created for his son."

Boom.

"Why?" Lucia pushed away from Sergio and stepped in front of Caspar. "Why leave him with the orb?"

"You have to understand, his mind and body were not as one. We feared what would happen with the orb's removal. Would he remain a man or stay locked within the lion... or become something in between? We couldn't take that risk. That is why we let him roam free, suspended in this world until he regains control of his shift or the time of the Guardians ends. Amal is aware of this, and until tonight, I wasn't sure he cared anymore."

Double boom.

"I'll—we'll help him," Lucia said.

"We're counting on that." Caspar's musical lilt eased Olivia's nerves. She had to tell them about Delilah, but the timing felt wrong. Tomorrow—

Zach cleared his throat and nudged her with his elbow. "Olivia needs to tell you something she's already shared with us." Olivia jerked her head toward Zach, widening her eyes as she stared at him. "It can't wait."

Her mouth turned dry when she found Melchior staring at her. "Well..." he cocked his eyebrow.

There was no easy way to say it. She exhaled, puffing out her cheeks.

"It's about Delilah. I meditated and found her."

Triple boom.

"You did what?" Melchior bellowed. "Why would you take such a risk?"

A flush crept up her neck from the intensity radiating off the Magi. "I needed answers that only she could provide. I asked Michael first, and he was with me—"

"Probably should have said that first," Bal muttered, stroking his beard.

"Let me back up. Delilah has been the center of everything since the beginning. I think she's the key to discovering Lucifer's next step. She said there is a more powerful force in Hell, stronger than Lucifer. Someone was coming, so I had to leave before she could tell me who or what the unknown force was. I have to go back and find out what she knows. But I want all of us together when it happens so you can see and hear for yourself and decide if she is lying or telling the truth."

"And what do your fellow guardians think about this?" Melchior's stare never wavered from her. "Zach?"

"That we have to take the chance. Olivia thinks Delilah is telling the truth. That works for me."

"Sergio... Lucia—you feel the same as Zach?"

Olivia lifted her chin, but inside she was a mess, wondering what Sergio and Lucia would say.

"Before the lion, I mean uh—Amal, showed up," Sergio sputtered. "We were waiting for Olivia to tell her we were on board. We agree that it's worth the risk to see Delilah and find out more about this other force."

Melchior's lips pressed into a thin line, but not before something Olivia couldn't quite grasp flickered in his eyes.

"Tomorrow. After school. My room. Let's hope she's not weaving another trap." Bal was not happy, but at least they could see her again.

"She's in a—"

"Stop." Melchior raised his hand. "I will see her through my eyes, not yours." Tension emanated with every step he took away from Olivia. His anger she accepted, but his disappointment cut deep. Caspar and Bal followed him, each giving a civil nod as they left.

"You've certainly stirred up the hornet's nest," Zach whispered in her ear. "They'll get over it, just like we did."

He kissed her temple. His gentle lips stirred memories of the deeper kisses they shared while the stars danced in the sky above them. Amal's arrival and Melchior's sharp disapproval of her actions overtook her life-changing moment. But here he stood, tall and steady. She leaned into Zach and gazed up at the fine line of scars mapping his jawline. Her prior error in judgment about Delilah resulted in Zach's scars. Could she be wrong about this, too?

"I guess we'll find out tomorrow. Melchior rarely—"

"I'm going! Stop trying to stop me and don't you dare follow me." Olivia's head swung around in time to catch Lucia storming out of the Weapons Room.

"She never listens to me." He threw his hands up and faced Olivia and Zach. "She's off to chase down, Amal. She's crazy, thinking she'll get more answers from him."

Olivia sent Lucia a mental fist pump. "Lucia needs to do this... by herself."

Sergio dashed away, muttering a stream of Spanish as he headed toward the stairs to his room.

"Come on, we should call it a night, too. We've got a big day tomorrow." Zach nudged her.

Olivia nodded as she stared off into the flames. Delilah's prison cell floated in her mind. Her stomach rolled, wondering what horrors they might find tomorrow. She turned away and followed Zach. Between what happened between her and Zach tonight and Delilah's situation, she didn't think she'd get much sleep.

CHAPTER
TWENTY-FOUR

DELILAH

N umb.
Cold.

Desolate.

Delilah felt dead. At times, she was certain the poison had finally taken her. But her heart maintained a slow beat, like each was a clock's tick counting down to the end of her life.

Her wasted life.

She curled in on herself; her legs like stone with the purple poison creeping up her body. Laying on her side, she stared into the space, envisioning the cavern's entrance and the freedom beyond it.

The darkness shifted as if a gust of wind disturbed the heavy air. She blinked, hoping to clear away another brewing hallucination to taunt her guilty conscience. Her eyes widened as a faint streak of green emerged, but then disappeared. Her senses weren't fooled. Someone entered the cavern. Regardless of who it might be, they all wanted her dead. She shut her eyes, not wanting to know who returned. Was it the traitor coming to kill her or Lucifer with demands for more answers? Could it be Asura back to mock her or follow through with her promise to kill her for her lover's revenge?

Death is a welcome gift.

She chided herself because she couldn't die yet. There was more to share with Olivia.

I have to stay alive, if only until she returns...

Her eyes snapped open. The visitor's smell was one she recognized and thought she'd never see again.

Zar...

Could it be him? She followed Zar's green glow along the cave's walls, his platinum hair like a floating spotlight. Desperate to be sure, she unfolded herself and crawled toward the bars, not caring how close she came to the snakes below.

"Zar," she licked her cracked lips. "Is that you?"

Are you here to free me or kill me?

The flap of his green streaked wings was like a whip's crack. He flew across the moat's purple glow, burning brighter by the snake's agitation. She gripped the bars and watched him land on the ledge in front of her. Leather bound legs stood so close; her hand itched to touch to see if they were real.

"Delilah," His voice rained down on her. She couldn't answer him, instead her eyes filled with tears she thought she could no longer produce. He crouched down, but she stared at his blurred boots.

"Look at me."

Slowly, her eyes traveled until they found his face hardened by anger. She sensed the pity stirring within him, filling her with shame.

"What has he done to you?" The disgust in his voice drew her deeper into herself. Whatever shred of dignity she had left was lost.

"Nothing I didn't deserve. But you know that since he sent you here. Have you come to kill me or gloat at my demise?"

"I knew nothing of this! I asked to see you." He jumped up and grabbed the cage's door. He shook it, rattling the unyielding metal. Angry hisses spit at him from the pit. He sneered down at the slithering occupants. "I have to get you out of here." He shook the door again, unyielding to his powers. He shoved away when they remained closed.

"Stop." She pulled herself up with what strength she had left.

Sagging against the metal for support, she leaned her cheek on the bar. "Don't bother. Why did you want to see me?"

He turned to her, body rigid. "Lucifer summoned me. He wants me to hunt the guardians again. He thinks I'm the one to find them. I asked to see you because I had to find out for myself what had become of you. I escaped to the mountains after I... I—"

"Whipped me? Shamed me as Lucifer displayed me above the Fallen for their pleasure?" He remained silent, but she knew his eyeless orbs were somehow assessing her. "I don't blame you." A humorless chuckle felt harsh in her ears. "You did what you did to survive."

"I took my disgrace out on you."

"I drove you to that point with my recklessness. You're right to hate me."

He shifted his feet. "I've tried so hard to hate you, but it never lasts. Our time in Heaven collides with our time here... memories sparring with one another."

"You... and I were wrong to take the Fall," Delilah whispered. "Yes, humans are broken, but so are we. Our only perfection was in Heaven."

"You're wrong—"

"Am I? Do you find pleasure manipulating humans to sin, or did your soul slowly melt away, leaving a black hole filled with hatred?"

"I lost my soul in the Mar of Sin and I have no problem with what I did to humans. You are the one showing regret not me. Don't throw me into your pool of self-pity."

Delilah's shoulders slumped, wishing Zar would abandon his anger and listen to her pleas. Unlike Zar, her time as a Fallen was short, yet illuminating. Evil lived in every fiber of a Fallen's being, in every thought they possessed, soaked through by their vile existence in the Realm. Her words may be futile, but she had to try, for herself and for him.

"I wish you had stayed with me in Heaven. Maybe things would have been different. I wouldn't have fallen for Conner—"

"And you could have come with me—" he took a step forward, "—and fought together... been together. But we both made our choices."

She shook her head. "And it all leads right back here. The past is done, but *we* can change the future. Our actions were selfish, don't you see? We hurt people, killed angels, and it got us nowhere. We'll never be in Heaven again, but at least we won't be like this: broken, hollow, alone. Lucifer is drunk on power. He may win a few battles, but he'll never win the war. I want to make sure of it." Her tirade left her breathless from her desperate passion to make him understand.

"What do you mean? You're in no position to stop Lucifer?" He scoffed.

"We can still right the wrongs we've committed—"

"Don't say we! You broke the silence! You gave Lucifer the knowledge. You—"

Delilah slid down and crumpled to the ground. The weight of her actions was too heavy, the cost of her revenge too high. "And I regret it all. If I could go back in time, I would have disappeared when I saw you that day outside the hospital. But I couldn't resist the pull to you... the temptation to quench a reckless need for freedom. To destroy everything, I once held dear because I couldn't be—" she closed her eyes as the shameful reality washed over her, "—human."

"You're more of a prisoner now than you ever were." Zar's harsh words were meant to hurt her. She could tell by the way his hands flexed into fists at his side.

She gazed up at him, remembering the striking neon green eyes that could see through her. Now scarred hollow sockets were aimed at her as if they could still see. "You should do well to remember those words."

His fist slammed against the cage. He paced across the ledge, growling in his displeasure. She lay motionless as she watched him stomp back and forth through the filthy strands of hair dangling down her face.

"The traitor. Why did you make an alliance with Sonneillon behind my back?"

Delilah tensed, not wanting to talk about the traitor. "It doesn't matter anymore why I met up with Sonneillon. He's dead because he got caught and got what he deserved... just like me."

Zar's face turned to stone. "Liar. Sonneillon was never the traitor. He's dead because Lucifer believed your trail of lies."

How does Zar know?

"So, Asura got to you—"

"I found his lair... his torture chamber deep in a mountain near here, littered with tattered remained of Lessors still chained to the stone walls. Know how I found it?"

Her blood pumped thick in her ears, wishing it was loud enough to drown out Zar.

"A wail awakened me, coming from deep inside the mountain. I went to flee, but a scent assailed me. One I've searched for since I first detected it subtly on you." She bit down on her tongue, forcing herself to not react to his findings. "Because I lost my eyes, my other senses are razor sharp. I could never figure out who it was. Never smelled it on anyone but you. I knew you had another alliance, but kept it to myself. When Sonneillon was killed and you were taken, I assumed it was him and the scent about you was from your mating. Lucifer didn't kill the real deceiver, did he? But you know that already." He cackled as he cocked his head. "He was who you were working with. I was still a pawn in your flawed game of revenge."

Delilah realized in a crushing fit of reality; she'd lost Zar. He would never help her because he couldn't trust her anymore. She slowly sat up, gravel shards biting into her hands. "Go. Believe what you will about me."

She waited for his retreat, but he stood ramrod straight, white-knuckled hand gripping the hilt of his sword. Was he going to kill her, after all?

"Why hasn't the traitor come and killed you?" He muttered, as if talking to himself. "You're a dangerous liability to him."

"Because the dead can't kill."

"Liar!" His condemnation ricocheted off the cracked walls. "You're incapable of speaking the truth."

"And you are incapable of seeing that Lucifer will be the death of you."

"He said the same about you to me." Zar scoffed and turned towards the cavern's entrance. "I won't help absolve you of your sins. That's pathetic and reeks of humanity. I have all I need to track down the traitor. I came here because I thought you would finally be honest with me. It sickens me I even entertained us—" His chest heaved, "—but that's dead now, along with you, soon."

"It's never too late to change the course, Zar. Humanity is worth more than our pride—our envy."

"Speak for yourself. My pride bled into the pit by the mutant's lash."

He jumped off the ledge and flew away with a streak of green. She released the dry sob she had held back while he stripped himself of her. She curled up into a fetal position, staring at Zar's fading light.

"Goodbye, Zar," she whispered. "I hope one day you will understand why I kept the truth from you."

Plummeted into a ghastly darkness, the purple glow throbbing with a life of its own. She waited.

Waited for the next stab of pain...

Waited for a one of her maniacal captors to return...

Waited for death's oblivion.

Waited for Olivia. The one she'd hurt the most was the only one willing to help her.

CHAPTER
TWENTY-FIVE

ZAR

I'm back...

Zar lounged in the driver's seat of a vacant car across the street from the high school the Guardians attended. When Lucifer sent him back to find the Guardians, he didn't have too many choices for where to find them. Olivia's house was out because he was sure goon angels were watching for him since he attacked her parents. The coffee shop was small, leaving him vulnerable to being noticed. He didn't know where the other Guardians lived, so he went to the high school. It was easier to hide here from any watchful eye. The high school parking lot was quiet. Waves of heat drifted off the asphalt.

His mind wandered back to Delilah, away from the school, blurring into the dank cavern, oozing with fear and evil. When he'd first sensed Delilah curled up on the dirt floor, her appearance shocked him. The lattice network of purple, seeping up her legs like ribbons of dye marked by multiple pairs of red welts. She dragged herself to the bars, her stub arm useless yet moving as if it could mirror its mate. The static like map of the cage painted a picture of torture and despair. He recognized that in himself. Her face glowed white against the ebony backdrop except for the jagged scar his whip slashed across her face. He flew over the moat and found the epicenter of the evil surrounding her. He sneered down at the agitated occupants, comprehending they were responsible for the markings on her legs.

Delilah was as disfigured as him, but he wasn't a prisoner anymore. Their argument had clarified this to him in a stunning fashion.

He was misunderstood, and that worked just fine for him and his purposes. The self-imposed exile to the fringes of the Realm was how he preferred to live. A loner, free to do as he pleased. Slipping in and out of the background, and answering to no one except Lucifer, was how it should have always been. Zar changed his behavior because he got sucked into Delilah's promises. His world quickly became full of strife and self-doubt. When he flew away from her, he was determined to shed himself of her and the shackles of an unattainable dream. With each angry thrust of his wings, he dismissed the nagging sensation that wondered if she was right. But looking back was futile, as was holding onto the notion they would share the same beliefs or a life together. The Fall doomed any chance of success when battle lines found them on opposite sides. He scoffed as he thought about trying to right their wrongs.

Whatever. I'm not her sucker anymore.

Turning his back on her was like walking away from her grave. She was dead to him. He felt dead too and welcomed back the hollow void inside that Delilah had filled. It was a relief knowing he was done with her.

Lucifer left him with one task. Find the Guardians' weak spot. Give the information to Lucifer and be done with it.

Until Lucifer storms Heaven.

The leather seats creaked as he shifted in the seat. His heart beat faster, excited about stalking humans again. He wished there was time to cultivate a weak soul for his purposes, but he didn't have the time to satisfy his needs. The doors flew open, kids funneled out and scattered to either their cars or a long line of vehicles wrapped around the parking lot. As the parking lot thinned, his frustration grew. The

Guardians were not showing themselves. Pounding his hand on the steering wheel, he wondered if he missed them. Were they still going to school or were there too many kids for his senses to map?

Wait a minute—

Zar jolted up. His grip turned white-knuckled as an aura he recognized emerged through the double doors.

Sergio...

The one who he'd brought humiliation upon Zar when he and Gabriel escaped from hell after he'd brought Sergio there as a prisoner. His upper lip curled, thinking of how he'd love to get his hands on both of them and right that wrong. Visions of revenge washed away as Sergio held the school door open. He glimpsed a girl in a wheelchair before a van blocked his view. He shook his head and wondered if his senses had made a mistake. Did she also have the same aura as Sergio, or had the glow spilled over to her? Tapping his fingers against the dashboard, he leaned forward, impatient for another look. When the van drove away, they were gone. Scanning the area around the school, it surprised him when he found no Angels lurking. The van stopped at the lot's exit before turning onto the street, giving him one last chance to map the occupants more closely if he dared. He didn't want to risk being discovered. Following the van was more important.

I've got you now.

Zar surrounded himself in his bubble, throwing the outside world into a blurry haze. He stepped out of the car and took flight, glancing over his shoulder to make sure he wasn't followed. As the van maneuvered inside a neighborhood, a tendril of doubt tickled his neck hairs. It felt too easy to follow them. Where were the goons? Were they in a bubble, too? Zar stopped and hovered behind a tree at the street's entrance. The van pulled into a driveway and parked inside the garage of a one-story house. His senses on high alert, he scanned the neighboring houses to find one where no one was home. A small grin thinned his lips when he found the two-story house bordering their backyard.

That will do nicely...

He crouched down to take flight, but froze when an Angel's glow emerged at the front of their house. The Angel stood still on the doorstep and scanned the area. Zar held his breath, ready to pull up his portal if the Angel zeroed in on him. He didn't move a muscle, even though the bubble should deflect the Angel's senses. The Angel paused and rested its hand on the sword's hilt. The front opened, startling both of them. Zar couldn't see who stood in the doorway, but the distraction was enough. Zar glided away from the tree and made a sweeping arch towards the vacant house. His heart pounded, worried more would arrive. He dove for the front porch and quickly portaled through the front door. Only the air conditioner's hum greeted him in the foyer. Certain he was alone, he raced for the stairs, taking them two at a time. There were three doors on the side of the house facing Sergio's back yard. He glanced into the first room, heavy with the odor he recognized as a teen-aged boy. Being inside this room held no appeal. The next room was a bathroom with a narrow window above the shower. Feeling his frustration rising, he tossed open the last door. A large bed dominated one wall, but the wall facing him had a large window.

Perfect.

He walked slowly as he appraised the view mapping out the back of Sergio's house. A few palm trees dotted the back fence, blocking some windows. Someone moved in front of the second to last window. Still inside his bubble, he stepped as close as he dared. Movement flashed again, sharpening his focus on the shape pacing behind the blinds.

Come on, show yourself to me.

As if hearing his command, the figure stopped and stepped into the window's light. Zar gasped as the girl's face unfolded in his mind. The girl from school, but not in a wheelchair. She stood and gazed at the backyard, an aura pulsing around her. Was this some trick? The night he had attempted to grab a Guardian, there were only three of them. In the desert, three Guardians arrived to battle. Who was she and where has she been hiding?

Sergio entered her room. His darker aura churned around him. She turned away and faced him. She shook her head and pointed to the door. Oh, how he wished he could get closer to hear their angry words. He realized how strikingly similar they were in coloring and facial features.

Brother and sister...

Of course, but—

Sergio stormed from the room, slamming the door behind him. He sensed movement in her room again, but she had moved away from the window. A pulse of bright light burst in the backyard's corner, stealing his attention. He sneered at the arrival of two more Angels, too close to him for his liking. A growl emerged as the desire to kill them tried to override his reasoning to leave. He was outnumbered and more were likely roaming that he couldn't detect. He looked back, hoping for the sister—

A flash of white stalked past the window. Rooted to his spot, he waited for it to pass by again. And when it did, he stumbled back until his legs collided with the bed. He raised his portal as the image tattooed in his mind.

The golden carnal eyes of a white tiger staring up at his window.

He jumped into the portal and slammed it shut behind him, fearing the imminent arrival of a goon angel... or the tiger. But Zar stood alone on the bridge near Lucifer's tower. The only thing that followed him through the portal was the feeling of dread. He reached up and rubbed the area of his shoulder where the tiger had nearly bitten off a chunk in their previous battle. Fear licked down his spine at the memory of the wet fangs seeking more flesh. A fuzzier memory turned crystal clear. Sergio's devastation when Zar stabbed the tiger. Words of revenge left Sergio blinded to his own safety. All this time, Zar had assumed it was a magical beast trained to work with the Guardians. The truth revealed itself through the window.

The beast and the sister were one.

He ran his hands through his hair, taming the desire to snarl at the question burning in his mind.

If I found this new Guardian, are there more?

Are they in hiding—waiting until the war begins?

He flew toward the massive doors, yawning open on the Throne Room's roof, dreading his next meeting.

CHAPTER
TWENTY-SIX

LUCIFER

"I won't disappoint you, Master." Mammon's frosty blue lips paled in a sly grin. "The Realm of Greed will lead you to glory." She took flight and left through the open roof doors. Her role in his next phase was critical. The time to prove herself had come. She was perfection, and he was certain he'd chosen wisely.

Or my plan is doomed before it even begins.

Asura stormed across the inky pool's walkway like a woman who took out her wrath on anyone who dared get in her way. Lucifer chuckled, imagining the wake of imbeciles she'd struck down while she searched for the true cause of her irritation.

Delilah is alive, and her mate is a traitor, leaving her to look like a fool.

Her angst secretly pleased him, but her impatience grated on his taut nerves. War was at hand. He was so close he could see it clearly before him. His victory lived in his dreams and his every waking moment. Nobody wanted to cleanse Heaven more than him. Nobody wanted the humans dead or slaves at his feet more than him. Nobody wanted to strike down Michael—or God more than him. This was his right. He had started the chain of events long ago.

And I will finish it.

"Is she dead yet?" The cracks in Asura's face sizzled like lava flowing beneath her skin.

Her fit amused him as she marched up the stairs, "Who, my sweet?"

She put her face close to his. "Don't play games with me. I'm not here for your entertainment."

"Then why are you here?" Lucifer cocked his head, his amusement layered thickly in his taunt. "There's nothing I enjoy more than watching your golden eyes spark, giving away the emotion you desperately try to keep hidden. It truly is part of your charm."

Heat rolled off her body as she vibrated with anger. "Answer my question or I'll go check for myself."

All humor deserted him. "You are never to return to Delilah."

"I'll go if it pleases—"

His hand snaked out and grabbed her arm, yanking her hard against him. "You are my queen, but I am your king. No one defies me. Did you not learn this lesson when you watched your beloved burn for his crimes?" He shoved her away. He'd hit the nerve he desired when her body deflated.

"My heart struggles to accept what my mind believes to be true," she hissed. "If he deceived me, used me to betray the Realm... then his death was just." Turning away from him, her glorious six wings blocked whatever else she wanted to keep from him. No matter. She can have her space. I've won this round.

She believes me.

"It pleases me to hear you say this." He reached out and touched her wild gold braids. His fingers ached to pull them aside and expose her sleek, ebony neck. His tongue flicked over his lips, ready to nip her flesh.

Abaddon rustled, breaking the spell. The dragon raised his head, his reptilian pupils sharpened at the roof's entrance. Lucifer's head snapped up as anticipation zipped through him. A green streaked Fallen glided towards the base of the stairs. Lucifer moved beside Asura and watched him approach.

"Zar. Were you expecting him?" she asked, crossing her arms.

"He's on a mission for me. His presence here had better bring good news."

Zar landed and bowed low at the waist. "My Lord." His black pits seemed to stare right through him.

He shifted to Azura. "My queen." His thinly veiled disdain wasn't missed by either of them. Her lips parted, but then pressed together. She simply nodded at him.

"I apologize for the interruption, but I felt my new discovery needed your immediate attention. If this isn't—"

Lucifer's nostrils flared at the hint of unwanted news. "Speak freely. She will hear what you have to say... she's our queen, after all." He walked a few paces and stroked his hand across Abaddon's hard scales. They rippled beneath his touch. The sensation soothed him, knowing the dragon was his kindred spirit.

"I went to the Guardian's school and waited in a car across the street. Olivia and Zack didn't make an appearance, but the Guardian Sergio did. There was a girl... in a wheelchair with him. They were picked up together. I followed them to his house and observed them from another house's window that faced their backyard. Goon angels arrived, but I hid myself long enough to get information until it became unsafe for me to remain. There is no element of surprise for the Fallen around their homes."

"Is this all that you have to report? I sent you to find their weakness. I need more than something I already suspected!" Tannin emerged in the pool; his tail fin slapped the water like a punch of frustration.

"I discovered something more." Zar placed his hand on his sword's hilt. "The girl in the wheelchair. I believe she's Sergio's sister."

"So what?" Lucifer sneered.

"She transformed—shifted into a beast." Lucifer's hand paused mid stroke as his head swiveled to Zar. "Into the white tiger... the one that nearly killed me in the desert."

"You must be mistaken. That was a heavenly beast you stabbed. I saw it fall, mortally wounded, as blood spilled from it." Asura's hand touched her side.

"It's survived. And if I'm correct, she isn't a magical beast. She's a Guardian. It explains how she survived and why she can be both human and tiger. There may be more Guardians waiting to be activated, just as these Guardians were."

"This can't be." Lucifer growled. "Delilah's deceit continues to come to light." He raised his fist, but the only thing in striking distance was Abaddon. He shot his hand in the air, his cold fury released in a sonic blast through the roof and into the dark sky. The boom ricocheted around the Realm.

"We have only ever faced three." Asura raced down the stairs to face Zar. "How can you be sure what you saw? You need eyes for what you say to be true."

A muscle twitched in Zar's jaw. "My vision—my mapping it is just as accurate as your sight. If it's what my senses mapped, it *is* what was in front of me."

"What if there's more... more of these wretched Guardians? What powers did God give the others? How do they work in His plan to thwart us?" Something like panic snaked up his spine and shook him to his core. This can't be right. Zar had to be wrong.

"We can't rule out that there are more hidden Guardians to protect the humans—"

"And the Mar of Sin." Azura spat.

Lucifer paced back-and-forth, his rage churning at a dangerous level. "I cannot have this. I will not have this treachery! It could ruin everything. Put all my plans to waste. I have to know if there's more. Now!" His vicious command ignited a fireball, glowing in Abaddon's belly. He aimed his wrath at Zar with a pointed finger. "Go back to Earth. I don't care what you do, but don't return until you find out if there're more Guardians." He barely held back the snarl on his lips.

"You get your wish today, Asura. I'm going to Delilah. I obviously didn't make myself clear to her when I told her to tell me everything she knew. Her lies will cost her everything."

"I wish to join you." Asura stepped toward him.

"No. This time, only I will go."

Zar shifted his feet. "I think Delilah shared all the truth she's been told. If Connor knew of more Guardians, he would've kept that from her. She does not know of this. It was too good for her not to have dropped a hint to me."

"I find it curious you would speak on her behalf." Lucifer's eyes narrowed.

"I'm not defending her. Delilah is a waste of time. It makes sense to me that for the safety of their identities, the Guardians would only know about the ones they would fight with. Until the Mar of Sin opens, *they* may not know how many are out there."

Fallen raced through the roof. The Seven Princes landed behind Zar. Their arrival stoked his burning wrath.

"Master, we came as soon as we heard the blast. Is there a problem?" Beelzebub asked, his hand readied on his sword's hilt.

"A problem—only your arrival when it is unwelcomed and not needed." He sneered at the Princes below him. "Are you questioning my ability as leader because I send a bolt into the sky? You insult me by your presence here." He felt his control slipping with his fury at the breaking point. "Be gone when I return."

Lucifer launched himself onto Abaddon's back. His massive hands gripped the black horns and pulled them back, signaling he was ready to fly. Abaddon took to flight. Everyone ducked as his claws hung dangerously low. He leaned over the beast, becoming one with every stroke of the dragon's wings. They burst through the rooftop. All the vibrant colors of the Realm exploded around him. But there was no solace found within its dark beauty. Instead, it mocked him as the lava pools hissed. How could he not have considered more Guardians?

"I'm so close," he seethed. "So close to making everything I've worked for, everything I wanted for the Fallen to come true. But now

—now is it all for naught? Is this a trap set for me? If we walk into this blind, we may get obliterated. It doesn't matter. I must go to war, no matter the losses. I'll not back down a second time to Michael or the Angels. Or to God, who didn't honor me. He only wanted me to adore him. It is I who will kill them and be adored!"

Abaddon spiraled high until he was far above the Realm. The smoke-filled haze that lingered below in a thick canopy blocked them from sight. Only up here, far from prying eyes, could Lucifer let his guard down and crumble under the weight of self-doubt and confront his fears.

And face the unthinkable truth.

Defeat.

CHAPTER
TWENTY-SEVEN

OLIVIA

The Persian carpet's intricate design blurred beneath Olivia's sneakers as she paced a well-worn path across its thick weave. She went to her room in Magi-land right after school instead of going home first. Mom and Dad didn't need to know she was going after Delilah. Some things about what she did were better off not sharing with her parents. It warmed her heart to see them so happy, having finally put the past where it belongs. But she didn't miss their fleeting concerned glances, well aware the Guardian's mission was more dangerous than ever. She had a job to do, and meditating to Delilah required her full concentration. She mentally ran through the list of questions she had for Delilah. This might be her last chance to meet with her.

A light knock at the door interrupted her internal monologue. "Can I come in?" Lucia's muffled question didn't hide the urgency within it.

"Of course—" The door opened, and Lucia slipped inside her room as if she was dodging someone in the hallway. The door closed with a quiet click. When Lucia turned around, her golden eyes were huge and luminous.

"I need to talk to you before we meet with the others." Olivia sat on her bed and observed her friend. To say something was bothering

Lucia would be an understatement. She stalked the same strip of rug Olivia had just paced, her emotions raw and barely contained. Her gut told her Amal was at the core of Lucia's turmoil.

"Spill it before you wear a hole in the carpet." Lucia stopped her prowling and gazed at Olivia with the same torment she recognized in herself when Zach's arrival had blown her world apart.

"It's Amal. He's hiding from me. I searched the forest. Nothing. I called out to him. Crickets. Nothing—*nada*. He could be anywhere, but I know he's close... watching me—"

"Whoa. Slow down." Olivia got up and grabbed Lucia's hand, guilt twisting her insides. Was he hiding from her because of what Olivia had revealed about her dad? "He's fine. Probably went someplace we don't know about here. Learning about a fallen angel spilling sacred secrets and Lucifer upping the game had to be a shock to him. He'll be back when he's ready after he's processed it all."

Lucia groaned and plopped down on the bed. "It's more than that. I... I have feelings for him. He's a kindred spirit, different from Sergio. When I see him, it's like there's a rope attached to my heart and he's tugging on it, pulling me towards him and away from everything else. That's never happened to me. It's scary because a part of me wants to lose myself to him... even if it means staying a tiger."

Nailed it.

"Well, you know that's a bad idea, right?" Olivia sat down next to Lucia. "You can't be a tiger for the rest of your life."

"I know." Lucia flung her head into her hands. "Ugh. I'm so confused. When I heard about his wife and baby last night, I felt horrible for him. Now his skittish behavior makes so much sense to me. When we shift together, he loses himself. When we're human, I understand now why there was confusion from him, a distance he put between us. And to top it off—he's like two thousand years old."

Olivia slapped her hand over her mouth, but the giggle escaped. Lucia peeked at her between her splayed fingers. She put her hands in her lap, a grin tugging at her lips. "Was that a bit dramatic of me?"

"Very." Olivia grinned, happy to see some of the tightness leave

Lucia's beautiful face. "I get it. What you're going through? Losing control of your sanity because someone comes in and steals your heart. Zach steam rolled me, too. No matter how many times I reinforced the wall surrounding my heart, Zach would come in and knock it down until... I didn't want a wall between us anymore."

"Does that mean what I think it means?" A mischievous gleam sparkled in Lucia's eyes.

Olivia's teeth tugged at her bottom lip before letting her smile of joy escape. "Last night, before Amal showed up, Zach and I went on a date," —Her fingers made air quotes, "—because he wants our relationship to be more normal, like other teenagers. I was still a little hurt when he got angry about Delilah, but I went to meet him. He was so cute, waiting for me under the bridge, all nervous and hopeful with a picnic basket. All my angst disappeared, replaced by that same desire to be with him. He took me up to this hidden grove on a hill and we gazed at the stars. He kissed me like he never had before and told me he loves me. Even though I hoped at some point this would happen, I froze. Love is a complicated word for me because my trust in it was crushed when my dad left us. My stomach did a few flops, but this peace just settled over me and I knew I was ready to return his love." Her throat constricted as she remembered their shared moment. "I felt free when I said I love you. Now I want to say it every minute to him."

Lucia threw her arms around Olivia. "I'm so happy for you," she whispered in her ear. "I knew you two were meant to be together."

Olivia returned her embrace, so thankful for Lucia's friendships and support. "Thank you," she pulled away and grabbed Lucia's hand. "When all this ends with Lucifer, I hope you and Amal can figure out your feelings, too. You two may be from different worlds, but you share one mission."

"I hope you're right. Now that he's in my life, I can't imagine him not being in it." Lucia sighed, a sadness pulling down the corners of her mouth.

"I know I'm right. The heart wants what the heart wants... it finds a way. It's our brain that messes everything up."

They both jumped at the knock on the door. "Liv?" Zach asked softly. "You in there?"

"Yeah, we'll be out in a minute."

They stood up, squeezing each other's hand before letting go.

"Thanks for listening to me. I feel better now."

"Good. That's what friends are for." Olivia reached for the door-knob, but Lucia surprised her when she grabbed her arm.

"Wait. There's something else I want to tell you. Today after school, something strange happened at my house."

Olivia turned around, confronted by the worry etched on Lucia's face. "Is it about Sergio?"

Lucia shook her head, although Olivia wasn't convinced. "I was in my room, thinking about Amal and trying to figure out my next move. I couldn't concentrate because I couldn't shake this feeling of being watched. I glanced out my window, but no one was there. The sensation didn't leave me. Sergio came into my room to say he was ready to come here. I told him to go ahead without me. I stood away from the window, but the hairs rose on my neck. When I felt that, I just had a feeling it was coming from the house behind us. I ran to the window and looked up and felt certain that someone was there. An angel appeared in the backyard just as I shifted. I was going to portal to the house, but the feeling was gone. I think a Fallen was watching me and my instinct is telling me it was Zar."

A jolt of fury struck Olivia. Zar had kidnapped her mom and beat her dad almost to death. She had a score to settle with him and didn't like the fact that he could watch Lucia. "We have to be very careful if he's back in the picture. Whenever he shows up, something bad is about to happen."

"My thoughts exactly. But why watch me instead of you?"

"That's the question we need to ask ourselves. Stay alert. Now let's go get some answers from Delilah."

"She better be straight with us this time."

"I'll make sure of it." Olivia opened the door, hoping her

certainty didn't turn into a disaster.

Olivia sat cross-legged on the plush, over-sized pillows strewed throughout Balthazar's room. Candlelight flickered over the walls, a musky scent hinted in the air. Normally, this would have calmed her, but her back was ramrod straight, palms moist in her lap. Mediating to find Delilah was risky, at best. Michael helped with the last effort, a shield of protection for when Guardians are most vulnerable to the hive's pull. Now, she faced Delilah with the Magi and Guardians watching her back. If anything went wrong, they would pull her out in time. Peace flowed from this thought, giving her confidence a much-needed boast.

We can face anything together.

They believe in me.

All eyes gazed at her; their expectation was clear as they waited for her to begin. "We'll watch for the Fallen so your fellow Guardians can concentrate on Delilah." Balthazar glanced at Melchior and Caspar. "If any of us tell you to leave, you must retreat immediately. You don't want to be discovered and give us away."

"I promise. Hopefully, we'll get enough time with her that I can get the information we need." She rubbed her palms against her jeans. "Are you ready?" The level of intensity raised as everyone nodded at her. She closed her eyes, slowing her breathing as she tapped into the orb beneath her mark.

Olivia broke through the tunnel and was assailed with the familiar odors of sulfur and decay. The purple swirl surrounding Delilah was the only light in bleak darkness. She sensed Sergio, Lucia, and Zach with her, but not the Magi. They must be out of her reach and didn't want to waste precious time searching for them. Instead, she zeroed in on Delilah thrashing on the dirt floor and a thick snake falling over the side into the pit from which it came. Her breath caught; fearing she found Delilah was in the throes of a seizure. Once glorious red hair lay across her face like a net, masking whether she was awake or unconscious. She gasped sharply as her back arched off the floor, then she collapsed, her body still and silent.

"Delilah—it's me, Olivia" She waited for a second, but got no response. She wished she could shake her awake. "Can you hear me? Please, Delilah—"

A soft moan emerged, but still no movement. A bubble of panic rose, knowing they didn't have the luxury to wait a long time for her response.

"Try to answer me. I don't know how long I can stay with you."

Delilah's hand twitched before she lifted it to her face. Shoving the tangled mass of hair aside, cloudy green eyes scanned the room. "Olivia? Is that you?" Her voice was like leaves crackling underfoot. "Or am I dreaming?"

Relief coursed through Olivia. "Yes, I'm here. I came back so you could finish telling me about—"

"Conner." Her voice was breathless. "How's Conner? Did Zar kill him?"

Olivia didn't want to waste time answering questions about her dad. "He's fine, fully recovered from Zar's attack. Now—"

"And your mom?"

So surprised, her body jerked back and almost snapped out of the connection. "She was not harmed."

"So beautiful. I was jealous of her, you know... of them and their love." Delilah's words grew louder but slurred as she slowly sat up. "I wanted what they had more than anything... even being an angel."

Stunned by her admission, Olivia didn't know what to say. Her parent's love had survived the war waged upon it. "They love each other now more than ever."

Delilah nodded, as if acknowledging something she already knew was true. Her eyes closed and her body swayed. "Wait, don't leave me. I have to know more about the other enemy, the one you told me about that's more powerful than Lucifer."

Delilah's eyes snapped open. "The Dark Prince," she muttered.

"That's what I call him. Hates Lucifer with a vengeance. Wants to kill him and take his place. He can't rule. He's more evil and ruthless than Lucifer. Having two souls has made him mad."

"Two souls... How can that be?" Olivia's pulse pounded in her ears. Was Delilah delirious? Her story created by the poisoning of her mind?

"Two souls. One body that fights for inner control. He hides it under a shell of obedience, but he wars with it as it tells him what he needs to do. It wants to be set free, but as long as he controls it and can stay as one, he's... he's unstoppable."

"You're not making any sense. No one can have two souls."

"He found the evil seed, a soul set free from its owner. It has been protected through the centuries, hoping to reunite with its original body when it returns to claim it. To come back and rule once more. The Dark Prince found the person harboring the soul and took it for his own..." Delilah laid back down as if the weight of her words crushed her.

"From who? Who had this soul?"

"A nun. He killed her and the Guardian Angel, who tried to save her." Delilah's voice was fading so quickly, Olivia wasn't sure she heard her correctly. "Ask Michael. He was there. Lucifer's ready for war. Don't let him find you... Zar—" Delilah's head lolled to the side; eyes closed to an oblivion only she would know.

"Wake up—"

"Pull out now!" Melchior's command cut through her. "Lucifer is coming."

"But she's not making any sense. Just one more question—"

A large hand grabbed her arm, its tug pulling her back to Balthazar's room. "Now, before it's too late."

Olivia pulled her mind away from Delilah's prison, leaving her broken body defenseless. A chill ran up her spine when a booming voice, dripping with disdain, echoed into the cavern before the meditation connection was completely lost.

"Oh, Delilah... I'm back for you. You've been a bad, bad girl."

CHAPTER
TWENTY-EIGHT

OLIVIA

Breathless, Olivia collapsed back on to the cushions. The dim light held no comfort from the horrors inside the cavern's oppressive darkness. Lucifer's sick call to Delilah, dripping with malice, clamored inside Olivia's head. He had deadly plans for Delilah.

"He's going to kill her. We can't leave her there. He'll do something awful to her, and I left her there."

Zach came into view, his brow scrunched. Olivia reached for the hand he held out and let him pull her up to a sitting position. Her shoulders were weighed down with guilt. There must be something more they could do to help Delilah.

"Her death, at Lucifer's hands, was sealed the moment she plunged into the Mar of Sin." Melchior's words of hard truth didn't ease the surprising wave of sadness for Delilah.

Had she caused Olivia and her parents much hardship?
Yes.
Did she feel like Delilah was sorry for the pain she caused?
Yes.
Did any being deserve to die at the hands of ultimate evil?
No.
A part of Olivia felt like Delilah wasn't fighting her punishment,

deserving this terrible plight by turning her back on good and choosing evil. Delilah was purging her own demons, and that's why she decided to help them as her one last act of defiance. Was it too late to undo some of the damage Delilah had done through sharing her knowledge of the Guardians with Lucifer? Olivia certainly hoped not.

"How are you feeling... any lingering effects?"

The concern from Zach squeezed her heart. She smiled, certain the love she felt for him was loud and clear to all in the room. "Just a little shaken by the encounter. Has the poison taken over? Her words were nonsense... some riddle only she can decipher. I wish I had more time with her." She shook her head, knowing how foolish her statement was considering the ramification of Lucifer catching them. "So, what do you think? Is she trying to tell us something or playing one last game before she dies?" She glanced around the room, hoping that someone could see Delilah in the same light as her.

"I saw someone in pain," Lucia said, holding her hand against her stomach. "There's sorrow for the choices she's made. I don't know how she's still alive. Those snakes... terrifying."

"*Loco*," Sergio twirled his index finger at his temple. "The poison has definitely done a number on her mind. A nun, two-souled Dark Prince, evil seed from the past? Hard to trust something so far-fetched."

"I don't know if we can count anything out," Zach said, shrugging at Sergio. "Look at all that's happened to us."

"*Si*, Boy Scout," Sergio scoffed, patting Zach on his back

"She's a shell of who we battled." Zach said, glancing at Olivia. "And I have a hard time believing her because of all she's done, but I can't shake this feeling that there may be some truth inside her delirium."

Olivia stood up and stretched, relaxing her shoulders. Caspar handed her a glass of water. She drank it in one long draw, letting the water cool her dry throat. She replayed the events and decided there was only one thing they could do.

"What do you think, Melchior?" Olivia looked inside her nearly empty glass and swirled the remaining water. She was afraid she'd look up and find his disapproval.

"I understand her desire to make amends after making a tragic mistake. The only question is whether she's in control of her mind or not. She gave you an avenue."

"We need to contact Michael. She said he knew about the nun. That's the only way we'll know if what she says is true or not." Olivia handed the glass back to Caspar; relieved Melchior supported her train of thought.

"Could it be a trap?" Lucia turned to Balthazar. "Any way they picked the link up that could lead them here?"

The Magi shook their heads in unison. "Olivia broke the connection in time." Balthazar ran his hand down his beard. "The Fallen are more focused, as if driven by a timeline. My fear is that it may not be long before Lucifer unleashes his plan."

"Or the Dark Prince unveils his own purpose." Olivia didn't like the sound of her own words.

"Then there's no time to waste." Melchior waved his hand at the door. "Sounds like we have a date with an Archangel in the Weapons Room."

The Magi filed first into the Weapons Room. Olivia was so preoccupied, she didn't realize there was another occupant until she heard Lucia's gasp.

"Amal," Lucia cried out, dashing toward him. He welcomed her embrace and whispered something in her ear. She flushed and stepped away, nervously glancing over her shoulder.

"What's he doing here?" Sergio asked.

"He came to us before the meditation began." Caspar replied. "It's important he's kept up to speed since it's his desire to help us."

"I know I left suddenly. It was not my intent to upset any of you."

Amal glanced down at Lucia. "After what I heard about Lucifer and the Angel, I was stunned and needed to think about how I would move forward—to be a Guardian again. I have been alone for too long."

"Are you going to runaway every time you hear something unsettling or have to be around us? Life moves fast here and you can't disappear when it gets too hard."

"Sergio—"

"He speaks only the truth, Lucia. I would ask the same question after my behavior last night. I am here ready to fight .. if you'll have me." He tilted his chin, staring at each of them.

Zach walked over to Amal and held out his hand. "We are honored you've joined us. I'm Zach and she's Olivia. We share the same angelic line. Guess that means we're related."

"We are indeed. The honor is all mine." Amal smiled when he returned the handshake and nodded at Olivia.

"It's good he's here," Olivia said, reaching for Sergio's arm. "He may know something, and besides, it makes Lucia happy to see him."

Sergio scowled. "I know, but it doesn't mean I have to be *happy* about it."

Zach walked back and leaned over to whisper in Sergio's ear. "You better get used to it. He's around to stay."

Before Sergio could reply, Michael emerged from within the fire pit's white flames. His magnificence never failed to leave Olivia stunned with a sense of awe. The cobalt blue feathers glistened against the fiery backdrop as if diamonds encrusted his wings. He scanned the room's occupants until his piercing blue gaze landed on Olivia.

"To what do I owe the pleasure?"

"Thank you for coming. We need your help."

"Tell me what troubles you."

Olivia swallowed before stepping in front of Michael. "I returned to Delilah in meditation—with the Magi and my fellow Guardians with me."

"I see." Michael's face remained passive, but she detected his wave of unease. "You had many unanswered questions when you contacted her. I'm not surprised you returned to her. I'm thankful for your wisdom in including your friends for their protection and prospective. Did you find what you were searching for?"

"Well, that's why we called you here. Delilah was barely lucid when she spoke, but said you knew the truth of her story."

Michael's eyebrows shot up. "Me? How strange of her to think I would have any idea of her truths."

Olivia glanced back at the group who had been with her, uncertain how Michael would react to the wild weavings of Delilah's story. She found Zach's steady gaze. He gave her an encouraging nod, steadying her nerves.

"She tried to tell us a story, but it was incoherent and hard to fathom. It was about a nun, her Guardian Angel, and a Dark Prince who stole the nun's soul." Olivia recounted Delilah's tale, sounding even more disjointed as she unraveled it. She was afraid Michael would find her disillusioned, once again a victim of Delilah's lies, but the shifting emotions on his face told her those fears were unfounded. His normally radiant calmness hardened, his features like chiseled granite. Something about Delilah's story must have sparked a memory in him. "Does any of this make sense to you? Can you help make sense of it for us?"

He turned and paced in front of the flames. The Weapons Room turned silent as if the walls also waited with bated breath. He glanced at them, misery shrouding his eyes. "I thought it was another random act of evil, striking down a devout young nun and her Guardian Angel. A cat-and-mouse game to make sure we never forget they find nothing sacred in our world. "I had no idea..." He had a faraway gaze, as if reliving an agony only he could see.

Not sure what to do, Olivia slipped back in between Zach and Sergio and watched the beloved Archangel work out the reckoning of the past warring inside of him. Finally, he stopped and faced the room, determination vibrating with such voracity, his wings quivered.

"This event, this abomination against all that is good, happened last fall before you received the orb. The nun's name was Anne. She was young, just beginning her calling. Her Guardian Angel was Meira. She was a warrior from the Choir of the Powers, of the Red Kingdom of Patience. We heard Meira's death cry and raced through the stars, but we—I was too late. Meira lay in a pool of her blood, glistening silver with the stars. He had burned the nun's body, her ashes lifted in the breeze that swept them away into the darkness. It appalled me, outraged by their senseless deaths at the hands of the Fallen. Hate and smoke lingered in the air. I followed the odor and saw a portal closing across the empty street. I lifted my sword and hurled myself at the source of her death. I'll never forget what he said. 'You're too late, Michael, but we'll meet again.' His words have haunted me, making me yearn for the day when he would come out of hiding and show me his face. My blood boiled as horrible images arose about the horror and fear the nun must have felt in the last moments of her life. But as I add Delilah's tale to these events, the picture becomes clearer."

"How so?" Olivia asked.

"A soul cannot be taken unwillingly. Somehow, he convinced Anne to relinquish her soul. I'm sure Meira came to protect her. She may even have become an unwilling pawn in the *Dark Prince's* game. He killed her and Meira, leaving no trace of this heinous deed."

"What do we do now? We don't know who the Dark Prince is, and I fear Delilah may not even be alive anymore." Her heart sank with the death and roadblocks facing them. There must be a way to find out more information, or they face an unknown nemesis with untold powers.

"Go back to the church and seek answers from those that remain. Ask for the Mother Superior. If anyone knows the nun's secrets, it'll be her."

"Won't you come with us? She might not want to share such precious information with teenagers she doesn't know." Lucia waved her hand at the group. "She'll have no reason to trust us."

"Give this to her." Michael reached inside his wing and plucked out a luminous blue feather. "Tell her it's a gift from St. Michael. It should free up any doubts she has about sharing what she knows. Come back here and wait for my return."

"Where will you go?" Olivia accepted the feather from him and twirled it between her fingertips.

"I need to think and seek counsel from Gabriel and Raphael. I have a theory, and if it's true... well, the consequences are dire."

"We'll keep a distant eye on the hive, just in case." Melchior said.

Michael nodded and raised his hand, opening an electric blue portal. "Go. There's no time to lose. Peace be with you."

Normally, when a portal opened for Olivia, her heart pounded with excitement. There was a hammering inside her chest, ignited by Michael's intensity and growing fears from learning the truth of an elusive Dark Prince harnessing two-souls, seeking the ultimate power.

"And also with you," she whispered, even though peace faded away as the past's truths unraveled their deadly secrets.

CHAPTER
TWENTY-NINE

OLIVIA

Dusk painted the sky in a soft purple glow, framing the red brick church. The portal closed behind Olivia, who stood under a grove of trees facing the church's courtyard filled with overgrown grass. A colorful variety of flowers packed the beds surrounding an old wooden bench. It created a pretty place to watch the water cascade from the tall fountain, bleached white from the sun, commanding the center of the grassy courtyard.

But something shrouded the serene setting with an uninviting air. A chill ran up her spine as she searched for any signs of demons nearby. Neither her mark nor her vision were aroused to intruders, but that didn't appease her unsettled nerves.

"You feel it, too?" Lucia whispered in Olivia's ear.

"Yep. Not the welcoming vibe I'd expect from a church." Olivia bit her lower lip. "Something is off about this place."

"Agreed. We'll keep a lookout for any unwelcomed visitors." Lucia nudged her as she walked past, followed closely by Amal and then Zach. He led the short distance to a wrought-iron gate, its black paint peeling away in patchy spots. Olivia gazed down the fence line both ways and found it connected with the rest of the buildings, with the courtyard in the middle.

"Looks kinda deserted," muttered Sergio.

"That must be the convent over there," Olivia pointed to the one-story building to their right.

Zach shoved opened the old gate with a grating squeak. "No one is sneaking in through here," Zach scoffed.

"Maybe that's the plan," Olivia nodded her head as they filed past Zach. His brows furrowed, closing the gate with another spine-tingling creak. A woman appeared from behind the fountain. Garbed in a simple beige sheath with a dirt smeared green apron around her waist. Sharp eyes watched their noiseless approach across the soft grass. They paused as they rounded the large fountain. Olivia found it curious that the woman held a small spade in her white-knuckled hand, more like a weapon than a gardening tool.

"Hi," Olivia waved and stepped forward. "I'm sorry to bother you, but I hope you can help us. We'd like to talk with Mother Superior. We have some questions we're hoping she can answer." Olivia caught the sadness flickering across her face.

"I'm afraid Mother Superior passed away a while back. Maybe I can help you. I'm Sister Clare, and... I'm unofficially in charge around here." She said as she glanced around the courtyard. "What's this about?"

Disappointment tugged at Olivia. They needed answers quickly. Hopefully Clare could help fill in the blanks. "We're here to ask about Sister Anne. Is there anything you can tell us about her or her background?"

Clare jumped up and shook her head. "You must be mistaken. We don't have a nun here by the name of Anne. If that's all..." She turned and hustled toward the church.

"Wait—don't leave," Olivia called out. "I have something for you. A gift from a friend."

Clare paused and peeked over her shoulder. Olivia grabbed the feather from underneath her shirt. She raised it, blue twinkling off its delicate edges against the fading sunlight. "Please... come back and talk to us. We mean you no harm and desperately need your help."

Clare froze, her eyes huge against her pale skin. She turned and slowly closed the distance to Olivia. Never taking her eyes off the feather until her trembling fingers reached out and gently took it from Olivia's fingertips. She twirled it and gazed at the play of luminous blues.

Olivia waited, wondering if the nun would now trust them. Clare brought the feather to her chest, her fingers tight around the quill. "Is this from…"

"Michael plucked it from his wing as a gift for you. He wants you to know that you can tell us whatever you know. Your secret is safe with us. We are on the same team, looking for the evil that killed Anne for their gain."

A sob escaped while tears slipped down Clare's cheeks. "Sweet Anne," she whispered. "Come with me." She headed toward the church without a backwards glance.

Zach elbowed Olivia. "Here's hoping she can give us a name."

"Or who this ancient soul is." Sergio muttered. "That's what I can't figure out."

"And how it could make this Dark Prince so powerful?" Amal said.

They jogged across the courtyard and met Clare as she pulled open a metal door. A dark entryway beckoned them before Clare waved them inside. "After you."

Olivia crossed the threshold first, the others followed close behind. Silence, so pure, wrapped around her as she glanced around the intimate chapel. The outside buildings may be run down, but not in here. The wooden pews gleamed from decades of regular polish; a fresh scent wafted from the newly mopped floors. No streaks or dust marred the bank of windows' serene view into the courtyard. Clare brushed past them and walked down the aisle, stopping at the last row of pews. She gazed at a marble font near the entrance, then turned and sat on the pew's edge. With her hands clasped in her lap, she raised her chin and cast her haunted stare upon them. "I wasn't certain anyone would come looking for her—Anne. We all hoped one day she'd walk through the door, trying to explain away the reasons she'd left the convent. But as the days turned into months, we knew something horrible had happened to her." She lowered her head. "That we failed."

"Failed?" Zach asked, glancing at Olivia. They all followed suit and sat in the nearby pews.

Clare stroked the feather. "Failed to protect her from the same evil that stalked her mother and brought her pregnant to our doors." Her voice hitched, but the meaning was loud and clear.

Evil had broken the barriers of this hallowed ground, along with the nuns' spirits.

"This must be horrible for you to relive again, but anything you know—"

"The truth needs to be told. I—we kept our silence, praying that wickedness would forget us and not return. It sounds so naïve, when I say it out loud, but we are remote and small. It was easy to fool ourselves into thinking she was safe." Clare sat up straight, resolute as she faced them again. "A little over twenty years ago, a young woman pounded on the back door late at night across from Mother Superior's room. She woke with a start and rushed to the door. When she opened it, Hannah—Anne's Mom, lay collapsed at her feet. She was in labor and already bleeding. I heard the ruckus and went to investigate. I found Mother Superior staring into the courtyard, gripping her crucifix. A wave of hate swept through the door. Fear gripped me as I rushed to help. We slammed the door, desperate to shut out whatever lay in wait, and dragged her into Mother Superior's room. The baby was coming, so I went to get supplies for the birth. I returned just in time to bring Anne into this world." The feather fell to her lap as she stared transfixed into her palms. "She was perfect—beautiful, wiggling in my hands. Soon after, Hannah died having lost too much blood. Of course, the childbirth had awakened the other nuns. We all stared at Hannah's lifeless body, stunned beyond belief."

"Wow, how frightened and confused you must all have been." Lucia reached over and squeezed Clare's hand.

"That's not all," Clare swallowed. "A demon emerged in Mother Superior's room, demanding to take the baby."

"Now that's scary," Sergio muttered.

"We fought the best we could," Her fingertips brushed across her throat. "He choked me near to death, before Meira arrived and saved us."

Olivia perked up. "Meira?"

"Hannah and Anne's Guardian Angel. She fought him in the courtyard. We watched through those windows right there." Anne pointed with a faraway look. "She was magnificent, fierce, like how I imagined Angels would be when battling evil. Mother Superior hovered Anne over the font, baptizing the child with holy water. Finally, Meira struck down the demon—saving us. She entered the chapel, gracing us with her presence, and asked for our help. We needed to protect Anne until she returned to divulge to Anne her life's purpose."

"Did she ever return?" Olivia asked.

"Not to my knowledge. We expected her when Anne became a woman, but—" she shrugged.

"Do you have any idea what Meira might have wanted to tell Anne?" Olivia pushed for more answers.

Clare rose and went to the font. She leaned over, transfixed by the empty basin. After a moment, she turned and leaned against it. "When I left to get towels for the birth, Hannah shared with Mother Superior who she was... a vessel harboring two souls. Her own and that of a dark angel who split his own soul. He inserted it into his wife's womb as she was giving birth to their child. The soul would transfer with each birth until he could come back and reunite with it to resume his vile works. But he never did. This went on until one mother heard Jesus speak and realized her child couldn't be used for this evil. She fled, protecting herself from this hidden cult. Since then, each generation has lived in obscurity, hiding this secret. Hannah begged Mother Superior to raise Anne under the church's protection. And we did... happily. She was a joy. Sweet, gentle."

"This harboring of the soul started before the time of Jesus?" Amal scrunched his brow as he stood up.

Clare nodded. "That's what Mother Superior told me."

Olivia rose and paced the aisle, her brain trying to fuse all the pieces of Clare's story into place. "Did Anne ever suspect she was... a vessel or know about her mom?"

Clare rubbed her arms as if she were warding off a chill. "We told her she was left on our doorstep with a note asking us to raise her. Not too far from the truth, but Anne never questioned it. Mother Superior shared Anne's lineage with me towards the end of her life. I found it hard to reconcile Anne's bright light with a dark seed lurking inside her. Mother Superior warned Anne repeatedly, almost compulsively, about demons and their desires to hunt clergy and nuns, but nothing can prepare you when faced with an evil that knows no bounds. Now it's your turn. What do you know?"

"We believe a powerful demon—" Olivia cleared her throat, "a Dark Prince killed Anne and Meira. He claimed the soul and became one with it."

Clare shoved herself from the font and rushed up to Olivia. "This melding of two souls is an abomination meant only to cause further destruction of the world God created for us. He must want war between good and evil. We'll be used as pawns and weapons against the Angels charged to watch over us, slaughtered before them. Humanity can't protect itself from what escapes from Hell." Clare grabbed Olivia's arm and squeezed. "Michael has to intervene before it's too late. Only God can help us."

The nun's fear shook Olivia's core, spilling her inner fears as if the nun had read her mind.

What if she's right?

What if we can't stop the Dark Prince from gaining control?

Then many will perish, including myself.

"I'm sorry," Clare shook her head and released Olivia. "Sorrow and anger have colored my thoughts. In my sadness, my faith weakened. Please, don't despair on my account. We all have a part in God's plan... in life and in death."

Zach came up beside Olivia and linked his hand with hers. "We'll do everything we can to make sure this never happens."

"I'm sure you will." She smiled up at Zach. "Now go. Find Michael."

"Thank you, and I'm sorry about Anne." Lucia said, rising from the pew along with the others.

The group started up the aisle, but Olivia paused. "One more thing. Are you being watched or had another encounter with a demon?"

Clare stiffened, clasping her hands in front of her. "There is a sense, every so often, of hate boring into my back. I ignore it, wrap myself in protective prayers, and the sensation fades. It's as if... something is checking in on me. A quick glance through the window. It's not unusual for evil to torment religious orders. Please don't worry about our safety."

Olivia smiled and joined the choir of goodbyes that rang out from the Guardians. They left the chapel, but Olivia wasn't satisfied with Clare's response about being watched and didn't feel good about leaving the nuns behind. Even though Clare validated Delilah's story, they still didn't have a name, which left an icy dread blanketing her.

Nobody spoke as they walked through the courtyard. Olivia wondered if they were also lost in thoughts of war and evil.

And whether any of the Guardians would survive.

Clare kneeled beside her bed, in the same room where Hannah had died giving birth to Anne.

Anne...

Dead because she was part of an unknown lineage of women trying to keep an evil seed from seeing the light of day.

And I couldn't help her.

Guilt wrapped around Clare like an old friend. Her worst fears came true with the arrival of an unusual group of teens bearing a gift from St. Michael. She plucked the feather from on top the bed covers and brought it close to her face. Its simple beauty and luminescence left little doubt that it was from him. She whirled it, watching it create a sparkling light inside the dim room. After the teens had left, she sat on the bench outside, replaying the visit while she twirled the feather. Maybe she was casting a line to catch the insidious watcher who dipped in and out of her life.

Today will be the last visit.

Prayers of peace, strength, and forgiveness flowed within her and reforged a vow she'd made long ago.

Protect Anne.

The skin between her shoulder blades burned as the familiar hate tried to burrow inside of her. She welcomed it this time. It will not feed on her fear.

Not tonight.

Never again.

She stood slowly, the stench of Hell making her gag. Her heart danced a frantic beat, knowing this meeting was different. Whatever had peered at her before had never brought a noxious odor.

He's here.

"You have a new treasure. Where would you ever find such a vile thing? Did it fall from the sky?"

"I had visitors today." Clare willed her body not to shake from his voice, deep with venom. "They gave this to me. A gift from St. Michael."

"Who visited you?" Her eyes slammed shut as a single finger ran down the length of her spine. Goosebumps trailed behind; revulsion threatened to close her throat.

But she would not hide.

"I didn't ask their—"

He grabbed her arm and tossed her against the wall. Pain exploded across her back, breath knocked out of her. Stars floated through her vision, but the light couldn't diminish the demon glaring at her. He was dressed in black, with a haze of smoke drifting around him. It blurred his features, but not his rage-filled hatred suffocating her. He bent over and grabbed her by the throat, his nails clicked behind her neck with his stranglehold complete.

"Teenagers perhaps?" Heated breath blasted Clare's face as he dragged her up the wall. Her sweat-soaked nightgown stuck to her skin and her lungs begged for air.

She remained resolute in her silence.

"How did they find out about you?" He hissed. "Who knew—"

Her body quaked in terror. Smoke coated her tongue, mouth hung open as she gasped for air. Black edges narrowed her vision.

Death is here.

Our Father, who art—

And then she was free, dumped to the floor in a heap. She crawled back against the wall, watching him between her strands of hair.

"No matter. There's nothing for them to find here but a rundown convent, full of heretics, no one cares about," he sneered, bending closer. "Another sign the world has given up on the Almighty and his book of lies."

Clare's hand found her small crucifix dangling from a chain around her neck and clutched it. Rapid fire thoughts of wasted time and fear clouded her mind, but she pushed away her self-pity. A new found resolve drove her to stand. "You think you're winning, but you're not. I've aired your secret, and soon Michael will know all about you!"

"No. No... NO!" She watched in horror, on legs barely able to stand. Two faces shifted, as if two bodies battled to dominate under one skin. "You know nothing!"

"St Michael will hunt you down and never let the evil soul you stole come to life." Hot tears rolled down her face. "I brought your treachery out of the darkness because you killed someone I love!"

Fireballs glowed in each of his hands. "He can't stop me. No one can!" He flung a fireball out the open bedroom door, crashing through the windows into the courtyard.

"My faith knows differently!"

"Faith is for the weak. Humans will have a new god soon. They will see who I am and fear me." He raised his hands, glowing orbs aimed at her.

An orange glow appeared above Clare's bed. She watched her Guardian Angel take form. "Leave!" She yelled, shaking her head. "Find Michael, it's too late for me—"

He launched the fireball at her and another at the fading orange light. A burst of heat slammed against her chest, knocking her to the floor. She thrashed against the searing pain enveloping her mind and body. A ferocious snarl filled the room as more bursts of fire slammed into the walls. The room became a blaze around her, thick with smoke and rage.

"Let it all burn to the ground!" He yelled before he disappeared among the licking flames.

Screams filled her ears as her world faded to black.

Her past played in her mind while the pain blissfully ceased as her soul separated from her body.

Regrets and unfilled dreams held no weight when the images ended.

Peace blossomed in those voids because her new and everlasting life was just beginning...

CHAPTER
THIRTY

ZACH

Zach stepped through the portal first, entering the Weapons Room under the watchful eyes of Balthazar, Melchior, and Caspar. Tension was thick, ramping up the growing anxiety coiled within him. Clare's affirmation of an ancient dark soul combining with an evil force, and Anne's lineage squelched the joyful relief of professing his love for Liv and her returning his feelings. Could the Dark Prince be more powerful than Lucifer? Just when he thought he had his past all within his control, it slipped away in a flash.

Caspar paced while the other two Magi stood still with their arms crossed. Liv, Lucia, Amal, and Sergio followed him as he approached them. Caspar paused, his frown lifting. "Finally. I was contemplating —never mind. What did you learn?"

All the details of Clare's tale looped through his mind.

Anne's mom dying during her childbirth.

A demon who tried to take Anne until Meira saved them.

The nuns raising Anne in secret protection.

The fantastical linage of women and the evil soul they each carried in secret.

Does this fit into what Delilah told them about a Dark Prince stealing the soul and killing Meira and Anne?

Yes.

"We have some new information, but Michael needs to hear it, too." Olivia closed her eyes and moved her lips silently. The fire pit's flames crackled to life as Michael emerged. He nodded to the Magi as he flew down the stairs. Michael's arrival should have calmed Zach, but the intensity burning in Archangel's eyes was an amplifier to his own nervous energy. He slid his hands into his pockets, hiding their tremors. Memories surfaced of when the same uncontrollable unease surfaced after killing the demon at Callie's house. He inhaled deeply and pushed away the night he'd lost his composure and unraveled in front of his dad.

Keep it together, man.

The team needs you.

"I hope this means Mother Superior had some answers." Michael glanced at each of them before returning to Olivia. "Did she tell you the name of who killed Anne and Meira?"

"No. Mother Superior passed away, so if she knew the name, the identity died with her. We found another nun, Sister Clare. She was cautious at first, but when we asked her about Anne, she literally turned around and high-tailed for the church. Only when I showed her your feather did she agree to talk to us."

"Clare must know something for her to be so nervous." Michael cocked his head.

"Scared is more like it." Zach licked his lips. "The vibe around the church was uneasy, gloomy... feeling of being watched. I thought a demon would pop out at any moment, but nothing showed up."

"We found out more about Anne and her mom." Olivia tucked her hair behind her ear. "Turns out they were a part of secret lineage Anne didn't know about before she died."

"What secret lineage?" Michael asked.

"A line of women who were vessels harboring two souls. Their own and that of a dark angel from ancient times. He split his soul, inserted it into his wife's womb before she gave birth to their child. This severed soul now transfers with each birth. Apparently, he will return and reclaim his soul and begin where he left off. Something happened because he never came back. One mother saw Jesus and fled to protect herself, her child, and hid the soul from being found. It worked until, somehow, a Fallen found out about the secret and killed Anne for it. I think this Fallen is the Dark Prince Delilah said is more powerful than Lucifer. He's plotting against Lucifer and plans to overthrow him and rule over the Fallen. Does this sound like it can even happen... this soul split in two, carried through the centuries?"

"Did she name any of the mothers from the past?" Melchior asked, pursing his lips.

Olivia shook her head. "Only Anne and her mother, Hannah."

Disgust rippled over Michael's face. "Only the highest of all angels, the Seraphim, can split their souls. If this legacy Clare told you is true, then our nature has been twisted for a despicable use. Like all secrets held for too long, the damage is costly and may be irreparable. We have to find who this Dark Prince is before it's too late. Did Clare say who else knew of this secret?"

Olivia shook her head. "She only mentioned Mother Superior, herself and Meira."

"Meira?" Her name exploded from Michael's lips. "How is it possible she knew this and kept it to herself?"

"I can't tell you. I only know that Mother Superior told Clare that Meira would return when Anne was ready and tell her the truth." Olivia's wide eyes glanced at Zach.

"She's right, Michael," said Zach. "Meira must have known about the soul if her plan was to return. Maybe she's been guarding these women all along, protecting them from being found."

"By all of Heaven and Earth, apparently." Michael paced at the foot of the fire pit's stairs. The flames grew larger, as if mirroring Michael's anger and confusion. "We could have helped these women with their burden, extinguished the evil that dogged them through the centuries! Meira was mighty, head-strong, and protective of those she guarded. Keeping this secret did more harm than good, and with her death, everything she knew died with her."

"We have to find out who the dark Prince is before it's too late," said Olivia. "I'll go back to Delilah—"

"No! It's way too dangerous now. Lucifer was coming for her. She's probably dead by now, anyway." Olivia gaped at Zach. "What? You can't be surprised. She started all this, and it was only a matter of time before Lucifer wised up. Her secrets—" Panic bubbled inside of Zach "—are why we are now in this mess searching for this unknown Dark Prince."

"I agree... his identity is crucial, but not through Delilah. We must find him first before he goes after Lucifer or this mystery angel comes looking for his soul." Michael gazed across the room. "Too many unknowns. Mysteries of time that we must unravel before their secrets catch us in their deadly webs."

"I have a secret."

What?

Sergio emerged from Zach's peripheral vision, breathless and pale under his tanned skin. "I have to go get it." Sergio backed up. "Just wait here... I'll be right back." He turned and ran, disappearing behind the shimmering veil.

What has Sergio been hiding?

"Lucia. What is he talking about?" Olivia spread her arms wide. "And why now?"

"It's been weighing on him for some time, but it's his story to tell, not mine." She crossed her arms. "I just found out about it by accident and I wasn't too happy with him when I did. Just hear him out."

Zach stood stunned by Sergio's admission. What has he been hiding from them all this time? He breathed through his nose and exhaled, trying to calm his nerves. Anything to get his control back.

"Are you okay?" Liv tugged on his arm.

"Not really, are you? First, we hear from Delilah about this Dark Prince, then Clare drops the bombshell about an ancient line of women harboring a secret soul that has made the Dark Prince more powerful than Lucifer, and now Sergio is going to share a secret he's been hiding from us? No. I'm not okay. I don't like surprises, especially when Lucifer could be so close to starting a war. I feel like we are back to square one and I don't like it one single bit!"

His outburst left the other Guardians speechless. He didn't care about their questioning gazes. Someone had to sum up the crappy events of the day. "I know that was harsh, but it's the truth we're facing."

"I get it. Honestly, what we learned today scares me, too." Olivia said. "It's a lot of information to take in, but I'm glad we know. Maybe we can flip all this to our advantage? Let's hear what Sergio has to say, and then we'll make a new plan."

Zach ran his fingers through his hair. His nerves were eased some from getting his worries off his chest. "Okay." Zach nodded. "Sorry I unloaded like that. I—"

"You only said what we all were thinking. I know my appearance has also caused you all some stress. But we should brace ourselves that more secrets will be uncovered before our journey is done." It surprised Zach to hear Amal speak. He'd been quiet most of the day, but he'd noticed Amal's watchful nature taking in the day's events.

Lucia put her hands on her hips. "When Sergio gets back, just listen to him before you guys get upset. It won't be easy, but—"

Sergio rushed back into the room, clutching a black bag.

What in the world is in there?

CHAPTER
THIRTY-ONE

SERGIO

I *have a secret...*

No one was more stunned than Sergio when he blurted out the admission he'd clung to for so long. Between Lucia's threats of revealing the ax and Michael's confusion over Meira not sharing her knowledge of the women carrying two souls, the pressure of his silence finally overwhelmed him. His legs felt like mush as he raced up the stone staircase, taking them steps two at a time. He threw open his bedroom door; the force slamming it against the wall. The bang exploded around the room, electrifying his charged nerves. He got down on his hands and knees and reached for the backpack under his bed. A tremor went through his hand, in anticipation of the illicit pull of the ax calling for him to cradle it in his lap and dream of the revenge he pledged to himself and Manny. He fought against it as his fingers wrapped around the strap, yanking the backpack from the darkness. Relief swamped him, knowing the object of his obsession... and his nightmares would no longer be his to carry alone.

Sergio flew back down the stairway, out of the hallway's cool confines, and into the heat seeping through the shimmering veil cloaking the Weapons Room. He held his breath and stepped through the enclosure, shedding his pride like a second skin as the veil slid over him. The weight of their stares almost made him stumble. Some were filled with confusion or curiosity. Others with a transparent weariness wondering what he would confess. The ramifications of losing his friends by keeping the ax a secret made his tongue thick and his heart pound. There was no turning back. He didn't know how or where to begin his plight.

How do I confess to Michael, my friends and the Magi that I'm a liar, no better than the Fallen we battle?

"*One word at a time,*" Bal's voice echoed in his mind. Sergio locked stares with his mentor, the one who had broken through his defenses and demanded Sergio's attention and earned his respect. Bal's expression was unreadable, but the gold sparking in his eyes told another story. "*Be done with this burden.*"

"Are you going to tell us what's in the bag—this big secret of yours?" Sergio absorbed Zach's hard tone and let it fortify his own armor. When he turned to Zach, he expected to find a sneer tugging at his lip. What he found was a wide-eyed guy, shoulders up around his ears. Zach wasn't looking at him, only at his bag. He'd never seen Zach look like this, and it unnerved him to think it was his fault.

"Sergio." Lucia came forward like a breath of fresh air and rested her hand on the one gripping the backpack. "Let me help you."

"No '*manita,*" Sergio whispered. "I made this mess, so I need to fix it—on my own."

"Just remember, you're not alone." Lucia smiled and squeezed his hand before she stepped aside. His throat clogged with emotion, but this time, it wasn't from anger, it was from his sister's love. He placed the backpack at his feet and took a deep breath.

You can do this mano...

"I don't really know how to begin, but I hope that when I'm finished, you'll—uh, be able to help me and... forgive me."

"We're a team," said Olivia. "We're best friends. Of course, we'll help you. Just tell—"

"But, that's just it. I haven't been a very good friend. Ever since —" He swallowed back the bitter taste in his mouth, "—since Manny died, I've been selfish, reckless, and full of hate. I was on top of the world that night before Zar came. I'd found myself, my purpose. I felt like I'd finally found equal ground with my brother. Zar would have taken Olivia, killed me and Zach, if it hadn't been for Manny gunning toward them with his headlights blazing. He always looked out for me, saving me from any potential danger. The irony was, I was the chosen one, and he, the human, still saved the day," Sergio grimaced, unwanted tears threatening to spill.

"Manny's a hero to all of us," Olivia replied, eyes bright with her unwavering compassion.

"He's also in my eyes, but those feelings couldn't outweigh my devastation at losing him. All I could focus on was the moment of his death. It's so clear to me, it's like I'm standing there reliving it again: the ax embedded in his back, blood blooming on his shirt, him collapsing without a sound. I ran to him and yanked the ax out of his back and tossed it under his car. I cradled him in my lap while the life faded from his eyes, feeling a part of me die with him. The void created in my heart flooded with hate and anger and visions of nothing but revenge. My world shrank to black lifelessness. Out of the corner of my eye, a streak of red—glowing on a black handle—caught my attention. At first, it repelled me, but... it was like it was calling me, demanding I grab it. So, I did. When my hand wrapped around the handle, it amplified all emotions, seeping its darkness into my every pore. Letting Manny go almost killed me. But as I set him free, I whispered a promise to him. A promise of revenge for his death with this." Sergio bent over and unzipped the backpack. He grasped the handle, hot against his sweaty hand. It glowed red inside the black bag, coming to life as if it knew its time had come. "The ax, the one that killed him."

"Wait—"

A collective gasp drowned out Bal's protest when Sergio pulled his secret from its hiding place. Red pulsed inside the handle and through the crescent shape blade. Sergio's heart skipped an erratic beat, still morbidly drawn to the weapon. An explosion of colors shot off the walls, blooming from the weapons shelved around the room.

The kaleidoscope of dancing light converged on him like a protective wave aimed at shielding the evil which permeated from the ax. He squinted at the force field; its frantic rays of light encapsulated the ax. The ax exploded vibrant red charges against the field, but none of its angry energy pierced it. The urge to hold it, to own it—to use it drained from him, replaced by a welcomed peace flowing up his hand.

"Bring it to me!" Michael shouted. The fierceness of his command broke Sergio's spell. Before he could move toward Michael, the ax was plied from his grasp, leaving a pinprick sensation shooting up his arm. His jaw fell open as the force swept across the room, as if in a tractor beam, to Michael's outstretched hand. His long fingers reached inside the force field and wrapped around the handle. Red sparks flew between his fingers, but Michael remained unphased. This seemed to only heighten the ax's flurry of electric charges, as if furious by Michael's taming. Red glowed off Michael's face as his blade and armor awakened in cobalt blue, recognizing his battle for control.

"I don't wish to be your master," he snarled. "But I can take you to him if you open your blade to me."

The red sparks tempered to a simmer. Michael nodded while his battle armor returned to its normal hues. The force field opened around the ax. The lights retracted back to its weapons like rainbows disappearing into their pots of gold, leaving behind a kinetic energy far from invisible.

No one spoke.

No one moved.

All in stunned anticipation of what could play out before them.

Sergio jumped when Lucia laced her fingers within his trembling ones. She held on tight, as if she knew her presence was the only thing keeping him from collapsing.

"What have I done?" he muttered.

"You can't question it now. God's plan is a mystery to us."

Lucia's attempt to comfort him was fleeting when Michael's gaze zeroed in on Sergio. Shame washed over him, but it wasn't because of what he saw in Michael. It came from knowing he had broken his promise to the people he cared for the most. The fire pit's flames burst alive as Gabriel and Raphael erupted from within, swords drawn, ready to fight. Each halted, fixated on the weapon in Michael's possession.

"Where did that come from?" Gabriel asked, taking the remaining steps toward Michael.

"Sergio," Michael nodded in his direction. "This is the ax that killed his brother. He's hidden it from us until now."

"The Fallen's weapons have always been destroyed when their masters are killed," Raphael said, frowning down at the ax.

"I believe that whoever brought this weapon to the fight was not its master. It still seeks the owner through the blood and feather at its core. If we can find out who that is, maybe we can get some answers." Michael brought the ax closer.

Sergio's mind raced as he remembered the night Manny was killed. Shouts of anger and fear blurred with his internal screams. A name pierced above the others. "Balik," Sergio shouted. "His name was Balik... the one who killed Manny. I remember one of the Fallen calling out his name."

"That's good, Sergio," Michael said as he turned the ax over in his hand. "Now let's see if the name matches."

"How?" Olivia asked.

"The same way it was revealed to you. I'll blow on the blade."

Michael raised the ax close to his lips. Sergio couldn't make out the mysterious angelic language Michael whispered across the blade. Light reflected off the half-moon silver edge, but it didn't reveal the scroll of the ancients. Sergio stepped closer, his breathing quickening, willing the ax to heed to Michael's calling. Intensity grew in Michael's chanting, his knuckles white as he clutched the handle. "Show me!" Air burst from Michael and swept across the blade. Red scroll bloomed on the steel with a flash of fire racing over it. Surprise awakened Michael's face, as Gabriel and Raphael gasped at the disappearing words.

"Who is it? Who owns the ax?" Sergio called out, unable to wait another second for answers he desperately needed.

They didn't respond to Sergio, as if his question went unheard. Instead, they shared glances between them, only they understood the answer. When Sergio thought he might explode with apprehension and fear, a large hand rested on his shoulder. Startled, he turned and found Bal.

"Patience," he whispered. "They'll tell us when they're ready."

Silence hung in the air; anticipation so thick it clung to Sergio. Michael nodded and turned away from Gabriel and Raphael. The three Archangels faced the group, but Sergio felt the weight of Michael's gaze. "His name is Symedek. He was the leader of the Watchers, betrayer to humanity and Angels. Amal lived and fought against his evil tyranny."

"Symedek." Amal closed his eyes. "That's a name I haven't heard in a long time and one I wish I never would again. He brought lies to the people, made himself and the other Watchers out to be gods, ones seen in their lives instead of in Heaven. He made our God out to be uncaring of their needs and desires, out of touch with the people while he lounged on a gold throne in Heaven. The wickedness he taught them turned their actions into sins, and in the end, he caused their demise."

"When God created the flood," Lucia murmured.

Amal nodded, sadness pinching his face.

"He and his fellow traitors paid for their sins. Banished for their deeds, sealed in darkness..." Michael's voice trailed off.

"Until they're freed when we open the portals," Olivia said.

"Why is this possible?" Sergio lurched toward the stairs. "Why would God make it so we could free the Watchers one day? They did nothing but hurt people, innocent people. What about the women who lay with them and created the Nephilim? It was all so wrong and now we could free them?" Sergio didn't care about the anger spurring his thoughts. He needed answers, some kind of explanation as to why the ax that killed Manny belonged to Symedek, the leader who set in motion the cleansing of Earth.

Michael came down the stairs, the ax dormant at his side. He stopped in front of Sergio and laid his hand on his arm. Warmth spread up the limb and calmed Sergio's racing heart. He closed his eyes and swallowed back the emotions taking over him.

"Whether we like it or not, the Watchers are a part of God's plan."

"I hate him, this Symedek." Sergio opened his eyes. "It's his fault. His ax killed my brother—"

"Yes, he's responsible for many evils, many deaths. When I captured him and brought him before God, his smugness—arrogance filled me with a deep fury. My hand gripped my sword, ready to rid the world of him. I was so blinded by it, I should have known he had something else planned. And now we know. Symedek must have thought there would be a way to escape or that God would forgive him for his crimes and set him free. There's something we have to consider."

"What?" Sergio asked, licking his lips.

Michael scanned the group as if reluctant to say his thoughts out loud. "He's the one who split his soul, something only Seraphim can do, and harbored it in his child. But he was banished and his soul kept moving from generation to generation, lost except to the mothers who would hold this horrible secret."

Amal stumbled forward, his eyes wide with panic. "Wait, are you saying? It's his soul that this Dark Prince has overtaken?"

"It's a strong possibility. He's a powerful angel who turned against God. He fits this ancient soul who would make this prince more sinister and the time line fits."

"No!" Amal crumbled to his knees. His hands covering his face, but it couldn't smother his mournful wail. Michael raced to his side and kneeled next to him.

"What is it?" Michael asked.

Amal's head fell back, tears streaming down his face. "When the Angels came for the Watchers, I went to the fortress where the battled raged. My sister was inside, so I wanted to get her to safety. I found her outside the fortress, on the run... with her newborn child. I got her to safety—to the ark." His body sagged like all the air had deflated out of him. "My sister—she was Symedek's wife."

CHAPTER
THIRTY-TWO

LUCIA

Amal's words echoed inside the room as quiet as a tomb. The anguish on his face tore her heart in two. Lucia remembered the night Bal shared Amal's painful past about his wife's death and helping his sister escape the battle. Never in her wildest dreams would she have believed his sister and Symedek's wife would twist into one woman.

"This is all my fault. In saving my sister, I put this nightmare into motion." He collapsed to his knees, his last words muttered as if they were his last.

"That's not true." Lucia cried. Sergio reached for her, but she rushed past him, leaving him grasping only air. She stopped in front of Amal, her stare demanding he return it. When he at last looked up, his eyes held no light. They were flat, reflecting his misery. "She must have known what he did to his soul. She had to have witnessed this act and willingly helped Symedek carry out his plans. Did she give you any indication she or the baby had been harmed or made to do something against her will?"

Slowly, he stood, staring over her shoulder.

"Tell us what happened when you found her." Amal's head swiveled towards Michael, who nodded with encouragement. "Any detail can help."

Amal ran his hands through his hair. "The skies were dark, heavy with unrelenting rain. Dirt streets had turned to muddy rivers, homes soaked from leaking roofs. People were trying to escape the city while the battle raged at the palace. They didn't know who or what was fighting or why, but I did. The Angels had finally come for the Watchers. Their time on Earth had come to an end. I'd made sure my wife and baby were safe. I told her I'd return soon with my sister and I would get them to safety." Amal's throat worked up and down, tears welling in his eyes. "She kissed me, saying they'd be fine and to hurry and find Arayana. It was the last time I saw her alive." Without thinking, Lucia touched his arm. "I raced to the palace. When I found Arayana outside the palace walls, she and her servant were drenched. She clutched a baby to her breast while her servant helped her walk. When I grabbed her, she was shaking, sweaty and asked me to help her escape. She'd just given birth. They couldn't be in the elements much longer, so I took matters into my own hands. I told the servant to go look for a donkey and cart. I maneuvered her out of sight and then opened my portal."

"Not the smartest thing to do, but I understand your desire to help her. You had no idea about the baby?" Michael asked.

"No, the baby was bundled up and quiet. My bigger concern was getting her out of there."

"Where did you go?" Her hand trembled when she removed it from his arm.

"The only place I prayed she would find true safety. I took her to Noah. We were friends, and he lived away from the city's chaos. I told him about the battle and asked him to watch after her until my return. But if I didn't make it back, I asked him to take care of her. He said yes, and we parted ways. Arayana never spoke. I assumed she was in shock, but she may have been too afraid to bring attention to herself or the babe. When I found my wife dead, I lost all reason and ended up staying here with the Magi. I don't know what became of Arayana or the baby, but they must have survived if the soul is still present today. Please forgive me—"

"There is nothing to forgive." Caspar stepped in front of him. "Lucia is correct. You had no reason to suspect your sister's deception. She took advantage of you and all who helped her along the way. She's a shrewd woman to have kept this a secret, and maintained it."

"We can't let Symedek find out his soul survived." Determination etched Olivia's brow. "I can only imagine the war he'd wage to reunite with his soul."

"I wish I could say you were wrong, but you're not." Michael said. "Symedek will not only want his soul back, but he and the rest of the Watchers will have something more to consider if the portal is opened. This is their final judgment, just as it is for Lucifer and the Fallen."

Between Sergio and Amal's revelations, Lucia's mind spun with the possible consequences for the Guardians and the future. It all circled back to the one crucial factor upon which everything hinged.

"We have to find out who the Dark Prince is first." Lucia said. All eyes turned to her. She tilted her chin up, casting a glance at Amal.

"Stopping Symedek is more important than finding the Dark Prince," Sergio replied.

"If we can find out who the Dark Prince is, we can stop him before he starts his war against Lucifer and before we release Symedek through the portal. Symedek won't have a chance to reunite with his soul, and we only have to deal with Lucifer. Him I can deal with. These two other evils in the mix..." She stopped as she weighed the outcome if they fought against all sides.

"The odds are bad for us... surviving." Sergio muttered.

"This Dark Prince is the key," Michael said. "We'll see what we can find out. Meanwhile, stay on alert. We know Lucifer is preparing for war."

Gabriel came down the stairs. Gold reflected off his wings like sparks. When he stopped in front of Sergio. "Secrets eat at the soul. You know this firsthand." Gabriel placed his hand on his shoulder. "I'm glad you found the courage to bring us the ax. Its burden is no longer yours to carry. Let go of any thought of guilt or hate this has brought out in you. There's no place for it in what you—all of you—have to do as Guardians. We'll keep the ax where it can't influence anyone anymore."

"Thank you." Relief washed through Sergio's face. "I'll not disappoint you again."

Gabriel squeezed his shoulder and followed Michael and Raphael through the fire pit, flames licking at their disappearing forms.

Lucia wrapped her arm around Amal and brought him over to Sergio. Olivia and Zach joined them.

"I'm sorry... so sorry I didn't—" Sergio began.

"Let it go." Olivia nodded towards the fire pit. "Gabriel is right. We have to concentrate on finding the Dark Prince."

"We need to find out something, and soon. If this keeps up, we may not survive until graduation." Zach raked his hand through his hair. "Time is running out."

Sergio squinted at him. "I know I screwed things up by keeping the ax to myself, but we have to believe the Archangels will find some answers. Evil can't win. Not now. Not ever."

Even though Sergio spouted his words with confidence, a chill went down Lucia's spine. The odds were stacked against them. She sensed the same fears weaving its thick roots deep within them all.

Lucifer.

The Dark Prince.

Symedek.

Any one of them is a dangerous foe, but three at once?

Deadly.

"I need some fresh air—to think." Amal took a few steps backwards.

"Wait, I'll come with you," Lucia said.

He shook his head, raised his portal and was gone before she could stop him. "I have to go find him." Her heart raced, not only in fear for his pain, but she knew her place was with him.

"He's had a huge shock." Olivia tucked a strand of hair behind her ear. "Maybe he wants to be left alone."

"Would you leave Zach alone?" She couldn't hide the bite in her words. "He's hurting and doesn't need to do this alone. He's come so far and I can't take the chance that he'll disappear again."

How could she make them understand when all these new and tangled emotions left her off balance, unsure if these feelings for Amal were real or just wishful thinking? It didn't matter if they understood. She had to go and find these answers for herself.

When Olivia wrapped her in a hug, tears clogged her throat. "Go find him," Olivia whispered in her ear, "and show him you're exactly what he needs."

Lucia nodded and ran for the back door. Bal's gaze followed her through the door. She opened up her mind briefly to Bal so he could understand where she was going and why. He dipped in and out before she shifted. He didn't stop her, but his worry lingered as she trampled the grass beneath her on the way to the forest.

Low-hanging branches slapped against her thick fur as if trying to hinder her search for Amal. Her roars were left unanswered, mounting her frustration. Each roar grew louder, causing wildlife to scurry away and birds flee through the forest's canopy. Lucia quickened her pace, fighting the need to shift back. She raced for the only place she knew to look. The stream where he had revealed himself to her. With the stream in sight, she gave in to her human form. She fell to her knees, the water gently lapping against the shore. She scooped up a handful and took a long drink. The cool liquid eased her dry throat. She stood and called his name. Silence greeted her, squeezing her heart.

"Why won't you answer me?" She cried out. "I thought we were at least friends!"

She threw her arms up in disgust, more at herself for believing he cared for her.

I guess it all was made up in my head. He doesn't like me; he likes the shifter.

Swiping away the tear slipping down her cheek, she turned her back on the stream and the bitter memory. Leaves crunched under her heavy footsteps in no hurry to find their way home.

"Lucia." Amal beckoned from behind her. "Please don't go."

She turned and found him a few feet away. Even the dark couldn't hide his tension and sadness, but his eyes told another story. Their green hue burned with longing, silently begging her to stay. When his arms reached out for her, she threw caution to the wind and stepped into them. Warmth radiated from him as he closed his arms around her. She closed her eyes and inhaled his earthy scent. This was what she wanted... needed, to feel him, be human with him.

"What took you so long?" Her question muffled against his chest. When he didn't immediately answer, she pulled away and looked up. His throat worked up and down before he answered.

"I guess I needed to work up the courage," he smirked. He lifted his hand and cupped her cheek.

"You have nothing to fear from me." She tilted her head into his warm palm.

"This is all new to me. You, the Guardians... even seeing the Magi. I've been alone for so long. I've forgotten how to share my thoughts—my feelings. My mind and my demons clash in constant turmoil. When all the facts came crashing down on me, I did what I was used to doing. I sought the solitude of the forest and let my insides rage. I ignored your roars at first, but when I heard you call my name, I couldn't deny myself anymore. You've awakened a part of me that wants to stay human again, to be with you."

Amal's admission played over her like a cool breeze, sweeping away her fears and self-doubts. Her life had been about playing it safe, but becoming a Guardian changed every possibility for how she lived. She put everything on the line daily, now it was time to put her heart on the line as well. Raising up on her tiptoes, she whispered. "Kiss me."

He hesitated at first, so she closed the distance. His lips were soft, a light kiss of tenderness that was nearly her undoing. She put her arms around his neck, deepening the kiss. An explosion of sensation flooded her. He moaned as his arms tightened around her. She threaded her fingers into his thick hair, wanting him to continue to unlock the ache growing inside of her.

She gasped when he pulled away and leaned his forehead onto hers.

"Why did you stop?" Breathless, she looked up at eyes sparkling with the same desire she felt certain reflected in hers.

A chuckle rumbled in his chest. "If I keep kissing you, I won't want to stop. And as much as it pains me, we have to. If we don't find this Dark Prince, there may be no more kisses for us."

She nodded as she stepped away, not trusting herself to speak. Kissing Amal had opened up a whole new world to her. There was no way she'd let the evil steal this from her. Armored with a new resolve, she took his hand. "Then we'd better go back and get to work."

"Wait." Amal gently tugged her back to face him. "I'm sorry I left like that. I promise you, I won't leave you again."

"I know." She dropped a quick kiss on his lips. "Because then you'd have to deal with the tiger." She grinned before turning away.

Hand in hand, they walked out of the forest and into uncharted territory for both of them.

CHAPTER
THIRTY-THREE

DARK
PRINCE

He slouched in his throne chair, bored by watching the Lessors drop black souls into his pool of lava. Bored by watching the Damned reborn with either surprise, horror, or pleasure upon arrival in their eternal damnation. What did they expect? To escape punishment in the afterlife?

Fools.

For thousands of years, the Realm had been building an army, collecting souls whose dark, selfish deeds on Earth earned their one-way ticket to Hell. Yet, they were stowed away in the mountains, eager to stretch their bodies in war and plunder. The restless need to execute his plan was getting harder and harder to deny.

Why do you continue to wait for Lucifer? We are greater than him.

The Ancient One broke through his brooding thoughts. "Because if I move too soon, I risk his discovery of who I am. We need the distraction of *his* war drums for cover."

You mean who WE are. You will not accomplish this without me. You'd be still stuck in his shadow if—

"And you would still be trapped inside the breast of a nun. I rescued you. Remember that."

And now all traces are burned to the ground. We

should have killed that nun sooner. Michael now knows the truth.

"He already knew a nun and Guardian Angel were killed. He was there and couldn't stop me. She knew nothing else or who I am. It was a waste of their time." He sneered.

Then why send Guardians?

"Cease with these idiotic questions. You worry over nothing. We've bigger issues at hand."

The Dark Prince lurched from his throne, not willing to let the Ancient One's concerns cloud his vision. He growled, disgusted by Lucifer's ineptitude tying his hands. He had to do something... anything to push Lucifer into action. Too many questions lay before him like land mines. The waiting was eating him alive, while the Ancient soul's constant internal prodding pushed him to the brink of madness. Torturing the Damned, while satisfying, didn't quench his thirst long enough to keep the madness at bay. He needed more, but that was a conundrum he'd yet to solve.

Delilah was no longer an option, if she was even alive. He'd returned to give her lies to plant, but when he flew into the mountain, he knew she was lost to him.

No snakes vying for the right to bite into her battered flesh.

No Delilah, broken and filthy, curled up on the dirt floor.

Only a whiff of her fear lingered in the stale air.

He'd flown away, the Ancient One berating him for risking everything on her. He hated it, but it was right. And that set his blood to boil.

One option uncurled before him. Maybe even riskier than Delilah.

Asura.

The Queen is dangerous. She keeps her own counsel. You don't know where her loyalties lie.

He gazed up at the sky, forever clouded by a layer of ash, and pondered the Ancient One's theory. Asura was an unwilling queen, forced into this alliance after her past lover had killed her mate...

falsely. Satisfaction burned within, knowing he'd fooled them all. He'd gone to Asura to offer his sympathies after Sonneillon's brutal death. As much as she tried to hide her feeling behind her veneer of pride and strength, pure fury burned behind her gold eyes. He recognized those eyes because he'd seen the reflection of his own. Lucifer may have her shackled to him in the pretenses of power and admiration, but he'd caged a predator who would kill him at the first opportunity.

He needed to add fuel to the flames, and her blind spot would do the trick.

Yes...

He lifted his massive wings, buoyant with a surge of excitement sparked by his plan. Circling above his Realm, the color vibrated once again.

The lava's churning lifeblood excited him once again.

The Damned a beautiful evil once again.

Taking a chance he could find her alone, he dove toward the mountain where she spent most of her time with her treasured Degasus, far away from Lucifer.

As he flew through the mountain's tunnel, the walls undulated with the colors of the Realm, but it was the display at the tunnel's end that mesmerized him. Colorful lights streaked behind the herd of Degasus flying over the cavern's floor. Heat swirled past his face and over his wings, bringing with it the tang of animal sweat. He dove over the side, dark from light, and into the fray of the herd. The creatures darted around him, not in an individual frenzy, but with the unified grace of a flock of birds. The leader was larger, a dominant creature, leading the others in flight. A sharp whistle pierced the air catching the lead's attention. They chased the magnificent beast to the floor. The Dark Prince gave chase as well, pleased when he found Asura standing proudly among the beasts. The chaotic air lifted her braids, hiding her face from view. Her stance was unguarded, arms lifted in the air, shrouded by the swirl of dust. He envied her wild, uninhibited nature and desired it. There was no mistaking when she sensed his presence. Her laser vision cut through him as if she could rip away his barrier and unearth his secrets.

Be careful—

"Stop chattering like an old fool. You'll only distract me," he mumbled.

He landed next to the walls, preferring to watch from a distance as she orchestrated the Degasus to their corrals burrowed within the walls. She ran her ebony hand over the back of her Degasus, then down its flank. Feathers and skin rippled at her touch. She turned and faced the creature standing proudly before her. Leaning closer, she whispered into its ear. He couldn't hear her words, but the beast's ear twitched while its front hoof stomped as if approving of what she said. When both sets of eyes turned to him, he arched one eyebrow and returned their inquisitive stare. Underneath, her intensity unnerved him, feeling an unsettling need to squirm. He locked his cool regard in place, making sure no cracks gave her entry.

"Home," Asura commanded. It flew away, leaving the two of them watched by an unwitting audience. She crossed her arms when he strode towards her, but her intense gaze never wavered. Stopping short, he let his arms hang at his side, his posture one of ease. If there was any chance of plying delicate information, her guard must be down.

"You're a long way from your Realm, Prince," she smirked.

"And you're a long way from your throne. Looks like we're both seeking a diversion." He waved his hand toward the corrals dug into the craggy walls. "You seem to find some peace among the Degasus."

A harsh laugh escaped her lips. "There is no peace here, only snippets of solitude before the next storm arises. So why are you here, storm maker?"

"I come as a friend, not a foe," he raised his hands in surrender. "Lucifer is the only one brewing up at a storm of his own making. I'm here out of concern for my Queen and the Realm. His obsession with these Guardians has skewed his vision, his purpose."

Her face remained a mask, but the golden swirls flared on her chest. "You've not shown the least bit of interest in me since he put the crown on my head. You coming here only makes me suspicious and I'm not in any mood to play games, least of all with you." She turned away from him, heading toward the old corral. He followed her inside, not allowing himself to be dismissed, more curious as she entered the place where precious beasts had been punished. He was surprised she hadn't sealed the entrance, leaving the horrors forgotten in the darkness.

She's leery of you. Choose your words wisely or—

A whip looped around his throat, squeezing with a fiery heat. The Prince's hand found the hilt of his dagger, while his other grabbed the lash. Blind fury pulsed at Asura's blatant disrespect for him. "Be still and release your weapon or you'll suffer your last breath." She hissed.

His hand dropped, but his desire to kill her didn't fade. Lifting his hands, he tugged against the whip ensnared around his neck. Everything inside of him wanted to shift and show her who she was truly dealing with. "Loosen the whip," he said between gritted teeth. "You have no reason to threaten me in this way."

"I'm your Queen and I can do as I please, threaten who I please, kill who I please. Lucifer would replace you as quickly as he did Sonneillon." The whip crackled like her braids glowing in the dark.

"And Mammon would wear the crown if you cease to please him."

"Yes." The whip unwrapped from around his neck and fell to the dirt floor. The tip slithered back and forth in front of him as a reminder she would strike again. "But she's only loyal to herself, not to the Realm. Not like me. That's why I let you follow me in here. I'll listen to your concerns, but not at the risk of your traitorous words being overheard. So... what is so pressing that you'd take the risk?"

Her words are true. She could tell Lucifer and have you killed.

The Ancient One's fear froze his tongue. Was it worth the risk of planting a seed of deception, or was he setting a trap for himself? He gazed at the beauty before him, contrasting the harsh surroundings with the magnificent gold swirling on her chest and arms, her braids alive like each strand had a will of its own. Her allegiance to the Realm over Lucifer was what made her a fierce warrior and a popular choice for the Queen.

But it was also her weakness, open for him to expose.

Asura's six wings snapped out from behind her, breaking his trance. "Having second thoughts about speaking freely?" She tsked, cocking her head. "I thought you were never one to have any fears."

"Choosing my words wisely as so duly counseled." He nodded at her. "What I'm about to say may not sit well, but I can be silent no longer. Ever since Delilah showed up, he's been obsessed with her and the over spun tales about these Guardians. He's lost sight of _our_ own power. He's relinquished any valiant victory by the Fallen, to controlling the Guardians' supposed powers... of which we aren't even certain they have or how many there are."

Asura stepped forward, eyes blazing like laser beams. "I've fought them in battle along with the Archangels," she spat. "Their skills match ours. If they weren't vital, why would the Heavens protect them?"

"I think the Angels are working with humans, equipping them with weapons and powers, because they know war is coming and they can't beat us again. We're too strong. We have the Damned—an army of ruthless killers. They have the Saints. Who's mightier? Who is hungry for revenge? We're destined to win, but Lucifer has forgotten this in the heated haze of Delilah's easy lies."

"Delilah holds no power over him anymore," Asura said. She paced like a caged animal... _good_. "She came to us, fell through the Mar of Sin, because she was just as deluded by God as we were. It makes no sense—"

"She's a sacrifice, Asura—a martyr. The Heavens are clogged with them." Asura stopped in her tracks and he knew he had her. "She is the only one who has spoken of this Mar of Sin. This gateway to Heaven. She's blinded Lucifer with the thoughts of an easy victory, when it could all be a trap to send us up through the vortex, slaughtering us, leaving us too weakened to win a war. Think about it... think carefully and you'll know I'm right. This could be Michael's doing."

"I think Lucifer isn't the only one obsessed with Delilah. Your tale is as extreme as hers." She flicked her wrist at him, but doubt simmered in her eyes.

"Is it? Who else has her precious knowledge? No one. And we can't seem to capture three teenage Guardians to find out the truth? Why? Because banished and lovesick Zar, along with Delilah, failed at every attempt. Too convenient for me. And now Zar is back from the shadows, whispering more lies in Lucifer's ear. Conveniently, according to Zar, there are *more* Guardians. This seed sent Lucifer into a rage, unsettled him, making him too unstable to cut a clear path of victory. How can Lucifer still trust him, after all Zar has selfishly done to the Realm? Is there no end to this?"

Silence hung thick, but Asura all but glowed. "Zar wouldn't lie about what he saw," she hissed. "To Lucifer or to me. He's atoned for his misguided ways—"

"Atoned?" The Prince laughed at the absurdity of the word. "Fallen don't atone. They're killed, imprisoned, or banished for their crimes against the Realm. You understand this more than anyone, don't you?"

A shadow of sadness rippled across her face as she gathered the whip back to her side. "What do you propose? Kill Zar now and forget about the Guardians?"

"Zar's life is for you to contemplate, not me. However, I think we should strike the Heavens now." He clenched his fists, taking a step closer to her. "Forget about these stories and start this war on our terms, now, before they can set anymore traps for us. We don't need the Mar of Sin for victory."

"And if the Guardians are real?" Her husky voice rolled over him. The question he'd been waiting for.

"*We* get them first to make sure Lucifer rides in glory through the Mar of Sin."

"Leave me," Asura muttered.

The Prince nodded and raised his portal, not wanting to push his luck.

Well done. She's taken the bait.

He stepped through the portal. The Ancient One's praise reverberated in his mind. She had taken the bait, but whether she acted on it, he couldn't be sure. It could mean the fruition of his plan or death for his treason.

"We must watch Asura carefully. We gave her much to think about, but she gave us little. There are many layers to our queen. We need to find a way to peel them back to our advantage."

Should we kill Zar ourselves?

"We shall see. Our Queen may answer this question for us."

CHAPTER
THIRTY-FOUR

ZAR

Cydanos skimmed the charred canyon walls, hugging the jagged terrain of the mountains beyond where the Degasus reside. Zar loved the freedom of riding on the beast's back. It cleared his head and sharpened his thoughts. That was the purpose of the ride today. He needed to finalize his plan, examine it from all angles to find the flaws—the perils of getting close to the Guardians again. He couldn't fail this time. If he did, he might as well never return and let Lucifer think he perished in his attempt to get more information about the status of the Guardians. Were there more of them, secretly waiting for the call to fight against the Fallen? Better to create chaos on Earth than to die at Lucifer's hands. He had no desire to feel the slashes of a whip or the deadly bite of a snake.

No. I've suffered enough torture in my lifetime.

I must succeed and retain the respect I've clawed my way back to earn.

I can't let anyone stop me now.

The beast dove for the black gaping entrance and flew into the tunnel, increasing its speed. Zar's platinum hair whipped behind him as he ducked lower. A smile stretched his hard skin as the pit's entrance grew larger in the distance. Cydanos plunged over the edge. The floor loomed in front of him. His legs tightened as he held onto the flaming mane, exhilarated by the daring ride. Their hearts pounded in sync. Zar let Cydanos take control, fighting the urge to command it to pull up, instead trusting it to understand its limits. A cry lodged in his throat, the floor so close, he could map out the rocks and pits. Finally, it surged up, wings of fire kicking up dust before it circled the pit close enough to graze the walls. Hooves stomped inside the corrals, as if applauding the daredevil entrance. Zar's heartbeat slowed as they descended in lazy circles.

"Showoff," Zar chuckled, patting its neck. "Can't resist making a grand entrance, can you?" A quick snort of fire from Cydanos left no doubt it was the intention.

Movement against the far wall caught Zar's attention. He turned his head and mapped Asura's angry stride kicking up dirt. It didn't surprise him she was here. What was strange was the fact she exited out of the old stables. They both knew the horrors of what took place there until she had put a stop to it. She made it very clear she would kill any Fallen who dare beat any Degasus for punishment or pleasure. One had ignored her edict and paid for his life. The beasts were now left for their purpose. To train for battle.

Cydanos landed near Asura, cutting in front of her path. Zar dismounted and patted its flank. The beast took off in a trail of fire, leaving them alone. He was glad to see her, eager to share his plan. But as he approached her, he sensed she didn't feel the same. He slowed, sensing something troubled her. What has her so upset? Could the lingering sadness of the old stables invade her mood, igniting an old simmering anger? Why would she go in there and put herself through the empathic pain, certain to upset her at the core? Only one way to find out. Ask at the risk her wrath.

"Hey," Zar nudged his chin towards the entrance. "Surprised to see you coming out of there? You look like the bad vibes still permeating from the walls have soured your mood."

"What I do or where I go is of my concern." She shoved past him. The heat of her anger rolled off and hit him square in the chest as if he caused her irritation. Zar's brows furrowed, trying to remember if their last encounter had caused distress toward him.

"Have I done something to upset you?" He turned and faced her hasty retreat. "And don't lie to me. We know each other too well."

She pivoted in silence, but she couldn't hide her inner turmoil. Zar let the silence lengthen, knowing it was not his turn to speak. Asura's hesitancy sent a signal of alarm down his spine.

"Some information has come to my attention, and I need to weigh it carefully before I act," she said, pointing back to her earlier path. "The stables serve to remind me of the selfishness of one's secret pleasures and what lengths they will go to fulfill them."

"Who is so important that what they whisper in your ear will grant your consideration? You've never wasted your time on idle gossip." Zar didn't like the way her gaze was trying to worm its way past his defenses.

"Being Queen of the Realm demands I pay more attention to what is happening inside of it... and as a protector of Lucifer."

Zar barely held back his laughter. "Since when has Lucifer needed a protector? He's quite capable—"

"Since you brought Delilah here with her grandiose stories of Guardians and storming Heaven through the Mar of Sin. It brought forth chaos, traitors, and death. Delilah has manipulated the very heart of the Realm, yet do we know her true motives, or are we supposed to continue to dine on her feast of lies? Many questions were brought to me along with information I find intriguing and hard to ignore, no matter how much I want to or how much it pains me to consider these paths."

He was stunned by her not-so-subtle accusations. "Information... about me?" He splayed his hand to his chest. "What could someone have said to you to make that comparison? The Realm doesn't care what I do anymore. Whatever Fallen gossip—"

"I care what you do and why. As do others. You're not as invisible as you think."

"Hhmm, I can fix that," he scoffed. "I can disappear at any time.

You can take me off your worry plate and look for the real traitors among us... living and breathing, not ghosts haunting your memory."

"That's what you do best, isn't it? Running away, no desire to face the hard truth of your actions. You choose to live outside the Fallen instead of facing their challenging stares. You keep your own counsel, find your own truths to match the chip on your shoulder. And when it doesn't fit your needs, you disappear and take all your secrets with you." A long, sharp talon was aimed at him, accusing him before he even knew what to defend himself from. "You're good at that... keeping secrets. But for whom is the question."

His lip lifted in a snarl, heat burning within at Asura for questioning his loyalty. "You're right. Delilah did mess with me. She tapped into old feelings I didn't know I had anymore. Made me crazy with jealousy while she trapped me in her web of lies. I'm not the only one to fall under her spell. Lucifer and Sonneillon did as well." Asura turned away in disgust, hiding the emotions certain to give her away. "But I paid for my mistakes, as did your mate. I thought I had your trust... your understanding of what this trial has brought on me as well."

She spun around and was upon him, her fury squaring off with his. "I don't feel sorry for you or your stupidity for believing her. I only care that what you're doing now will bring glory to Lucifer and the Realm—nothing else matters to me." Asura shouted.

When the echoes of fury stopped reverberating around the pit, an icy dread settled on him. Someone had turned an ally into an enemy, and it wouldn't be long until she shared it with Lucifer. Finding out who this was became vitally important to his safety.

"I assure you that is the plan, my Queen."

Asura stepped back, lifting her chin. "Then stop wasting your time here and go do as Lucifer demanded."

"I know what my job is, but it seems as if I'm not the only one wasting time. For all your profession as Lucifer's protector, you sure spend a lot of time away from his side." He steeled himself for the strike of her clenched fists. Instead, she turned away and leaped into the air, her silent departure as effective as a slap. It wasn't until after she entered the tunnel that he realized he'd been holding his breath. He replayed their conversation in his head, searching for clues about who would have the influence to change her thinking. He turned and cocked his head toward the entrance. Had this meeting just taken place? There was only one way to find out.

He stormed over to the stable entrance, ignoring the unease he felt. Once inside, the complete darkness matched the bleak despair his heightened senses still picked up. He pushed those aside and concentrated on the faint odors lingering in the dank air. Asura's scent was clear to him, but others brought his heart racing. Neither one specific enough to capture, like they were melted together, overlapping with the smell of terror stamped into the walls, creating something new. He gasped and spun around, needing some fresh air to clear his nostrils. He fled in the same manner as Asura. With haste and without looking back.

Once Zar escaped the tunnel and departed the entrance, his head cleared. But fear lingered as he allowed himself to paint the picture of what he'd sensed. Asura had definitely met with someone.

And if his senses were right, he was in trouble.

And she was a traitor.

CHAPTER
THIRTY-FIVE

ZAR

The street was quiet. It was as if the houses all took a collective sigh, recovering from the hectic morning of families hustling to get out the door and start the day. Zar's focus was on the single-story structure, the home of his nemesis. Sergio, and now his sister Lucia, caused the friction in his life. Their constant ability to escape his grasp had fractured his world, splintered him from the Fallen, made him an outcast. After his unsettling run-in with Asura, dread had formed a sickening knot inside him, leaving him desperate for the information he needed to satisfy Lucifer and get back into Asura's good graces. However this day played out, he must get answers or die trying.

Today is not my day to die.

The garage door opened and a small silver car backed out, maneuvered out of the driveway and away from the house. The elderly woman who lived with them rarely left the house except for one day every week. From a distance, safe inside his bubble, he learned the routine she rarely deviated from. First, she went to a florist and bought two flower arrangements, followed by a slow drive to the cemetery. He only stayed for the first time, hairs on his neck prickling from lost spirits wandering the grounds. She strolled down the sidewalk, turned onto the grass, and stopped in front of two matching headstones. He sneered at the square white marble; certain it held the name of the intruder who saved the Guardians on his first attempt to bring them to Lucifer. Hatred pulsed as she kneeled and placed the flowers in a vase beside each grave. Brown, thin hands pulled at tuffs of grass around the headstones, all the while talking as if she were having a conversation. As much as he wanted to grab her and punish her, he knew an Archangel had to be nearby. Sweeping the grounds again, he left before his presence was detected. He returned to the house regularly for the next few weeks, until he was certain this was a routine he could count on. It was now time to act upon this opportunity and go investigate.

His portal took him into the living room, quickly submerging himself back inside the bubble. One of the curious things he'd learned was when the house was empty, it was not guarded. Instead, the goons followed the family. It worked out fine for him, but he didn't want to take any chances. While he waited for her return, he snooped to find anything of interest. Mapping the walls, happy smiles beamed back at him. His hands itched to hurl the frames and rid his mind of their joy, but doing such a thing would raise an unwanted alarm. Sneering back was the best he could do as he continued to the kitchen. Snippets of paper fluttered as he passed the refrigerator. One caught his attention. He took note and moved on to the hallway. The first door he opened must belong to the woman. Sparse and tidy except for the expanse of crosses on the wall above her bed. It became clear she was a grandmother to the Guardians from the pictures on her dresser. He carefully searched the room, opening drawers and the closet, finding nothing of interest. Disappointed, he turned to leave, but an odd sensation washed over him when he neared the bed. Shoving his hands under the pillows, a wicked smile emerged when his fingers wrapped around a handle. He pulled out an angelic knife. Could she be part of the old line of Guardians? The desire to keep it burned, but her finding it missing wasn't worth it. He put it back and moved to the room across the hall.

Lucia's room.

The shifter...

Hers most intrigued him. Why was she a shifter and a Guardian? Could the others have this same power, but keep it hidden? He didn't think so, but he didn't want to underestimate them again. He turned the knob, but paused when the garage door rumbled open. A growl vibrated in his throat as he put his back against the wall.

No one should be back...

Gripping the hilt of his sword, he steeled himself for the possibility of Lucia or Sergio. He couldn't leave without something for Lucifer. The back door opened and closed quietly. A small woman emerged, keys rattling in her hand. He relaxed when he recognized the grandmother. She muttered under her breath as she quickly headed toward the living room. Dropping his bubble, Zar chose his knife instead. He lunged for her, slapped his hand over her mouth and easily brought her back against his chest. A muffled scream brought satisfaction to him as he put the knife to her delicate floral scarf wrapped around her neck.

"Shhh. You stay quiet and I won't have to kill you." Her struggles stopped when the sharp blade's edge sliced through her scarf and pressed into her flesh. "You answer a few questions and I'll let you go. You fight me, and I'll take you through the portal and you'll never see your family again. Nod if you understand me."

A quick nod was her answer, but her body remained tense against his. In a swift move, he spun her around and pinned her between him and the wall. Her eyes grew huge as he felt a tremor move through her body.

"You recognize me, don't you?"

The sharp scent of fear filled his nostrils as she nodded. "Good. So, you know I keep my word." He pushed closer until his armor could prick her skin. He lifted his hand. "What is your name?"

When she remained silent, Zar added pressure to the blade.

"Camilla," she uttered. "What do you want? I know nothing."

"Don't be coy with me," he sneered. "I found your little weapon under your pillow. Angel made I suspect—just for you. You're a past guardian and don't waste my time denying it. We've learned your powers are passed down through the family. You're not much of a fighter now, old—useless, a burden to your family."

She puffed out her chest, no longer playing the victim. "I was a fierce warrior." A proud smile spread across her face. "Killing your kind brought me much pleasure."

His hand snaked up and slapped her cheek. She gasped; blood trickled from her lip. "As it will bring to me when I kill the Guardians."

"You're no match for them. They've already proved that." Her hatred for him laced her words.

"There's only four of them. How hard can it be, unless there's something more you're keeping from me?" His face moved closer as his thumb smeared the blood across her chin. She tried to jerk away, but he pressed his body deeper against her petite frame. "Are there more of you?"

Camilla's brow furrowed for only a moment, long enough to give herself away before she answered. "I'll never tell you anything."

"Fine," Zar shrugged. "Death it is." He raised his hand to open his portal when a blast of energy tore him away from Camilla and threw him into the living room. The table smashed beneath him, leaving him sprawled over splintered wood on the floor. He frantically mapped the Angel standing in front of Camilla. Zar recognized the short, spiked orange hair matching his orange-dipped wings. It was one of the goons protecting the house. The lean face held orange eyes, seething with hate.

The Angel nudged Camilla into her room as he grabbed one of his two swords hanging from his hips. "It will be your death I'll celebrate, Zar."

A chill zipped down Zar's spine. If he was here, then others were sure to follow. It left him with few options, and possibly his demise, but angel blood would also spill.

"My death will not be by your hands." Zar sprang to his feet and leaped behind the couch. A bolt of hot air ruffled his feathers, narrowly missing him, shattering the glass door instead. Glancing over his shoulder to check on Camilla was the goon's mistake. The Angel filled his visual map, wings spread wide, arms raised with his sword pointed at him. Zar turned and threw the knife, still clutched in his hand, aiming at his vulnerable midsection. He cried out and crumbled to the floor. Blood bloomed as shock spread over his face.

"Got you," Zar sneered and pulled out his sword.

The Angel lurched to his feet and blocked Zar's blow with his sword. They clashed again, but Zar didn't have time to spar. He was faster than the wounded Angel. He spun and struck the Angel's thigh, sending him to his knees.

Zar grabbed him by his hair and yanked his head back. He placed the tip of his sword against the angel's heart. "Tell God we're coming." It angered Zar even more when he scoffed back at him.

"Why would he care what a Fallen has to say?"

And with that, Zar plunged the sword deep, gleeful as the Angel's lifeblood spilled over his hand. "Because we bring war."

"Bring it... you'll lose again." He said before gasping his last breath. Zar released him as his dead body crumbled to the floor.

"Not this time."

Electric energy filled the air. He raised his portal, hoping he still had time to get away.

"No!" Camilla's soul crushing wail had him glancing behind him. Her body vibrated, and he could sense the warrior she once was.

"You live to see another day, old woman," he chuckled, stepping into the portal. He welcomed the heat and ash engulfing him, smiling at his victory. He lifted his chin when he thought of how Lucifer would be pleased with his newfound knowledge and death of another Angel in one fell swoop.

Finally, a victory I can savor with him...

As the portal began to close, he heard the whoosh of the blade sent through its opening.

The battle cry of a woman he'd underestimated.

The pain exploded in his back from her knife, splitting through the bones of his wing, pinning it to his back. Zar turned and sent a wave of energy at her. There was complete satisfaction as it sent her crashing into the wall and crumbling to the floor.

It wasn't until the portal closed that the acid-like burn seeping its way to his bloodstream caught his attention.

"Lucifer," he cried, before his world turned black at the foot of Tannin's pool.

CHAPTER
THIRTY-SIX

LUCIFER

W*here are you?*
Zar should know something by now?

The Seven Princes stood at the foot of the steps leading to where Lucifer sat on the throne. Each vibrated with the colors of their Realms, specializing in the specific sins that whittled away at man's goodness. They each followed their mission well to build and train his army of the Damned. Beelzebub, his closest ally and Prince of the Realm of Pride, nodded at Lucifer. His muscle ladened broad chest rippled with golden ribbons over his brown skin. Mammon's blue lifeblood, like fine etchings under her pale skin, honored the Greed Realm. Leviathan's black dreadlocks looked like a mane while his bare black chest glowed Envy green with tribal-like tattoos. Berith with his long black hair, flat face, narrow eyelids harbored eyes burning red. His jet-black wings swirled with red like the magma surrounding his Wrath Realm. Asmodeus, Prince of the Realm of Lust with her waist length, wavy dark brown hair, flowed down her shapely body clothed in her hot pink electric webbing crackling from head to toe. Gressil, Prince of the Realm of Gluttony, her bright orange eyes burned wide-eyed within the sharp angles of her face as if eagerly waiting for the next thing to feast upon. Astaroth's purple forked tongue flicked over his black lipped mouth, reminding Lucifer of the snakes he'd gotten from the Sloth Prince to use against Delilah.

Delilah...

Where would I be if she hadn't landed in my lap?

She gave me a way to start this war, but has she also sabotaged me?

He willed his body to relax and not worry about the possible fallout of her story. Exuding the confidence of the supreme ruler of the Realm was all his Fallen wanted—needed from him. It came naturally, allowing for his complete and utter control of their destiny.

But inside?

His blood flowed, thick and hot, like the lava coursing around his domain. He'd called them here for a status report of their Realms, not that he needed to hear it from their mouths. Many spies kept him abreast of the armies gathered, built for the war nearing with each passing day. He wanted to observe them in a different light to see if his suspicions were correct.

Asura stepped next to him and laid her hand on his arm. "Forgive my late arrival. Time slipped away from me." A small smile graced her beautiful face, but it didn't quite reach her eyes.

"No doubt time with the Degasus is more exhilarating than a status report of the Realm." Lucifer said.

Her focus sharpened with a golden spark. "Nothing is more important to me than the Realm, my lord."

He grabbed a fist full of braids and gently brought her closer. "One day I will hold that honor," he whispered.

To his surprise, she nodded and whispered, "Maybe one day."

Pleased she was softening toward him, he let the braids slip through his hand. She was critical to his success and his vision for the Realm's future. The Fallen admired her and would follow her into battle. He'd need her leadership on the battlefield soon. Focusing his attention back to the Princes, he had studied their faces from the beginning of time, watched them grow into their powerful roles. Their tells and the things which brought them pleasure or disgust were clear to him. As he studied them now, he found a mixture of impatience, adoration, and excitement. Something else lurked underneath the room's energy. A brief undercurrent of animosity, sharp and poignant, gone as quickly as it surfaced. He straightened in his chair and remembered the unsettling shift, something he hadn't felt since Sonneillon.

Are one of you seeking to fill the traitor's shoes or was there always two of you?

Underestimating me will be your demise and my victory...

"My Queen and I are ready for the status from each of the Realms. We'll soon be at war with our enemies and must be on high alert to move at a moment's notice. Beelzebub, share the triumphs of your Realm." He leaned forward in his seat as if attentive to his words, but the disgust hovering within him pulled his attention away, back to when he'd cracked in front of them not so long ago.

Despicable.

His hand curled into a fist at his side, not able to deny his actions when he'd fled his Throne Room on Abaddon's back. The dragon had flown him high above the Realm and into the far-reaching corners, where he unleashed all his pent-up emotions and flung it out over the ash and smoke. He considered taking it out on a Damned or getting lost in Asmodeus's debauchery, but prying eyes would see this and take notice. They couldn't doubt his sanity or grip on his emotions. It would have led to discontent, and he'd already dealt with that... or had he?

In the end, he tackled it alone. Once all his conflicts were exhumed from within, clarity seeped into the void. Little things he hadn't concerned himself with before tickled his subconscious. He brought them to light and examined their possibilities for truths gone unnoticed. With this clarity came a heightened vision, a clearer path to the future...

And a lurking shadow standing in my way.

With a magnified mental lens, he checked the cracks and fissures of each of his Princes. Each examination brought the possibility each would be motivated to conspire with Sonneillon, except for one.

Mammon. There was no falsehood about her. She was cold, ruthless and didn't fight for attention because she knew she already had it.

I like it.

"The Greed Realm has doubled the souls brought here with our renewed efforts on Earth. Humans hunger for more money and few have qualms about how to achieve it. We give them what they want even though they know the cost." Mammon stepped back, her gaze level with his.

"I'm very pleased with—" Lucifer paused when a portal opened at the back near Tannin's pool. The Princes turned, each resting their hands on top of their chosen weapon, but Lucifer recognized Zar's platinum hair emerging from within.

"Looks like Zar barely escaped again," Asura said as she started down the stairs.

A female scream erupted through the portal's opening. Zar arched, face etched in pain. He turned and stumbled to the floor. Raising his hand, Zar shot a blast of green energy into the portal, silencing the scream before the portal closed.

"Lucifer." Zar said before he collapsed at the pool's edge.

Lucifer took flight with Asura behind him. When he landed, an angelic knife was embedded in Zar's back.

"Guardians," Lucifer hissed as he bent down to pull the knife out. Asura knocked his hand away, pushing herself between them. "What are you doing? The knife must come out for him to heal."

All the Princes had gathered near where Zar lay. "Don't touch it! Look at his feathers." Asura pointed to Zar's back. "They're sizzling, melting as they fall out. There's poison in the blade, maybe the handle as well."

"How dare they!" Lucifer aimed his hand, palm out, at the knife. An energy beam took hold of the handle, pulled it out and flung it against the wall, and set it aflame. Red fire consumed the knife, melting it until nothing was left. His gaze shifted to Zar, who laid still at his feet. Lucifer knelt down and nudged his shoulder. "Zar... wake up."

After a moment, Zar moaned through blood crusted lips.

"We have to do something quick or he will die." Asura bent down beside him.

"I can only think of one thing. Stand back—all of you." Lucifer commanded. He pulled out his knife and plucked a feather from under his wing. "If it's not too late," he muttered.

"I'll hold him down," Asura said, glancing between the feather and knife. "If it works, it will burn like hell."

"Better than death," Lucifer shifted over the top of Zar.

Asura moved to the front of Zar. Using both her hands, she pressed down on his shoulders and nodded at Lucifer. The knife's edge glinted as he brought it to his hand. With a quick slash across his palm, blood bloomed and dripped off the side. Lucifer put the palm above the open wound and let the blood flow into it. Zar twitched, his skin sizzling as it accepted the blood. Lucifer clenched his fingers into a fist and forced more blood into the wound.

"That's it," Asura exclaimed. "A little more..."

Lucifer's nostrils flared, anger burning inside at those who attacked Zar. When enough blood had seeped into the wound, he slammed the feather's quill into the wound as far as it would go. Zar arched again as the ebony feather dissolved into the gash. His blood-curdling scream left Lucifer wondering if the potion was too much. Convulsions shook Zar's body. Leviathan rushed over and bent down, his large hands clamping down on Zar's calves.

"What is happening to him, my lord?" Leviathan asked.

"By entering my lifeblood into his, along with a healing feather, the poison should dissolve and give him a chance to survive. If not, he'll be dead soon." Lucifer wondered if he was too late as he watched Zar's body slowly stop its spastic movements. Water lapping against the pool's edge was oddly deafening against the hushed quiet from the Princes. Asura's head fell as if she'd accepted Zar's fate.

"Get your hands off of me or I'll cut them off." Zar uttered.

Asura and Leviathan released their grip and stepped back. Zar slowly sat up, wincing his back. "What happened? I feel like I've been thrown into a pit with Hell Hounds."

"You tell us," Lucifer said, trying to hide the relief in his voice. "I was holding a meeting in the Throne Room when you came through your portal with a knife in your back."

Zar ran his hand through his sweat drenched hair. "I can't remember—"

"A woman was screaming from the other side," Asura touched his arm. "She may have been the one who stabbed—"

"Camilla," Zar's upper lip peeled back. "She'll pay for that."

"Whoever this Camilla is, almost killed you with a poison laced blade." Zar turned his head towards Leviathan, who put out a helping hand. "Welcome back." Zar took his hand and rose slowly, scanning the room.

"Camilla is Sergio's grandmother and former Guardian." A volley of outrage and questions rained down on Zar, but Lucifer raised his hand.

"Quiet! Let him speak." Zar faced Lucifer and waited until the silence was complete.

"As you ordered, I went to discover more about the Guardians. I went to Sergio's house when it was empty, and the goons weren't around and searched their rooms. Before I could finish, their grandmother returned early. I was about to kill her when a goon Angel from the Kingdom of Temperance arrived."

"I can't wait to battle them and—"

"The pleasure was mine, Gressil. He's dead. There're others from your old kingdom you can battle." She growled and stormed away, cracking her orange whip against the stone walkway.

"After I finished him off, I opened my portal to escape before more arrived. The last thing I remember was her scream and fire stabbing me in my back. And now, a different fire fades from inside my body." Zar cocked his head. "Did you save me?"

"Yes," Lucifer replied. "Now tell me what you learned."

"What we knew was true. They passed the Guardians' powers down through the families."

Lucifer took a step closer. "Are there more of them waiting for us?"

"When I asked her, she refused to answer, but I sensed her confusion and denial. I don't believe there are other Guardians. I'd stake my life on it."

"We can't trust his *belief* in something. There's too much at stake!" Berith shouted, putting his hand on his sword's hilt. "And with the death of Jehidiel and the witness he left behind, they'll know *we* are behind it. You should have let him die."

Once more, Lucifer raised his hand. "I sent him because his presence wouldn't be such a cause for alarm. They are all well aware of his desires to get revenge. Unlike if I were to send one of you." Lucifer weighed Zar's words carefully before speaking. When he came to his conclusion, it really didn't matter if Zar was correct.

"Learn anything else of interest before I decide what to do?"

"I did, my lord." The corner of Zar's mouth lifted in a sly grin. "I know exactly when and where all the Guardians will be together, in public, for us to grab and erase from the world."

A jolt of excitement ripped through Lucifer. "Tell me."

"Their graduation from high school. We can get them there before they even know what hit them."

This was the information he needed. What he waited to hear for so long.

"You've done well, Zar. With this knowledge, we can do what we've wanted to do since He shoved us down the Mar of Sin. We'll not only take the Guardians. We'll strike first and start our war against the Heavens. It is time for the Fallen to take back what we've lost and build a new world for us!"

War cries erupted around him. Lucifer absorbed their adulation as he allowed the full force of his vision to unfold.

"Go ready your Realms! Gather the Damned! Our victory is soon at hand!"

CHAPTER
THIRTY-SEVEN

CAMILLA

Awareness came to Camilla as the light's warmth caressed her face. Her eyes fluttered open, resisting a heaviness beckoning her back to a safe darkness. She sunk back into her pillows and turned her head away from the source of light, too bright for her dry eyes. There she found Javier's gaze upon her. Heavy lines creased his forehead and dark circles revealed a sleepless night.

"Mama," he whispered. "How do you feel? We were so worried about you." He grabbed her hand and brought it to his lips, dropping a light kiss across her knuckle.

"Oh, *hijo,* I'll be fine, but—I couldn't save him." Tears sprung and leaked from the corners of her eyes when she shut them tight, trying to stop the memories threatening to drag her back to the terrible moment when Zar plunged his sword through the Angel's heart. "I was too late." Her sob tore free, but the grip around her heart only tightened.

"Shhh. You're safe here with the Magi." Javier's muscular arms wrapped around her and brought her against his chest. She inhaled his musky scent while her hands clutched his soft t-shirt. The ever-present wall between them slipped, bringing forth tears from her grief. She'd desperately missed her son, the rock in her life since her husband died. The wall between them held no appeal, leaving her with the only option left. Share the truth about the night of his father's death. Javier stroked her back and rocked her quietly until her tears dried up.

"*Lo siento.*" Camilla tried to pull away, but he didn't release her.

"You have nothing to be sorry for. He died protecting you and would do it again, even if he knew the outcome."

She knew he was right, but it didn't ease the heartbreaking loss of an Angel. Another freeze frame memory surfaced through her haze, bringing with it a spike of joy.

"I hope I killed him." This time when she pulled away, Javier released her and helped her lay back against the bed.

"Killed who? What happened?" He asked, pushing her hair away from her face.

She didn't answer immediately as the frightening memory washed over her. "*Por favor, necesito agua.*"

Javier nodded and quickly brought a glass to her lips. She drank greedily, relishing the cool liquid soothing her throat. "*Gracias.*" Her fingers grazed her neck, the silky material comforting her. She exhaled deeply, knowing her time had come to tell the truth.

"I returned—"

The door opened, and Sergio's head peaked around the corner. "*Abuela?*" When their eyes locked, he threw open the door and rushed inside, followed by Lucia, Zach, and Olivia. Javier stepped back when her two grandchildren sat on the edge of the bed. Lucia leaned over and hugged her.

"*Nieta*, you're choking me," Camilla chuckled as Lucia loosened her hold.

Big brown eyes raked over her. "We were so worried about you! Michael summoned us and told us about the attack. Are you okay... hurt—"

"Slow down." Camilla ran her hands up and down Lucia's arms. "I'm fine. A little sore and my head hurts. Don't worry any more, *si?*"

Everyone nodded, but Sergio radiated an anger that she needed to squelch. "Who hurt you?" He asked.

She licked her lips, knowing her revelation would turn the room into chaos. "I will tell you all I remember, but you must promise me you'll not do anything rash. Because what I have to say is more than about what happened." The room grew still. It didn't take much of a leap for them to think it was Zar, but she needed them to be calm.

"Go ahead, Mama. We'll all behave," Javier winked.

She closed her eyes and sent up a prayer for peace.

"I left for the cemetery and library like I always do, but I forgot a book in Lucia's room. I came inside and was grabbed from behind. When he turned me around and pinned me to the wall, I recognized him from your descriptions. It was Zar."

It was as if a bomb went off with no sound and slammed against Camilla in waves of unspoken outrage.

"I knew it," Sergio sneered. "How—"

Lucia squeezed Sergio's knee. "What did he say—was he looking for us?"

"Zar asked me a question, and I found it odd. Of all the questions he could have about us, he wanted to know if there were more Guardians. Those black pits of his were inches from my face. It was like he could still see my face. I told him I would never answer his questions." She left out the part about his slap. "He must have been searching the house because he found my knife under my pillow. Taunted me about being a past Guardian... too old now to be useful anymore." Camilla chuckled, remembering his cry of surprise before his energy force slammed her into the wall.

"He certainly doesn't know you well at all."

Camilla glanced at Javier and found a knowing smile softening his worry lines. "I made him pay for his disrespect."

"*Bueno.* I would expect nothing less."

"What did you do? Please tell me you killed him." Lucia's face was so hopeful, Camilla wished she knew if the poison had worked.

"The Angel arrived and tossed him onto the table. He pushed me into my room for safety, but I was so mad. I unsheathed my knife from under the pillow and went back into the living room, only to see

Zar plunge his sword through the Angel's heart. Zar turned and laughed at me as he raised his portal. Called me an old woman before he stepped inside. I couldn't believe this evil had come into our home and killed an angel who had only been trying to protect us from harm. Fury boiled, and I screamed at the closing portal, hurtling my blade at him. I felt great satisfaction when I heard his cry. He sent an energy blast through the portal that hurled me into the wall and I blacked out."

"Good for you, *Abuela*. He'll never forget you." Lucia wrapped her long fingers around her grandmother's hand and squeezed.

Camilla thought about the dichotomy of Lucia's youthful hand comforting hers compared to her smaller hand, marking the passage of time with the dark spots and veins riddling its surface. "I may be past my prime, but I still have a few tricks up my sleeve. I laced the blade with poison, so unless he got help as quickly as Olivia did, your wish may come true."

Whoops and hollers filled the room as Lucia snatched her into another bone-crushing hug. "*Guerrera feroz*," she whispered into Camilla's ear before pulling away.

Camilla laughed, but a stab of pain in her ribs made her flinch.

"Mama," Javier rushed to her side. "Lay back and rest. We'll go—"

"No, please. I'm fine. I need to tell you something else and I want you all here when I say it. I wish Balthazar and Gabriel were here, too. What I have to share includes them, but I guess they'll find out soon enough."

Camilla remembered Gabriel emerging in Olivia's backyard, his gold wings fluttering in the wind, a memory filled with the joy of his miraculous recovery. Her heart flip-flopped in her chest as she recalled looking up at Sam; her friend, her confidant, her fellow Guardian. Conflicting emotions tussled inside her, nervous to unpack her feelings dormant for decades.

A knock on the partially open door pulled her away from the past. "You called... May I come in?" Bal's request coincided with a gold orb opening in the room. Gabriel emerged, ticking Camilla's rapid pulse higher.

"Of course." Camilla replied. Between Bal and Gabriel's imposing bodies, the oversized bedroom suddenly felt small. She'd thought of Gabriel before and he never appeared. Now that he was here, all she wanted to say clogged up in her throat.

"It's so good to see you well. You gave us a scare.' Gabriel laid a hand on her shoulder, sending a soothing heat through her body.

"I'm so sorry about—"

Darkness shadowed his face. "Evil caused his death, not you. He'll be remembered for his bravery and dedication to humankind. You've quite the audience here." He smiled and glanced around the room. "Is there another reason for this gathering?"

The room grew quiet, waiting for her response. She twisted the sheet between her hands as she struggled with how to begin. Backing down now wasn't an option. She licked her dry lips and prayed she wouldn't make things worse.

"Thank you both for coming. After my run-in with Zar, I realized I needed to clear the air about what happened to me long ago. I've made some grave mistakes for which I'm forever sorry. Zar coming into our home must mean Lucifer is desperate or close to starting a war. Either way, I hope what I have to share will help the young Guardians face this evil and the sacrifices it will demand, and forgiveness from those I love." Her gaze turned to Javier. He tensed, a protective mask slipped into place.

"You've always been so wise, *Abuela*."

"Oh Lucia, that comes with age and hindsight. When I was a young Guardian, my emotions and stubbornness blinded me, especially when it came to family."

Her fingers trembled as she reached up and untied the scarf around her neck. Cool air brushed across the skin, only ever uncovered when she slept. She lifted her chin and exposed the scar she'd left to remind her of her mistakes. Lucia gasped and Camilla didn't blame her. She knew the jagged scar marring her skin was startling.

"Where did you get that? How—"

"In a battle that almost killed her." She didn't miss the disappointment in Gabriel's response, but was surprised by his gentle touch. "And took her husband."

"What is he talking about?" Javier raked his hand through his hair. "Papa was mugged, killed for his watch and money. I'm sure a Fallen was part of it. You should have sensed it and been at his side."

She nodded, letting his words tear open the wound, never quite healed. "I was." She muttered.

Javier stumbled back as if her simple revelation had shoved him. His faced paled as he shook his head. "But that memory wasn't given to me."

"No. I begged Bal to block it from you. I didn't want you to see my failure and your Papa's demise."

"I'm confused," Sergio blurted out, starting a low rumble of voices around the room.

"Let her finish," Bal's deep voice returned the room to silence. "You'll understand when she's done." He nodded at her and she returned the sentiment.

Camilla ignored the anger vibrating from her son and pushed forward.

Please let him understand and forgive me...

"I wasn't very good at juggling being a Guardian, parent and wife. There were times where I didn't give my family the best of me, especially as we all got older. When Javier went to high school, I understood that my time was nearing its end. I wanted to do as much as I could, rid the world of as much evil as my time allowed me. With that singular focus, I was gone far too much, especially at night. You were busy with sports and girls, but your Papa became lonely and—"

"Papa would never cheat on you! I won't believe—"

"He had a mistress. It was the horses. I didn't know until his gambling had gone too far."

Javier's shoulders slumped; sadness replaced his anger.

"I'm sorry, *hijo*. His demise was my fault." Camilla held back tears that were too late to shed. "Your father was a good man, but everyone has their breaking point. Gambling filled the hole left by my absence. He didn't seek this addiction. Instead, it took control as time marched on."

"How did you not see it and stop it in time?"

Camilla slumped deeper into the pillow, wishing it would swallow her up and deny the pain and shame of this moment. "I've asked myself that question every day since his death, raked myself over the coals for missing it. All I can say is he took care of the money, so I never saw the money dwindle away. I also never felt a demon with him... until the end. He also didn't want me to know. We had gotten very good at living on the edges of our marriage instead of working with each other to make it the most important treasure in our world. I took for granted his patience, love for me and my mission. I fully accept the blame. I hope you can understand, on some level, the delicate balance of our lives."

Javier's silence was crushing, as was the flexing muscle in his jaw. She'd hoped she said something that would strike home, help him understand her better.

"Marriage is the fabric of my life; the edges may fray or dull, but I could never cut it in half, making myself the most important piece. I wanted more for me and Sofia." Javier sighed. "But I'd be an arrogant fool to think I haven't hurt her or that she wasn't lonely. We aren't perfect in this world. Tell us the rest."

Relief loosened her inner knots, freeing up some of her doubts. "I came home late from a battle. When I went to the bedroom, the essence of a demon drifted around him. I woke him up and asked him where he'd been and he said nowhere, but I knew it was a lie. I told him a demon had been near him, but he continued to deny any wrongdoing. We fought... I saw the guilt on his face. He told me not to worry about him and to leave him alone. His words cut me, but I didn't let it go. I searched our bank accounts and found money missing, along with a few crumbled betting receipts in his pockets. I continued as before, but I didn't go hunt. Unknown to him, I stayed close to home to watch over him. After a week, he finally left the house one night. I followed him to a casino parking lot. Guilt clutched me as my fears came to life. He was gambling. Before he got too far, two men emerged from the shadows, each with a demon latched onto them. An argument broke out, so I called my armor and went to battle. I fought the Fallen inside the bubble. Anger and fear dulled my moves as the men shoved him around. I killed one gluttony demon, but when your papa cried out, I turned in time to see a punch land on his jaw. The force—" Camilla closed her eyes to shut out the brutal image, "—sent him off balance and reeling backward. His head hit the concrete with a sickening thud. In my horror, I froze, the Sloth demon forgotten. She jumped on my back, pinned me to the ground... cackled in my ear that I would watch him die before she killed me. Her talon dug into my flesh, ready to tear open my throat. I couldn't fight back, and in that moment, didn't care. His eyes stared lifelessly back at the sky, the men escaping into the shadows. She whispered *too late* into my ear and slit me open."

"But you're here?" Lucia's quizzical gaze matched the question Camilla had many times asked herself.

How did I survive?

"Only because Gabriel arrived. The demon portaled away in time, thinking she'd completed her tasks. Between my healing and Gabriel laying his hands on my wound, I survived. But it was too late for *Abuelo*. And I never forgave myself. At first, all I wanted was revenge. I'd hunt, but the guilt of leaving you alone was too much. So I backed away, and Sam and Helen took over most of the duties. Sam was also learning about his wife's illness. We leaned on each other and our friendship got me through some dark times. I'd hoped that after you became a Guardian, you would understand this bond and know there was never anything more between Sam and I. In my healing, I realized I had a new purpose. To help you and your future family, never be left alone. That's all I've ever wanted, Javier. To protect those I love. And I did. The Sloth Fallen that arrived in

Lucia's room was the same one that attacked me. We fought, but it was Manny who killed her."

"It all makes more sense now. I thought you lived with us because I was handicapped, but it was deeper," Lucia said. "But why did you feel like Gabriel was mad at you?"

She grabbed her granddaughter's hand and squeezed. "I thought the shame I felt would extend to everyone, even an Angel. He tried to help me, but I shut him out... said some hurtful things to drive him away. And it worked. He gave me the space I desired. But when you love someone, doing what they ask can come at a significant cost to oneself."

Unchecked tears finally spilled down her cheeks. Exhaustion swamped Camilla. The emotional release of her story left her limp. Had she made herself clear? Did they understand how sorry she was for all her mistakes?

A soft thud landed next to her. She turned her head and found Javier's blurred face as he kneeled next to the bed.

"Why didn't you tell me this before?" His voice cracked. "I had a right to know the truth."

"At the time, I thought it best to keep the dark side out of it. Your guardianship was coming, and I didn't want it tainted with hate or revenge."

"I get that, *Abuela*," Sergio said. "My feelings about Manny's death almost ruined my chance to be a Guardian. I'm glad Papa didn't have to feel the same as me."

Javier reached around Lucia and cupped Sergio's neck. "You make me proud... both of you."

"All of you have put your lives at risk for a greater good. When Zar came into our home and attacked me, I felt in my bones that everything our lineage has fought for is coming to its ultimate challenge. Lucifer is coming for mankind. He wants this world gone and to destroy Heaven. You all will graduate soon and can go your separate ways, yet still be Guardians. I urge you to stay close, trust one another completely, and never give up. Each of you are in my prayers.

But never forget, there will be sacrifices you'll have to make and the cost may be great in order to defeat evil."

"Thank you for sharing this with us. We're in this together and graduation doesn't change a thing. We're ready for Lucifer and the Fallen. We have the Angels with us, so I think Lucifer will lose it all again." Lucia leaned down and hugged Camilla. Her heart swelled with the love she felt from her granddaughter. "We love you."

Camilla pulled away and smiled. "Me too. Now shoo... let me rest these weary bones."

Everyone left the room with a chorus of goodbyes, except Javier, who hung back.

"I'll be back to check on you." Yet, he didn't move. She held her breath, fearing he was about to unleash his unhappiness on her. "Mama—"

"You don't have to say—"

"I'm sorry about the past. I can't change it. I don't know if knowing about Papa would have changed me as a Guardian, but as a parent now, I understand why you did it. Even though my emotions are so conflicted, I want us to move forward. The kids need us. That's what's important."

"Right before Zar plunged his sword into the Angel, he said war was coming and that they wouldn't lose this time. Whatever Delilah told them has given them a confidence that worries me. I'm scared for them—all of us."

"The Guardians will do their part to make sure that doesn't happen. Sleep well, Mama."

Javier slipped out the door quietly. She sighed and drew the covers up to her neck. Her fingers ran along her scar, raising goose-bumps along her flesh.

But at what cost, hijo?

How many will we lose in order to defeat evil?

CHAPTER
THIRTY-EIGHT

OLIVIA

O livia slumped against the metal seat, the tassel swinging on the right side of her graduation cap. The arena was packed with cheering parents and excited graduates whispering about their future festivities. Soon, this season of life would be behind her and she could fully concentrate on Lucifer's war. She reflected on her high school years: soccer team, her injury, her friendships, the classes she liked and didn't like. Becoming a Guardian overshadowed everything. All the memories were amazing except they were shrouded by her dad's absence. It tossed her world upside down when he returned, but his arrival made her confront her anger and resentment. When the burden of those emotions lifted, it opened her world with a fresh lens.

And fully become a Guardian

Ironically, it was Miss Thomas's turn at the podium when it was time to call out her name. She grinned at Olivia when she walked past to collect her diploma. Miss Thomas may have pushed Olivia's buttons at times, but at least she'd cared enough to approach her when she noticed a change in her behavior. Her actions may not have shown it, but Olivia knew Miss Thomas had the best intentions. She remembered the loud cheer that went up when Olivia's name was called. The three families sat together and clapped like a proud clan. Camilla had fully recovered over the past week and sat happily wedged between Sergio's parents, clapping and cheering. Zach's family waved long, foam glow sticks wildly in the air. Dad stood up and whistled with a smile so big his face should have cracked. Sam and Mom clutched each other in a big hug. Tears filled her eyes, touched by the delightful pleasure she felt from their tremendous support.

She twirled the rolled fake diploma in her hand as she scanned the area around the large semi-circular stage. Zach stood not too far to her left in a long line down the aisle, waiting to make his way to the backstage entrance. She could find him anywhere, even dressed in a cap and gown. It was an energy between them, an invisible tether connecting mind, body, and soul. As if sensing her, he turned, and they locked eyes. She smiled and sent him a finger wave. His handsome face stretched into a wide grin. Her face flushed, knowing their relationship together was as much a part of her future as the Guardianship.

"I love you," he mouthed.

"Love you, too," she whispered, not caring if anyone around them noticed. She turned her attention back to the brightly lit stage. Rows of metal chairs filled with members of the faculty faced the crowd. Tall pillars created from school-colored balloons stood in front of the massive, drawn black velvet curtains. Olivia couldn't help but chuckle at the on-stage antics of some students. Most walked tall and waved at the crowd while others strutted or did a little dance. A part of her wished she felt that carefree. Even with all the distractions, she couldn't shake the feeling of something unholy in the air.

Something is wrong...

I can sense it...

But what is it?

She'd been nervous all day, but it wasn't about the ceremony. Their last mediation into Hell had been quick and shocking. The hive was working as one at a fevered pitch. The skies were so full of Lessors and Fallen, it felt like she was dodging them even though she wasn't physically there. They'd never seen such intense activity there before, which explained why their hunts had been essentially fruitless. The Fallen were staying close to home, and that definitely wasn't normal. The Guardians decided to keep their links open to each other in case something bad happened and they needed to find each other quickly. They couldn't take the risk anymore, their safety overrides their privacy.

When the ceremony is over, I want to meditate.

We have to get more info... maybe I should seek Delilah again?

Sergio emerged at the curtain's edge, pushing Lucia in her hot pink wheelchair. Olivia sat up straight, waiting for their names to be called.

"Lucia Camilla Mendes." Her name was met with a loud round of applause. Her beautiful smile graced the crowd as Sergio pushed her on stage.

"Sergio Juan—"

The arena was plunged into darkness. Cries of surprise rushed through the crowd. Olivia stood, heart pounding in her chest. Was this some prank or something more devious?

"Liv!" Zach called out as he pushed his way back towards her. She moved down her row towards him.

"Hey, watch it!" A girl cried out.

"Sorry," she whispered, but it didn't slow her down. Zach grabbed her hand, pulling her close.

"This doesn't feel right," He muttered as he scanned the building.

"I don't think so either, but my mark—"

Bright colors exploded across the arena's roof. The circles crackled, sending an ominous sizzling into the air. When the centers began to open, her mark flared on her chest. Heat billowed into the dark arena, smothering it with the putrid smell of sulfur and smoke. Panic erupted as people bolted from their seats, madly trying to reach their children or push their way to the exits. Horror ripped through Olivia when the first of Fallen emerged, careening down into the room like a flaming bird diving towards the crowds.

"They're here!" Zach cried out.

"And in the open. They want to be seen by us! Why here, why now?" A green portal bloomed on stage behind Sergio and Lucia.

"Because they're here for us."

"Hurry—we have to get to the stage!" Olivia shouted over the screams. A sudden heat scorched her back. She turned her head as a blue whip's electric end snaked through the portal and wrapped around her waist. An invisible force tugged the whip and pulled her toward the dark abyss, hissing from within. She pulled against with all her strength.

"Grab my hands!" Zach cried out. Her hands wrapped around his wrist. He pulled back, gaining momentary traction against the whip. The tugging around her waist only got stronger.

"I won't let you go. Don't you let go of me!"

She grunted against the force, feeling her hands slipping.

And then she was free. The whip around puffed into ashes and disappeared into the air. Zach stumbled back, absorbing her body being slammed into his with a shocked look on his face. "What the— Miss Thomas?"

Olivia turned and couldn't believe her eyes. Miss Thomas held a red sword gripped between her hands and red tipped wings erupting from her back. The portal sizzled closed.

"You—you're an Angel?" Olivia couldn't believe her eyes. "Why didn't you say anything?"

"You couldn't treat me any differently. We live among humans; our identities must remain a secret. Get out of here and do what you are called to do. Go... more help is coming!"

"Thank you." Was all Olivia could muster in her disbelief.

Miss Thomas winked and flew toward the melee.

"Armor on!" Olivia's sleek black armor materialized and wrapped around her body. Her sword, Sandalphon, and a dagger hung from her hip, throwing stars glistened on the harness around her chest. She and Zach shouldered their way through the panicked, wide-eyed teenagers, barely glimpsing at them as they shoved past. She felt her own panic rise as the Fallen snatched random people from the floor and flung them across the room. Bolts of lightning erupted from other Fallen, striking groups seeking escape. Olivia glanced up to where her parents had been. Through the filtered smoke, she found their row of empty seats. She didn't have time to be thankful or wonder if they made it outside.

"Look!" Zach pointed to the stage.

Zar emerged through the portal. Sergio's armor was wrapping around him as Lucia's body blurred between flesh and white fur. Zar grabbed her shifting form and dove back into the portal. Sergio's face was frozen in a snarl as he leaped in after them, his feet barely making it through before the portal snapped shut. Everyone had deserted the stage, folding chairs askew with papers scattering the floor. Lucia's wheelchair knocked over, vacant under the spotlight.

"No!" Olivia cried and raised her sword. "He has them!" She looked back at Zach and saw a green female Fallen charging him.

"Behind you!" He turned; their swords clashed in mid-air. She opened a portal behind him, trying to back him into it. Zach pushed back; their swords blurred into a flurry of metal. Olivia threw a star at the Fallen. It struck her cheek, momentarily distracting her, allowing Zach to deliver the killing blow through her chest. She exploded into ash; the portal slammed shut.

Olivia braced her feet, and she raised her hands. She pulled from the orb, channeling the elements within her. Blue bolts of flames shot into the air, aimed at the demons shamelessly attacking those still desperate to escape. The flames licked across the Fallen's wings, leaving a singed path as it danced over their armor. Their cries of delight changed into shrieks of pain. Some portaled out, while others fell to the ground. Zach joined the fight, launching green, glistening boomerangs that sliced through their bodies. This took the attention off the people below, but put an even bigger bullseye on them.

"Faster!" yelled Zach.

Olivia moved in a circle and pushed more fire through her hands, trying to create a barrier around them. She wasn't sure how much longer they could hold them off when new orbs brightened the arena. They exploded into glorious Angels, bathed in white armor, weapons raised high. Weapons of all types clashed as good and evil battled above them. Bursting kaleidoscope of colors erupted above them like the grand finale of a firework show. As quickly as the Fallen arrived, they soon retreated from the fight, diving through portals closing behind them. The Angels hovered in the air; weapons raised for the Fallen's return. Cheers burst from those inside, their faces pictures of awe. A wave of peace flowed down from the Angels. Some people fell to their knees, clinging to one another in relief. Others cried out for their loved ones as the frantic search began.

An Angel dove for them, gold streaking from the white wings. Zemira landed in front of them, her flaming gold sword in her hand.

"Excellent work using your elements. You saved many today." Olivia's Guardian Angel nodded at both of them. The three scars marring the skin over her milky eye crinkled as the other eye sparked with gold. "I'm very proud of you both, but this is just the beginning."

"Thank you," Olivia exhaled, trying to settle her racing heart. "Your arrival made the Fallen retreat. Lucifer's started his war and took Sergio and Lucia."

"We can't stay here. A new wave of Fallen could appear." Zach tugged on her arm. "We have to tell the Archangels about Lucia and Sergio."

"I'll stay here in case they reappear, but I won't be far from you today. Now go." Gold swirled in Zemira's white armor before her wings lifted her in flight.

Grief squeezed her heart as they ran for the exit. Are Sergio and Lucia already dead or hostages somewhere for Lucifer to torture? Anger blurred her vision, but determination pumped in her veins. They would find their friends and make sure Zar never touched another soul ever again.

Michael...

Zach shoved the metal door open, bathing them in bright sunlight. She inhaled the fresh air, needing to cleanse the Fallen's reek. Her brow furrowed as she scanned the eerily quiet skies while havoc rained around them. People ran to their cars, crying and hugging each other over the nightmare that had destroyed what was supposed to be a day filled with treasured memories. The parking lot became a traffic jam. Cars honked and drivers yelled out their windows in their desperation to flee. Accidents clogged the arteries of escape. Some stayed inside their cars while other fled on foot.

"I don't see our parents." Olivia raised her hand to shade her eyes. She found her dad's truck still in the space where he'd parked it.

"I'm sure they escaped through a portal to Magiland. We made sure they always had their talisman with them." He squeezed her hand. "They'll be safe there no matter what happens today."

She nodded, but tension coiled inside. "We can't just stand here. Lucia and Sergio are gone. Zar took them to Lucifer. I don't want to think about what's happening to them. If Delilah told him what she knows, he won't kill them. He needs us to open the Mar of Sin. The Fallen will be back for us soon."

"Maybe we can use that to our advantage. Set a trap—"

Michael, Gabriel, and Raphael appeared before them, their white armor a beacon of hope. Olivia flung herself into Michael's open arms. "They're gone. Zar snatched Lucia from her wheelchair right on the stage. Sergio dove through the portal after her. The Fallen tried to get us, but we escaped." She pulled herself away. "We have to go after them."

"We'll return them to you."

Olivia stepped back in disbelief. "I'm not staying here. I'm going with you. This is what we've trained for—this day! I'm not hiding any longer from Lucifer or the Fallen! He wants a war, he's got it."

Michael regarded her with little emotion. "If any of the Guardians die, then the ability to open and close the portals dies, too. Hell is too dangerous and unpredictable."

Olivia crossed her arms, unwilling to accept her plight.

"Are we supposed to stand around and wait?"

"We don't know when or if Lucifer will strike again. Go to the Magi. Your parents are there. You can prepare for the next stage." Raphael said.

The skies grew dark behind the Archangels. Black clouds billowed and bloomed as if blown by a mighty force. Michael, Gabriel, and Raphael turned, the wind blowing back their hair. The center grew open like a massive mouth yawning, ready to exhale the foulness within it. But no gentle breath exhaled, instead smoke and fiery rocks spewed from the gaping hole.

Leaving Olivia wondering if Hell wasn't coming to them first.

CHAPTER
THIRTY-NINE

SERGIO

N *ot again.*
   I swore I'd never return...
But Zar, snatching Lucia off the stage, changed everything.

Smoke burned his eyes, and the Fallen's screeches bombarded his ears, but there was no way he was letting go of Lucia's leg. Zar glared back and snarled at him, but could do little else but hold on to his tenuous grip on Lucia. Her shift complete, she roared and lifted her paw. She took a swipe at Zar, but missed as he released her, leaving them free falling through a massive opening in a roof. He remembered this building. It was Lucifer's tower—his domain—and they were streaking right for it. Stone walls blurred as they hurled toward the floor, precariously close to a dark pool of water. He prepared for impact, hand on his sword's hilt, hoping he could still fight when they landed. Lucia's angry roars told him she was ready for battle as well.

And then they jerked to a stop, suspended above the floor. Lucifer was laughing below them with his hands raised. Sergio tugged at his sword, but he couldn't move. Fear rippled through him as he tried again. They were stuck inside some kind of suspension force... at Lucifer's mercy.

"Welcome back, Sergio. Miss me?" Lucifer chuckled as he slowly brought Sergio to the floor.

"Never!" Sergio yelled inside his echo chamber. He glanced over, expecting to find Lucia next to him. He gasped when she wasn't there. She was being lifted over the pool. Sergio fought against the invisible force, but nothing he did penetrated it. He couldn't even put his hands together to make an air bomb. He was as helpless as Lucia, hovering over the water, growing turbulent beneath her. Black ropes materialized from the ceiling, spinning down to her like vines. The tiger blurred and Lucia appeared without armor. Sergio feared she must not be able to call up her armor inside the force field. The ropes snaked around her wrists, wrapping her body and ending at her feet.

"No!" Sergio screamed as he was yanked toward a huge stone pillar and pinned against it. He seethed as the same type of ropes lashed him onto it.

"You won't escape so easily this time." Lucifer dropped his arms to his side, releasing whatever beam was holding him.

"You won't get away with this. They'll come for us." Sergio wrestled against the ropes, to no avail.

"That's exactly what I'm counting on." Lucifer smirked and walked up the stairs, greeting the black dragon waiting for him at the top. Sweat broke out on Sergio's brow as he remembered being chased out of Hell by the same beast. The one who almost burned Gabriel alive. As if it had read his thoughts, the dragon sent a fireball through the open roof.

"I think Abaddon remembers you. Tell me... did Gabriel survive the blast?" Lucifer ran his hand over the opaque scales, leaving a trail of ripples in its wake.

"Of course he did! It takes more than dragon fire to kill an Archangel." Sergio yelled, wrestling against the ropes. "He's ten times stronger than you could ever hope to be."

"We'll see about that. Zar, relieve him of his weapons." Lucifer flicked his wrist at Sergio. "And teach him some manners."

From behind him, Zar appeared and took Sergio's sword and dagger. He examined them each closely, like he had all the time in the world. Zar's hands on his weapons made him feel sick, vulnerable. He sent the sword skittering across the stone floor, landing at the foot of the fire pit running along the stairs. "I'll take this dagger as a souvenir of our time together. Too bad I don't have something of your brothers, but I think your sister will make up for that."

"Don't you touch her—" Zar's fist plowed into Sergio's stomach. The armor absorbed most of the blow, but his jaw took all of Zar's next punch.

"Sergio!" Lucia cried out. Sergio gasped for air as he looked up at her. Her eyes burned gold, but her efforts to free herself had done nothing but leave her swaying above the water.

Zar grabbed a fist full of Sergio's hair and cracked his head back against the pillar. He moved so close; Sergio could see the thin scars in his black eye sockets. "I'll do whatever I please to Lucia. She intrigues me. Maybe I'll keep her. Train the tiger... and the woman."

A red haze blurred the edges of Sergio's vision. He lashed out with his teeth, hoping to take a chunk out of Zar's smug face. He moved away quickly and rewarded Sergio's efforts with another blow to his cheek. The skin split, blood trickling down his face. Sergio's body vibrated with rage and the helplessness he hated feeling. How long had he dreamed of getting his chance at Zar? Here he was, so close and yet powerless once again to kill him.

"You'll pay for that, Zar!" Lucia's threat rained down from above. Sergio's heart swelled at her bravery, knowing she certainly felt the same as he did. He glanced at her again, horrified by the way she hung from the ceiling, her body so small against the great chasm of the room. Fallen dive bombed the open roof, catching his attention. The smoky skies were packed like flies swarming a carcass. He suddenly realized he didn't want Olivia and Zach to come for him or anyone else... The Fallen were ready this time.

The trap is set and we are the bait.

"I don't think so, tigress." A faint smile tugged at Zar's lips.

Water lapped over the pool's edges when a long, red fin glided across the surface. Long spines fanned across its back, testing the space beneath Lucia. Sergio watched her chest rise and fall rapidly as it made another pass. This time, it revealed itself. A serpent with reptilian eyes trained on Lucia. She struggled again, but the movement dropped her lower. She cried out as it swam beneath her, bringing the tall spines closer to her feet.

"Not yet, Tannin." Lucifer called out. "Your hunger will soon be satisfied."

Lucifer lifted his face toward the open roof. "Come."

And they did.

Seven huge Fallen flew inside. But these weren't just any Fallen. These were the Seven Princes Sergio had caught glimpses of during meditation. In person, their presence was completely dominating, each one dripping with the evil that nurtured their Realms. Sergio could only wonder how magnificent they were when they were Angels, closest to God among the Heavenly Hosts. Now they served Lucifer, who somehow, out matched them all. His evil was pure, his power over them unmatched. But Delilah had warned of a Dark Prince who could rival Lucifer. He sized each of them up, but found each lacking in the end.

"We've gotten what we longed for." Lucifer waved his arm at Sergio and Lucia as if they were shiny new trinkets. "Two are here. The others will come soon on the heels of the Angels, running to their rescue. Let them come or not." He shrugged. "We'll capture the other two on Earth if need be. They're only pawns in our war. They have no idea what we have built with our sweat—our blood. Our time for vengeance has finally come. There will be *no* mercy. There will be *no* escape. There will only be the death of our enemies on this day!" Spittle flew from his mouth as the Princes roared their approval. "Let us unleash the Damned."

Lucifer shot his fist into the air. The roof peeled away from the walls, like a tornado shredded it apart. Lucia's mouth hung open; her terror unheard in the noise. Sergio's throat felt raw as he screamed for her, his eyes unwilling to turn away from the sight of his sister becoming part of the carnage. When the skies cleared of wreckage, her body was as it was before; dangling from the ropes gripped now by claws of a gigantic Fallen. Sergio sagged against the ropes as the stench of Hell washed over him.

"Put her down! You have what you want!" Sergio just needed to keep Lucia alive until help came.

"You have no idea what I want... yet."

The ground beneath him shook as a deafening rumble seemed to come from all corners of Hell. With the roof gone, Sergio watched some of the mountain peaks explode, like they finally released the immense pressure from within. When the smoke and rock cleared, out poured flying beasts mirroring some Heavenly creatures Sergio had seen before. But these blazed with an unearthly fire. Landslides opened gaping cave entrances. What once were humans flowed out like a waterfall, scrambling over each and the arid landscape.

"Mammon. Berith. Ride your dragons to Earth. Take the Damned and Fallen from your Realms. Destroy all you see. When the Mar of Sin is opened, meet us in Heaven."

The two took flight into the frenzy above. Mammon mounted a black dragon with wings of blue flames. Berith climbed on a red dragon with black spines and a flaming tail. Lucifer opened a massive portal. Hordes of blue and red disappeared into the portal, coming from all directions. It felt like the flow of terror to Earth would never stop, but the portal finally shut, leaving the rest of the Fallen waiting for Lucifer's next move.

Anguish consumed Sergio. Bloodshed was about to happen, and there was nothing he could do to warn anyone.

"Oh, how I wish I was with them," Lucifer mused. "But I have some last-minute business to attend to that has plagued me for too long. Saxem, bring them in."

Blood rushed in Sergio's ears as he stared at the huge wooden doors beyond the pool. Who could possibly be on the other side?

When the doors swung open, Sergio's blood froze.

A disfigured mutant lumbered through the entrance, his body filling up the doorframe. Behind him, he pulled on a thick chain whose end remained hidden in the dark hallway. Anger flared when the traitor who started it all finally came into view.

Delilah.

CHAPTER
FORTY

DELILAH

The mutant lumbered in front of Delilah, half-dragging her down the hallway. There was no use in struggling against her destination. She scoffed at the irony of going back to the Throne Room, the place where she'd first told Lucifer about the Guardians and the Mar of Sin. As the massive doors yawned opened, she faced her destiny to confront Lucifer and the consequences of her actions for the last time. Her recklessness had been her demise. She could never have outplayed the ultimate evil. His place as ruler of Hell was entrenched the moment they landed. Becoming a Fallen would never make her an equal in their minds. He knew that and had played her naivety perfectly. He may have strung her up in the Main Hall and had Zar whip her, but her own rope of envy had bound her to defeat.

But she had one more card to play before her inevitable death.

Now was the time.

Unless the scene she was about to witness indicated it was too late.

Delilah tucked her head, keeping her face hidden behind her matted hair. What was once glorious red flaming hair surrounding her beauty now lay in dirty strings over her scarred face. Gaps between the strands allowed her to glance around the Throne Room. She jerked back, stumbling at her ominous fate. The roof was gone, exposing a sky thick with Fallen and Lessors. A girl dangled from a rope above a stalking Tannin while Sergio was lashed to a pillar.

"You—this is all your fault!" Sergio yelled at her, struggling against his restraints. "How could you betray us?" His panicked gaze darted to the dangling girl, exposing his vulnerability. Of course, Lucifer used a loved one to crush any resolve to fight against him.

Five of the seven Princes stood guard at the foot of the stairs where Lucifer and Asura lorded in front of Abaddon. The dragon snorted emitting, black smoke from its reptilian nostrils. Finally, her eyes fell on the Fallen next to Sergio.

Zar...

As the mutant had dragged her across the bridge, Zar stood frozen. Delilah wasn't sure if Zar realized his hand moved to his sword's hilt. Was it fear or a need to kill the creature who had caused him so much pain and shame? It didn't matter. He wouldn't come to her rescue or comprehend her motives. He made his position very clear. He fought hard to get back into Lucifer's good graces, and she wasn't worth risking his valuable place in the inner circle.

The last time Lucifer came for her, she thought she would draw her last breath. Instead, he freed her from the cage. He took her from the horrid mountain's depths, the swirling glow of the purple snake pit fading from her sight. His silence had been deafening, yet his anger at her was so red hot, it should have scorched her cold flesh. He didn't take her back toward the Realm. Another desolate mountain awaited. When the metal door of her new prison slammed shut, his fateful words still played in her ears.

"The next time I come for you, it will be your last."

She believed him.

The groans and cries from the Realm crashed down on her and overwhelmed her senses. She wanted to cover her ears, but it was useless with only one hand. Her recent days had been filled with damning thoughts running through her head or the echoes of the mutant's stomping when he made the rare occasion to check on her. He never said a word when he paused at her door, only cocked his head and glared at her with dead eyes. He would then return to his lair, leaving her relieved to escape the same torture he exacted upon Zar.

But death was coming. At whose hands was the question, she wasn't sure she cared about anymore. She had one mission left. One chance to possibly undo the harm she'd caused and maybe stop The Fallen from winning the war.

Her bare feet left the smooth walkway and crossed onto the stone floor. Tannin swam near the edge, its tail splashing hot water over her feet as if to say *don't forget about me*. A chill shot down her spine, knowing her destiny with death could very well lie in the serpent's belly. She remained silent as she passed Sergio, his hateful stare boring between her shoulder blades. Her platitudes couldn't undo what she'd done, but maybe she could change things with her actions.

"Delilah," Lucifer crooned. "I wish I could say it was good to see you, but your decline is not pleasing to the eye. It reflects your disloyalty." Asmodeus snickered, the feathers on her hot-pink wings ruffled as if preening at Delilah's hideous state. Delilah paid neither her nor the other Princes who held similar looks of disgust any attention. Under all their contemptuous glances, one of them lingered upon her. Was it curiosity she felt or a touch of unease?

You'll soon find out.

"As you can see, we have visitors today. I believe you know, Sergio and Lucia—both Guardians." Delilah glanced up at the girl; fear plainly etched on her face. "They're here because it's time for them to share their secrets. Once the others arrive, either by my Fallen or because they attempt to free their comrades, I will have them open their portals. You see, the war you so richly wanted to start with me has begun without you. Berith and Mammon have taken their Realms to Earth. The other Realms will join me in Heaven and then we'll finish off the human race together."

The mutant's ragged breathing grated on her nerves. Green electric sparks crackled from the ends of the rods embedded in both forearms. He seemed ready for the battle at hand. As Delilah listened to

Lucifer, she took stock of the Throne Room's master. He had already put his plan in motion and captured two Guardians. Yet there was still something missing, an anticipation as he leered down at her.

"What is she doing here?" Asura did little to disguise her hatred for Delilah. "I thought you killed her. She's done nothing but lie and manipulate you and the Realm—"

Lucifer snapped his head to Asura. "Silence. There's been much manipulation going on behind my back... games of deceit in the scramble for my throne. Don't think I don't know about who you meet up with when you're off with your Degasus." Asura's full lips pressed into a thin line as she stood defiantly next to Lucifer.

"I have nothing to hide from you, my lord."

Lucifer cocked his head as if he considered challenging her. Asura was many things, but Delilah believed her statement. "I think time is better served unpacking Delilah's secrets," he replied.

A cold grip of fear seized her when his eyes of fire landed on her. "The time has come for you to share your knowledge."

Delilah swallowed as she lifted her chin. Her hair fell away. She gazed at Lucifer with heated green eyes. "I have told you all I know about the Guardians."

"That information is useless to me now. You told me everything I needed the first day Zar brought you to me. After that, I kept you around to see who would come sniffing at your skirts for personal advantage. You were a toy to me. A simple pleasure and a beautiful lure to those who wished to gain power. And many came, didn't they?"

The room seemed to close in on her, as she knew her end was near. She'd been a colossal fool in thinking she'd evaded his spies, but she could still help Heaven.

"Yes."

The mutant's arm lifted; a green whip snapped at her feet. "Time to share, Angel. No more lies. No more tales about the Guardians. Give me the truth I desire." Lucifer sneered.

From the corner of her eye, Zar took a step forward. If only he still had eyes so she could read his motives. Would her admissions shock him or would they further his hate for her?

"I'll share what I know freely with you. I have kept many secrets, although most served only me. I thought coming here to you... to Hell —was my destiny. To finally be free of the restraints of being an Angel. In my fury at Conner, I wanted to do as I pleased and ruin him and all he loved. When I went through the Mar of Sin, I desperately wanted to become a Fallen, and share my knowledge to ensure your rule over Heaven and Earth. But it wasn't until I lay broken, snake bites slowly killing me, I came to a shocking realization. I was created for this moment. I was *meant* to bring you the knowledge and selfishly deny my original being so I could, when the war truly began, help the *Heavenly Hosts* to defeat you. And that's what I'm going to do."

Lucifer threw back his head and laughed into the smoky skies. "You're still so delightfully arrogant. I once found it charming." All humor left his face when he locked eyes with her again. This time, the mutant turned and lashed Sergio across the chest. He cried out, but his armor absorbed the whip's energy. "But I tire of you now and want my answers. Who were you working with?"

Delilah raised her arm and pushed the remaining strands away from her face, revealing the ragged scars of lashes and torture. She glanced at Asura, then scanned each Prince. A peace fell over her as she exhaled a final, deep breath.

Let it be done...

"I'll tell the truth you're looking for. You were wrong about the traitor's identity and killed the wrong Prince. The traitor is alive and in this room. He wants your place on the throne and will do anything to achieve his goal. Even steal another's soul. You'll never win the war because someone will always be there to ruin you." She raised her hand and aimed a single finger at her foe.

Lucifer stood, enraptured, not surprised by her revelation.

Asura's armor ignited in a golden swirl, her upper lip peeled back.

The Princes moved away, shock and disbelief at what they heard and who she condemned with her aim.

Zar crept slowly behind her, hand clutching his glistening dagger. She closed her eyes and braced herself for the jarring stab between her shoulder blades. It made sense to her that Zar would be the one to kill her. Lucifer probably gave it as another reward for bringing the Guardians to him.

It doesn't matter.

He'll make it quick...

CHAPTER
FORTY-ONE

DARK PRINCE

The Realm's noise of violence vibrated around the Dark Prince as it rained down from the open roof in the Throne Room. Lucia hung above Tannin's pool and Sergio's anguish was breathtaking. Mammon and Berith departed with their Realms through the portal. The sight was awe-inspiring, igniting the fires of built-up anticipation, born of his own bloodlust to rid the world of humans. Lucifer finally started his war, but soon he was in for a rude awakening. A power Lucifer could never comprehend would overtake him. All the plotting, the eons of waiting and pretending to be his ally, were about to end. The Dark Prince could almost taste Lucifer's blood when he imagined plunging his sword into Lucifer's heart... laughing at the surprise in his eyes that he'd killed the wrong traitor.

Our time has finally come.

No more hiding who we are.

Free to rule when we lead the Fallen to destroy Heaven.

He growled in response. His timing must be perfect in order to succeed.

"Go away. I need only my thoughts when I face Lucifer. I must do this without error." He felt the Ancient One slip out of his mind. For once, the soul had listened. It understood they would both die

269

today if they weren't careful. The Dark Prince had to play along only a little longer. Once the Mar of Sin opened, he would kill Lucifer in the chaotic vortex and emerge in Heaven with the Fallen behind him. They would follow him into battle, gaze upon his glorious dominance, and exult him as the new ruler when they won the war.

"Saxem. Bring them in." Lucifer's command brought him out of his visions. The Dark Prince turned when the enormous doors slowly swung open. His skin crackled with his Realm's vibrant energy as his eyes narrowed in expectation of Olivia and Zach emerging.

He was wrong.

The mutant lumbered inside, dragging the one person who could ruin all his well-laid plans.

Delilah...

She's not dead. He lied to me!

Did she tell Lucifer about me?

The scene played out before him. Lucifer, forever a puppet master, putting all his pieces in place. Whatever the Realm's master thought he knew; he wasn't prepared for the actuality of what was about to be exposed.

He *felt* the silence of the unknown pressing upon him.

He *watched* her pathetic form move over the bridge; felt her smug, icy gaze flicker over him.

He *listened* to the accusations slung between her and Lucifer; felt words of rage building behind his pressed lips.

He *smelled* her rank fear; felt the need to destroy all in the Throne Room burn inside of him.

"Who were you working with?" Lucifer asked.

She exhaled and shifted to face the Princes. His boiling fury at her treachery burst when she stared at him with a haughty peace in the lifting of her chin. She raised her hand; her accusing finger etched a path to his chest to expose his traitorous heart.

He touched the hardened flesh on his chest; felt his own peace about his rightful place as lord quiver beneath with the need to set it free.

"There you are." Lucifer's face twisted in disgust. "The coward finally shows his face. My oldest, most trusted ally has become my newest, most unworthy foe. The Prince of Pride succumbed to his urges, blinded by your assumption that no one can be better—do better than you."

"Here I am." Beelzebub's body crackled with gold as he faced Lucifer. "I *will* be a greater ruler of the Fallen than you ever could be. You brought us here, demanded our allegiance to you. And then what? You did nothing! We waited and played war games among ourselves, turned sinful humans into the Damned. And still nothing for thousands of years. All the while, you grew soft and complacent. Did you ever really want a war between Heaven and Hell? No. I think you just liked the power you had here and were ultimately afraid of losing another war."

"You really are a fool to think you are more powerful than I— smarter than I in the ways of war and leadership. It was me who was most supreme next to God, not you!" Lucifer yelled, his body growing into his truer, more evil form. When his transformation was complete, Beelzebub was certain he would overshadow him with a truly terrifying being.

"It isn't only I who comes to rid the Realm of its tired, pathetic ruler. I'm one with Symedek, the Dark Seraphim Angel who ruled over the Watchers... who had the courage to stand up to God and corrupt humans. I claimed his soul as mine—a soul who has made me more powerful, more ruthless than you ever will be."

Lucifer stepped forward as Abaddon rose behind him. Lucifer's face tightened in anger, but the flair of fire in his eyes flickered briefly with fear. "Not only are you a traitor, you're a liar. Symedek is gone, banished by God for his deeds against Him. There's no way you could have possession of his soul. No, you sowed your seeds of infidelity until I finally brought you out into the light." Lucifer sneered at him, placing his hand on his sword.

"You never even considered me—killed Sonneillon because you were blinded by Delilah's lies." The Dark Prince let the Ancient One stir inside of him. He wasn't afraid of Lucifer. It was the red glow coming to life in Abaddon's belly that he had to escape. The Princes moved away from him, not wanting to be caught in the melee.

"Cowards—all of you! I come as a greater force and you shy away instead of fighting by my side. I'll kill and replace all of you!"

"You are delusional if you think any of us will let you rule. You've earned nothing from us but our distrust. You'll die today." Leviathan's tribal markings glowed green as he pulled his sword from its sheath. "Abaddon burns bright for you."

Lucifer's audacious laugh bellowed at him. "The traitor doesn't even realize he's been the target of my web all this time. I knew Sonneillon wasn't the traitor. He was too loyal—a lapdog. When Asura claimed his innocence, I understood the perfect way for him to help me was to make an example out of him. To display my ruthlessness to the Fallen, and replaced him with a true warrior. I also gained a Queen worthy of the Realm. All the while, I continued to hunt for the real culprit... the one who made the gross error of working with Delilah."

Even though the Realm percolated with war, an ominous disbelief fell upon its inhabitants.

I told you she would ruin it for us. You should have killed her when you had the chance! We're now dead because of your blind pride.

"How could you?" Asura rushed in front of Lucifer, her black skin crackling gold with her fury. "Sonneillon wasn't a tool to kill in your twisted games! He was—"

Lucifer pushed her to the ground and raised his sword to her neck. "You may be Queen, but you will not defy or question me about how I rule the Realm."

This is your chance...

Beelzebub opened his body to the Ancient One. The unholy orb within smashed into him at long last, fully uniting the powers of both evils. His body morphed, shifting... mutating into an enormous being of bulging muscles and expanding talons. When the six wings erupted behind Beelzebub, the only Fallen feature left were his gold eyes and sharp teeth dripping with saliva. More beast than Fallen, he roared and took flight as those below scrambled from his path.

"Abaddon!" Lucifer yelled, his face in full disbelief. "Kill him!"

Beelzebub shifted; missing Abaddon's burst of flame. He had to kill the dragon and the rest would fall.

As Abaddon turned to take aim again, bright lights erupted in the sky. Angels riding Heavenly beasts rained down as more flew from a larger portal, pouring heinous light into the depths of Hell.

Perfect.

As all eyes and weapons turned to the skies, Beelzebub stayed focused on his target, and Lucifer now perched on its back.

Kill them!

CHAPTER
FORTY-TWO

OLIVIA

The Red Rock mountains were obscured as the menacing black clouds rolled over them like a tidal wave about to crash into the valley. The first to emerge from the darkness was a female, ice-blue Fallen on a black dragon, its wings fanned with blue flames. Beside her, a striking male red Fallen rode a red dragon with a tail of red fire. The dragons spit flames to the ground, lighting swathes of fire across the terrain filled with homes and unsuspecting people. High in the air, they circled above as the horde of Fallen burst into the valley. They scattered in all directions on unnatural beasts or in flight. Sulfur and smoke assaulted her as thick ash fell in their wake. The clouds stopped rolling when the puffy ends touched the ground, allowing a new breed of evil to expel from hell. A turbulent mass of wingless beings with markings of blue or red scrambled over the ground, spreading like ants in all directions. Once the portal had relinquished its bounty, the center closed, yet the black clouds remained, smothering the mountainside, encircling the city.

"Are those the—?" Olivia gasped. She understood this day could come, but the actuality of it happening here, in her hometown, crushed her soul. Her sense of responsibility for the death of innocents could have crippled her. Instead, she let it ignite an unyielding will to fight that exploded in outrage and a determination. She would do whatever needed to be done to bring an end to Lucifer's war.

"The Damned. Lucifer has awakened his army of the dead—those who's soul went to Hell upon their deaths. They'll receive no mercy." Michael looked over his shoulder. "It's begun. He has sent Mammon and Berith to lead their Realms in battle or to find you. Other Realms may have been deployed to other places. Leave here while there's still a chance." Michael yelled over the screeching war cries erupting from above.

Michael raised his sword, blue electricity ran from tip to end. The Archangel's wings expanded, blocking Zach and Olivia from view. He looked back, brows lifted when he found them still there. "Olivia, go to the Magi! Now!"

Olivia shook her head as she raised Sandalphon. The hilt felt warm in her hand as the blue sparks traveled down the long silver blade. "I'm not leaving to have others fight in a war between Heaven and Hell. Zach and I are going to free Sergio and Lucia. Lucifer won't harm us. He knows if we die, there's no chance for him to open the Mar of Sin and get to Heaven. But he will try to kill every Angel who comes to fight him."

"She's right," Zach shouted. "We're the only ones who can bring them out alive. Even if he captures us, he'll demand we open the portal. When the other two portals open, we'll have the element of surprise. It's the only way."

Warrior Angels flooded the skies, streaking toward the incoming Fallen like colorful comets. Some rode on magical beasts and battled in the skies, while others fought to protect those fleeing the reign of terror in the city. Horrified people ran in all directions, hysteria taking hold. Others stood covering their ears, screaming, unable to comprehend the sight before them.

"Watch out!" Zach cried as a red Fallen dove toward them. Gabriel sprang into flight and met the Fallen's sword in midair. The flurry of blows soon ended with the Fallen turning to ash. Others followed, but more Angels appeared and fought them off. Olivia caught glimpses of Sealtiel's purple wings and Barachiel's opaque pink wings landing near them. Land and air were full of clashing weapons.

The war is here.

Michael turned and grabbed Olivia by the arms. His face was its own battlefield of emotion until it finally settled with a sigh of resignment. "Can you link with Lucia and Sergio?"

"Yes!" She nodded, heart pounding in her chest. "We opened our links to each other because we were worried something like this could happen."

"Good. Call your beasts. When I open the portal to Hell, go directly to them. Let the Angels do battle. Your only concern is to get them and get out. Then open the portals at once. But you have to stay together so you can be ready to close them when you see the sign."

"What... what's the sign—what are we looking for?"

"You'll know when you see it. Just promise me one thing before I go?" Michael asked, giving her arm a quick squeeze as he glanced at Zach next to her.

"Anything! Whatever you need." Tears blurred her vision as a foreboding overtook her.

Was he telling me goodbye?

"That you won't forget to look up."

"I don't understand." Olivia shook her head, needing to shake away the clouds of doubt.

"You will." He turned his gaze to the sky. "I'll open the portal, and then I have to leave."

"You're not coming with us?" Zach asked as he glanced at the chaos growing around him.

"No. Raphael will lead the Angels here and Gabriel will go with you. I have another destination. I'm going to the Watchers." A muscle twitched in his jaw as he released her. "It's time they learned of their fate."

"You'll convince them to do the right thing, I'm sure of it!" Olivia knew Michael wouldn't fail.

"Call Aureus and Malik. Ride them through the portal and let them lead the way. Focus on Sergio and Lucia. Stay focused and trust the Angels to protect you." He seemed to want to say more, but instead, he launched himself in the air, crying out in the language of the Angels. Two portals sizzled open. One blazed with a bright spotlight, illuminating the murkiness of Hell. The other opened to a black void of nothingness.

"Aureus!" she cried. A portal opened and her beloved Aureus flew through it. Malik appeared through another portal. They both climbed upon their mounts, the magical beasts stomping their front legs in readiness.

Gabriel landed next to them. "We've only seen Mammon and Berith here. That leaves five Realms Princes lurking somewhere. Uriel will aid in the fight here. Jehidiel will join us. Let's be quick about this."

Gabriel didn't need to say the rest. They were likely flying into an ambush. Or worse, Lucia and Sergio were nowhere to be found.

"We will. Don't worry about us. We'll be right behind you." Zach smiled wide, gleaming with the same eager anticipation she had to free her friends. Olivia's heart swelled at the confidence he displayed on top of Malik. The Pegasus was glorious underneath him. Together, they would do whatever it took to free Sergio and Lucia.

With the portal fully open, Michael sent Olivia a quick nod before he flew into the inky tunnel, his blue wings immediately engulfed and disappeared.

Peace be with you, Michael.

Warrior Angels dove into the other portal's illuminated smoky haze, daring and heedless of their potential death. They understood the gravity of this day and the power they faced once before in a war that shook the Heavens. Their war cries sounded of vengeance and bravery.

Olivia and Zach followed Gabriel towards their awaited fate. As she entered the portal, nothing could have prepared her for what lay before her or the new evil presence stalking Lucifer.

CHAPTER
FORTY-THREE

SYMEDEK

Time had lost its meaning, bleeding into one endless existence. All sense of reality had leeched away in his eternal damnation of ice and darkness. Along with his fellow Watchers, Symedek floated with translucent chains of bondage latched around his wrists and ankles. His wings were useless, shriveled with brittle feathers mangled inside the withered folds. He longed for the weight of his once majestic six wings, but without his Seraphim essence, they embodied the consequences of his defiance. His desire for greatness, to be a god to humans on Earth. His plans had succeeded until he'd reached too far, landing him in this prison.

My Nephilim.

My children.

My greatest sin.

In the beginning, his rage against the Nephilim's certain death burned within him, along with losing Arayana and the enduring love they shared. Did she make it out alive with his child, or was she cut down in the ravages of war? He screamed into the abyss, echoing the wails from those around him, who also mourned the loss of their children, their wives... their lives, so glorious in adulation and power. Once those emotions were exhausted, he turned his fury at God and the Angels who certainly annihilated the Nephilim protecting his kingdom on Earth. The tides of time swept away that fury, too.

One can only cling to hate for so long. The fires fanning it burn out when memories no longer bring forth the faces of those you love. Time pounded his spirit and will until he felt invisible, with no mind or matter left. Yet each day, his body remained.

Only the barest of spark flickered. The hope that his soul survived through generations across the centuries.

But what if it did?

Did Beelzebub claim it for himself?

If so, I'll never reunite with it.

Only one body can hold it.

The thought of Beelzebub returning to Earth and claiming his soul was the only heartache left to endure. It was reckless—so desperate of him to have split his soul. Hubris to think God would set him free or exact little retribution for his heinous deeds. If he'd known what was in store for him, he would have never done it. If Beelzebub had indeed claimed his soul, would Lucifer still rule in Hell?

Was there a war between Angels and Fallen?

Am I to blame for their deaths?

I'll never know.

A pinprick of blue light emerged, snapping a streak through the opaque air. It pierced his ears like the shattering of thick glass. Symedek squinted at the portal opening before him. Long dormant blood began to pump at this intrusion. Was there really someone walking through the portal or had his mind now begun the decline into wishful hallucinations? Steam rose around the figure like a halo, accentuating his presence and the blue-dipped wings, so gloriously full and vibrant. As excited as he was, this arrival from the Heavens could mean only one thing.

Michael brings his death... at last.

The Archangel's brilliance cast a glow across his fellow Watchers' faces. Some were in awe, others in shock, but most revealed

Symedek's resignation that their deaths were at hand. Michael scanned them all until his bright blue eyes settled upon him. He turned and flew closer, causing Symedek to wince against the shock of his light. He fought against his desire to turn away in shame. Instead, he let the Archangel's light seep warmth into his body, feeling it come alive like a bloom's first thrust against the hard soil after a long, cold winter.

"Symedek," Michael's deep tenor boomed. "It is time for your trial."

Symedek lifted his chin, eyes burning as he gazed at his foe. "I don't fear you or whatever trial you'll hold. My judgment is for God to decide, not you." The lack of emotion in his voice didn't surprise Symedek. His time here had left him void of passion.

"I'm God's envoy to you and the Watchers. I come to tell you the fate of the world you left behind."

"Why should we care?" Symedek scoffed. "When you locked us in this retched prison, whatever happened out there has nothing to do with us. If you've come to gloat about your works, spare us."

"You're wrong. You set in motion a collision course for us to meet again when you split your soul and placed it within your child."

Symedek's mind and body sparked to life upon hearing the only thing that mattered to him. What had become of his soul? If Michael knew, it could be his greatest fear has come true.

"How do you know this—what happened?" His voice sounded like gravel being walked upon.

Michael was silent for a moment as raspy murmurs floated between the Watchers. "Someone has taken it for themselves."

"What is this, Symedek?" Eonlysis's accusation rose close to him. "Is what Michael is saying true?"

There was no reason to deny it. They'd all be dead soon and his unholy deed would die with him. "I split my soul and put it into my child, born right before our capture. It was my goal, my purpose, to come back and retrieve it. I would be whole again and ready to fight to regain our reign over humanity. I did it to preserve what we built. I never imagined that we would spend eternity here. I did it for us—for our children!"

"Did you ever wonder why you weren't killed?" Michael's questions silenced their discontent. "Why you were sent to this prison of ice and eternal darkness?"

Every single day...

"That's simple. So we could languish here with our sins. Punishment for our teaching... the birth of our children." Symedek couldn't think of any other reasons for their imprisonment.

"When God passed His judgement, I thought that, too. Eternal damnation." Michael nodded. "But His infinite wisdom is grander, more complex than simple punishment. When Lucifer's Fall occurred, God set in motion a plan for redemption and forgiveness, including you and your fellow Watchers."

Symedek felt a blow to his heart. His breath stilled as he tried to comprehend Michael's revelation. The Watchers had done too much harm to be forgiven.

"You come here to tell false truths... to heighten our despair. You cannot increase our misery by teasing us with simple hope."

"I'll take my leave soon, but not before I share man's plight and Lucifer's impending war."

The sound of Lucifer's name aroused grumbles and curses from the Watchers. "Lucifer would never be so foolish as to really go to war... unless something has changed." Scenarios ran through Symedek's head, but none of them made sense. How could Lucifer think he could win a war against Heaven?

"The secrets of the Mar of Sin were exposed to him... by an Angel who took the Fall. He will storm Heaven with a massive force burning for revenge, mightier than when he left." Michael let the words sink in before he finished. "What Lucifer doesn't know is when the Mar of Sin was created, two other portals were also made and lay dormant. Each of these portals has a purpose. One portal opened and God put you here." Michael waved his arm around the vast darkness. "The other was made for Heavenly souls to escape and fight on Earth. When four young people come together and reveal their powers, they will open all three portals to fight Lucifer and seal them forever when Lucifer is defeated."

"I don't understand this. Why would He have humans and portals—us as a part of this war? With a flick of the wrist, He could kill the Fallen in an instant."

"Because this battle between Heaven and Hell is for the souls of mankind! Their free will—our free will! The time has come to choose a side. Good or evil. This decision can't be made for us by Him. It has to be claimed, fought for, or our choices become meaningless for us and humanity. We have to help defeat Lucifer because the rule under him would be one of tyranny, death, and no free will."

"So, are you telling me that a portal will open and God wants us to fight for him after he sent us here?" Symedek peeled back his upper lip. "I don't think God wants me in his army."

Michael raised his hand, and a blue flash appeared. When it faded, he clutched an ax, spiting red sparks from the crescent blade. Recognition flooded Symedek.

"Raum!" Symedek cried out. He went to grab it, but his chains held firm. Memories cratered open to the last day he had possession of the ax, and who took it from him. "How do you possess it? It was stolen from me before you came—"

"Was it Lucifer?" Michael pointed at him, accusing him with Baum's edge.

"No!" Symedek bellowed. "It was one of his Princes. One who would come and whisper guidance in my ear while we were on Earth."

"Tell me his name."

"I will not. He has my soul, and it is for me to take back. If I tell you his name, you'll leave and kill him. That will be my doing!" The ax shook in Michael's hand. Symedek wasn't sure if it was because the ax wanted to come to him or because Michael wanted to kill him with it. Michael closed his eyes and fought for composure. When he opened them, anger simmered, but reasoning won.

"The poison you've spread can't be undone, but what you choose to do now can help win our fight over evil. If the Guardians are successful on their mission, the portal will open soon. Your bonds will disappear and you'll all return to your former selves." Excited shouts and wails of relief ricocheted in the void. "But—"

"What?" Symedek asked. "Of course, there's a condition for our freedom. What is it?"

"No condition. Just a choice. Who will you fight for? Lucifer or God? Because which side you take is up to you, but you'll not live past the war. Once the portals close, so does your life."

"And if we stay here?" Eonlysis shouted.

"This prison will disappear and all who stay behind will perish. You have the opportunity to help the humans you so wanted to rule over, the ones you once loved, to beat Lucifer. If you fight with us, we can defeat the evil of this world and you'll have died truer to your original essence. Angels created to serve man, not rule over them."

"And if we choose to fight with Lucifer?" A Watcher called out from behind Symedek.

"Then you'll die fighting for evil. Is that who you truly are, what you were created for? This is your trial. To die in battle, as every warrior desires. This is your opportunity for redemption. The side you chose is the judgement you hold for yourself. Are you good or are you evil? Do you love humanity as you professed, or was it just the power you had over them? Stay here, if you choose, and die a coward, unable to confront your true self. In order to pick a side, demands you be bigger than yourself."

Once again, silence fell among the Watchers. Symedek understood they waited for his reply. His decision would have a significant influence on theirs.

Symedek also knew he never wanted humanity in Lucifer's clutches.

"Time here has cooled my rage, the pain of my losses. I *will* fight on the side of good, but not because of you or the Heavenly Hosts. I fight only for *humanity* because they do not deserve to live under his evil rule. Their future is the only thing worth fighting for."

"I, as well, will fight for mankind," Eonlysis replied. One by one, each of the Watchers gave their alliance to humanity.

"Thank you." Michael scanned the room. "When the portal opens, I'll free your bonds. Your weapons were destroyed, but you'll receive new ones."

"I wish to have Raum back. I have some unfinished business to take care of."

"I couldn't hold on to it if I wanted to. It's been searching for you."

We have much to do, old friend, before our time is up.

CHAPTER
FORTY-FOUR

OLIVIA

I t's worse than I remember...
   Or could have ever imagined.

A terrifying snapshot burned in her mind. One that would haunt her for however long she lived. Fallen filled the smoky sky as they clashed against the Angels streaking through the portal. Lucifer's Throne Room no longer had a roof, allowing her a bird's-eye view of the horrors happening within the massive walls.

Over a black pool, Lucia hung from a rope gripped by the talons of a huge Fallen. Olivia had seen the serpentine beast that owned the murky depths.

Sergio was tied to a pillar, struggling to free himself.

Delilah stood in front of Zar, a dagger raised in his hand. A grotesque troll-like beast loomed next to them with green whips snaking out from his forearms.

Lucifer perched on Abaddon's back. Fire erupting past its jagged rows of sharp teeth, aimed into the sky.

But it was the enormous black beast of a Fallen, with gold running through his skin like lava, that demanded her attention. Its manifestation could only mean one thing.

The Dark Prince had emerged. He had his blazing gold sword raised high on an arcing path toward Lucifer. His were the only eyes not set on the battle above them. A triumphant snarl appeared as he neared his target. But it was too soon to count his victory. Abaddon flicked its tail and struck The Dark Prince on his side, sending him flying against the wall. Stone crumbled around him as he crashed to the floor. He shook his head as he slowly raised himself up. A few Fallen around Lucifer shifted in form, doubling in size. They took flight into the melee. Lucifer lifted his face and roared into the sky, his malignant presence exemplifying his evil domination.

"Go to Lucia!" Olivia commanded. If she and Zach had any chance of freeing Sergio and Lucia and escaping, they had to act fast. She created a bubble around herself, hiding her arrival. Aureus dove toward Lucia. Gabriel led the Angels, flanking her on all sides, acting as an added shield and cover for her. Their war cries rallied her, giving her hope they would succeed. She blocked out her thoughts of how Zach would free Sergio, but faith in his speed and determination gave her peace.

"Get right under Lucia," Gabriel shouted, glancing over his shoulder. "Once you're there, I'll cut the rope. Get out of here and don't look back." He shot up above Lucia and raised his sword. Olivia was so close she could see the fear etched on Lucia's face change to hope. Olivia threaded her fingers deeper into Aureus's thick mane. They'd only get one shot, and she could not miss it.

"It's a trap!" Lucia yelled. "Get out of here!"

"Not without you!" Olivia maneuvered Aureus under Lucia. "When Gabriel cuts the rope, land on Aureus's back."

She looked up in time to see Gabriel cut the rope. Lucia gasped, spread her legs and landed with a thump behind her. Olivia glanced over her shoulder to make sure Lucia was safely in place. The Fallen holding Lucia screeched and dove for Gabriel, but an Angel swooped down and sliced its neck, sending its exploding ashes raining down on them.

"I can't leave without Sergio," Lucia's voice was hoarse, filled with urgency.

"That's Zach's job. You and I are out of here. Hang on!" Olivia urged Aureus back toward the portal. Her heart pounded as the sky was thick with Fallen between them and the portal. Her mark throbbed; panic threatened to take hold. Lucifer had to be close, but maybe he had his hands full with the Dark Prince.

"Look out!" Lucia warned before Olivia felt Lucia ducked down behind her. Olivia looked up as two Fallen strafed them. Both of their swords sliced the air, injuring two Angels. The security of the bright portal was obscured by another Fallen. Pink eyes blazed as its taloned hand reached inside the bubble for Lucia. Olivia released a hand and grabbed a throwing star from her chest. She tossed it and heard a satisfying screech when it impaled one eye. But before she could re-grip the mane, a powerful jolt hit her shoulder and knocked her off Aureus. She fell out of the bubble for all to see. Her arms and legs were weightless and flaying against the hot, thick air. She looked up and heard Lucia cry out, the rope still dangling from her wrists. Lucia tried to grab her, to no avail. An unfamiliar roar came from beneath her from the black pool. Her body turned cold as she imagined the serpent's jaws opening as it surged above the water. She couldn't let panic take control. This time, a familiar roar echoed as her heart synchronized with another.

Aureus.

Olivia fought against the air torrents and flipped her body, only to find her projection was true. The serpent's red fin rippled across the water like a line of fire. Its head rose, water rushing down its shiny, black scales. Its jaws yawned open, ready to catch its prey, but suddenly it snapped its head away from her. Then Aureus's golden coat filled her vision.

"Olivia!" Lucia was where Olivia first sat, her body pressed over Aureus's neck, giving her as much room as possible to land on his back.

I've done this before...

Olivia landed on his back, but her balance was off. She gasped as she slipped down his back legs. She desperately reached for his thick tail. Her hand grasped the end and she hung on for dear life. She brought her other hand forward and gripped it tightly. The chaos of roars and clashing metal bombarded her. Aureus flapped his wings with all his might as more Angels gathered to fill in the gaps of those lost.

Arms grabbed around her waist. "I've got you!" Gabriel yelled in her ear. Olivia let go, and he placed her behind Lucia. Just as she wrapped her arms around Lucia, a black bolt raced through the sky and hit Gabriel's wing.

"No!" Olivia yelled as Gabriel tumbled through the air. Angels raced toward Gabriel, battling their way through the blood lusting Fallen, seeking their prize. White wings closed around her, blocking her view of Gabriel's fate.

"Turn around," Olivia shouted.

"We must get you to safety above all else," an Angel said. "That is our mission."

Olivia sagged against Lucia, resting her head between her shoulders. Tears threatened to spill, but she squeezed them shut. If she let her fears take hold, she would be useless in battle. When she opened them, determination burned bright, along with a vow to win today at all costs.

He has to live... please let Gabriel come home.

"Are you okay?" Lucia's question filtered above the noise.

No, I'll never be okay again.

She couldn't admit the truth. Too many Angels have perished, and the battle has only begun.

"Fly home!" Olivia commanded in a cocoon of white wings as they aimed for escape. The portal was still open, but what waited for them on the other side was more Fallen.

And more death.

CHAPTER
FORTY-FIVE

DELILAH

The sharp pain of the dagger piercing the vulnerable skin between Delilah's shoulder blades never came. Nor did the lashes from the mutant's whips. Instead, the room froze for a fragile moment while Beelzebub morphed into a being borne of nightmares. Even Lucifer was transfixed as Beelzebub grew in size and malice. Only Abaddon rose to the challenge and bellowed a burst of fire at the transformed enemy. The dragon missed when Beelzebub took flight just as a blinding white light erased all the shadows in Hell. Screeches of surprise turned to outrage. Angels rained down upon Hell with weapons raised and war cries of their own. Good and evil collided above her in a whirling mass of light and dark, the colors exploding off their weapons and bodies.

War is here.

Overwhelming grief filled Delilah. She'd been the catalyst for Heaven and Hell battling in the smoky skies. Even though she believed this fight was inevitable, the fact she was a factor in its beginning left her wanting to weep in guilt. But the fighting left her with the opportunity to escape. Could she be saved in this moment? Would the Angles have mercy on her and free her from Lucifer? Could she find a way to make amends?

"Delilah," Zar appeared next to her. "We need to leave right now if there's any chance for your escape." He grabbed her arm and pulled her toward him. She pushed back against his chest; uncertain she could trust him.

"Why do you want to help me? You were getting ready to kill before they arrived."

Zar shook his head. "I wasn't going to kill you. I was going to kill the mutant if he—"

A searing pain lashed across her back. She cried out as she collapsed against Zar's chest. His face contorted with a rage she'd not seen in him before. When Zar shoved her behind him, it was then she faced the source of her pain. The mutant's whips crackled as he raised them to strike again.

Zar pulled his sword out. "It's time you received your punishment." The mutant's deformed lips spread in a macabre smile as it lowered its arms, the whips arching down from above. Zar spun, but the whip's tip caught the edge of his wing. An electrical current swept over it, but it didn't deter Zar. He took flight and brought his sword down, slicing one of the mutant's arms off above where the whip was bolted into his flesh. He screeched and fell to his knees, staring at the black blood pulsing from the stump. Zar swung once more, slicing through the creature's thick neck. Its beady eyes flickered wide before its head tumbled to the floor. Its massive body collapsed next to Delilah, shaking the floor beneath her.

Delilah gasped and scurried away from the twitching body. With the mutant gone from her view, she returned her focus to the war's ferocity raging around her. With the wound on her tattered back now weeping down her legs, she got up to run, and came face-to-face with Sergio still tied to the pillar. He glared at her, first in anger, then defiance. Her first instinct was to save herself, leave him. But if she did that, he'd remain as Lucifer's prisoner. She had to help free him and do what she could to help him escape. In her weakened state and without a weapon, she wasn't sure how she might accomplish the task.

"I don't know how I can free you. I don't have—" A hand shoved her aside. She stumbled, but threw herself in front of Sergio. She glanced up, but Sergio wasn't looking at her, but over her shoulder.

"You're such a coward, you would kill me while tied up instead of fighting as equals." Sergio struggled against his binds. "You killed my brother, and I want vengeance!" Veins bulged in Sergio's neck.

Delilah shielded Sergio behind her. She turned to Zar, hoping she could stop him. "You can't kill him. The only way Beelzebub and Lucifer lose is if the Guardians stay alive and use the gifts God gave them. War has started. You're a Fallen. Do you want subjugation under Beelzebub? Let this play out. Give the Guardians a chance."

Zar stilled, the dark blood of the mutant glistening on his sword. "Our world is over. It doesn't matter who rules it." His eyeless face turned to her. "I believe what you said about your part in this, which means I have a part to play, too. Maybe if we'd stayed partners instead of pitting ourselves against each other, things could have been different—we could have been different. If I cut him loose, will you come with me?"

Disbelief bloomed inside Delilah. After everything she'd done, Zar still wanted her, just as he had so long ago in Heaven. "Yes."

Relief rippled over Zar's face. He went behind the pillar to cut Sergio free when a Pegasus with a flaming orange mane landed next to him. "You touch him and I'll kill you." Zach yelled with a dagger readied in his hand. Angels swarmed above, granting him cover.

"Zach, wait." Sergio pleaded. "He's freeing me." Just then, the ropes slipped to the ground. Zach lowered the dagger as the Pegasus pranced impatiently beneath him. Sergio stepped away from the pillar and jumped up behind Zach. Angels flew around them, fighting off the Fallen. Sergio turned to them, his brow furrowed as his gaze flickered between Zar and Delilah.

"This isn't over—"

An Archangel appeared, orange wings spread wide, the tip of his sparking gold sword aim at Zar. "It is for now. You need to get back to the others."

"Jehidiel," Delilah murmured.

The Pegasus, Zach, and Sergio shot into the sky toward the portal before becoming encapsulated in a bubble of invisibility. A cocoon of white wings surrounded them and raced through the crowded sky with swirling rainbow contrails in their wake. Fallen bombarded them from all sides, Angels battling against them.

"Your choice here will not be forgotten." Jehidiel nodded at them and took flight. Delilah felt an old familiar warmth rekindle inside of her.

Goodness.

The short time she'd been a Fallen had buried those feelings. Anytime they tried to surface, she slammed a door on them. They weakened her fortitude to fulfill what she'd thought actual power was... freedom to do as she pleased. Freedom was never achieved in the gripping shadows of the ruthless and selfish. It was an unattainable obsession that chained her to evil. Lucifer used the lure to entice her in a partnership for a future. It wasn't real. He used her. Too late did she realize the freedom in Heaven was given in love in order to aid in a greater good. How Delilah would find peace again, she didn't know. As she looked down at her scarred marble hand with talons hooking from the ends, she understood she could never be an Angel again, but that didn't mean she couldn't still aid in Heaven's cause.

Full circle...

She glanced at the pillar, sensing Zar's scrutiny. She smiled at him and reached out her hand. Quick strides brought him next to her and his hand in hers. "We must go—portal out of here." Zar's urgent tone underscored they were still in grave danger. She nodded and squeezed his hand in return.

"Fate has always brought us back together. I'm sorry—" Her unspoken words stuck in her throat as Angels began to disappear from the Realm, taking with them their precious light.

Zar led Delilah behind the pillar. "We don't have time to discuss this now." He waved his hand to open his portal. "The portal will close soon. We'll go to Earth—"

A clawed hand grabbed Delilah from behind and yanked her out of Zar's grasp. "She's not going anywhere with you. Her time has come to an end." Beelzebub turned her around and lifted her to his chest. The only thing recognizable in him was his burning gold eyes boring into hers. He cackled as he took flight with her cradled inside his massive arms. "You should have kept your mouth shut."

"I only wish I had done it sooner!" She cried out, struggling to break free, but it was of no use. There was no escaping him. She heard Zar's cry of denial, afraid he took off after them. The floor beneath them went from stone to black, churning water. Terror ripped through her when Tannin broke the surface. The serpent swiveled toward them. Her body shuddered; mind frozen on the reality of her death swimming to greet her.

"You'll never win. The Fallen won't follow you because you stole the dark soul." She turned away from her pending destiny with death and funneled all her hatred for Beelzebub through her fiery green eyes. "You're a traitor who only wants what is best for himself, not the Realm."

"They *will* choose me when Lucifer is dead at my hands and I lead them to victory in Heaven." He sneered at her as his grip loosened.

"You'll never step foot into Heaven. God would never allow you back in."

"We'll see about that."

Then she was weightless. Her legs flailed, body slipping through the smoldering air.

Time stopped for a precious instant as her surroundings collapsed into one last frozen moment.

The terrifying roar beneath her.

Beelzebub releasing a gold electric current, sending Zar hurdling to the floor.

The portal closing, returning the Realm to its murky, harsh den of evil.

Delilah succumbed to a numbing realization. She wasn't destined for Heaven. She would die without saying the sentiment she wanted to shout back at God when she originally jumped into the Mar of Sin.

I love you, too.

Tannin's teeth closed around her, slamming her into darkness and silence, entombing her declaration and body forever.

CHAPTER
FORTY-SIX

ZAR

D*elilah...*
   Not now...
   Not after we're so close to getting away from what held us captive.

Zar tumbled across the floor as gold sparks ran over his body, seething at Beelzebub as he flew away with Delilah toward Tannin's black pool. Temporarily left stunned, he had no control over the zapping currents preventing him from rescuing Delilah before Tannin's jaws snapped her body in two. He strained against the fading energy, desperate to get his body to respond. When his legs and arms jerked awake, he expanded his wings and took flight toward the pool, only to be greeted by the horror of Delilah falling into Tannin's gapping mouth lined with rows of razor-sharp teeth. If Delilah screamed, it was lost in the triumphant roar of the serpent. Water cascaded down its black scales as it launched its long body into the air at the prey careening toward it. As quickly as its jaws opened, they slammed shut around Delilah, dragging her below the pool's inky surface.

Zar dropped to his knees and screamed into the murky mists, releasing his rage and despair of her death by Tannin. Delilah despised the serpent, had a premonition that her death was entwined with it. Lucifer had threatened her death by it so many times, she lived in constant terror of even being in the Throne Room. All the beatings, the torture, the snakes... none of those broke her. She survived them all through sheer will. Beelzebub knew of her fear and sent her to her grisly death as punishment and to crush Zar for helping her.

I couldn't save her.

If only she'd told him about Beelzebub. If only she'd trusted him with the truth. Maybe she'd be alive and Beelzebub would be dead in the bowels of the beast. But he hadn't earned her trust back in time. He was so filled with jealousy and petty hurts that it kept a wall between them... until the very end, when they'd both decided to set it all aside and try to survive the chaos together. The fragile dream shattered before it began. And with it, any desire to live without her. But there were a few things he'd do before he left this world.

Kill Tannin and destroy those truly responsible for her death.

Zar dove into the center of the circular wake left by Tannin's retreat. The screeching of the Throne Room muffled when he hurled himself down into the black abyss. He wasn't afraid of the dense, inky water. His world had turned dark long ago, and he'd learned to thrive in the deep gloom. Letting his mapping scan the depths, he picked up swirls of the serpent circling beneath him. He sped faster toward his target, his wings pushing him through the water. Tannin's snout snapped up in his direction. Zar pulled out his sword and stilled, floating in the water as the beast flipped his tail and moved toward him. Zar raised his hand, his heartbeat steady as Tannin grew larger. It opened its cavernous mouth in anticipation of another meal.

You've had your last meal.

Zar released a hail of green bolts from his hand. It lit the surrounding water in a hazy emerald color until the bolts found their target inside Tannin's mouth. The serpent jerked away from Zar, roaring in pain. Red blood trailed behind him as it swam away. Zar launched at it, moving faster than the wounded serpent. Black scales raced beneath him, urging him to swim faster before Tannin lashed out. When the back of its reptilian head moved within range, Zar raised his sword and plunged it into the vulnerable area at the base of its skull. It bucked, then froze as its eyes rolled back in its head. Zar pulled the sword out and thrust it in again with all the fury he possessed. He buried it deeper until the serpent moved no more. He pulled his weapon out and sliced away a hunk of the red spiked fins spanning its back. Zar floated in the bloody water until the black depths engulfed Tannin, sending him to his deep watery tomb.

Zar raced for the surface, feeling no remorse for the serpent's death, only regret that Delilah's last moments were defiled by a horrid beast she couldn't escape. The water grew clearer as the surface neared. Lucifer would have heard the death cry of Tannin, but with any luck, he was locked in battle with Beelzebub and he couldn't escape to attack Zar in retribution. If not, at least he'd killed Tannin before his own death. With the souvenir of spines clutched in his hand, he broke through the surface and raised his portal. Tension released from his shoulders when there was no one waiting to kill him. When Zar glanced at Lucifer's throne, he understood why. The fight had begun. The outcome made no difference to him or to the inhabitants who dwelled in the Realm. His journey—his life—was no longer attached here. It lay on Earth and the vengeance he sought.

Satisfaction coursed through him as he hurled the trophy of Tannin's death at those gathered around Lucifer's throne. A familiar sharp gaze turned to him. Asura yelled his name, but he didn't respond. Instead, he flew through the greens sparks of his portal and let her angry shouts be cut short when it slammed shut.

Asura made her choice by standing with Lucifer. He held little hope for her survival or for the Fallen. It could all burn for all he cared.

And I don't care.

His only allegiance was to the memory of Delilah and her last wishes.

Zar stared at the bloody battle raging before him. Angels and Fallen clashed over the city's skyline. Streets and homes lay in ash and ruin while the center of the city burned. The portal brought him to the church where he'd found the Guardians. It was a hollow shell with gaping holes in the roof. Death and abandoned cars were all that remained from the carnage of the earlier battle. Zar's mission to capture Lucia had been successful. He got his prize. But ultimately, the cost turned out to be higher than he was willing to pay.

He expanded his wings, feathers rippling as if in anticipation of what lie ahead. He took flight, determined to exact his justice. He inhaled, seeking the scent of those he needed to find. His nostrils flared when he found their unique smell. Heading in a direction away from the city, he planned out his next moves.

And of who would die first.

CHAPTER
FORTY-SEVEN

OLIVIA

A ureus flew through the portal, away from the depths of Hell and all who wanted a piece of the Guardians for their own malicious desires. A shiver ran down Olivia's spine when she thought of how close she'd come to death by the serpent. She'd never forget Lucia dangling over the pool, Sergio lashed to the pillar and the Dark Prince and Lucifer about to have their showdown. Had Zach gotten to Sergio and made it out safely? Was Gabriel hurt badly or worse? She squeezed her eyelids tight, forbidding the memories of the Angel's deaths, who perished protecting them. If she let those images come alive, the heartache would be too overwhelming. The time to mourn them properly would come later when Lucifer and the Fallen were defeated.

Give us the strength and wisdom we need to see this through.

Olivia opened her eyes, expecting to see the Vegas valley in smoke and ruins, with battles raging all around her. Instead, the Angels had spread out their protective cocoon to reveal the red, rocky terrain of the Valley of Fire. It was hard to believe they were back where their journey began when, with each passing minute, more Angels were dying in a battle they should be fighting, too.

"Liv!" Zach shouted. She turned, her heart skipping a beat when Zach and Sergio both waved as they flew side-by-side. Zach's confidence buoyed her own with his hand gripping Malik's orange flamed mane, his hair swept back from his flight. He'd overcome his guilt, his fears of being unworthy. He leaned over, whispering into the Malik's alert, pointed ears and stroked a hand down its neck, radiating how much he cared for his magical beast. In this moment, she loved Zach more than she thought possible.

"Thank God Zach got Sergio out of there. I've never been so scared. I felt so helpless hanging there while Lucifer used us against each other." Lucia's voice hitched. "I don't know what I would have done—"

Olivia's arms gently squeezed Lucia's waist. "Don't think about it right now. We're all safe, but not out of danger. We must open the portals and fight until we can close them and end this. We can do it." Olivia wondered if she was saying this more for her benefit than Lucia's.

"Look! There's the Magi... and Amal!" Lucia pointed to a wide-open area where Aureus and Malik were both headed.

Olivia straightened, tightening her grip with her knees as Aureus prepared to land. "They'll provide cover if the Fallen show up." Her mark wasn't inflamed, but the Fallen would find them soon enough. Too much was at stake for the portals to remain closed. Lucifer had started his war and wanted the portals opened to finish it.

Were they doing the right thing?

Are we helping Lucifer more or further crippling ourselves?

Michael must be successful with the Watchers, or we'll have more enemies than allies.

Will the Heavenly warriors be any match for the Fallen or will it only lead to more slaughter?

Opening the portals is all we have left.

Red dust flew up as the magical beasts landed and galloped toward the Magi. Sunlight glinted off the swords hanging from their hips. Olivia jumped off Aureus and was soon scooped up into Zach's open arms. One hand threaded into her hair while the other held her close. "My heart stopped when I saw you fall. You scared the life out of me." Zach's voice quivered with relief and a hint of anger. "Don't ever do that to me again."

"I promise to never fall into the open mouth of a serpent again." Olivia chuckled and pulled back to gaze at Zach. "But I can't promise I'll never scare you again. I'm not built that way."

His warm hands cradled her face. He sighed before he leaned in close. "One of the many reasons why I love you." His kiss was gentle, but an urgency burned beneath. She wanted to deepen it, be free to take what she longed for. Instead, she pulled away and glided her fingers over his lips.

"I love you, too."

"Olivia... Thank goodness you made it back to us." Melchior called out from behind her. She let go of Zach and welcomed Melchior's arms wrapping around her. His steady heartbeat beneath her ear calmed her own racing heartbeat. "You gave me quite a scare —all of you." He said over the top of her head.

"But that's over now." Balthazar's deep voice rolled over her. Sergio had his hands on his hips, staring at the sky. Lucia and Amal stood next to him; their fingers entwined. "It's time to open the portals. Raphael brought you here to buy some extra time to open them uninterrupted. It won't be long before the Fallen discovers your whereabouts. They know your scent now." He left the rest unsaid, but Olivia understood what it meant. Their brief respite of peace would not last long.

They will hunt us mercilessly until this is over.

"You won't have this same quiet landscape when the time comes to close the portals." Caspar came up next to Zach, laying a hand on Zach's shoulder and squeezed it. "You must all stay together so you can act immediately when the portals need to close. We'll be here, fighting with you."

"What if they don't open the portals? Maybe Lucifer will retreat again—" Amal asked, glancing at Lucia.

Melchior shook his head. The creases around his eyes deepened. "Lucifer has unleashed the Damned. We need the warriors in

Heaven and the Watchers if we are to win. This war is here. There's no turning back. The longer we wait, the more innocent lives are at stake. Right now, only part of his army is on Earth. He kept most with him to charge Heaven. He'll continue to unleash more of his army on Earth to force you to open the portal. Our advantage is that he doesn't know about the other portals. You've trained for this moment. You're ready."

"Why aren't we in Magiland?" Zach glanced at more Angels arriving and creating a circle around them. It was like standing in the center of a rainbow. "It's safer there."

"Our home is not of this world. The portals are only open for you on Earth." Melchior waved his hand in the air. "You may not see Orion in the dusky sky, but the lights on his belt will soon be bright beacons of hope in our battle against evil. Now, gather round."

A gold portal came to life. Gabriel stepped through; his wing was intact, but an area of feathers remained charred from the black bolt.

"Thank goodness." Lucia whispered.

"They're coming." Gabriel's warning sent a chill down Olivia's spine. Looking over her shoulder, the distant sky had turned hazy like a fog rolling in from the sea. Her mark flared as it reacted to the evil speeding toward them.

The Guardians gathered in a circle. Olivia's heart pounded as she reached for the dagger at her hip. The blade twinkled as the blue hilt surged with energy.

"Armor down." Olivia said. Her armor unwrapped enough to reveal her mark and necklace.

"Ready?" She glanced at her friends. Each had their daggers poised, determination gleaming in their eyes. Whatever fears and uncertainty they each had were swept aside. This was the moment they were made for. What they were called to do. Open the portals and save the world.

No problem.

The Fallen's shrieks were growing louder. Bursts of lights erupted like small bombs going off around them. Sulfur and smoke filled her nostrils, but were swept away by the arrival of more Angels. The Magi raised their hands, creating a massive tornado of red dirt. Inside the vortex, it muted the chaos and the fight building outside the spinning walls.

"Ready!" Zach, Sergio and Lucia shouted. Olivia nodded as she turned over her left hand. Sweat glistened as a tremor ran through her fingers. She ran the sharp blade quickly across her palm. She hissed as sweat mingled with blood, but the adrenaline held the pain at bay. The Fallen would be upon them soon. There would be no second escape from Lucifer, no wondering about what he would do next. They were running out of time.

"Hurry!" Olivia thrust her hand in the middle of the group. "Let's show Lucifer who we are! We're the Guardians of Orion!"

"To the Guardians!" Zach yelled, clasping her hand for a moment before he let go.

"To the Guardians!" Sergio followed Zach.

"To the Guardians!" Lucia followed suit until each of them had their fellow Guardian's blood on their hand.

Olivia lifted her hand, smeared with the blood, and grabbed the metal capsule hanging from her chain. An instant heat flared inside her fist. The necklace detached itself from around her neck. She opened her hand, eyes widened as she gazed at the dissolving metals pooling inside her palm. Steam rose as blood and silver swirled around the gold nugget, mixing until the elements became one. A thick, iridescent puddle remained. The roar in her ears was not from any battle, but from the anticipation of what came next. Heart pounding, she looked up and found all eyes on her.

Place it on your mark—now!

Melchior's command thundered in her head, snapping her out of reverence. She inhaled sharply and slapped her hand over her mark. A bright light exploded behind her eyes, a blue aura wrapped around her. Falling to her knees, she gazed up to the sky, its brilliant blue like the crystal-clear waters off of a tropical island. Her shoulder felt alive, as if every cell inside awakened from a deep slumber, amassing together within the orb. A brilliant light erupted from her mark. She grunted, flung her arms wide as her back arched, becoming nothing more than a vessel to the power of the orb's essence. The beam shot from her like a rocket straining to break the bonds of Earth. Three more beams shot out next to her, but she couldn't tear her gaze away from the sky to see what was happening to her friends. Her breath shortened, feeling as if her core might shatter with the pressure bursting from within her. Hot tears scalded her cheeks as she watched the beams soar through the sky, heading toward their long-awaited destiny.

Would the portals open and do as foretold?
Would Lucifer's reign of evil finally be crushed?
Would mankind be saved on this day?

Suddenly, the light stopped projecting from her mark, the beam no longer visible. The sky turned dark as if day had switched to night, illuminating a canvas of stars above them. But they only served as a sparkling backdrop for the one constellation dominating them all.

Orion.

The hunter, the warrior, their protector—burned with a brilliance worthy of the secrets hidden within his stars. Olivia gasped when the three stars of the belt exploded, and their beams streaking down to Earth, ends open as if a tunnel to a glorious destination. The vortex collapsed, along with her exhausted body. She rolled over, tasting the grit of the red dirt as she licked her lips.

"We did it, Liv." Zach yelled, as he crawled to her side.

"Yes..." She sat up as Zach's arm went around her.

"It worked!" Sergio shouted. He and Lucia joined them. A collective relief bubbled to the surface as their incoherent shouts of joy were lost inside their tightly held embrace.

"It's not over yet." Olivia disentangled herself. "It's only just beginning. Armor on."

The others did the same as she took stock of their surroundings.

For a moment, the engagement was a snapshot of the battle between good and evil as all combatant's heads snapped up and gazed upon the three beams and their unimaginable meanings. It was as if everyone held their breath in anticipation of what might happen next.

But not all eyes were transfixed by Orion's belt.

One narrowed in on its prey.

The other upon the predator.

CHAPTER
FORTY-EIGHT

LUCIFER

Abaddon glided through the smoky mists billowing above the roofless Throne Room. Lucifer relished the delicious chaos before him. The Seven Realms were alive; their lava pools churning, their mountains relinquishing the Damned, and all the beasts who would take them into battle. Angels and Fallen were locked in battle, fighting for their chosen leader. Abaddon blasted red fire balls at their enemies, keeping them at bay so he could see who came to rescue the Guardians. His plan all along had been for the Guardians to escape so they would open the portals on Earth. He'd sent a command through his link to let the Guardians be rescued, but the Fallen could kill as many Angels as they desired. The purpose had been two-fold. Push the Guardians into action and find the traitor.

Beelzebub...

Lucifer had feared it was him, but hoped until the very end that it was another one of his Princes. The look of surprise on Beelzebub's face had been worth the ruse, but his oldest ally had a trick up his sleeve as well. How he'd gotten Symedek's soul, Lucifer may never know, but it stirred an inkling of admiration for his depraved creativity and ruthlessness. Beelzebub's new form was impressively formidable. Lucifer wasn't worried. He was confident Beelzebub was not long for this life. Were there any more surprises in store, or had his new enemy played his only hand?

If only he'd done it for me, for the Fallen.

No.

Pride would never allow it.

He sneered at the Guardians, thinking they had outsmarted him as they escaped on the backs of their magical beasts. They would die soon enough, never knowing they were simply pawns caught in an eternal state of warfare they could never truly appreciate. As the portal's heinously bright light closed, Lucifer zeroed in on his target. He must defeat Beelzebub before the Mar of Sin opens. To kill this new defector in front of the Fallen would embolden them into the greatest battle they would ever face. This skirmish is but an early taste before the true victory when Heaven crumbles at their feet. He swelled with a malicious satisfaction that his plan was coming to fast fruition. Revenge was at hand. Heaven and Earth would soon be under his rule.

Beelzebub fought off his opponents with an easy slash of his sword or a golden bolt striking its mark. Abaddon's scales ripples beneath him as he circled lower in tune with whom Lucifer tracked. A red fire burned the length of the dragon's body, ready to strike on command. Beelzebub turned his focus on something else. Lucifer's eyes narrowed when he discovered the target.

Zar and Delilah. Holding hands like forlorn, star-crossed lovers.

What a joke.

They never had a chance. Beelzebub ripped Delilah away from Zar and flew towards the pool. He blasted Zar and then released her. Lucifer almost cheered when Tannin broke surface and snatched her midair before sinking back into the pool's depth. Zar's cry of despair grabbed the attention of the Fallen close to him. Lucifer felt nothing. Her death was long overdue and was a fitting end with the creature who had truly coveted her flesh most of all.

Tannin.

When Zar dove into the pool after Tannin, Lucifer scoffed, remembering what he'd told him.

Delilah will be the death of you.

But Zar became a fleeting thought when Beelzebub scanned the skies and locked eyes with Lucifer. Blood lust burned as he took flight toward him, staying out of Abaddon's range.

"Will you stay on Abaddon's back or come fight me without your dragon's flames?" Beelzebub's voice boomed, casting his taunt for all to hear. "I challenge you for the throne, for the right to lead the Fallen."

Lucifer threw back his head and laughed at him. "Your challenge means nothing to me. Being the harbinger of two souls doesn't make you worthy of *my* throne. It makes you worthy of death by whatever means I see fit."

"You're old—a coward who rules on a dragon's back." Beelzebub pointed his sword at Lucifer, his accusation bold in front of the Fallen. "When is the last time you raised your sword and fought? The Fallen must have faith in their leader during battle." With the Angels and Guardians gone, the Realm's inhabitants had gathered with a watchful eye. Their collective anger vibrated toward Beelzebub, but some Fallen, most crackling with the Realm of Pride, watched their Prince with curiosity. Lucifer couldn't lose any of the Realms now. He must end this with Beelzebub and stop any seed of doubt.

Asura emerged from the gray haze, glorious upon her Degasus, her golden braids whipping behind her. The regal crown on her head amplified the warrior stature of her armor-clad body, created a captivating vision. But there was no queenly love or adoration in her golden eyes. As she sped closer to Beelzebub, sorrow and hate burned. Abaddon swiveled his head. Smoke bloomed through his nostrils as he opened his mouth.

"No. Let her fight. I need—"

A gold bolt of lightning struck her chest, throwing her off her mount. Shrieks of outrage echoed as her motionless body tumbled.

Two Fallen swooped from the sky and carried her back inside the Throne Room's walls.

Beelzebub aimed his hand at Lucifer. "Don't worry. The bolt was not enough to kill your precious queen." His lips twisted in a wicked smile. "Asura wants my blood, but it's hers I will draw first."

It was then that Tannin's death cry echoed out of the black pool, igniting the last spark of an infernal rage ready to explode.

Zar will pay...

Many times, Lucifer's veins pumped thick with hatred and malice. But Beelzebub's betrayal ripped open a depth he thought was reserved for his heavenly enemies. "You've harmed my queen and threatened me for the last time!" Lucifer's six wings erupted, lifting him off of Abaddon. Lucifer spread his arms wide, hovering mid-air as Abaddon blasted a shield of fire around him.

"You shall now see who you're confronting. Did you think I would attack Heaven in this form? I, too, have a power inside of me begging to surface." Lucifer dug deep and opened a part of him only he possessed. "As the highest Angel supreme above all, I could channel all the Kingdom's powers. As Lord of the Realms, I'll channel all their powers once again. Wrath!" A swirling red rope of lava rose from the churning pool. Blazing through the air, it struck Lucifer's hand like a lightning strike.

"Envy! Lust! Sloth!" Lucifer roared over the thundering cheers that grew as each Realm was named. "Gluttony! Greed!" When each was summoned, a new slithering ribbon of lava emerged from the pool. "And now, the Realm you've dishonored—Pride!'

"No!" Beelzebub cried out when the gold lava swirled toward Lucifer's outstretched hand. "That is my Realm!"

Lucifer was lifted above Abaddon; lava ropes of vibrant colors suspended him in a magnificent display above the Realm. His body absorbed the powers infused inside the lava, feeding him with the malignant power born of the seven sins. He welcomed the tearing of his old flesh to rebuild an unparalleled, undeniable being of pure evil. His body grew immense, his awareness crystal clear, like each of his bodily fibers drew its own breath. As more lava poured into him, he arched his back and felt invincible. When the last tendrils of lava snaked into his hands, his gaze swept over the Realm, welcoming their fanatic cheers of approval. He found Beelzebub, rage and defiance burning in his former Prince's eyes.

"It was never your Realm to own, only yours to breed the Damned I desired. You failed me and you *will* die."

"I'm not afraid of you." The crowd roared as Beelzebub took flight. Lucifer raised his sword, glowing with the light of the Seven Realms, fearless of this impostor who had worked against his reign. Beelzebub would soon learn his dual-soul body couldn't defeat the powers channeling within him.

And then it happened.

What Lucifer had waited on for so long, he thought it may have truly been a ruse at Delilah's hands. A gigantic shaft of light appeared in the far corner of the Realm, followed by a blast of air too pure—too fresh for this world. He gasped as a part of him, on a visceral level, responded to the growling vortex, calling him to fly to its light and bask inside of it. The Fallen froze as if they also inhaled the sensation, stirring memories of a different time and place.

The home of my enemies.

"The Mar of Sin! Let's finish what we started!" Repulsed by his own reaction, he mounted Abaddon and urged him into flight. He aimed for Beelzebub, who must die before Lucifer continued his charge into Heaven. But the roars of another vortex made him turn and glance over his shoulder. His brow furrowed as another portal opened, but no light shone through it. Instead, a frigid blast swirled through the gaping black opening.

"What is this?" Leviathan yelled as he and Asmodeus emerged next to him on their dragons.

"Another trick from our enemies. I don't know what it holds, but I'm not staying to find out. I must get inside the Mar of Sin before there are any more surprises."

I won't let it stop me—I'm so close!

Translucent black forms with long black wings darted out of the opening. They moved like shadows and engulfed the sky. Their immense bodies and wingspan shifted among the smoke, creating rolling contrails behind them. Lucifer sneered as he felt a stir of remembrance of the beings he once knew but couldn't place. He understood one thing: these were no friends, but forgotten adversaries.

"No! Not you!" Beelzebub's roar jarred Lucifer. "Your soul is mine now, Symedek! I'll not allow you to take it." He turned and flew toward his old Realm with a solitary Watcher giving chase.

The Watchers...

Fallen raced to fight the invaders, but their shifting forms, like ghosts of lore, made it difficult for the Fallen to kill. The Watchers moved quickly, striking down all in their path.

"It can't be!" Asmodeus turned to Lucifer.

"And yet it is. Freed from their prison to fight against us through a secret portal. If there is one, there may be more. Two can play this game." Lucifer punched his hand, opening a new portal. "Astaroth and Gressil! Take your Realms to Earth and destroy everything in sight." Purple and orange Fallen rushed toward the opening. Earth's blue sky quickly filled with evil.

"Our numbers diminish with Sloth and Greed's departure, my Lord," Leviathan's armor pulsed with green.

"More Angels will need to leave Heaven to protect the humans, leaving it more vulnerable. Maybe the Watchers will follow to Earth as well. We must go now!" Lucifer raced for the Mar of Sin, sending the link for the rest of the Fallen to follow him. He couldn't think about the Watchers or of their place in this war. He was only consumed with his destination, his destiny to finish the conquest he started in Heaven.

Nothing will stop me.
Not Beelzebub.
Not the Watchers
And not Michael.

Not this time.

Lucifer glanced down as he passed over the Throne Room. A section of Tannin's spines lay in a heap at the foot of his throne, serving as a quick reminder to him that loyal companions will be lost today... only the strongest, most cunning will survive to revel in the new world he'll create and rule for all of eternity.

CHAPTER
FORTY-NINE

SYMEDEK

When the Watcher's prison rumbled and his shackles disappeared, the first blush of Symedek's freedom was a sense of nakedness. Vulnerability and choice. He'd forgotten the wonder of it. A beam of light shattered the dark, demanding he turn away, but he couldn't. The light was freedom, just as light always was. But with the light came the stench of sulfur and a smoky haze at the portal's core. They weren't going to freedom; they were headed for their deaths, but at least it was their choice—his choice.

And his destiny with an enemy who stole his soul.

I will get it back.

Michael hovered at the opening, light sparkling off his blue wings. Symedek wished he had time to marvel at the Archangel, to absorb a fraction of the beauty his mind held only in memories.

"Weapons!" Michael called out.

Symedek held Raum in one hand, and a sword appeared in the other. No Kingdom's color from Heaven energized the weapon.

"No Angels willing to give their lifeblood or feather for us?" Symedek raised his sword at Michael. "Are we not worthy because we're doomed to die or does the Heavenly Host still hold a grudge?"

"Doubt still lurks in your heart." Michael raised his magnificent sword and waved it over them. "I had these made with my blood. We fight together on this day, so it's only fitting you should have my blood." Lightning erupted from the tip of Michael's sword. It shot off into separate streaks, touching the tip of each weapon until all were alive with blue bolts and electric sparks.

Symedek gasped, not only from the power vibrating in his hand, but from the humility flooding him. "I misjudged you, Michael. Thank you—"

"Don't thank me. Your death is at hand today." Michael pointed his sword at the portal. "Hell awaits you along with the Fallen who seek to ruin everything in their path. They'll attack you while Lucifer takes an army into the Mar of Sin. If a portal opens to Earth, you may choose to follow the Fallen who flee there."

"And you?" Symedek asked.

"My place is in Heaven to greet Lucifer. The Heavens will know of the valiant choice all of you made." Michael scanned the Watchers floating in the vast wasteland, their sentence here ending. He thrust his sword into the blazing light. "To victory!"

Their war cries roared above the portal's vortex's groaning opening. Symedek flew past Michael and into the milky mist, churning as it speared a path through the stars. He expanded his wings, energized by the glorious sensation of his feathers gliding in flight. His essence had lost all color, his lifeblood drained as he languished in the cold abyss. Heading into the portal, he embraced his shadow-like form. The Watchers may look dead, but they were very much alive and deadly in purpose.

I'm coming for you Beelzebub.

The portal shifted from light to dark as they neared the exit. By the time he burst out of the tunnel, every fiber of his being was fully awakened. They shifted with ease, dodging the blasts of energy from the Fallen. The Damned had little protection from them, making them easy targets. Eyes of confusion and fear narrowed as the Watchers spread out into the skies above their foe. Symedek was emboldened by the chaos their presence caused and the quick deaths in their wake. His fellow Watchers made rapid work of the Fallen. Their shadowy bodies were swift, deft against the enemy, who didn't understand the intruders they fought against. In the distance, a massive dragon with a rider took flight toward the Mar of Sin. Symedek didn't recognize Lucifer's new manifestation, but the pure hatred and evil could only emanate from him. But Lucifer's zeal for revenge was not his purpose. It was more personal. Symedek opened an ancient sealed pathway inside of him and sought the missing part of his soul that he ripped away that fateful night so long ago. He fought through the flurry of the Damned. Their lack of skill made them easy to kill, but would reign terror upon Earth. A flush bloomed in his chest as if a returned heat had found its origin. He followed the invisible source. It didn't take long for him to find it was Beelzebub glaring back at him.

My soul...

Waves of sorrow swept through Symedek. His soul recognized him, even as it was smothered inside Beelzebub's murderous rage and warped sense of self. His sorrow quickly shifted to anger, realizing his soul had been tragically influenced, determinately manipulated by Beelzebub's maniacal evil and visions of grandeur.

Lost.

"No! Not you!" Beelzebub yelled. "Your soul is mine now, Symedek! I'll not allow you to take it back!"

Symedek dove for his enemy, who never had any intention of helping his lineage or keeping his soul safe for his return.

I was a fool to strike that bargain.

And now I have to kill my soul.

"It doesn't matter what you want! The soul is mine and I'll not have you use it!

His fellow Watchers flew past him toward the Fallen charging the Mar of Sin's entrance. Their larger bodies intimidating as their energy blasts laid large swaths of the Damned to ashes. If they could diminish the Damned, the Angels could concentrate on the Fallen. His brothers and sisters in battle wouldn't distract Symedek. They knew their death was carved in stone for this day, making their fighting even more courageous.

Beelzebub raised his sword and roared at Symedek like a crazed animal. "This is my day. Not yours. Not Lucifer's. Mine!" He bellowed and took flight.

No fear churned within, only determination steeled Symedek's heart and weapon as they sped toward each other. When their swords clashed, a thunderous clang erupted. He wasn't as large as Beelzebub's hideous new form, but that only forced him to dig deeper for the strength needed.

"Leave now and I'll let you live," Beelzebub yelled through the sparks of their swords.

"I'm already dead." Symedek lowered his sword and spun to the side. Surprise rippled across Beelzebub's face when Symedek's sword sliced a gaping gash over his back. "Release my soul! Now!"

"I'll never release it! It's mine now—we are one!" They exchanged blows, each dodging their opponent as they neared the rocky ground. A plume of black dust surrounded them when they landed, but the fighting only grew more intense. Some blows hit the mark; others landed steel against steel. Symedek's arms grew weary, his body weakening from the battle and the energy needed to heal. The same struggle burned in his opponents' eyes, motivating Symedek to keep fighting. Their combat was a blur over the skirmishes happening across the Realm. He vaguely wondered if Lucifer was in Heaven destroying the place Symedek had so recklessly found beneath him. The thought of Angel's blood flowing in Heaven ignited a burst of energy he didn't know remained. He shoved his sword into Beelzebub's stomach, angry he'd missed his heart. Beelzebub staggered back, taking the sword still lodged in his belly with him.

"You never had good aim." He chuckled, mocking him while he pulled out Symedek's sword and tossed it to the ground. The only weapon Symedek had left was Raum burning red as it hung from his hip. He pulled it out and steeled himself as Beelzebub raised his sword and launched toward him.

"But I do!" Came a cry from an unknown voice as a gold lightning rod of a weapon sliced through Beelzebub's wing.

"Asura, this isn't your fight." Beelzebub snarled as his head swiveled between his two opponents.

"Your lies are the reason Sonneillon was killed. I knew he wasn't a traitor. He was used to make a point. Now it's my turn to make a point!" Asura swung her sword, but Beelzebub pivoted.

"You can't kill him. He's mine!" Symedek cried out.

Beelzebub jabbed his sword at Symedek while he hit Asura with a gold lightning bolt. She turned, her wings absorbing the energy.

Beelzebub turned to Symedek. "I tire of our battle. It was entertaining to watch you think you could beat me and get your soul back, but—the Ancient One has completely become one with me. When you split yourself in two, you should have known you would never be whole again."

An ache tore from the inside as Symedek's dream of reuniting with his soul extinguished. Symedek tightened his grip on Raum as Beelzebub gloated in front of him. A part of him wanted his own death at this moment, no longer having a reason to live. All whom he'd ever loved were long gone, and he'd never see them in the afterlife. He hadn't earned that privilege. The other part of him was more persistent, pushing him to do what he had thought was unthinkable. Bloodied, but not beaten, Symedek raised the ax that had found its way back to him.

For this purpose...

"Be free," Symedek whispered before he launched his ax. It spun end-over-end and hit its mark; Beelzebub's heart. He fell to his knees and screamed, but it was cut short when Asura's sword cut across his neck. Beelzebub's severed head fell to the side, disbelief etched upon it before ash and oily blood exploded into the air. Beelzebub's body disappeared, taking a precious part of him, too. Symedek gasped, struck his chest as a searing pain ripped through him. Killing a part of himself had become the ultimate sacrifice, but better this than to have it used by Beelzebub's diabolical—delusional purposes.

Symedek waited for the pierce of Asura's sword, but when the ash cleared, she was gone. He spied her golden trail heading toward the Mar of Sin.

It's over...

But I didn't win.

Symedek shook off the fog of Beelzebub's death and took in the vicious war taking place in every corner of the Realm. Watchers and Angels were in combat with the Fallen and Damned desperate to follow Lucifer into the Mar of Sin. Sparks of color encompassed the Realm as the forces clashed in a war destined to occur since the beginning of time. Lucifer underestimated how heavily he'd be contested, or he maybe he didn't care about the losses. The Fallen fought blindly for a leader whose sole purpose had always been for his personal glory. Symedek hadn't promised Michael he would fight for more than his soul, but as he watched his brave comrades, a resolve grew within. He must continue the fight until he was killed, or the portals closed.

His fate sealed.

His soul lost.

But humanity still needed him.

He faced the portal to Earth, inhaling the rushing fresh air he treasured so long ago. The sin he'd inflicted on humankind couldn't be erased, but he could fight the evil who would never love or understand them like he did.

"Eonlysis!" Symedek found his sword, its hilt igniting in blue sparks when his long fingers gripped it. He retrieved Raum lying nearby.

His oldest friend appeared, a satisfied smirk on his face. "Have your soul back?"

"No. Beelzebub corroded it. Once he transformed, it became lost it me. A fool's errand for the biggest fool of all. But he's dead and can no longer use it. I need you to take a group of Watchers to Earth. They need our help."

"As you wish. What about you?"

"I'll stay here. I have a last battle to undertake."

Eonlysis followed Symedek's gaze. "The Queen." He turned back, but Symedek didn't return his stare. "I want to say—"

Symedek shook his head. He reached out and gripped Eonlysis forearm in a familiar handshake. "Be victorious, my friend."

Eonlysis returned the gesture as more Watchers streaked toward them. "And you as well."

His comrades flew into the portal, certain to find carnage waiting on the other side. He propelled himself toward the battle, bottle-necked at the glorious pathway back into Heaven. He'd long since lost the privilege of that passage, as had the duplicitous Queen fighting at its gate.

CHAPTER
FIFTY

OLIVIA

The pause of the portals opening lasted for one beat of Olivia's heart, but with the next brought an onslaught of heinous shrieks from the Fallen. The red terrain of the valley reflected their outrage as they descended upon the Guardians with a renewed energy that shook Olivia to the core. How could they withstand such an onslaught long enough to close the portals?

We have to fight back.

Olivia mounted Aureus, raising her hands, sending bolts of fire exploding from her palms. She called on her orb for more power, urging her flames higher into the air. She was rewarded with angry shrieks and raining ash. Zach jumped on Malik and hurled his spinning boomerangs, slicing Fallen in two. When Sidra, Sergio's magnificent red Phoenix, appeared, he leaped on her back and launched a concussion of air bombs. Lucia and Amal shifted and prowled around them, striking down the Damned who dared to engage. The Magi were blurs of flashing swords, fighting fearlessly. Together, they held their ground with the Angels, waiting for the reinforcements they needed from Heaven.

It was a scant breath of time to wait. As the action around Olivia slowed, her movements became crisper, her thinking sharper and clearer than ever before. She moved as if guided by another, tuning her reactions. This focus brought an understanding of this new self; dawning as a sublime gift. When the orb was awakened by her blood and the essence of Melchior's gold gift of the Magi, her body also became enlightened, shifting to another level of awareness and ability. She embraced it, knowing she would need every ounce of these combined majestic powers to stay alive long enough to close the portals.

We can do this......

Gabriel zoomed above them on a white dragon with enormous gold wings carrying him across the sky. Fiery gold flames erupted from its mouth, clearing a path through the Fallen. Sealtiel, Uriel, Barachiel and Raphael circled above them on their similarly glorious white dragons, matching their virtuous colors. Together, they each held out a hand, palm aimed at where the Guardians battled, still vulnerable to the Fallen massing around them. An energy field bloomed, crackling with their colors, creating a dome surrounding them. The Magi, Amal, Zemira, and some warrior Angels were enclosed with the Guardians. Around the force field, Angels circled as a last defense, fighting the Fallen who dove to kill their enemies at all costs.

"The Fallen think they're winning," Melchior said. "Now that the portal is open, Lucifer's orders are certainly to kill you and keep the portal open forever."

"But three are open. Where are the Heavenly warriors? Didn't it work?" Despair clawed at Olivia as Angels disappeared from the sky along with Fallen. She couldn't hear their cries inside the dome, but the orb within her ached as if it absorbed each tragic death.

As her anxiety heightened, iridescent beings emerged from the middle portal, rushing out like water from a faucet. They held weapons of all colors, using them to split the Fallen's forces and clear the sky above them. The Damned, who clamored heedlessly against the force field, shoving against each other to get inside, were swept away, obliterated, before they recognized another type of deadly warrior had entered the field of battle. The Heavenly warriors' arrival gave them the advantage they desperately needed to survive.

Red and blue Fallen Princes upon their dragons swooped down, spraying the force field with blue and red fire. The field flickered, but held. They looped back to make another pass, but Gabriel and Uriel turned their dragons and attacked with a force of their own.

"Lucifer sent two Princes to Earth?" Zach asked, turning to Caspar.

"Mammon and Berith. He sent his most lethal Realms to hunt you down." Caspar replied.

Uriel urged his dragon to cut off Berith's path, circling around to make another pass at the Guardian's weakening dome. The Kingdom of Forgiveness and the Realm of Wrath were on a head-on collision course, the champions of good and evil vying for dominance. Uriel's long mane of black hair streaked behind him like a tail whipping in the wind. His white armor scrolled red with the same pattern fanning across his forehead. He let go of his dragon's horns and raised his broadsword in one hand and held his long whip in the other. Berith met the challenge with equal force and might. The dueling dragons bellowed fire at each other, igniting the sky in a canvas of red flames. Uriel cracked his whip's length, the end wrapping around Berith's weapon. He yanked it free as they drew alongside each other, like jousters galloping to clash together in one mighty blow. With Berith weaponless, Uriel sprang from his dragon in a glorious burst of bright red wings. Both his hands gripped the hilt of the sword, plunging into Berith's chest. The Prince of Wrath's scream of outrage was caught in the wind, along with his ashes. A horrendous collective screech shook the dome as the Wrath Realm registered their Prince's death. Some scurried away, others became easy kills in their confused state of disbelief.

"Incredible! The Wrath Realm is running away!" Zach marveled.

"With their Prince dead, they run like rats. Lucifer is the Master of the Realm, but Berith is the one who molded their evil, brainwashed their thoughts to be his collective. They'll regroup soon and reunite under a successor Fallen and be back with a vengeance." Balthazar stared at the sky as if looking for red streaks of evil.

"Lookout, Gabriel!" Sergio pointed his finger over Olivia's shoulder.

Gabriel and Mammon were also locked in a fiery battle of gold and blue flames. They probed each other in the air, seeking the other's weakness. Gabriel pulled out a smaller sword from his hip and threw it, piercing the dragon's eye. It bucked, throwing Mammon off balance. She jumped off the beast and dove toward the Fallen fighting beneath her. Gabriel's dragon blew one long blast across the back of the wounded, unmanned dragon. The beast let out a death cry before turning to ash. Gabriel circled, pursuing his search for Mammon.

Olivia marveled at Gabriel and Uriel's prowess. She felt useless under the dome. She understood it was for their safety, but it was getting harder and harder to watch the combat and not be a part of it.

"Be thankful," Melchior whispered in her ear. "This barrier may not last forever under the barrage of attacks."

That's when a new portal yawned open. Swathes of orange and purple Fallen burst forth, converging on the battle with a frenzied zeal. And just when the Angels seemed to have gained the upper hand, the tide turned back in the direction of the Fallen.

"I can't stand this!" Olivia shouted, pointing to the sky filled with death. "We have to fight! We can help." She pulled out her sword, hand trembling, to open a portal.

Zach grabbed her hand and locked it inside of his "If we die, this battle will rage and more Angels will perish because of it. We must stay here, under the protection until we see—"

A loud explosion brought all the chaos from the battle outside within the dome as cracks splintered the protective shell. Olivia's head snapped up in time to see the orange and purple dragons bellowing not long streams of flames, but massive bombs of fire exploding on the already weakened dome.

"It's not going to last much longer!" Olivia cried out.

"Lucifer released Gressil and Astaroth. I wonder if this means the Watchers are winning the battle in Hell."

Sealtiel jumped from her dragon as Astaroth passed beneath her. She landed behind him. He turned around, his forked tongue lashed at her but she sliced it off. She flashed her iridescent purple wings. Feathers ruffled as she cut off his head.

Gressil stalked behind Barachiel. Her dragon turned, shooting pink flames, but missed as Gressil was upon them. The dragon's orange tail swept over and knocked Barachiel off. Gressil flew after her, sword in front, ready to ram into the unconscious Barachiel. When the sword pierced Barachiel's chest, orange sparks traveled over her body. The Archangel disappeared, leaving her light pink feathers floating down over the battle, too beautiful for the surrounding evil.

"No!" Olivia shouted, just as the dome gave way with a final blast from Gressil's dragon. Gressil retreated in a snarl of victory, flying toward her Realm of Fallen.

The Guardians harnessed their magical beasts, and the army of Angels reinforced the area. A sea of Fallen bared down on them, red dust in their wake. She remembered the Defender video game and the surreal battle scene that had overtaken her. It seemed so real at the time, and maybe it was. Had it been a premonition of her future, of what would happen if she accepted the guardianship? Had it tried to scare her away from her destiny or steel her for the monumental moment of life and death she would face? Raising her sword, she channeled the fierce warrior she saw who charged into that battle, ready to fight even if it meant her own death.

I'm ready......

I will not back down.

But the memory faded and reality took its place as her weapon collided with an orange Fallen's fiery sword. Angels and Heavenly warriors beat back the evil bombarding them from every angle, swarming them in a chaotic mass.

"Stay with me, Liv. Don't leave my side." Zach yelled. Aureus roared beneath her, his tail and wings batting away the encroaching enemy. Soon, the Angels had beaten them back, only to have another wave of the Damned racing toward them.

Lucia and Amal were fighting near Sergio. A chill shot up Olivia's spine when Lucia's roar turned to a cry of pain. She turned and found her face down on the ground, a deep gaping gash down the length of her back. They raced to her. Sergio was already kneeling at her side, crying out her name.

Mammon cackled as she circled above. Lucia's red blood glistened obscenely on her sword. "Now, for the rest of you!"

Sergio threw his head back, veins bulging in his neck as he faced Mammon. "You'll have to get through me first!" But another emerged from the fray, a Fallen whose white hair had been a beacon of evil in this from the beginning.

"Zar!" Olivia shouted, aiming her hand, ready to blast him with fire.

Zar moved so swiftly, its bolt wouldn't have mattered. He lifted his sword, gaze fixed on his unwitting victim. His wings lifted him into the air, allowing him to bury his sword in Mammon's back. Her ice-blue eyes widened; grip loosening on her weapon as Zar shoved until his swirling green blade pierced her heart. Mammon's ash and blood rained down on Zar. His chest heaved as he turned to them, forever scanning with his black pits.

"Why?" Olivia asked, holding back her bolt.

"Delilah is dead. She wanted you Guardians to have a chance—to finish what has begun." Olivia glanced over her shoulder when Lucia moaned. When she turned back, he was gone, melting into the melee. The battle spread away from them, the Angels and Heavenly warriors turning the tide their way once again. She didn't have time to ponder Zar's unlikely deed right now. But none of it mattered if Lucia died.

Olivia and Zach crumbled to their knees next to Sergio. Sweat caked Lucia's thick hair to her face, her eyes half open as she took

Sergio's hand. Her head rested against Amal's bent legs; his hand trembling as he cupped her cheek.

"It's the only way. You must take my orb before—" Lucia muttered to her brother.

"No, you'll be fine. You're healing powers—"

"Stop Sergio. I can't close the portals like this. Please do as I ask before it's too late."

"Two become one." Sergio said, face crumbling as the realization hit home.

"Yes. Just like Gabriel said." Lucia whispered, her strength fading quickly.

"You have to do it before—" Tears streamed down Olivia's cheeks.

Sergio's crestfallen face turned to Olivia. "What if it's the orb keeping her alive?"

"Life is bigger than me walking through it. This battle is bigger than all of us." Lucia grabbed his hand and placed it over her mark. "Call for it. Hurry."

Olivia hated how Lucia's pool of red blood grew larger in the red dirt. "It's the only way, Sergio. We must be ready to close the portals."

Sergio nodded and closed his eyes, pressing his hand down on her mark. Light burst between his long fingers, splayed yet rigid, as if trying to help pull the orb from her. Lucia's back arched off the ground as the orb appeared under Sergio's palm. She released a shuddering breath and fell limp back onto Amal's legs. Sergio slammed the orb over his mark. Anger and pain dueled on his face as the orb disappeared beneath his armor.

"I'm taking her to the Magi's home." Amal scooped her up and cradled her close to him. "They have healing supplies I can use if I get her back in time."

"Find her father. He'll know what to do." Casper said. A gash in his arm and filth from fighting couldn't hide his sorrow.

Casper raised a portal. Amal carried Lucia's depleted body through without looking back, her arm dangling from her side.

Sergio yelled, releasing his rage. "She can't die!"

Olivia came to him and grabbed his arm. "You're one with her now. Share in her courage so we can beat the evil that is trying to steal our world. Make it count!"

"We'll hold on for Lucia—I don't know how much longer we have to fight until we see the sign, but we'll do it." Olivia drew strength from the determination chiseled on Zach's face

Olivia scanned the red desert, a wasteland of charred earth and trampled terrain. Smoke rose in the distance, signaling her city was still in the throes of war. Even with all the death on both sides, the fighting was still ferocious. The Warrior Angels had turned the tide of battle, but it was far from won. Gressil led a charge of Fallen toward them, but Raphael was hot on her trail. Olivia thought about leaving, going to another place, but they would just follow and bring death there.

This is where we make our stand.

Olivia climbed back onto Aureus. The three of them kept in a close circle, watching the skies for a sign while fighting off their enemies with their powers and swords. She watched Bal strafe a row of Damned with gold bullets and Caspar flinging shards of green water glass at their enemies. Realizing she hadn't seen Melchior recently, she scanned for him, her heart pounding when she couldn't find him.

"Melchior!" Her call went unanswered.

"What's that?" Zach aimed his sword into the sky at the massive, shadowy black forms emerging from Hell's portal. "I hope that's not more Fallen Lucifer's been hiding until this day."

"We're about to find out!" Sergio shouted as the new wave dived for the trio.

CHAPTER
FIFTY-ONE

LUCIFER

I *made it!*
Abaddon escaped the Realms turmoil and entered the Mar of Sin's spinning gray vortex, roaring around Lucifer like a beast enraged he dared to enter its lair. Blood pounded in his head. Taloned hands gripped Abaddon's horns as they ascended in their vertical climb back to where it all began. A pinpoint of light grew wider as they raced higher, deeper toward Heaven. The cries of the Fallen buoyed him as they flew in his wake. They were just as eager as him to revisit Heaven and battle for the revenge they sought. As the light grew brighter, he recoiled against the memories of his place in Heaven, taunting him and what he lost.

Highest next to God...

The serenity and unity among the Angels...

The vastness of Heaven with iridescent waterfalls into the stars—

"Get out of my head! You betrayed us!" Lucifer yelled at the opening, spittle spraying from between his snarled lips. Did these memories surface because of God's meddling, or was there a deeper part of his soul that yearned to be back in the Heavenly fold? "I'll never forgive you!" The message of outrage burned to the Fallen through their shared link. The renewed frenzy of deep-seated need for bloodshed rewarded his surge of hatred. Lucifer shifted his focus to his memory of God showing his new creation—his abomination to the Heavenly Host.

Recoiling at being told the Angels would serve humanity...

A siren's voice whispering in his ear that he wasn't alone in his repulsion and he should rebel against God.

Others will follow if you lead them

The shame and resentment of being cast out of Heaven into a pit of darkness and damnation.

"I *will* destroy all you love above us!" Lucifer bellowed, his heart pounding with the elation that all his planning, his patience in creating the Damned, stroking the fires of hate and revenge, were coming to a grand finale.

Leviathan and Asmodeus rode close on each side, worthy of the royalty he'd bestowed upon them. He snarled when he thought of Beelzebub and his treachery. How could he have betrayed him so blatantly when Lucifer had given him everything he wanted? He channeled this deceit into his outrage at the treachery of the Watchers being released into his domain to fight for God.

Hypocrites! Their sin is no worse than mine!

It didn't matter what happened between Symedek and Beelzebub or the outcome of their battle. If they lived, he would kill them.

And anyone else who stands in my way.

"Ride us to glory, Abaddon! Let the souls in Heaven burn in your fire!" Abaddon roared, his belly glowing red, stoking its furnace.

Lucifer burst through the opening. He shuddered, his body recoiling against Heaven's vibrant, vast terrain before him. It was all as he remembered; God's grand throne was high up the crystal mountain, Angels adoring him from its clear cliffs. The force of love and beauty struck his chest, but Lucifer wouldn't allow it to dissolve the crust of evil hardened by the fires of the Seven Realms. He rejected it with all his will and envisioned how soon this place of illumination would reflect the bowels of Hell.

"It's still as I remembered," Leviathan shouted. "It sickens me."

"Let it be the fuel to your fire, my friend."

They rode on a wave of smoke, their wings snapping in their vengeful flight. Everything Lucifer had worked for had come to this point, this war he'd dreamed of since he fell through the Mar of Sin.

"Be ready, Abaddon, for today's vengeance will be sweeter than when I whispered in Eve's ear." Lucifer let the pleasure of Eve's demise wash over him, feed his certainty of the unworthiness of humans and the love and adoration they were so easily given.

"Stop Lucifer!" God's voice boomed. "You shall come no further and desecrate this ground with more blood." A white web burst from the mountain top, sizzling with the vibrant colors of the seven virtues winding around it and reinforcing it. The net rose and wrapped around the Mar of Sin, blocking their escape or forward progress.

"Burn it, Abaddon!" Lucifer raised his fist and shook it. Fire from Abaddon, Leviathan's and Asmodeus's dragons erupted from their mouths. Their rows of teeth glowed like shards of glass as they aimed at the web blocking the Fallen's progress. The flames were rejected by the web. Instead of burning away, the magical fibers absorbed the heat, making the ropes thicker.

Lucifer couldn't believe it. Wrath boiled in him like the day he saw humans for the first time.

"You're a coward!" Lucifer raised his sword toward the mountain. "You set this all up—for my return, and when it happens, you deny me and hide behind your power? You truly are afraid of me and the army I've brought!"

"I don't fear you, Lucifer." God spoke over the Fallen's anger shouts. "My love for you has never stopped. When you left, you used your free will in a way that tore my heart in two, but I couldn't stop it, for if I did, I had to change it in humans as well. This day has arrived as it was meant to be. A day that will transform everything."

"Because I shall destroy you and everything you love."

"We shall see. It will not be as you intend. You and Michael will finish the battle you started. If you win, I'll lower my shield and you can have your war. If Michael wins, the Fallen will return from hence they came."

A white dragon streaked across the sky, flaming blue wings quickly closed the gap, with a rider perched high behind its head. Lucifer sneered at Michael and welcomed the unfinished fight that haunted his dreams. As his nemesis drew closer, a low murmuring arose, growing louder until Lucifer could finally understand what it was.

"Do you hear that?" Asmodeus covered her ears. "Those are prayers asking for help. I can't stand their endless whining."

Lucifer wouldn't listen, letting the drumming in his ears drown them out. "Stop your *whining* or you're no better than them."

Michael hovered before the netting, his eyes blazing as he returned Lucifer's stare with matching disdain. "Notice the prayers aren't for you, Lucifer? They plead for Fallen's death and to be saved from the evil you bring upon them."

"They'll bow to me soon enough and learn that prayers will be punished in my world."

"Not if I can help it." A hole materialized in the web. "You and Abaddon may pass if you accept the challenge."

"With pleasure." Lucifer turned to Leviathan. "Be ready and have no mercy."

"Lead us to victory, Master."

Lucifer nodded, guiding Abaddon through the opening. It crackled around him as if straining against a need to close and split him in half. The shock felt like it was peeling back a layer of his skin, draining the powers he'd manifested from each of the Realms. He wanted to cry out, but he clenched his teeth together. No complaint would leave his lips. Yet, the gleam in Michael's eyes dared him to strike back. When he fully emerged, the opening sizzled closed, but Lucifer felt as if he'd been stripped clean.

My blood is still black.

"Your grotesque powers will not work here. You'll fight as you were when you left. A disgraced Seraphim, not a depraved Fallen who sucks up the energy of the wayward souls and the hate that festers in that pit." Michael's dragon snorted, smoke erupting from its nostrils. Its reptilian eyes narrowed, staring at Abaddon as if to remember when it had been a part of the beasts that roamed Heaven and were repulsed by him.

"Whatever tricks make you feel better." He guided Abaddon away from the shield. Each dragon moved in tandem, circling each other, starting the dance of assessment, looking for the slightest sign of weakness to strike first.

"No tricks to play here. Fair fighting is an art you've probably lost sulking in the dark."

Lucifer scanned the floors of Heaven, disgusted to find the number of souls and Angels smaller than it should be. "Of course, you've hidden the human souls. His precious abomination was always more important to Him than to us."

"Assuming the negative has always been your weakness. Warrior souls of the past have chosen to go to Earth through one of the portals the Guardians opened and are wiping out your army on Earth as we speak. They fight for the free will you want to destroy. You aren't the only one with an army of souls."

Lucifer waved a hand toward the web. Their sound had grown muffled as he and Michael ascended into the sky, but their malicious energy vibrated to him—within him. "The Fallen have free will—"

"You created slaves to follow your weak logic—your jealousy!" Michael unsheathed his sword. "They became limited, pathetic, trapped in the warpness of their sin. That isn't freedom. That's tyranny."

Lucifer had heard enough. "Fire!" Abaddon's red flame missed its target because Michael had already taken off, soaring away from the audience below. He chased his fleeting form, never more certain of anything than wanting to kill Michael. The white dragon slipped into the clouds hovering above them. Lucifer didn't blend in with his black armor riding a black dragon, but fearlessly surged upward at finally having the fight he'd longed for.

Abaddon shrieked as blue flames struck his underbelly, fanning around its ribcage, licking up to the feet of its evil rider. He returned a burst of red fire, catching the tail of the escaping dragon. Ripples of pain rolled through the scales under Lucifer's legs.

"Michael!" A weakened but fearless Abaddon chased them back through the clouds. Lucifer saw a streak of blue to his right in time to turn Abaddon to blast another fiery salvo. Red and blue flames collided and created a wall of flames between them. Michael emerged with his wings spread wide, flames like a halo surrounding him, stunning even to Lucifer. But the moment was shattered when Michael dove and sliced his sword across Abaddon's throat. Black blood sprayed over the clouds as Michael swooped down into the clouds toward Heaven's floor. Abaddon's flames stopped, but his massive jaws hung open. Pain ripped through Lucifer as if the sword had pierced him. The dragon's body went from tense to limp beneath him.

"Abaddon—No... *No!*" In a free fall spiral, Lucifer jumped off his dragon's back, no longer able to control him. He scanned the sky for Michael's dragon, but he couldn't find it. He descended the clouds next to Abaddon. "He'll pay for this." A yell ripped from his chest. "You hear that, Michael—You'll pay for this!" Abaddon bled out the last of his black blood as they broke free of the clouds, turning to ash over the inhabitants trapped inside the web.

Michael stood waiting for him, his long sword a light in blue flames. Lucifer landed and launched himself at Michael. Cheers from both sides roared around them as their swords clashed and sparks of flames showered in their wake. Their battle pushed Lucifer to his limits. He noticed the web getting closer, wondering if he could somehow slice it and make an opening for the Fallen to escape through. This slip of focus was his undoing. Michael jumped, twirled, and brought his sword down, slicing across Lucifer's shoulder. He cried out and dropped his sword, the only weapon he carried.

Instead of Michael delivering a killing blow, he slashed across Lucifer's thigh, bringing him to his knees. He pointed his sword at

Lucifer's chest, forcing him to lean back toward the web. The sizzling behind Lucifer grew louder, as if in anticipation of devouring him in licks of electricity.

"You coward, ending our fight! Too tired to go on? Give me my sword and let's continue. Or are you playing games with me?"

"No. The Fallen will go back to where they belong. Back to the pit."

"Sending me back as well? I'll be back. I *will* never stop." Lucifer stared at Michael and fully exposed all the hatred he felt for him. He was wounded, but the Fallen would go back to the Realms. They would regroup and destroy what God loved. "We'll always be locked together. You and I."

A new creature's cry pierced the air. It came from within the puffy white clouds billowing down God's Mountain. Another one rang out, louder, closer than before. The Angels fell to their knees, but Lucifer didn't notice. He couldn't tear his eyes away from the sky flashing with lightning, electrifying the enormous white horse racing toward him, filling his vision.

"My bondage to you ends today. I made the horrendous mistake of once letting you live. I *will* not make it again. It's over Lucifer. Your reign of evil has corrupted its last soul!"

Lucifer didn't feel the plunge of Michael's sword into his heart or know that his body turned to ash and oil, lost in the swirling Mar of Sin.

He didn't see how his death turned the Fallen into a chaotic mob, fleeing in crazed desperation to the only place they ever belonged— the depraved sanctuary where they would hovel out an existence without him.

Hell.

Because in the last second of his wasted existence, an explosion of pure light emanated from the face of the resplendent rider astride the white horse, blinding him with the revelation he should have under- stood when God enlightened the Angels with His beloved creation.

Humans

Lucifer's tyrannical rule over them was only an outcome in his skewed sense of ultimate purpose. All of what he had diabolically executed was just a sliver in a magnificent eternal plan he could only perceive in his final gasp of life.

The end of wicked rule—his insignificant death... was the majestic catalysis for humans and the future of their glorious new world.

CHAPTER
FIFTY-TWO

OLIVIA

Vast amounts of the shadowy beings obscured the sky, circling above the decimated red desert. Olivia stood in the middle of the war zone; feet braced with Sandalphon raised to face this new nemesis. Her body ached from the battle blows she received, her head pounding with the horrid screeches and wails of pain bombarding her from all sides. Fear gnawed, twisted her insides, that their survival was tenuous, and the Fallen could triumph. She fought back the exhaustion, the horrors of the day, to stay alert and fight with all she'd been given and all she'd learned. Letting Sergio and Zach down was not an option. If any of them failed to do their part, the world as she knew it would be lost forever. Anxious anticipation for Melchior's return didn't help. She needed him while they waited for the sign to close the portals. She cast out one last furtive glance, but his silver hair was nowhere to be found. Maybe he got swept up into another area of battle?

He would stay close to me...

Their shared link was still intact, but he could be in trouble and need her help.

The shadows were flying above them, catching the attention of the Fallen, confused by their presence.

"My mark doesn't hurt when I focus on them," Zach said as he put his back against Olivia's. "It's too crazy here—unpredictable. The Magi are spread out, and the Damned just keep pouring out of Hell. I don't know how much longer we can hold out waiting for this ambiguous sign that's taking its sweet time to show up. We should just close it before one of us gets hurt like Lucia."

"Lucia will be fine. She's not dead." Sergio came closer until they were in a tight-knit circle facing the enemy. "I would know. What if we went into the mountains? We could hide in the caves. If the Fallen think we've left, maybe they'll go back."

"I don't want to get trapped in a cave. The portals are still open and we have the upper hand with the souls from Heaven."

Gabriel and Raphael landed next to them. Their white armor covered in red dirt, dents in the links spoke of near misses. Both had slashes healing on their hands and faces.

"The Watchers are here!" Gabriel pointed as the Watchers flew closer, their wings beating back the Damned who cowered in the face of this unknown presence. One swooped down, striking down a line of Lucifer's army with his blazing blue sword. She looked at Sandalphon, noticing how the blue burned pure like hers, not infiltrated by a dark nature.

"I didn't know what to expect, but—"

"They look like all the light was leeched out of them." Zach finished her thought.

"That's it." She nudged him as more Watchers landed around them, pushing back the army on the ground and cutting down the Fallen striking from above. "You can almost see through them. Michael must have convinced them to fight on our side."

"Thank goodness, because they're terrifying," Sergio said. "Where did they get those swords?"

"Michael made them with a drop of his blood. He felt it was only right because he approached them with their choice." Gabriel nodded. "One of them is coming over."

"Where is Michael?" Olivia asked as she braced herself for the Watcher's arrival, her pulse rushing despite his obvious allegiance.

Their appearance had given them and the Angels a reprieve from battle, but it would only be momentary as the Fallen reinvigorated their efforts to break through the Watchers' reinforced barrier.

"His fight is in Heaven with Lucifer." Raphael said, green sparking from his raised sword.

"Are you the Guardians Michael spoke of?" The Watcher asked. Gabriel and Raphael maneuvered themselves between him and the trio, but remained silent.

"Must be if you two are protecting them," he chuckled. The sound was hollow, as if traveling a great distance. "I'm Eonlysis. We mean them no harm. I needed to meet the humans brave enough to take on Lucifer and the Fallen. And to thank you—" He gazed down at his sword "—for freeing us."

"We're thankful you chose to fight on our side." Olivia said, stepping out from between the two protectors. "I don't know how much longer we can hold them off before—"

"Michael will do everything in his power to defeat Lucifer. We'll stay here and fight until you close the portals—"

"And bring an end to your existence, right?" Olivia said, saddened by the thought of their abrupt end.

Eonlysis lifted his shadowy face to the sky and sighed. "My life will vanish in the light of day, not in my opaque prison of shame. Do *not* feel sorry for me, young heroes." He suddenly shifted, raising his weapon as a heavenly being slipped through their barrier.

"Manny?" Sergio gasped, stumbling forward and shoving past Olivia. "Is that you?"

"Wait!" Olivia lurched after him, but stopped when she also recognized the warrior soul before them. Manny stood proudly with his sword flaming green by his side. His features were the same, but he loomed taller, more intimidating than he ever was on Earth in his spectacularly iridescent form.

"Manny!" A strangled cry escaped Sergio as he reached out a hand toward Manny, but he stopped short out of Sergio's reach. "You're here... fighting with us."

"*Si, mano.* I told you I would always protect you."

"I miss you so much." Tears streamed down Sergio's face, clearing a track of battle dirt in its path. "I'm so sorry—"

"No. It was all a part of your journey. It made you stronger to help Lucia, conquer your own fears and harness your anger. I'm proud of you. You're a worthy Guardian, *mano.*" Manny took a step back and then another. Sergio lunged for him, but Manny shook his head.

"Don't leave me again." Sergio cried out.

"I was always there, but you have all you need here with you now." Manny smiled as his body began to fade away.

"Come back—"

"It is time." He said, and then he was gone.

"*Manny!*" Sergio dropped to his knees, his arms reaching out for the brother he loved so much. Olivia and Zach rushed to his side, pulling him away from the ever-shifting battle line.

"Come on," Zach said, leading him back to the Archangels. "We need to stay together."

"He was with me all along." Sergio muttered, eyes still frantically searching for the return of his brother. The wind gusted around them, sweeping the hair back from his forehead.

"Doesn't surprise me. He always had an eagle eye on you. Remember when Manny interrogated us before we went to Red Rock?" Zach patted Sergio's back. They shared a quick smile.

"That feels like a lifetime ago." Sergio muttered.

The winds continued to pick up, white clouds billowing like a fast-moving thunderstorm. It wasn't only the skies that were changing. The Fallen's swords moved at a faster frenzied pace, the horde of the Damned hurling themselves toward the Guardians in a renewed effort.

"Olivia." An anguished cry came from behind her. She turned just as Melchior stumbled through the Watchers' barricade and collapsed to the ground.

She ran to him, the wind whipping around her furiously. Falling to her knees, she placed her hand on his blood covered chest. "Hold on just a little longer. I'll get Raphael. I need you with me. Something is happening—"

Melchior's large hand cupped the side of her head, his thumb brushing away her tears. "You never needed me. You only needed to believe—trust in yourself and others." Then his hand fell away, vacant eyes staring over her shoulder.

"NO!" she yelled, shaking his shoulders. "Melchior!" She threw her arms around his neck, sobbing as she rocked his lifeless body in her lap.

Come back to me...

"Liv!" Zach crouched down, placing a hand on her shoulder. "Liv —I'm sorry, but you've gotta let him go. Something is happening. Look up."

She shook her head, not willing to believe he was gone. But she knew he would not want his death to stop her from doing what she was created for. She looked up and saw the sign. Their time had come.

White clouds surged so close, she felt she could touch them. The Fallen shrieked, cowering as if they understood what was happening before she did. They took to the skies, retreating to escape whatever could possibly terrify evil. Olivia's jaw dropped when a massive white horse emerged, chilling her to the bone.

"I love you," she whispered in Melchior's ear before she slipped his head off her lap. She stood and let Zach's arms embrace her.

"He loved you, too." Zach whispered.

The clouds encompassed every inch of sky, Angels rode in its wake as the Damned clamored over each in their desperation to get back to the portal. The Fallen flew through first, abandoning their allies as the disposable creatures Lucifer intended.

"He's coming!" Gabriel shouted; his face crumbled in joy. "Close the portals!"

She pulled away and glanced over her shoulder as Sergio joined them, but Melchior was gone. The trio then faced each other.

"Ready?" Olivia asked, her voice raw from battle and death.

"With every fiber of my being." Sergio declared.

"I love you, Liv," Zach said before he placed his hand over his mark. Sergio nodded and smiled at her, peace finally glowing in his golden-brown eyes.

"I love you, too. Both of you." she whispered. Her palm heated above her mark, seeking the precious essence she held within. Her mind linked with the mark, reaching deeper for the orb.

Release what was given...

She said the mantra again, this time out loud. Sergio and Zach repeated it with her. As one they chanted, beckoning the orb forth to reveal itself for the last time. A burning sensation bloomed under her mark. She gritted her teeth as muscle and skin shifted, separating to relinquish the vessel that had become embedded in her.

Will I die?

It didn't matter. Her life... their lives... had lost significance compared to the deaths of the day. She would gladly sacrifice her life to save her fellow humans from ever again facing what happened today.

The orb sprung free, the same bright blue as the day she remembered seeing it for the first time before Melchior slammed it into her mark. She held it out in her palm, anxiously watching as the swirling green orb released from Zach. Sergio brought his orb forward, larger than theirs, swirling with gold.

Olivia gasped when the orb lifted and hovered above her palm. The orbs rose in unison above them, electric charges firing off between their surfaces. They began spinning so fast that the colors blurred into one new, united orb. Zach laced his fingers between hers as their heads fell back, eyes glued to the orb's growing surfaces. The air crackled with a static charge, her hair slapping her face. Finally, the electric charges stopped. Three brilliant lights exploded from the orb, shooting into the sky toward the portals. A ring of light grew from around the orb, expanding like a ring around a planet. Time froze as the world around Olivia turned white. The brilliance blinded her.

"Get down!" Zach yelled, but it was too late. The shock wave's blast struck her, bulldozing through her body. It lifted her and threw her off her feet, the boom splitting the air. She landed with a heavy thud, her head smacking the unforgiving red ground. She watched the shock wave travel over the terrain. It washed through the Angels like a wave, but when it hit a Fallen or Damned, it swallowed them up, devoured by the blast. She saw Eonlysis raise his arms, welcoming the wave that swept him into oblivion. Her vision tunneled to black, but not before the white horse and its glorious rider glided above her.

It's done.

CHAPTER
FIFTY-THREE

SYMEDEK

A sura fought with a cold assuredness rivaling any creature Symedek had ever had the pleasure of watching or fighting against. Her moves were sure and swift, with no hesitation or doubt against her opponent. Gold streaks ignited in her armor and along her ebony skin, running like lava, a life force embodying her preeminent place among the Fallen. Queen, regal, yet deadly. Her ostentatious crown perched securely on her head, the mass of her thin golden braids lifted by the Realms heated drafts. Symedek could have fallen in love with her too, but Lucifer had laid claim to her eons ago in Heaven, and she to him. The virtue of Humility never suited her, but the sin of Pride, with its corruption of gold, was perfection on her.

Symedek easily defeated the Fallen who dared approached him. Most were of the lower hierarchies and were no match for a Seraphim. He watched Asura, assessing her strategy before confronting her. Lucifer and his army had flown through the Mar of Sin with such certainty that they would overrun Heaven with their advantage of surprise.

But was God ever surprised?

Only the purely narcissistic would dare make that assumption.

Lucifer was definitely delusional, and his war would forever leave a tragic mark on history. How humanity fared after his death, only time would tell. He wouldn't be there to witness the transformation.

I have one last mission.

As he worked his way closer to Asura, he allowed the sadness and regret of his past decisions to wash over him one final time. Not in self-pity, but to reinforce why he fought against the Fallen this day, and strived to bring them down. They loved nothing but their selfish desires. Humans were just toys to entertain them. What Lucifer was trying to accomplish right now in Heaven, spilling more innocent blood, was an effort to fill his abyss of rage. He would never be satisfied.

It must never happen.

The Watchers had loved God's beautiful, naïve creation. Humans were good and faithful. They wanted to please the Angels who were supposed to guide them in their service, in their of love for God and their fellow man. But the power of this adulation had been intoxicating, transforming Symedek's mission on Earth. He had yearned to replace God, even defiling himself by tearing out a portion of his soul and hiding it, so he could come back and rule on Earth. Shame burned a hole in what was left of his essence, reigniting what he wanted—needed to do, before his time was up, whether at the hands of Asura or the portals closing.

If they are closed...

He felt certain Asura was aware of his presence the whole time, but he allowed her coy game of avoidance. When her golden eyes finally locked with his, they sparked with hatred. But the ripple running down her wings betrayed a hint of fear. She faced him, waving away the army between them.

"I saved you once, traitor. I'll not do it again." Asura sneered.

"Why did you help me with Beelzebub?" Symedek kept his sword in front of him, keeping his body relaxed. He didn't want to fight her just yet. "He stole my soul. It was my right to kill him."

"Beelzebub wanted to *steal* the Realm for himself. He's the reason Sonneillon, my mate, was murdered. His death should have been by my hand, not yours." Asura glanced behind her. The Mar of Sin's entrance remained unchanged, bottlenecked as if the Fallen couldn't go through.

"But Sonneillon wasn't your true mate, was he?" Symedek cocked his head. "You've been eternally bound to Lucifer since the beginning of our time."

Her chest flared gold as if his words hit an old wound. "Lucifer grew tired of me, and I of him. The possibilities within the Realm changed our wants and desires."

"Hmm... I think you're lying to me and to yourself. You're the reason this pit—the Realm was created."

Her six wings snapped, cracking the surrounding air. "What do you mean? It was Lucifer who led the Fall... had the courage to stand up to God and confront Him about His hideous creation."

Symedek shook his head, inching closer to her. "You forget that I was also near Lucifer when we were shown humans. He remained stoic, but it was you who whispered in his ear. It was your chest swirling in defiance, just as it does now. You poisoned him with your fears, planted the seed of their unworthiness to be served by Angels. Weren't your words to him... *I find them beneath you?*" He shrugged. "Whatever you said changed his heart, his nature. I watched him become tainted by you. Do you deny this?"

Emotions shifted her chillingly beautiful ebony face. First surprise, then suspicion turning to denial with a slight lifting of her chin. But ultimately, a smug smile stretched her full lips. "I always wondered if anyone else noticed my influence over him. I should have suspected you, always observing in the background. It was easy to turn him. Didn't take much persuasion. What Lucifer desired was already lurking just below his superior surface."

"And what did he want that he didn't already have?"

"Power. Isn't that what we all wanted?" Asura scoffed. "Without the restraints of God? Being closest to that force makes it even harder to deny oneself. Lucifer should have known it was Beelzebub... he was his closest ally until I came became Queen."

"Yet it was you all along who really worked against him."

Her silence was all the confession he needed.

The Mar of Sin's swirling vortex grew faster and louder. Symedek spied the opening, wondering if it was ready to expel the invaders or disappear all together.

"Why aren't you fighting next to your King?" Symedek asked, moving closer.

"I'm to stay here to defeat the invaders, including you." Asura moved with a speed he admired and would have been caught by her killing blow, but his body moved quicker, lighter, having wasted away in his prison. He met her sword at the top of the arc, spraying sparks when their weapons clashed. He shoved her back, enjoying the surprise flickering across her face.

"You stayed here because you knew he would lose, die in his ridiculous siege in Heaven. You were going to pick up the pieces, weren't you, as the Queen of the Realm? Lucifer wasn't the only one who devised a plan when the Guardians arrived, was he? You suspected Beelzebub wanted to overthrow Lucifer because that's what you would have done. Were you working with Beelzebub? Did you help kill him to keep your secrets?"

Asura raised her sword, her chest heaving as she faced him, fanning out her six wings. "I killed him because I am the Queen of the Seven Realms and he had no right to usurp it from me." She snarled as she lunged for Symedek, aiming for his chest. He spun and slashed her wing. She cried out and dove for the floor with her damaged wing hanging to the side. He could have finished her, but not until she witnessed the truth of her fate.

"The Fallen are coming back!" A cry rang out in the Realm.

He glanced over his shoulder to find the army rushing out of the Mar of Sin's opening. Some of the Fallen shouted angry unintelligible words, others were silent in unspoken fear and dismay. He chased Asura, sensing his time was nearing an end.

She raised her sword when he landed before her, but her eyes shifted focus beyond him as she watched the Fallen flood Hell... again. Symedek marveled at the filaments of gold stitching healing her wounded wing, recovering enough for her to soon return to flight. She braced herself to battle him, but her attention kept switching between his sword and the Mar of Sin.

"Looking for your King?" Symedek smirked. "I doubt Michael will set him free again."

"I'm counting on that." Asura threw a lightning bolt at Symedek. It struck him in the chest, knocking him to the floor. He rolled to the side, barely missing the tip of her blade. He jumped up and grabbed a handful of her wild braids. Slamming her back against his chest. He brought his blue blade under her chin. Asura froze and dropped her sword.

"My fight is not with you." Asura shouted. "Go before I summon all the Fallen upon you."

The floor quivered beneath them; the mountains rumbled as if to erupt. "It has begun," Symedek whispered in her ear.

"What—"

Symedek yanked on her braids, silencing her. "The end of the Fallen," he hissed. "The portals not only open, but the Guardians will close them at Lucifer's death. A new, glorious era will begin for the human race with His second coming."

"No—that can't happen! I am to rule the Realms!" Her decry was lost in the roar expelling from the Mar of Sin. Symedek's eyes widened as the vortex grew narrow, spinning faster until it finally snapped closed, leaving the wails and outrage of the Fallen in its wake.

"The gates of Hell are now closed forever." He tossed Asura from him. She stumbled to the floor, losing her footing as the ground shook violently. "Evil never wins. We all die here today for the pain and suffering we imposed upon humanity. You lost, Asura. You will *never* rule Hell because its existence is no more."

A blur of green light and whipping white hair flew over him. The

Fallen was astride a black Degasus with a flaming red mane. He circled above Asura, brandishing his sword, swirling green around the lethal blade.

"Nooooooo—" Asura screamed with all her fury, snarling in hatred as the surprising cohort's weapon arched through the air and sliced across her neck. Gold braids entangled her head as it tumbled through the air. Her body slumped to the ground before exploding in a spray of blood and ash. A sweeping wind claimed her remnants, devouring the being who was truly the most diabolic of all.

The white-haired Fallen landed next to Symedek, Asura's blood evaporating from his blade. He lifted his face, eyeless pits taking in the destruction around him. He sheathed his sword with a sense of satisfaction in his swift movement.

"You assassinated your Queen." Symedek spoke it as a statement, not a question.

"She was never my Queen."

The mountains rumbled, exploding with boulders and rocks hurling into the sky. Lava boiled over its banks, and the buildings of the Realms crumbled in the deafening destruction of the malignant abyss that would never again consume another soul.

Hell is lost...

The gates are closed...

Forever.

Symedek swiveled when an ear shattering boom pierced the air in the direction of where the Mar of Sin had been.

"It is done." Symedek whispered, raising his arms to receive the fate of his death. He didn't have long to wait. The shock wave obliterated Hell and all the vile creatures in its path speeding towards them, obliterating the Realm from dark to light. As the wave surged toward him, the white-haired Fallen soared into flight on his Degasus, meeting the blast for his one final clash. He, along with the rest of the inhabitants, evaporated inside the brilliant light.

I love you, Arayana.

Please forgive me.

Symedek felt the wave strike him. The radiance slammed into him, its colossal force eviscerating him and all the evil left in its wake.

CHAPTER
FIFTY-FOUR

OLIVIA

Muffled voices broke through Olivia's fog. Her head felt as if it could split in two. A part of her wanted to ignore the outside chatter and stay safe in this haze. But a nagging inner voice forced her to confront the realties floating just outside her memory's reach. Something she didn't want to acknowledge was real.

Fallen stampeding toward her...

Angel blood pooling on red dirt...

A bright explosion...

A heavy body draped across her lap—

Her eyes flew open. "Melchior..." Olivia pushed away the hands gripping her arms. She shook her head, but the ringing in her ears wouldn't stop. "Where's Melchior?"

"Livvy, drink this." Her dad was squatted down next to her, nudging a glass of water into her hand. She licked her dry lips before gulping down the refreshing liquid. Sighing, she handed the glass back and gazed over her dad's shoulder. The Weapons Room glowed around her, filled with faces she knew and loved, but one was missing.

Her mom rushed to her other side and wrapped her willowy arms around her in a bear hug. "Olivia—thank God you're awake. I was so scared." Mom's wet cheeks rested against hers. She sniffled and gave her a quick peck on the cheek. "I'm so proud of you and so relieved you're back in one piece. Are you hurt, honey?"

"My head, but I think everything else is just sore. Can you help me up?" Her parents each put a hand under each arm and lifted. She scanned the room again and with each face she appraised, fresh memories flooded her.

"Melchior disappeared after—" She turned to her dad. "Did someone bring him back here?"

"No, honey—" his eyes bright with unshed tears "—he didn't survive."

"I thought maybe..." Olivia couldn't finish as pain slashed through her. She squeezed her eyes shut, trying to block the memory of him dying in her arms. "I can't believe he's gone."

"Liv!" Zach barreled through her parents and scooped her up. She threw her arms around him, burying her face in his neck. She wished she could burrow inside of him and let him ease the ache in her heart. "We did it, Liv. We closed the portals. It's over." She felt him smile, his warm breath reassuring her as it caressed her ear. He pulled back and cupped her face in his warm hands. "I'm sorry about Melchior. I wish it turned out differently. I love you." He leaned down and kissed her. She returned it with the raw emotion swirling within her, wanting to feel alive instead of sinking into the sorrow of the deaths of the day.

Dad cleared his throat. "Someone else wants to see you."

When Olivia and Zach separated, Lucia stood between Amal and Sergio, her large eyes bright within her pale face. "Lucia... I knew Amal wouldn't let you die." Lucia shyly glanced at Amal. Olivia walked over and hugged her gently. The bandages peeking out from under her shirt were a stark reminder that Lucia fought for her life as a human, not with the help from orb's essence.

"Between my *familia* and Amal, I was in the best of care." Lucia slipped her hand into Amal's, their fingers lacing together. Olivia grinned, happy for her friend. She turned to Sergio, his thick hair falling across his forehead.

"So, Manny…" Olivia reached for his hand and squeezed it tight. "What a gift."

"Yeah." Sergio's throat worked up and down. "I miss him so much, but to know that he's… there—waiting and watching." He ran his fingers through his hair. "It's a big relief."

The fire pit's white flames bloomed behind Sergio, their tips licking the ceiling. The crowd separated and faced the circular stairs leading to the fire pit. Olivia's heart raced in anticipation. Her brain buzzed with so many questions, it was hard to hold a single thought. When cobalt blue sparkled from within the flames, she released a breath she didn't realize she'd been holding. Michael stepped out and walked down the stairs, followed by Gabriel and Raphael. They glowed with the powers of warrior Archangels, but there was an air of sadness to them as they scanned the room. When Michael's gaze found hers, a dazzling smile stretched across his face.

"Guardians, please come forward." They exchanged puzzled glances before the four of them approached the base of the stairs. When they stopped, Olivia wiped her hands down her jeans. It was then she realized her armor was gone. Where was Sandalphon?

"The Heavenly Hosts owe you each a debt of gratitude for the bravery you displayed today. If you had faltered, the world would be a much different place." Michael bowed his head to them.

"What happened after the orbs connected?" Olivia asked.

"You mean exploded, right?" Sergio said with a lop-sided grin. "It blew me off my feet!"

Michael chuckled, easing the tension in the room. "When your orbs combined, it sent out three beams of light. Those lights triggered the closing of each portal."

"I remember seeing that, but I wasn't sure if I imagined it or not." Zach shook his head. "It gets foggy for me from there."

"Once the portals closed, their energy sent out a shock wave that destroyed the Fallen, the Damned, and Hell. The Watchers were also taken." Michael sighed like the weight of the world had finally lifted from his shoulders.

"The Realm? Wait back up," Olivia stepped forward. "What happened? Did Lucifer wage war in Heaven?"

Michael scanned each of them before he spoke. "Lucifer charged Heaven, but God didn't allow his entry. Too much blood had been shed on the hallowed floor already. Instead, he and I fought, and I defeated him." A loud cry erupted, along with a round of applause. Michael held up his hand, and the room quieted. "My heart is heavy with the losses, both human and Angelic, that occurred today, and every day since Lucifer tore our kind in two. His death—his defeat—marks the end of a dark, horrific period of our history. Now we move forward in a life of peace and goodwill. A new era has arrived for humanity. All thanks to you and the undaunted warriors who fought next to you."

"What does that mean?" Olivia asked.

"You'll find out for yourself when you return to your normal lives on Earth. You're now free of the Guardianship. There are no Fallen to battle, no evil roaming the world seeking the ruin of souls."

An unsettling yet reverent silence fell across the room.

What will my life be like without the Guardianship?

"Why did this all have to happen?" Olivia swept her hand back towards her friends. "Why did we have to lose people we love?"

"We'll all die someday. How we live our lives in this precious moment in time we've been given, can make our journey one of beauty or one of ugliness. God has always wanted humanity to choose good, choose love, choose eternal life without demand or fear. When faced with the reality of both good and evil... a definitive choice—a line was drawn for all participants. Symedek and the Watchers fought for good because they understood what a world under Lucifer's rule would look like. Humanity revealed what they wanted today through their prayers and by standing for what they loved. In this new communion of souls, all will unite and rebuild a world where no evil will ever touch them again."

"Then it was worth it, all the sacrifices across the generations to get to this point in our history." Olivia spoke through the sob threatening to let go when she thought of Melchior.

"And for our future." Zach whispered in her ear. His lips touched like butterfly wings against her sensitive skin.

"Balthazar and Caspar. The Magi." Gabriel waved them over. The two approached the stairs with a heavy step, as if Melchior's death weighed upon them. When they stopped before the Archangels, sorrow was etched in every crevice of their faces, in every breath they took. "We're also forever in your debt, thankful for what you've accomplished with each Guardian we put in your charge. You're fearless warriors who taught them how to fight, and your wise counsel showed them how to win. But now, your work here is done, and it's time for you to go home."

"Home?" Balthazar's deep voice rumbled as Caspar shook his head as if confused. "This is our home."

"Not anymore." The Archangels parted, revealing Melchior emerging from within a burst of white flames.

"Melchior!" Olivia cried out, running up the stairs. She stopped short when cobalt blue wings unfurled behind him. She gasped, placing her hand over her mouth.

"Wings—you have your wings back!" She raced the rest of the way and flung herself into his waiting arms, headless of the tears streaming down her face.

"Yes," Melchior said, squeezing her tight. Smiling at her, he let her go. "It's time for the Magi to leave this place. My friends and I will now return from where we came."

"Back to Heaven?" Sergio asked as he closed the distance between himself and Balthazar. "But I thought you'd always be here?"

"Me too," Balthazar chuckled, stroking his beard. "This was never the home of my heart... of my essence." Lucia wrapped her arms around him like she wasn't going to ever let him go. "But it *is* a place with memories I will cherish forever."

"I'll never forget how you helped me with Cody," Zach said, extending his hand to Caspar. "And all the rest of it."

Caspar shook his hand, a vibrant smile lighting up his face. "I'm glad your head's all cleared up now." He tugged Zach close, hooking his other arm around Zach's neck. "Because the past need not drag you down in your new life. You and Olivia have a bright future ahead of you."

"Thanks," Zach laughed, untangling himself from Caspar's headlock.

Olivia turned back to Melchior. "I'm going to miss you."

"I have something for you." Melchior lifted his wing and plucked a blue feather. Then another feather materialized in his hand. A gold plume that could only belong to one creature. Gleaming next to it was the cobalt blue stone that was embedded in the pommel of sword. The triangle etched in the smooth stone burned bright, just like it did when her fingers wrapped around the blade's grip.

Melchior, Aureus and Sandalphon.

My mentor, magical beast and cherished weapon.

The heart and soul of my Guardianship.

"Something to remember us all by." Melchior placed them gently on her palm. She closed her fingers, smiling as a familiar heat swept up her arm.

"I'll never forget you and what we accomplished together. You taught me so much, helped me believe in myself—and in others.." She barely got the words past the huge lump in her throat. "Thank you."

"I won't be far." He hugged her one last time before stepping away and joined Balthazar and Caspar at the foot of the stairs in a flurry of hugs and goodbyes from the rest of the families.

"It is time, friends." Michael motioned to them in the fire pit's direction. As Balthazar walked past Gabriel, wings of gold erupted from his broad back. Caspar froze as Raphael waved his hand, bringing his emerald green wings to life. Olivia didn't think she'd ever seen anything more stunning than the magnificent plumage of solid blue, gold and green ruffling on the wings as the Magi walked up the stairs. Melchior entered first, waving before he disappeared. Bal and Caspar whispered something and then walked through, disappearing with tears gleaming in their eyes.

The air was sucked out of the room with their departure. The Magi were bigger than life. She couldn't fathom her days without them or the Guardianship. "What will happen to this place?"

"Once you're all safely back home, Magiland—" Michael's lips twitched "—will also close. Its purpose is now complete. The magical beasts will return with us and the weapons will be destroyed."

Sandalphon and Aureus gone forever?

Olivia's heart sank, but she grinned when she thought about her majestic Griffin dominating the stunning sky in Heaven. Would he gaze out and think of her while he soared through the serene terrain? She felt deep in her bones that neither of them would ever forget their precious time together or the fierce battle they conquered as one.

"Amal—" Lucia stuttered.

"Is welcome to return with you and live out his days on Earth." Michael said.

Amal frowned and touched his chest. "What about my orb—the lion?"

"Its presence vanished when the orbs exploded. You're fully human, but you're entering a very different world than the one you knew. I'm certain the Mendes family will help you acclimate to your new life." Amal and Lucia smiled at each other as her family gathered around them.

"You should take Alisha up on that ice cream date, Sergio. We'll have lots of time on our hands now." Zach nudged Sergio's shoulder.

"Whatever, boy scout." Sergio smirked, rolling his eyes, but Olivia noticed the flush blooming on his neck.

"I guess it's time to go?" Olivia gazed at Michael, taking in every phenomenal detail of him to carry with her always.

"We're never far away." Michael raised a portal, crackling with blue as it grew before her.

Olivia remembered the first time she walked through the portal into Magiland to begin her journey. Now, she walked into another for the last time. The world was a new place, uncharted for her and her friends, but she knew Zach, Sergio, Lucia and Amal would be a part of it forever. As the portal's electricity traveled over her skin, she heard Aureus cry out his farewell to her.

Goodbye my friend...

Olivia reached over and pulled down the corner of her shirt. There she spied Orion still tattooed on her chest. The Hunter would always be a triumphant reminder for her about how to navigate through the rest of her life.

Through my burdens...

Through my blessings...

Remember...

The beauty is in the living, in the choices I make, and in fighting for who and what I love.

The End

PLEASE WRITE A REVIEW

Thank you so much for reading *Hunt for Orion!* I hope you loved reading this book as much as I enjoyed writing it! I would like to know what you think about the book, as would others. Reviews breathe life into an author's spirit and help others in their quest to find their next entertaining book. Please write your review on Amazon and/or Goodreads. Thank you so much!

Amazon:
https://www.amazon.com/gp/product/B0C22T4VJ6/

Goodreads:
https://www.goodreads.com/author/show/19692005.
S_L_Richardson

DON'T MISS OUT!

Never miss any future sneak peeks or updates on any of your favorite characters, happenings, or my upcoming books! Go to my website at www.slrichardson.com and sign-up for my newsletter and receive a ***free*** prequel, *Trials of the Guardians*! You'll be kept up-to-date on the fun and intriguing insights about the *Guardians of Orion* series and my writing life. I'd also love it if you'd drop me an email on my *"contact me"* page with questions or what you think about my books. I'll get back to you. You're the best!

TRIALS OF THE GUARDIANS

Get your FREE copy of Trials of the Guardians, a thrilling gritty prequel to S.L. Richardson's YA fantasy series, Guardians of Orion. Conner has come-of age as a Guardian of Orion, and is charged fight against the Fallen in their quest to ruin humanity. Little does he know, his first battle is to save his best friend from a succubus bent on ruining him. Is Conner ready for the challenge?

You'll love this thrilling adventure filled with jaw-dropping surprises and age-old battles.

ACKNOWLEDGMENTS

My heart goes out to each of you for staying with me and our Guardians. Never in my wildest dreams did I think it would take me three years to finish *Hunt for Orion*. The pandemic ruined my concentration and muse. I'm very empathic and was driven into a dark place during that time. All I could do was hunker down while I watched my family and the world suffer sickness, death, virtual schooling, and loss of jobs. I muddled through the writing process, but it wasn't until 2022 that I could finally find my joy of writing again. 2022 was filled with weddings, vacations, and a few surgeries, allowing me to fill my cup back up with joy and peace. The words and story flowed once more. I'm so thrilled to have the trilogy finished and into your hands. Thank you for all your support and love along the way.

My family is my core and purpose. My husband pushed... and sometimes dragged me across the finish line while my children cheered me on. He's an amazing editor and patiently listened as I worked through the characters' final arcs. Our four children never gave up on me and have always motivated me to never give up. I love you all so very, very much.

I'm very blessed by the support of my family. My mom reads the first draft and my dad is the last one to read it before it goes to print.

Their insights and inputs are invaluable. My brother, Orin, is a huge cheerleader and loves to help me with ideas on a character's physical features. We had lots of fun talking about his ideas, most of which I used. Jim and Aunt Marie gave me much needed encouragement that I will be forever thankful for. All my love!

I have a core group of friends that I leaned heavily on during this time. My two lovely Lisa's, Barbara, and Mary never shied away from my phone calls and always had a glass of wine ready when I needed it. Love you so much!

Finally, I want to thank Natalie at Original Book Cover Designs for your gorgeous cover art, Roxana for your brilliant editing, and Cait for formatting them into lovely books. I could do it without you and I'm forever grateful.

I leave you with my favorite prayer. It has given me solace, guidance and peace. It is probably the most popular and commonly know prayer, but there is nothing common about it. As always, thank you God, for giving me the strength, perseverance to write this trilogy and for proving the muse to get it done.

THE LORD'S PRAYER

Our Father who art in heaven,
hallowed be thy name.
Thy kingdom come.
Thy will be done
on earth as it is in heaven.
Give us this day our daily bread,
and forgive us our trespasses,
as we forgive those who trespass against us,
and lead us not into temptation,
but deliver us from evil.
For thine is the kingdom and the power, and the glory,
forever and ever.
Amen.

ABOUT
S. L. RICHARDSON

When you don't find her reading the latest YA fantasy or thriller or running her high schooler to his various activities, she is at the computer writing the next book in her trilogy, *Guardians of Orion*.

Being an author has been a dream of hers, but like running a marathon, thought it would never happen. After hitting 50, she chased the dream (not running a marathon, but writing), and released her the trilogy, *Mark of Orion, Light of Orion and Hunt for Orion*.

When she's not writing, she loves cooking, gardening, going to Houston Astros baseball games, and walking her German Shepherd (or maybe he walks her).

She lives in Texas with her incredible and supportive husband and is blessed with four amazing children

Get my other books:

Amazon: https://www.amazon.com/S.-L.-Richardson/e/
B07ZN9M8K2

Join the fan page:

Facebook: https://www.facebook.com/slrichardsonauthor

Follow me on:

Instagram: @authorslrichardson
Twitter: @_slrichardson
Pinterest: authorslrichardson
Goodreads: https://www.goodreads.com/author/show/
19692005.S_L_Richardson
BookBub: https://www.bookbub.com/profile/s-l-richardson